Every Beautiful Mile

Ashley Manley

WILDFLOWER
BOOKS
LLC

Identifiers:

LCCN: 2024901519 (print)

ISBN: 979-8-9899682-0-6 (paperback) | 979-8-9899682-1-3 (eBook) | 979-8-9899682-2-0 (Barnes & Noble Paperback)

Book Cover by Mary Ann Smith

First edition: May 2024 | Wildflower Books LLC

To Kevin, who's written on *almost* every page.

To myself: Ashley, you wrote a damn book. You go, girl.

Prologue

THE DAY I DON'T know the difference between sadness and anger is the day I drink half a bottle of whiskey for breakfast.

Standing behind the wooden podium of the church, swaying side to side, I catch the looks on my teenage kids' faces—their eyes, bloodshot from crying, are also wide with horror as they watch me.

I'm numb enough not to care.

Leaning heavily toward the too-tiny microphone, my mouth collides with it. I feel the thick, sticky slur of my voice before I hear it.

"Hellooo." The word comes out like molasses—oozing across the crowd. Hanging.

I tug at the neck of my dress, squinting at the fuzzy words scribbled on the paper in front of me. Nice words. Loving words. The thought of reading them in front of all these people makes bile rise in my throat as the dress I'm wearing actively tries to strangle me.

I'm trapped like a dolphin in a net that gets tighter whenever it moves.

In this dress.

In this nightmare.

I clear my throat to make room for my smeared words.

"You are all here because of the best person we have ever known, Travis—" I stop, glaring around the room at all the familiar faces.

I can't do this.

I won't.

Not because of breakfast whiskey—because of *them*.

I hate them.

I shove the paper off the podium. It floats through the stuffy air until it lands on the faded maroon carpeting, earning a wave of gasps and whispers from the jam-packed pews.

They're shocked.

Good.

I tug at my sleeves, desperate for air, but the dress only gets tighter.

I bring both hands to my neckline and pull.

Again.

And again.

It rips—*finally!*

The small amount of relief I get is enough to keep me going. Every inch of torn fabric feels like a prize.

The ripping sound cuts through the air and bounces off the stained-glass windows until I have torn a hole all the way from my neck to the seam under my armpit.

Black pieces of cloth sag off my shoulder just enough for my skin to feel the relief of the air.

I smile proudly as the taste of burped whiskey fills my mouth.

"Sorry about that." I squint to refocus the faces that gawk at me and my half-bare chest.

"You know what?" I ask, tone sharp as my smile drops. "I'm not sorry—I wouldn't be wearing this damn dress if it wasn't for all of you!"

I grip the podium so tightly my knuckles might split.

"You claim to love Travis?" I scoff. "Well, I call bullshit! This," I hold my arms out toward the altar covered with ridiculous flower arrangements that surround me, voice strained, "is you giving up on him."

I wipe my nose with my sleeve as I swallow the sob that feels like shrapnel in my throat.

"You all can sit here in your stupid black clothes and sad faces and do nothing, or you can go look for him like I've been telling you!" My voice cracks.

The priest, who has been sitting quietly, is now walking toward me, undoubtedly plotting to throw holy water on my face and begin an impromptu exorcism.

I have to get out of here.

I lean into the microphone one last time, pause, then croak, "You can all go to hell!" and let tears fall that I have no power to stop.

I stumble down the aisle by every pew filled with every person I've ever known until I push through the heavy doors.

After being in the dimly lit church, I flinch from the brightness outside.

I hate the sun for even existing on a day like this.

Straight ahead, I see the marina and the turquoise water of the Gulf of Mexico only blocks away.

That's where he is.

There's no time.

I kick my heels off in the middle of the parking lot and start to run.

The hot pavement mixes with tiny rocks beneath my feet and cuts like shards of glass with every step, but I don't care.

I don't stop.

Not when my feet start to bleed.

Not when I hear someone yell my name.

Not when the roughness of the road turns into wooden planks of a dock beneath me.

When the planks end—I don't hesitate—I jump.

It's only seconds until I hit the water, my dress instantly ballooning around me like a black jellyfish as I try to paddle and kick.

My lacerated feet feel like they've been lit on fire by the salt water, and everything goes heavy. I barely move.

The land has an invisible leash on me and will not let go, no matter how hard I fight it. With my chin barely floating above the surface, my small tears become drops in the big ocean.

"Penelope!"

Gabe?

My head turns as he drops his suit jacket on the dock just before diving into the water.

"Go away, Gabe!" I try in vain to swim again. "I'm going to get him!"

As I shout, the taste of saltwater fills my mouth in gulps.

He's too fast, and I'm too drunk. He catches me within seconds, hooks an arm around my waist, and drags me back to the same dock I had jumped from as I scream belligerently and thrash wildly. My elbow hits his face—blood spraying out of his nose in an instant.

I don't know what he says because I'm yelling through sobs, water filling my ears and eyes and mouth with every word.

We're at the ladder—he drags me up. My soaked dress clings to my legs like a wetsuit, ripped fabric drooping heavily off my chest.

Gabe bends over next to me in his dripping wet clothes, hands on his knees, panting.

"Jesus Christ, Nel! What the hell are you doing?" He spits the words out as he looks at me, blood running down his face. "You pulled that stunt back at the church, and now *this*?" He jerks to a stand and points to the water we were just swimming in. "You could've *died*!"

He shakes his head and rubs his forearm under his nose. The bright red blood spreads across his soaked white shirt and stains.

Looking at my brother, I don't feel a drop of guilt, only rage.

"*You!*" I grit my teeth, jabbing a finger into his chest. "You did this! You and everyone else in that goddamned church! You gave up—all of you!" My voice cracks, fresh tears streaming down my face making him look like a blurry blob. "It's barely been two weeks, and you're just going to give up?" Every single word burns my mouth. "Who has a funeral without a body, Gabe?" I demand, voice loud. "He's out there, waiting for us!"

He's silent.

A group of tourists on a boat tied to a nearby dock in the marina point and stare. A woman—wearing a wetsuit with goggles on top of her head—points a cell phone in my direction, recording me.

I smile coldly through my mascara-stained face as I raise both fists and wave my middle fingers.

Assholes.

People from the church are here.

My mom is on the dock next to me.

Where did she come from?

"Honey, you're scaring me," she says softly.

Nothing makes sense, but I lean into her anyway. She's the only thing holding me upright while my entire life washes away like grains of sand in an outgoing tide.

"Mom, why?" I ask in a hoarse whisper. "Why won't anyone help me find him?"

"Shhhhh." My mom hushes me as she gently rubs my back. "He's gone, Penelope, he's gone."

I want to argue. I desperately want to scream the words I know are true, but they don't come. Somewhere between the blurred lines of grief, anger, and smoke-flavored liquor, I know my mom is right.

The scream that comes next is a throat-shredding, ear-piercing sound that takes me to my knees and drains me of my ability to breathe or think. I don't notice my kids crying beside me or the car that shows up to take me away.

The only thing I know at this moment, the only thing I'll ever know again, is my husband of seventeen years is gone.

One

One year later...

I STARE AT A pelican sitting on a post and focus on my breathing. *Inhale for four, exhale for four.* Yet another bullshit technique I read about in one of the many books on loss I was given after Travis... After Travis.

Except I'm not trying to breathe through loss. I'm breathing through a conversation with a man who is very much in front of me. As per usual, breathing doesn't work.

"Say that again, Dad, because it sounds a lot like you hurling insults at me for no damn reason."

My teeth grind as a headache thumps at my temples.

He runs a hand through his more gray-than-blond slicked-back hair with a heavy sigh.

"Nelly, we've been trying to say this for a year in the nicest way, but you refuse to listen, forcing me to be blunt. You're stuck—unhappy—and you need to do something about it."

My mouth opens, then snaps close.

As we sit in my dad's office of the day—a table he randomly selected under the large palm frond thatched roof of his restaurant—I'm speechless.

He taps his knuckles on the colorful magazine spread open in front of us, as if to emphasize his point.

I frown as my eyes drop to the open pages.

"Dad. We were voted the most fun restaurant by the *American Restaurant* magazine for the second year in a row. What the hell else do you want from me?"

I feel like a cartoon character with eyes bulging out of its head.

"Read it," he says, his usually jovial voice firm. He takes a swig from his beer and raises his eyebrows, white mustache twitching.

My nostrils flare, but I do as he says.

"While most bars strive to make nightlife the center of their entertainment, the Crow's Nest in Key Largo works to create a vibe that's focused on a daytime audience having just as much fun. Their bartenders are known for wowing patrons with an assortment of tricks and unique specialty drinks crafted by island native Penelope Crawford, or, as the owner and her father, Richard Evans, refers to her, Queen of the Cocktail." I roll my eyes as I read—he's never once called me that. "They have live music most afternoons as well as local teachers and nature guides that lead kids' activities for a few hours on the weekends. Locals describe it as a summer camp with top-notch drinks and grouper sandwiches. Surrounded by turquoise water and the sounds of palm trees blowing in the breeze, every visit to the Crow's Nest feels like dinner and drinks being enjoyed on vacation. It's a place where life is lived on a seven-day weekend."

I look at him with a slight shake of my head, my wordless *and?*

"Nelly, that's the same thing they said last year when we won. Same activities! Same cocktails! There's no way they will vote for us again next year if we don't make a change."

He shrugs his shoulders, which are covered in an obnoxiously bright flamingo-patterned shirt and shakes his head.

I try to calibrate my thoughts as I look back at the magazine. He's complaining because we won, but *might* not next year? Unbelievable.

The pictures of kids playing with hula hoops under palm trees while parents sip colorful drinks smack my face, along with the flood of memories that follow.

Last year, I was in one of the photos, laughing on the beach as I spun one of the hula hoops around my hips. Last year, Travis bought the bar a round of drinks and made a toast when the magazine came out.

Last year, he got in his airplane, flew into a storm, and never came home. Travis is gone, and so is the person I used to be.

I find the pelican again, still on his same perch, and imagine how easy life must be for that bird.

My dad leans against his forearms on the table. "Listen—"

Thankfully, whatever he wants to say next is interrupted by a friendly smack on his back by a seasonal regular, Doug.

"Richard, you're keeping my favorite bartender away from us out here!"

Doug's outfit nearly matches my dad's, and I have to squint through the brightness. They are the most cliché retired men I've ever seen.

My dad's smile is instantaneous as he stands to shake his hand. "Doug, how are you, man?"

Doug gestures at the tropical scene around us. "Who can complain here?" His eyes twinkle as he grins. "Sadly, we head back to snow-covered

New York next week. And Nel—" his gaze drops to mine, "—we've yet
to see that pilot husband of yours this year."

He doesn't know. I don't know how to tell him.

My dad's lips press into a tight line as I spin the wedding band around
my finger with my thumb.

"He's..." I try to find a word that isn't a lie or the bitter truth.

Doug laughs. "That sonofabitch never comes out of the air, does he?"
He shakes his head. "Well, if we don't see him, tell him we say hi."

I only nod and look anywhere but my dad.

"Nel, dear!" From behind Doug, his wife's heavily New York accented
voice calls. "Can we convince you to make us some of your famous
daiquiris before we call it a day?"

She leans slightly to the edge of her stool to catch my eye.

"Anything for you, Claire," I say with a smile and lift of my chin. "Let
me know when you're ready."

Doug gives me a wink that's programmed into the eyelids of retired
men everywhere before saying goodbye to my dad and walking away.

I close my eyes. I don't need to look at him to know what I'll see. The
conversation with Doug proves every point he's trying to make.

He doesn't miss a beat as he sits back down and picks up right where
he left off.

"When's the last time you went to that market you love in Homestead
to get ingredients for a new cocktail?" he demands.

I drop my head forward and huff out a breath. He knows how long
it's been, and I refuse to answer.

"What about the kids? When was the last time you, Finn, and Marin
did something together? Had fun?"

I push my chair back from the table and jerk to a stand. I am *not* talking
about the kids.

I hold up my clipboard. "I have to finish taking inventory."

Much to my dismay, he follows me. "I know Gabe invites you out on the boat with him, Jenny, and the boys. You never go, Nelly."

I shake my head and round to the back of the bar, where I immediately start counting liquor bottles. He sticks to me like flypaper—annoying and relentless.

His voice lowers and there's a hint of sadness in it. "I'm worried. We're all worried."

My eyes flick to his, and he somehow looks older than he did minutes before. Concern fills every line of his sixty-seven-year-old face.

I soften just slightly. "I'm alive and well, Dad."

I hold my arms up as evidence.

He frowns at the oversized gray sweatshirt that hangs sadly from my arms, baggy from a year of my grief-induced withering away.

"You don't have fun." He says it like it's a fact, and it makes my entire body tense.

I wish I was that damn pelican.

"Travis was the fun one," I argue.

"Travis wasn't the *only* fun one."

I don't budge—he's wrong.

Travis was the better half of every good time. The kids used to turn to him when they wanted to do something adventurous, not me. I'm just Mom—drinking wine and laughing nervously from the sidelines as they make bottle rockets and snorkel with sharks.

Three hundred and eighty-three days after he left, and the only thing I know how to be is empty. Fun is a pipe dream.

"Your ideas are what made the bar what it is, but the last year..." he pauses, clears his throat, and adds, "I don't know what I'd do if I lost your mother. I'm just saying maybe it's time to take some steps. Go through his things. Let yourself have fun. Let your kids have fun *with* you. Let him go a little. He wouldn't want this."

Let him go?

The words hit like an anvil to the sternum, making all my emotions bleed together.

The weird thing about grief is that one minute, I feel fine, and the next it's as though my heart is being scraped across a cheese grater.

Peace. Pain. Peace. Pain.

It's a sick cycle that doesn't make sense. Time hasn't made it stop, just created longer intervals between the two extremes. The moments of peace will always be followed by devastating blows of pain. Even knowing that doesn't prepare me for how abruptly horrible it feels. How easily my heart can be shredded, over and over again.

"Your kids need you, Nelly," he says, softer this time.

I close my eyes and try to rein in whatever feeling is thrashing wildly beneath my ribs.

"I don't know how to give them that." It's the most honest thing I can say.

His unexpected smile is instant—like this is what he's been waiting for—and the tone of his voice fills with optimism.

"That's why I'm going to help you." He claps his hands together loudly. Smiling.

My eyes narrow as I slowly put the bottle of vodka I've been holding on the bar and search his face for some kind of explanation.

He takes a final sip of his beer, foam clinging to his mustache, before his eyes meet mine with a steely determination.

"You're taking the summer off," he declares.

My eyes widen as I suck in a sharp breath. "Dad—"

I start to protest, but the hand he holds up effectively cuts me off, reminding me he is the adult, and I—even at forty-one—am the child.

"You're taking the summer off, and you're figuring this out. I don't care what you do, but I'm not going to sit here and watch you disappear on my watch. I'd let you go now, but we're too damn busy, and you're too damn good."

The look on his face tells me there's no arguing. Richard Evans has spoken.

For the second time in this conversation, I am completely speechless.

"And Nelly?"

I swallow hard as I look at him. He drops the copy of the magazine on the bar top, a piece of paper sticking out from between the pages.

"There's an article about restaurants across the country that base their menus on local and seasonal items. I'd like you to contact one of them that interests you and see if you can find out the logistics. I want to refresh the menu."

I puff my cheeks up with air before blowing it out slowly.

The world feels like it's spinning so fast, it's making my throat ache.

Take the summer off? Get yourself together? Refresh the menu?

I want to scream, but instead, I do as I'm told. Begrudgingly.

"I thought you were retired?" I mutter.

"Only sometimes."

Then he winks, because of course he does, and turns to make small talk with the guests like he didn't just flip my world upside down.

My jaw clenches as I turn to the marked page and skim over it quickly before choosing a restaurant in Maine. I've always imagined the coast there would be gorgeous—ruggedly beautiful with its rocky shores—and quiet. The kind of quiet I could go for a heaping dose of right now.

The owner, a man named Ethan Mills, is pictured wearing blue jeans and a flannel in his photo, and his write-up checks all the boxes of what my dad's looking for.

Done.

The truth is, after everything my dad just said, I don't have the capacity to think about this beyond just picking one. Maine or New Mexico, I just don't give a shit.

"Daiquiris, Nel!" I hear Claire call from down the bar in her thick accent.

I drop the magazine, smile, and grab the bottle of rum.

The rug may have gotten yanked out from underneath me all over again today, but if there's one thing I can count on, I can still make a damn good cocktail.

Before I head home for the day, I send the email.

> To: ethan@mainelylocal.com
> From: penelope@crowsnest.com
>
>
> Mr. Mills,
>
>
> I'm reaching out because I read your write-up in *American Restaurant* on local ingredient sourcing for Mainely Local. I'm wondering if I can pick your brain on logistics. We have a restaurant in Florida that we'd apparently like to change.

Thanks,
Penelope Crawford

Two

THE WORDS MY DAD says stick in my head like an annoying song I can't shake all afternoon and into the evening as I make dinner.

Go through his things.

Let yourself have fun.

Let your kids have fun with you.

Let him go a little.

I look around the familiar kitchen. The same kitchen Travis had walked into every afternoon of our entire marriage. Like every day in the last year, my heart waits for him to walk in while my head knows he never will.

"Well, Nel..." he would say, loving the way the words rhymed. "Tell me how you broke the hearts of every man on this island today."

Then I'd laugh and pretend I didn't love how he thought that's what happened when I was behind the bar.

The fabricated memory expands then pops like a bubble with a lash to my heart.

As I grab the carrots from the refrigerator, a faded newspaper clipping beneath a gaudy seashell magnet catches my eye.

Key Largo Pilot Travis Crawford Aids in Hurricane Irma Relief Efforts

The title is bold, just like he was, above a picture of him with his token broad smile as he leans against his seaplane wearing a Columbia shirt. His sand-colored hair is handsomely messy, and permanent dimples are carved into his cheeks. It's not in color, but I can imagine the green of his shirt, the tan of his skin, and the gray of his eyes against the bold red stripe of the plane.

I wipe my hand on a dishtowel and trace the faded lines with a finger.

Most of the time, he had flown private charter planes in and out of the Keys, but when a hurricane hit a few years ago, he used his seaplane to help in relief efforts to deliver supplies to islands with closed bridges. He became a hometown hero.

The sound of the front door opening and closing pulls me back to reality.

"Hey, Mom!"

Marin drops her backpack on the floor and tugs at the scarf that ties back her stylish blonde pixie haircut.

I drop my hand from the clipping and smile at her. "Hey, kid! How was school?"

"Meh. The usual. Girls are dramatic, boys are idiots, my teachers are clueless."

Her strawberry-colored lips smile, dropping when she sees the cutting board I've been working at.

"You cut a cucumber?"

It's more of a question than a statement as her blue-gray eyes—Travis' eyes—widen slightly, and she steps toward me.

"Umm, yeah." I clear my throat. "I'm making a salad to go with burgers tonight. I thought we could eat on the patio and grill."

I try to say it nonchalantly. I try to say it in a way that ignores the fact that for a year, most of my cooking was in the form of boxes of macaroni and cheese, frozen pizza, or reheating something I brought home from work.

"Okay," she says, dragging the word out with skepticism.

She looks between the bowl of chopped vegetables and my face then gives me an unexpected hug—as though I've done something amazing—before wordlessly walking to the table and spreading her books across it to start her homework.

I stop, mid-rinse of the carrots, and look at her.

Between her spunky hair, small nose dotted with freckles, and heart-shaped lips, she looks like a fifteen-year-old fairy that hasn't yet grown wings.

Unlike me, she handled the loss of her dad like someone who had written volumes on healthy grieving. She spent the first days by my side in my crusade to find him, convinced just because they found his plane shredded to smithereens didn't mean he wasn't alive.

"I've read about people that get in accidents and walk away without even a cut all the time!" she insisted.

After a week of dive teams and recovery efforts relentlessly looking for him and investigators explaining all the reasons they had for declaring him deceased, she accepted their words. While I continued to cling to hope and Google things like *how long you can survive treading water,* she read sad poetry and then went back to living her life. Meanwhile, I entered a monogamous relationship with misery and stayed fully committed.

When the front door opens and closes again, Finn steps into the kitchen, stack of books under one arm. I turn, shooting him a smile over my shoulder with a "Hey Finn," before peeling the carrots at the sink.

"Mom's cooking," Marin says in a way that implies something else. Like disbelief.

He snorts but says nothing.

As usual.

While Marin is everything easy for me, Finn is not. Gone is the talkative little boy who loved me more than life itself, and in his place a reserved young man who would rather have a lobotomy than a conversation with his mother. Travis had bridged the gap, but with him gone, it's become staticky radio silence between us most days. At seventeen, he's at an age where he knows more than me. Every conversation I attempt ends with something that teeters on being an argument.

Don't take it personally, Nel, Travis told me once.

I hated that advice with a passion. Isn't the way a mother and son interact the epitome of personal?

Finn runs a hand through his shaggy brown hair and watches me from the doorway, face slanted in annoyance, wielding his superpower of silence.

"I'm making a salad, and I thought we could grill burgers and eat on the porch tonight," I tell him, playing my favorite game of answering questions he never asks.

"I didn't know you still knew how to cook." The bored tone in his voice makes me want to scream. Instead, I exhale.

To a fly living on the wall of this house for the last year, there would be no denying I appear to be a woman who has no clue how to cook anything that isn't gelled together with preservatives.

"Well, don't say that until we see if it's edible." When I chuckle, he walks away.

Down the hall of our tiny bungalow, the only response he gives is the click of his bedroom door as it closes.

The searing pain in my chest from the sound feels like water boiling.

For the millionth time in the last year, Travis' absence is so incredibly loud, I almost have to plug my ears for fear of going deaf.

***

"Your grandpa told me today I'm stuck."

I don't know why I say it, but dinner is too quiet, and my brain is too loud.

Marin chokes on her bite of cheeseburger while Finn says nothing.

Of course.

I take a sip of wine and stare out of the patio to the hedge of sea grape leaves that fan out like waxy veined saucers.

"Well?" I demand, knowing damn well their silence means they agree.

"Mom, what do you want us to say to that?" Marin asks gently, scrunching her freckled nose. "Everyone grieves differently. It's just..."

Her voice trails off only for Finn to pick up where she leaves off.

"Let's see, *Mom*," he starts, without hesitation. "You freaked out on an entire church full of people because you thought Dad was alive after two weeks of being out in the middle of the Gulf of Mexico. Then, you spent the last year of our lives moping around while also pretending he was just out running an errand. So, yes, I'd say Grandpa got that right."

Finn's amber-brown eyes look at me like he's challenging me to a duel.

Here's the thing I've learned about being a parent to teenagers—half of the time, I love them so much it hurts while the other half I wonder if shoving knives under my fingernails would be more enjoyable.

"Finn!" Marin hisses, but he's unphased. He simply shrugs.

"Tell me how you really feel," I mumble, stabbing a fork into my salad.

"I think what Finn was trying to say, Mom, is that you don't seem to... have fun anymore. You go to work, you come home, you wear a lot of gray."

Her eyes drop to my gray shirt, and I don't miss the look of disgust she fails to hide.

"And we never talk about Dad," she continues. "As much as we all miss him, it's like we have to pretend he never existed."

The words sting like a well-deserved slap.

I can't argue with any of it. I had freaked out on an entire church. My wardrobe does resemble that of a warm weather undertaker, and I do avoid talking about Travis. But do I mope?

I scoff. "I don't mope."

"You don't mope?" Finn clasps his hands together over his plate as he leans against his elbows on the table, eyebrows raised. "Marin, you know all these fancy words. Explain to Mom what moping means."

"Sad. Gloomy. Low spirited. Sulky. Broody," she says, ticking the words off on her fingers.

Damn her and the books she's always reading.

I have no defense. They're right, and so was my dad in his obnoxiously cheery retirement garb.

I look back to the leaves as they rustle in the breeze and try to figure out how to handle this news.

"Well, what am I supposed to do about it? He was supposed to be here, doing all this with us. It's hard not to be *low spirited* when it constantly feels like he keeps forgetting to show up."

My voice comes out in an almost whine even I feel annoyed by.

"Really, Mom?" Finn scoffs. "He didn't *forget to show up*. He died. Though seeing how miserable you're acting, I wouldn't blame him if it was his choice."

If he wasn't my kid, I would have kindly told Finn to fuck off.

Marin whips her head towards him. "Finn!"

I hold up my hand and bat his comment away, refusing to feed into the argument he's looking for.

"Stop right there." I fight to swallow every ugly word I want to hurtle out of my mouth. "I got it. I suck at this. Your thoughts are noted, Finn. Apparently, you both think Grandpa is right, so I'll work on it. Happy?"

I cross my arms over my chest, pouty child mode fully activated.

"Maybe we could go on a vacation or something?" Marin offers, hopefully.

I force a smile, but the idea of a vacation without Travis makes my temples throb. I consider telling them about my dad essentially firing me for the summer but force it out of my mind. I don't have the mental capacity to handle that conversation on top of the *lovely* one we're already having.

There's a long pause that seems to go on for hours as we take bites of our food and live in our own heads.

"How about we share a favorite story about Dad?" I suggest. "We can't go on a vacation tonight, and I can't change the fact my wardrobe rivals the Grim Reaper at the moment, but I can do better about talking about him."

It's a moment, albeit an ugly one of sorts, where I need to show them I'm willing to pull myself out of whatever mud pit I'm stuck in and keep living alongside them. I know my kids will look back at the year after Travis left and remember how poorly I handled it. But I can't let one year turn into two, turn into a lifetime of me being a shell of a woman.

"Me first!" Marin's squeal almost makes me laugh, and God bless her, she's beaming.

"Today's favorite story is when I was six and in ballet. Do you remember?"

Finn and I nod as a silent truce forms between us from the lightness of her words.

"I was so scared to go on stage, so Dad stood with me backstage. When it was my turn to go out, he just hoisted me on his shoulders and danced with everyone else." She laughs. "All the parents were so shocked, and the other ballerinas were giggling, but I felt like a queen up there."

Her hands are over her head as she finishes talking. She looks every bit like the six-year-old girl who twirled on top of her daddy's shoulders.

"I remember how pissed that mom sitting next to me was that he was stealing the show from her daughter." I say over the rim of my wine glass, making them both laugh.

"Finny, your turn! Tell us something good."

Marin takes a bite of her burger while she stares at her brother like he's about to reveal the secret of life.

"When I was fifteen, I got invited out to the sandbar with some friends, but Mom said no because she didn't trust them." His eyes meet mine, but shockingly, there's no contempt in them. "Dad knew everyone was going to be out there, even Emily, who you know I was convinced I was in love with." He wipes his hands on his napkin. "Anyway, Dad felt bad I couldn't go, so he took me up in the seaplane and landed near where everyone was, letting me get out and swim for a little bit. *Boats are a boring way to arrive at any party,* he told me. And then we flew home and never told anyone about it. On Monday, nobody could stop talking about it. Even Emily. Who I wasn't even in love with, apparently."

He smiles again, and my heart expands and collapses with the grotesque beauty of it all.

"God, that sounds like your dad. And he had a knack for finding loopholes when I told you guys no, didn't he?" I smile, shaking my head.

"Your turn, Mom!"

I wouldn't be surprised if Marin's enthusiasm had an actual pulse.

"Hmm...."

I have a collection of encyclopedias worth of stories I can tell, but I know, in my heart, all the good ones start at the beginning. I set my wine down and lean back in my chair.

"I was home from college, working at the bar, of course." I smile as I say the words, feeling like I'm there again.

I'm twenty-one without a care in the world, working at my dad's bar for the summer. I can smell the fish and feel that sticky dryness of my skin that only happens after way too much time in the ocean. I can see the pelicans that line the docks as they wait impatiently for whatever scraps the fisherman will throw their way.

"I was behind the bar at the time of day the fisherman and day drinkers started trickling in, and in he walked, taking a seat on a stool and ordering a beer. I noticed him, but I knew better than to think beyond him buying beer. I chatted with him the way I did with all the customers, teasing and swatting my bar rag at him, trying desperately not to get lost in those gray eyes of his. But he stayed on that barstool all afternoon, flirting relentlessly. When he finally stood to leave, he asked my name. Nel, I told him. He smiled his crooked smile, laid cash down, looked me dead in the eyes, and said, 'Well Nel, I bet you break the hearts of all the men on this island when you're behind that bar.'"

They both look at me—almost fascinated—as a wet sheen forms over my eyes.

As bad as it hurts to relive the memory, it feels good. *So* good. They knew we met at the bar, of course, but they had never heard the story of why he always said '*Well Nel*' at the end of every day.

In this moment, I desperately don't want to feel sad. I'm so damn sick of sad, it's suffocating. I want the magical spell of happiness we had cast over the table for the first time since he left us to stay.

So, I reach for it.

Spinning my wedding band around my finger, I blink back my tears and lean against the table.

"And then we made out on the dock where they unload the fish after I got off my shift."

My grin is so big it hurts my face.

Finn shakes his head and rolls his eyes while Marin snorts and throws her napkin at me.

"Way to ruin it, Penelope."

I laugh—both at the use of my name and the reaction.

I don't bother telling them what happened a few weeks later on their grandpa's boat. I figure some stories would always be just ours.

***

As Marin and Finn do the dishes after dinner, I open my computer to finish the work my dad derailed me from earlier. Opening my email, I'm shocked to see there's already a response from the restaurant owner in Maine.

Penelope,

```
Thanks for the message. I'm no ex-
pert, but I'm flattered by the ques-
tion and happy to help. Ask away.


Also, I have to know—apparently?


Ethan
```

I was so annoyed by my dad's request I almost hoped my email was as far as this was going to go.

Clearly, he picked up on said annoyance.

I blow out a breath and hit reply.

```
Mr. Mills,



Thank you so much for this. I'm not
exactly sure what to ask. My area of
expertise is the bar, and my reaching
out to you is regarding the restau-
rant portion of our business. We
currently order from distributors for
most of our food—do you do the same
by finding ones that are Maine-based,
or do you go smaller than that and
```

```
find local-to-you farmers and go from
there?


No rush to respond—we won't be making
changes until our slow season anyway,
which is summer.



Thanks,


Penelope
```

I reread, making sure I've asked questions that will help whatever it is my dad is trying to do, then add,

```
P.S. If you don't understand my use
of the word apparently, then I'd say
it's pretty apparent you aren't in
business with your dad. That's an
experience that really expands your
vocabulary.
```

Three

I YAWN INTO MY hand as the coffee drips slowly into the pot, my body humming with the foreign sensation of excitement.

Between the ugly words Finn said to me and the beautiful ones we shared in our stories, something shifted in me ever so slightly. Like a weight had lifted just enough to remind me how it feels to not constantly carry something so heavy.

After Marin and Finn went to bed, I forced myself to open Travis' closet. The first time since he left. I did laundry the day of his crash, hung everything up where it belonged, then closed the doors and never looked in there again. As far as I was concerned, it was a sealed tomb not to be disturbed for all eternity.

It was, like everything else in my life, an echo of what used to be. His salty, citrusy smell didn't linger, his voice didn't whisper from the rustling of his shirts, and his familiar arms didn't reach out to hug me. It was just a closet of stuff.

I easily bagged most of them up to donate, but when I got to his t-shirts, I couldn't let them go. They were just so *him*.

"How else will I remember this place?" he would ask with a grin.

Whether we were on a big vacation or just down the street at a restaurant, if there was a t-shirt for sale, he was buying it. After almost two decades of the habit, he had nearly achieved hoarder status with his ridiculous collection.

I went through all of them and smiled as I remembered each story. One from a hotdog stand just a few miles outside of town. *Dinghy's Dongs*, it said in big loopy letters, making me laugh out loud. Like a teenage boy, he bought it because he thought it was insanely funny. I closed my eyes when I held it, and I could see his face and hear his voice so intensely from the day we went there for lunch.

"Would you like a dong today, Nel?" he had asked with a wolfish smile as he leaned against the counter at the window.

Every shirt pushed a button to start a slideshow of memories in my brain, taking me back to the scene like it was unfolding in real-time. I spent hours last night lost in the faded cotton artifacts that made up our whole history. I spent as much time crying as I did laughing.

I take a sip of my coffee and cringe. For seventeen years, Travis made my coffee every day, and somehow, after over a year of having to make it myself, it's still never a guarantee I'll get it right.

Honestly—it's mostly wrong.

I look around the living room. The house—far from modern—is a little bungalow built in the 80s we slowly remodeled. The walls are painted in jewel tone colors of blues and greens, dotted with paintings by local artists. The floor is tiled, but most of it's covered with natural fibered rugs and oversized tropical houseplants shoved in every corner.

Even in my year of misery, I managed to keep them alive.

The lime green velvet sofa in the middle of the room is now covered with stacks of Travis' t-shirts I laid out to look like a department store display. Somehow, despite the chaos of all the colors and ridiculous graphics, they look like they belong.

An alarm goes off from one of the bedrooms followed by the sounds of drawers sliding open and closed. In minutes, Finn and Marin will see what I've done. I go to the mirror in the hall to give myself one last look.

"God, you look awful," I mutter to my reflection.

Even after I purposefully tried to look alive by skipping my usual shades of gray for one of the shirts I found last night—a bright green favorite of mine from the Everglades—I'm homely. My skin is pale, my hair is dull, and I look every bit of my forty-one years and then some. The braid in my hair doesn't make me look like the cool kind of mom I hoped for and the mascara I had swiped on somehow makes me look more dead than alive. Mostly dead.

I shake my head, laugh so I don't cry, and then wait by the couch where Marin and Finn meet me with confused looks on their sleepy faces.

"Mom? What's going on?" Marin asks, yawning into her hand and taking a step toward the clothes.

Finn doesn't move, but his eyes drop to my shirt.

Travis' shirt.

"Morning!" I raise my mug of disgusting coffee in mock cheers, suddenly aware of how nervous I am. "So, after dinner last night and those great stories about Dad and everyone telling me how depressing I am, I got to thinking about everything, you know? And maybe it's time I do something..."

Their response comes in the form of silence and blinking.

"Anyway, the stories made me think of all your dad's ridiculous t-shirts, and how much he loved them, and what a waste they were just sitting in his closet." I pause, not sure if I make sense. "What I'm trying to say is, I went through your dad's clothes last night. I kept a few t-shirts for myself, my favorite ones, but I wanted to see if you guys wanted any of these. To wear or keep or whatever."

I spin the gold band around my finger and look at them, waiting for something... what? Confetti? I forgot to think that far ahead.

Marin silently picks up one of the shirts, pinching the shoulders so it unfolds in front of her, revealing a large lobster.

I take another sip of coffee then fill the silence they seem to not notice.

"And as you can see, I picked the one from the Everglades. Remember that trip? We spent all that money to watch that toothless man feed raw chicken to a gator. Your dad thought it was hilarious, but we were all too covered by mosquito bites to even watch."

I trace the line of the alligator standing on hairy legs with dark green blocky letters that say *Sasquatch is a Gator* that covers the shirt I'm wearing.

I swallow hard, twice, then wait.

Finn finally says, "Dibs on the one from the owl sanctuary."

And while he doesn't fully smile, his lips tip slightly enough to ease the tension in my shoulders. I remember the shirt exactly: *Hoot for Hooters* written in a red scripty font above a cartoon owl.

"Mom!" Marin gasps. "This is so fun! Let's all wear one today. Dress like Dad Day! Dress like Dad Day!" Her chanting makes me laugh as she wildly digs through the shirts.

"I'm going to make breakfast. Blueberry pancakes?"

"Sure," Finn says, lifting one of the shirts without looking at me.

As I mix ingredients in a bowl, listening as they tell stories, my chest tightens. Happiness over the t-shirts being worn clashes with the devastation of Travis not being the one to wear them.

Four

Me: *I'm taking the day off. Got Jade to cover the bar, let me know if you need anything.*

Dad: *Sounds good, Nelly. Everything okay?*

Me: *All good. Also, tell Mom I'm mad at her for not telling me I look like shit all the time.*

Dad: *She says she knew you'd realize it eventually.*

The playful laughter of the morning wraps hands around my heart and squeezes just enough that it starts to pump again. It's faint, but it's there. Like for the last year, it's just been a useless organ sitting in my chest for show, but today, it beats in a way that propels me forward.

Other than clothes in a closet, the only other space Travis claimed was a large, detached pole barn we have in the yard. Our modest house sits on a double lot, a rarity on the island, and we built the pole barn, the shed as he called it, for a boat shortly after moving in. Eventually, Travis moved the boat to a slip in the marina, and the shed became a place for him and his friends.

I wander back to it, coffee in hand. A thick hedge of tropical, leafy foliage lines the property, creating a feeling that we're on an island all our own even though we're really in a small neighborhood. A string of unlit lights hangs under the rafters—half of the bulbs broken from neglect—and a stack of folding chairs leans in one corner, unused since before the funeral. I look to the other half, where a boat once parked, and frown.

The Avion.

Three months before the accident, Travis saw a 1978 Avion camper for sale on the side of the road for $6,000.

"It's a steal, Nel! The guy who owned it used it for his work truck. The engine runs like a top. The inside just needs to be fixed up."

He had said it with so much displaced pride.

I remember seeing the inside for the first time and thinking we had been swindled. It was barebones with raw plywood. The only thing salvageable was the bathroom with running water and a toilet—not that I was using the same grimy toilet the previous owner had. It looked like a kill room from a murder movie, and smelled like mothballs, salami, and mildew. It freaked me out to the point I never went back into it after he brought it home that first day.

Now, it sits like a dinosaur—big, bulky, and outdated. The whole exterior is a 70s shade of cream with thick orange-brown stripes wrapping around it. A truck cab sticks out from under a windowed storage space that connects to the rest of the living area.

Unlike modern campers I see on the road with sharp edges and clean lines, this one is rounded, with tinted windows floating around its body like a lava lamp. Walking closer, I can see through the windshield that the two bucket seats are covered with brown beaded seat covers.

Of course.

I'm not sure if they came that way or Travis put them there, but neither would surprise me.

I set my coffee on the hood while I walk around to face the entry door. It takes three pulls, each tug harder than the last, until the door finally swings open, and my breath gushes out of me.

What the hell?

I shake my head, not quite believing what I see as I step inside.

It's still unfinished, but it looks nothing like the kill room on wheels I had seen the last time I was in here. The floor is now covered in some kind of planks, hiding the exposed plywood that was there before. The small kitchen space now has blue cabinets with a butcher block countertop and a small sink. There aren't any appliances, but empty spaces have been allowed for them. Across the aisle is a dinette without any cushions that backs up to the wall of the bathroom. I open the door with one eye closed, but once again, I'm surprised. The shower and small vanity are the same, but there's a new toilet.

I laugh.

Travis knew I'd never touch that other one.

I step out of the small bathroom and turn toward the back. Two twin-sized platforms have been built with small doors to storage spaces beneath. I sit on one of them, easily imagining mattresses there for Marin and Finn.

I bring a hand to my mouth in disbelief as I look around again. From this angle, I can see into the cab of the truck, above which is a loft-style bed, maybe queen-sized, with a ladder resting on top of the mattress.

Our bed.

It still needs work, but I can see it. I can see us on stupid trips buying stupid t-shirts. I can picture Travis driving, me in the passenger seat, playing old music while the kids play cards at the table. I can picture the fridge filled with road trip foods and margarita ingredients. I see us dancing under an awning with cheesy novelty lights twinkling around us in the middle of some wooded campground while it rains.

It's yet another plan for a future life that doesn't exist. Plans shattered and scattered with the debris of an airplane across the waters that surround us.

My chest aches with the pain of all the Travis-sized memories that will be missing from my life for as long as I live, and he does not.

The space is instantly too small—my lungs can't get enough air. I pull at the neckline of my shirt, but it doesn't help. The walls are closing in. I feel it with every strangled breath I try to take.

I need to go, clear my head, and figure out how to get rid of this thing.

I push myself off the platform and rush by the bathroom, then the dinette, where a faded US map falls as I walk by.

I pick it up—a small piece of notebook paper slips out onto the table. *Forced Fun Road Trip* is scribbled across the top, and I recognize Travis' handwriting immediately.

A pit forms where my stomach used to be as I rub the paper between my fingers.

It's a list.

I take a seat in the cushionless booth and unfold the map that takes up the whole table. Highlighted lines cover roads from the Keys to Oregon to New York and back again. Towns and cities circled across the country.

I move my finger along the roads like a car traveling the country at warped speed. He was planning a trip.

"Well, Nel. Think of all the adventures we could go on in this thing. We can see the desert, the Pacific Ocean, and the tops of mountains," he had said, leaning against the hood the day he brought it home.

I rolled my eyes.

"Travis, that thing is creepy as hell. There's no way I'm going anywhere in it, much less sleeping there," I told him, arms crossed.

"You'll see, I'm going to make it so pretty you'll be begging me to stay in it forever!" he insisted.

There was no talking him out of it. The damn thing was already in the driveway, and his mind was made up.

I don't know how long I sit reliving those conversations with my finger sliding across the map. Minutes or hours, I have no clue. Ideas I can't even fathom start to form in my head, and like a line of dominoes falling in succession, I can't stop them once they start.

Yesterday, my dad told me I wasn't allowed to work all summer. Last night, Marin suggested we take a vacation. Though I'm sure this wasn't what she had in mind—here it is. My chance to come back from the plane crash that somehow has taken so much more than my husband.

I don't know how to have fun, but Travis did. I fold the map back up and take it with me as I walk to the door. I pause briefly, giving one last look at the change that had happened without me knowing.

Dammit, Travis, you win.

Five

I ALMOST PACE THE skin off my feet in the living room while waiting for the kids to get home from school. My latest display puts the morning of t-shirts to shame.

Finn's Jeep tires crunch over the gravel driveway followed by the sounds of doors opening and closing along with Marin's muffled, cheery voice. My throat is bone dry, but there's no time for water. I only have seconds.

I eye the wall—the whole scene looks like something from a suspense movie where the lead investigator gets so obsessed with finding a killer that he destroys his house with pinned-up pictures of the victims and crime scenes. Instead of crime scenes, I have landscape photos, and instead of victim statistics, there are distance calculations.

The door opens.

Here they are.

Speechless.

I swear five whole years pass in the silence that follows.

Marin drops her backpack instantly, walking to the wall. Finn looks at me hesitantly, eyebrows pinched, then wanders over behind her.

Marin's eyes are wide as they bounce between me and the highlighted map that takes up most of the wall. "Mom? What is all this?"

I drink the entire glass of water I forgot I was holding as moisture puddles in my armpits.

"I went in the old camper," I say, like that explains everything.

They blink, confused.

I shake my head and try again. "I went in the camper, the one Dad bought before... before. I don't know if you knew, but he started doing work on it. He never really talked to me about it, probably because I told him over my dead body would I ever sleep in it because it was so creepy. But he made it... better. It's not finished, of course, but it's close. Then I found this map." I point to the wall. "And those notes," I nod toward the small scraps of notebook paper pinned next to it. "Your dad was planning a trip. For us." I fumble with my braid in my fingers. "I thought maybe we should take it. We could spend the summer going to these ridiculous places he picked out for us. I just thought we had so much fun talking about him last night and looking at his shirts today, and Marin, you did suggest a vacation..."

The silence is heavy as I spin my wedding band around my finger.

"I scheduled it out. We could take ten weeks to see it all and still get back in time for you to have a week here before school starts. And I know that's a whole summer away from your friends. I know what I'm asking." I pin my eyes to Finn. "Finn, you're going into your senior year next year, and this is our last big shot to do something like this. And I know that might sound awful, being trapped in an old camper with your sad mom and little sister for ten weeks, but I think I might need you to do this for me. I think my heart won't survive if we don't try. He wanted this, and I don't know how to be anything right now without him guiding me. I don't want to be the mom that freaked out at her husband's funeral and never recovered."

There's a desperation I feel at the tip of every nerve ending in my pause.

They eye the wall again.

"And we don't have to only go to the places he wanted. We can choose our own adventures, too. God knows ten weeks of his kind of weird might drive us all insane." I laugh under my breath with the final words.

"Ten weeks, Mom?" Finn rubs his finger down the bridge of his nose. "I have baseball!"

"All summer? Who needs that much practice?" I laugh, he doesn't. "I mean, I can call the coach and see what he says..."

He ignores me, arguing further, "And I wanted to get scuba certified!"

"That one's easy. Someone has that course offered almost every weekend. We can sign you up for one in August."

I smile, hopeful.

With his hands held out, frustration fills his voice. "What will I even tell Abby?"

Marin groans and drops her head back. "Oh my God, Finn. *Abby*?"

Who the hell is Abby?

"I don't know what you see in her besides her boobs. Which, big deal," Marin says, rolling her eyes.

I scrunch my nose. "What are we talking about here?"

"My girlfriend? Abby?" He says it like I'm an idiot, but I'm too consumed with the fact my son has a girlfriend that I didn't know about to care about his shitty attitude.

"Abby..." My voice trails off, wondering what advice I can give about a girlfriend I found out about three seconds ago. "I'm sure she will understand."

I am actually *not* sure she will understand because I have no clue who she is.

How long have they been together?

What does she look like?

Is she nice?

Oh. My. God.

Are they having sex?

My stomach drops to where my bare feet meet the cool tile floor beneath me. For the life of me, I cannot remember if Travis talked to him about how to be safe when it came time. The thoughts spiraling inside of me have the force of a hurricane and threaten to wipe me out in the middle of the living room.

Finn points a frustrated hand toward the map. "Marin, you seriously want to do *this*?"

"A ten-week road trip, and we can go anywhere we want? Are you kidding me? Of course, I do, Finny! This is something people talk about doing when they retire. We are just teenagers, and mom's paying. It will make us cool and worldly."

Her vintage skirt floats through the air as she twirls theatrically.

Finn rubs a finger on the bridge of his nose again, squeezing his eyes shut before blowing out a long breath.

"Can't you go without me? I can stay with Grandpa and Poppy. Or Uncle Gabe!"

The words hit like a wrecking ball. Not only does he not want to go, he wants us to go and him to stay. Ten weeks away from each other? I'm not sure if I want to cry or scream.

The entire island of Key Largo might pity me, but my son does not. If anything, he has taken whatever the opposite sentiment is and then gone a step further.

My jaw clenches. "No."

I barely recognize the hard edge in my own voice.

Marin sucks in a breath, and there's turmoil in Finn's eyes. A thick quiet hangs in the air between us, but I refuse to look away first.

His shoulders sag as he shakes his head, muttering, "If you don't care if we want to do this or not, why are you even asking?"

I almost choke on the frustrating anger that burns through me.

"Ignore him, Mom. This is going to be great!" Marin says.

Then, like her brother and I aren't one breath away from triggering the start of World War III, she pokes him in the ribs and makes him chuckle through a groan in a way that defuses the situation just enough.

We stare at the map, and I let out a long exhale.

"We have three months to plan. I thought we could start by writing down places we want to go and see how they align with what your dad already wrote."

Marin sits cross-legged and eager on the floor by a whiteboard with the marker as Finn flops heavily on the couch.

I raise a suspicious eyebrow at him.

"I can't let Marin come up with every stop, or it'll be ten weeks of vintage stores and weird art galleries. If you're forcing me to do this, I'm making sure it isn't a total waste."

He rolls his eyes in annoyance but props his feet up on the coffee table.

I bite back a smile. Because, dammit, if this doesn't feel like the slightest bit of a win.

By dinner, there is an explosion of lists over every flat surface and sticky notes all over the map.

"What about the bar, Mom? Does Grandpa know about this idea?" Marin asks between bites of pizza.

"Funny story," I say, not thinking it's funny at all. "Grandpa told me yesterday he wasn't letting me work this summer because I needed to fix myself." With my confession, I pivot. "I'm going to ask Gabe to teach Finn and me to drive the camper. Your dad's life insurance paid off the rest of the mortgage. The money also let me set aside accounts to pay for your college, and the rest I put in savings for... whatever." I pull stretchy cheese strings off my pizza. "Ten weeks of seeing things we've never seen before seems like a pretty good reason to spend it."

Marin and I study the wall of chaos in front of us as Finn hammers out a text on his phone.

"So, Finn." I wipe my mouth. "I didn't know you had a girlfriend."

"Yep," he says, popping the *p* without looking at me.

"Are you guys—you know—serious? Or doing serious things?" I ask as nonchalantly as possible.

Marin snorts into her cup.

"Yeah, we aren't having this conversation." He stands up without looking at me. "I have homework."

"Right. Of course. Goodnight. Thanks for doing this."

I smile but know it does nothing to hide my disappointment.

He's already down the hall, the too-familiar sound of his door closing landing heavy on my chest.

"He'll come around, Mom," Marin says softly.

My eyes burn as my stomach sinks. The boy I had put Band-Aids on and read picture books to looks at me like a stranger. Hell, maybe I am. It's a reality I'm not prepared for.

Travis died and time kept going, but I had stood still. For the first time in a year, I feel an emotion I hadn't before.

Ashamed.

Ashamed, I've been so lost in my own grief I didn't pay close enough attention to these two amazing creatures that live right under the same roof as me.

I look back at the map. This will either be the thing that breaks us for good or the one that stitches us back together.

Six

Three-months later...

"THEY'RE HERE!" MY MOM yells as she waves her arms and scrambles down the steps of their stilted canal-side house.

My dad is in his usual attire—blindingly bright floral shirt and flip-flops—while my mom floats across the yard in a long skirt and paint-splattered sleeveless shirt. Her hair is long, wavy, and wild, like her, and her eyes twinkle as she claps her hands together with a gasp. She gazes at the camper in her driveway like it is the most magical thing she has ever laid eyes on.

"Penelope, this is simply wonderful." Her tone is pure whimsy, like she's imagining a thousand fairy tales playing out. "I came to the Keys in a van a lot like this in the 70s. I was going to find my big break as an artist, you know. Instead, I found your dad. He cared more about a good time than art, but still, it was love at first sight."

Her face fills with a dreamy smile.

I shake my head. I've heard the story a million times, but my mom's love of it never really gets old.

Marin beams as she shows my parents the new and improved Avion in the driveway. It had taken us three months, but we made it. After tireless hours scouring flea markets and thrift stores, the Avion had returned to its 1978 glory.

We painted the inside a creamy white and layered on textures of polyester, macrame, and a burnt orange shag rug. It almost makes me laugh at how good it looks after I hated it so much when Travis brought it home.

Finn leans on the side of the hood, disinterested, as he scrolls his phone before wandering into the house.

I try to ignore how that simple gesture lashes yet another shallow mark across my heart.

My arm hooks through my mom's as we walk.

"Thanks, Mom. I can't believe we leave tomorrow. It feels surreal."

The truth is, I'm nervous as hell. Even though the trip has Travis' engineering behind it, he isn't here to execute it—I am. The person who doesn't like driving long distances or living dangerously is in charge of keeping us alive as we drive thousands of miles away from home. Over mountains and through deserts. To another ocean. As excited as I am for the time with the kids, I am scared to death I'll fail. That I won't translate Travis' plan into an actual meaningful experience.

"You don't come back here until you figure it out," she says, turning to look at me when we get to the top of the steps. "You are going to get out there and want to come back when things feel hard, I know you. It *will* feel hard, and you'll think it was a mistake. I want you to keep going. I want you to see what you need to see until you can come back here and breathe easy. Until you find yourself again, even if it's just miles and miles of pavement."

I hate how well she knows me.

I let out a long exhale. "Finn doesn't want to go."

"Ahh. Well, he's seventeen, would you?" She laughs softly, her wild hair blowing in the breeze. "Remind him how fun you are. He'll come around. You lost your husband, but he lost his dad, and his mom didn't fully walk away from that crash either." She wraps her arm around my shoulder and leans her head against mine. "Some people say time heals all wounds, but I always thought laughter was the real salve for a wounded soul. You all need to go out there and find some."

Her familiar lavender scent envelops me.

"Now let's get a glass of wine, and I'll show you some new stuff I've been painting. I've been exploring nudes."

She gives a sinful smile and wiggles her eyebrows as we step into the kitchen.

Gabe meets me there, shoving a glass of tequila in my hands.

"You'll need this to soften the blow. She's already shown me," he says, face puckering. Mom slaps him in mock offense before disappearing down the hall.

I take the glass and give him a hug. "That bad?"

"Just wait."

His dark eyes widen so dramatically, I laugh.

Gabe's wife, Jenny, walks into the kitchen and squeezes me in a hug.

"I'm so excited for you!" she says in a near-squeal as we pull apart.

She's a little thing—a former cheerleader with a blunt brown bob, shiny blue eyes, and a huge smile. If she wasn't my sister-in-law, I would have hated her for how adorable she is. The red polka-dotted dress she's wearing would make me look like a clown, but she pulls it off effortlessly.

"I can't wait to hear about every single place you see!" she says, leaning into me. "And I'll vicariously live through you."

As if planned, one of her boys screams from outside, and she rolls her eyes then gives me a look that silently sums up the chaos of parenthood perfectly.

Again, I laugh.

"I will. I know, I really can't believe it. I'm sure Gabe here has told you what an excellent driver I've become," I say, shooting him a look.

"We'll be lucky if they make it off the island," he teases.

I flip my middle finger toward him with a fake smile, knowing he isn't entirely wrong.

"That's not fair. You never stopped yelling at me," I argue.

"Because you never stopped hitting the curb! For the sake of everyone, I hope Finn drives the whole time."

He rubs a hand over the stubble on his jaw, but his expression stays playful.

"That's not—"

My mom appears in the kitchen and destroys the rest of my words.

She's holding a large canvas of a man—a very nude man—that looks exactly like my dad.

I spit tequila.

"Yikes, Poppy!" Marin screeches, using the first name my mom insists on, and shoves her palms into her eyeballs.

"Christ on a crutch, Mom! Is that Dad?" I shriek, turning away as Gabe and Jenny groan and do the same.

"Don't be such a prude, Penelope. It's art!" She points to the penis—my dad's penis—that is highlighted with shades of turquoise and yellow. "It's very difficult to get the male anatomy just perfect with these colors. It took me hours. Hours! And you won't even look. Imagine how that makes me feel to know I raised you to be so unappreciative of the efforts of others. The human body should be celebrated!"

I don't know why, but I glance back at the painting again, this time
with a gag.

Then groan.

"I'm going outside, Mom. I love you, but never show me this again.
I'm sure you painted dad's... pieces... great, I just never *ever* want to see
them."

I hold my glass up to Gabe, signaling the need for a refill.

He obliges.

Poppy is a woman who lives and speaks the taboo, but even as her
daughter, the shock of that never fades.

Outside on the deck, the coastal breeze licks at my skin as the shock of
my mother fades. I watch as Finn throws a football to his cousins in the
grassy yard below. My heart squeezes. I catch a glimpse of my sweet little
boy playing and laughing in his almost man body.

I had always been so excited to have a teenage son. I imagined we
would have this funny banter and deep connection. But I screwed up,
or life screwed up, and that's not the relationship we ended up with.
Another dream lost.

Gabe leans on the railing next to me. "Kids," he says.

"Kids," I echo.

I turn to him and sip my drink. "How's work?"

"Fish are biting." He grins. "I had a good season with the snowbirds,
and the spring breakers survived in all their drunken glory. Can't complain about much."

Gabe owns a local fishing charter business, and it's as though it's what
he was made for. Like there's no place else he'd rather be.

He's a year older than me, but we could pass as twins with our brown
hair and amber eyes. Where my skin is pale from my year of self-inflicted
isolation, his is tan from a million hours on a boat.

"Thanks for all of your help, Gabe. I mean it." I turn my attention back to the kids running below us. "I wouldn't be doing this if it wasn't for you. Hell, I probably wouldn't have survived the last year without you. Or the funeral..." my voice trails off with my unspoken *when I tried to swim away.*

"We're all glad to see you doing this. Something fun." He taps his finger on the railing, smile pulling at his lips when he adds, "Randy Miller is hoping you're going to be ready to date when you get back."

He takes a sip of his beer with a cocked eyebrow.

I slap him on the arm and groan.

"Okay, first, how many times has Randy been married? Like four?" I ask, offended at the mere thought of *Randy Miller.* "That man cannot keep his thing in his pants. And second, I can't imagine ever dating anyone again, but *if* I ever do, please know, it won't be one of your disgusting friends from high school."

Gabe laughs as I down the rest of my tequila with a shudder.

"Also, are we going to talk about Mom's new art, or are we just pretending that isn't happening?" I ask.

"I'm good with pretending," he says with a grimace and too-long gulp of his beer that makes me snort.

When my mom yells, "Dinner!" it's the familiar smells of grilled steak and citronella candles blowing in the breeze as we settle around the table.

My dad raises his glass.

"To our Nelly, Finn, and Marin. May the road treat them well, and they return to us with only the best stories."

"And may Nel keep four tires on the highway," Gabe chimes in with a lift of his beer.

I shoot him a look that makes everyone at the table laugh.

As we clank our glasses, emotion sits like lead at the back of my tongue. I'm nervous as hell and have no idea how we will manage it all, but I know I need this more than anything. I need to leave with my broken pieces and come back mended.

After laughs and plates of good food, Finn and I are the last ones sitting at the table.

I study him, his brown hair longer than I realized. "You going to be okay with all of this? I mean, I know it's a lot, believe me, it's just that—"

"I don't want to do this, Mom," he cuts me off. "I don't think that's a secret, but I'm not going to fight you on it if that's what you mean." He pauses with a puff of a breath. "And I know you look for him, I see it. You miss him differently than Marin and me. You miss him in an out loud way all the time. I miss him when I hear an airplane buzz overhead. You miss him when you see there's an airplane *or* when you see space maybe an airplane *might* be someday. I just... I'm worried you think we'll find him waiting at a random truck stop along the interstate, even though we won't. He's gone. Whether we like it or not."

Surprisingly, the expression on his face isn't annoyance, it's concern.

He's right.

"I know."

I spin the ring around my finger.

"Me too." He nudges me with his elbow, lips lifting slightly. "Plus, I'd do anything to get you to stop being so weird. You're freaking the whole island out."

I throw my napkin at him, but there's no use denying it.

"You got smart, kid." I look at his face like it's the first time I've seen it in years.

"I know."

Then we turn and watch the sunset in silence.

Seven

"NELLY."

My dad's voice stops me as we climb into the Avion after dinner—Finn in the driver's seat due to Gabe's generous portions of tequila.

"I have something I want to give you."

He holds out a small box, and inside is a simple gold chain.

It's dainty—pretty—but not what I expect before setting off in a camper for the summer. He grabs my hand, his thumb and index finger gently tugging at my wedding band without pulling it off.

"Travis was a good husband to you, Nelly. I don't know if he ever told you, but I met him at the marina before you did. I had been out fishing for mahi, and we had a cooler full at the table cleaning them, drinking a couple of beers, and up walks this kid, looking like he just hopped off a damn surfboard. His parents had just moved to the area, he told us, and he'd never seen such a big fish. He ended up standing there talking to us and drinking my beer for an hour."

My dad laughs, but the look in his eyes is far away, like he's standing right in the marina with twenty-three-year-old Travis.

"I told him, '*I have a daughter you should meet, but only go see her if you want to fall in love.*' He shook his head and said, '*I have too much to do to fall in love! I'm going to be a pilot.*' He was so damn proud. I told him where to find you at the Crow's Nest the next day if he changed his mind."

I don't know if a heart can stop beating while a body continues standing upright, but I'm sure mine had. I wasn't there, had never heard this story before, but I can see it happening so vividly, like I'd always known.

"This ring, Nelly?" His eyes search mine. "It isn't him. Sometimes I watch you, laughing with some of the customers, and then you spin your ring for some reason, and a wall goes back up like you feel guilty for living. It weighs you down like an anchor. I don't want you to forget him—nobody could—but he wouldn't want this either."

There's a pause, slight chuckle, then, "The man didn't have a serious bone in his body. You know that as well as I do. Hell, he was probably smiling like a damn fool when that stupid plane of his went down. He'd be crushed to see you so sad." He shakes his head, a small smile on his face as he lets go of my hand. "I got this in case you think, somewhere out on the road, you're ready to at least take it off your finger."

He squeezes his hand around the one I'm holding the box with. His unspoken *you can do this*.

"Dad..." My voice is barely above a shaky whisper.

He holds up a hand and shakes his head. He knows. He's watched me carry all my shattered pieces in every way I stopped living since Travis left. He's heard everything I've said and didn't say in a way that only a parent can.

He wraps his arms around me and squeezes me in a tight hug. "You're stronger than you think, Nelly. Those kids are damn lucky to have you."

Tears drip down my cheeks as I hug him back.

"Love you, Dad." I squeeze my eyes shut. "Even though you fired me."

His body vibrates with a laugh. "For your own good. Love you, too, Nelly."

Necklace in hand, I wipe my cheeks, get into the Avion, and wave to everyone one last time.

***

That night, as I go through checklists of what we've packed and everything that needs to be taken care of for the bar, I scan through my emails and tie up every loose end I can find. I cringe when I come across the last one from the restaurant owner in Maine—Ethan Mills—I haven't responded in months.

I rub a hand on my forehead as I re-read it.

Penelope,

I try to source as much as I can
from local-to-me farmers, but that's
not always possible, especially with
protein, so I get as close to Maine
as I can. Yes, sometimes that's a
distributor. Produce, with the excep-
tion of lettuce, are all from local
farmers, most of whom I've met over
the years at local markets and built

a relationship from there. Does that
help?

I laughed at the family reference.
I made that mistake one time with
my brother—never again. The only new
vocabulary I learned was four-letter
words. Is it a whole family business?
Siblings? Husband?

Ethan
(please stop calling me Mr. Mills,
I'm only 43, and I think I have to
be at least 60 for that title)

A small laugh mixes with my exhale. I would love to see Gabe behind
the bar with my dad—they'd kill each other.

The word husband stands out like a neon sign, highlighting everything that's gone. I spin my wedding band around my finger, reading the
email again, then hit reply.

~~Mr. Mills~~ Ethan,

Sorry, I'm just circling back to
this. Life got hectic the last

few months. This is all very helpful. Farmers markets were always a
big source of my cocktail creation
process as well, so I can appreciate
this approach. However, I'm curious,
why the specific mention of lettuce?
Also, I read in the article that your
menu changes regularly. That sounds
like a lot of work. How do you manage?

I've worked with my dad since he paid
me under the table. Four-letter words
are actually the only words I speak
most days. No husband and my brother
was smart enough to find a different
profession.

Penelope

Eight

"HOW ARE YOU SO calm?!" Barely awake, I'm already stress sweating.

Finn strolls into the kitchen and leans on the counter coolly as Marin and I fly around the house like hummingbirds jacked up on too much caffeine.

"Mom, we've been planning this for three months, and I've watched you go through your crazy checklists five hundred times. What is there to do?"

He pours a cup of coffee, and I freeze mid-flip of the pages of my list-filled notebook.

"You drink coffee?" I ask, stunned as he grimaces with the first sip.

He shrugs.

"Yes, though typically not the kind that tastes like piss."

"It does not," I scoff defensively, too shocked to say anything else.

He raises his eyebrows as if saying, *does too*, and casually shakes his hair out of his face.

I don't respond, only staring at him a beat longer. Finn drinks coffee; yet another thing I missed.

"Mom! Let's go!"

Marin's voice pulls me from my thoughts.

Through shaking hands, my heart pounding like a drumbeat, and multiple attempts at talking myself out of it, I get into the driver's seat and point the Avion north.

"We're doing it, guys!" I bounce on the bead-covered driver's seat as we cross the bridge to the mainland. "We're going on an adventure! Six hours to Tarpon Springs, where we can eat the best Greek food outside of Greece and see sponges straight out of the water."

Marin and Finn are silent, staring out the windows from the dinette table in the back.

Six hours turn into eight when I realize we are driving through the Everglades and insist on stopping at the same ridiculous attraction we went to years before with Travis. To the surprise of no one, the prices are still too high, the mosquitoes are still hungry assholes, and a shirtless man feeding raw chicken to alligators still isn't impressive.

The t-shirts we buy are just as absurd.

***

After five horrible attempts, I still can't get the Avion backed straight in our spot at the campground.

Finn shakes his head, frustrated in the reflection of my side mirror.

"Mom, get out and let me do this. Didn't Uncle Gabe show you how to back up?"

Annoyed, I do as he says, irritated as he backs in perfectly on his first try with a smug smile on his face.

Once we're set up—attaching cords, hoses, and pulling out a few chairs—we only have a couple hours to explore the small town of Tarpon Springs. We walk by piles of sponges that line the docks fresh from the water and eat the best baklava I've ever had. A street performer plays lonely songs on a violin that Marin twirls to as we wander down the sidewalk after dinner. Finn keeps his eyes on his phone and any other day, it would annoy me, but today I'm just happy we made it.

When we get back to the camper, the rush of adrenaline from the day is gone and leaves me exhausted.

Marin pulls out a deck of cards.

"Rummy?" she asks, shuffling them.

Finn nods and takes the seat across from her. I shake my head with a yawn.

"I'm tired," I say, dropping kisses on their heads.

"Night, Mom," Marin says, dealing the cards. "Love you."

"Love you guys."

Finn lifts his chin. The closest thing I'll get to *love you, too* from him tonight.

Inside, I bumble through a quick shower in the too-tiny bathroom and climb the ladder up to my coffin-like loft bed. When I pull the little curtain closed, I breathe a sigh of relief.

We did it.

I smile until I realize I'm spinning my wedding band. I slide it off my finger, the faint light from the window reflecting off the shiny gold.

It weighs you down like an anchor.

I reach into the small space between the mattress and the wall and grab the box my dad gave me.

"Travis," I say out loud, snapping my mouth shut instantly at the sound.

Wrapping my fingers into a tight fist around the ring, it feels like holding my own heart in my hand.

"Travis, I'm talking to you. I know you aren't here, I know that, but along with everything else you were, my best friend was a big one. And, you know, your job as my best friend is to listen, so here we are. Me lying in the cramped bed of a camper you bought while I talk to you when you aren't actually here. So that's how I'm doing..." I laugh under my breath, closing my eyes to let the next words come out in an unfiltered stream of consciousness. "We are going on the trip you planned. Or kind of planned. And I let the kids pick some of the stops, and we decorated the camper to match the 70s time period. Can you believe you can still buy shag carpet? Leave it to Marin to be able to find it."

I smile but my throat burns, cracking my voice.

"Dammit, Travis, I still miss you so much it physically hurts. I miss you so much, over a year went by, and I couldn't tell you much of anything that happened until we started working on the camper. I might as well have been on that plane with you because I'm a ghost in my skin. Like a Travis-sized piece of me is missing. And since you were bigger than me, I guess that means I've just been missing."

I swipe at my eyes as I stare at the too-low ceiling above my face.

The words I want to say next feel like they might split me in two, but I know I have to say them, anyway. I have to move forward and telling him is the only way I know how to start.

"I don't want the kids to remember me this way. I want to be normal. *Happy.* I want to go to farmers markets and scream over the seasonal fruit or the smell of herbs. I want to laugh when I make a cocktail. I want the kids to *want* to be around me. I know the only way I'll be able to do that is if I stop letting your absence consume every second of every day.

"Finn told me I miss you out loud and look for you everywhere, and God, if that kid doesn't see me better than I see myself sometimes.

"I'm going to put your ring on this necklace so I can stop looking for you everywhere we go. I'm going to have fun with them and buy stupid t-shirts and make memories that are only ours, even though they are because of you. I love you, Travis Crawford. Thank you for loving us so much it hurts."

Before I change my mind, I slip the ring on the chain and fasten it around my neck.

As the kids laugh outside, I cry every tear my body can make until I finally fall asleep.

Nine

SOMEWHERE AROUND TALLAHASSEE, MARIN can't handle the fact that 1978 Avions are not Bluetooth enabled and insists on us stopping at an antique store. Fifteen minutes later, she proudly walks out with a box of cassette tapes. The collection includes Mariah Carey, Tom Petty, Janis Joplin, Johnny Cash, Creedence Clearwater Revival, and my personal favorite, Hootie and the Blowfish.

When we finally get to our campground outside of Fairhope, Alabama, I am convinced by the shack-like structure and hand-painted sign that says OFFICE, we are going to get murdered.

"Is this place safe?" Marin hisses as her face pales with the distant sound of a revving chainsaw.

Yes might be a lie so I don't respond.

The rickety screen door has holes and hangs loosely on the hinges, squeaking loudly when we open it, slowly stepping inside.

There isn't much in the space—a few shelves of fishing tackle and a cooler of drinks line one wall, nets and buckets on the other. There's a dim lamp in the corner behind a counter with a register. An old man with a wiry beard sits propped up on a stool, wearing faded overalls, eyes closed. A golden retriever is sprawled across the floor, sleeping, legs moving with little whimpers as he dreams.

Marin grips my arm tighter. "Oh my God, Mom! He's dead!" she croaks.

I freeze, Finn laughs, and the dead man startles to life. Hand to my chest, my heart beats like a jackhammer.

"God, sorry, we thought you were dead!" I gasp, trying to catch my breath. "Sorry. We have a reservation for tonight."

He eyeballs me, then the kids, as if assessing if we are who we claim to be.

He nods slowly as he says, "I see. Wha' brings ya down to de bay?"

His voice surprises me—instead of the southern accent I expect, he sounds almost Cajun. Shuffling through papers, he doesn't take his eyes off us.

"Y'all here to fish?"

He looks amused as he says it—like he doesn't believe it's a possibility. I bristle at the implication even though I don't even like fishing.

Finn clears his throat. "Actually, yes. I've been looking at the weather—you think there's a chance of a jubilee in the next couple of days? I know it's early in the summer, but temps are unusually high for this time of year from what I've read. Wind doesn't seem to be blowing."

My eyes widen as I look at Finn. *A jubilee?*

A surprised look that mirrors my own covers the old man's face.

"Y'all know' bout our jubilee, den. I call it de rush, myself. Eitha' way. Smart boy ya got here." He looks at me briefly. "I usually start checkin' for de signs abou' June one, but we only a few days early. Guess we could check tonight if you gonna get up and help."

He points a crooked finger at Finn, who in turn, looks at me.

Stunned, I just shrug my shoulders. Because—what?

Travis would have volunteered to join, no doubt. The thought makes me blurt, "We'll all help."

Finn's eyes go wide, Marin's fingernails dig into my skin, and amusement fills the man's face.

"Okay den, all y'all need to be here, dressed and ready in de mornin'." He peeks over the counter at our flip-flop-covered feet. "And no toes. If ya don't have no boots, ya better wear somethin' over de toes for when ya have to shuffle round wit de gig." He lets out a chuckle. "Name's Dickey, by de way. A jubilee comes when we least 'spect it, tonight seems good as any. Ya boy's right with de signs, but we gotta check de tide." He flips through some papers. "Yep, comin' in right on time." He looks up, a twinkle in his old eyes. "Course, I guess de tide's always on time."

He pauses—as if he's just been very wise—then we all stand in the shack in an awkward silence until he continues.

"Anyway, here's all de information for de campsite. You gonna wanna loop round de back side der." He points to a map with all the campsites laid out. "And just back on in den. Y'all got wada, sewah, and 'lectric all right at de site. Just come'n get me if y'all have any trouble."

I take the papers and start toward the door, pausing.

"Dickey? I don't think you said, what time in the morning should we meet you to go..." my eyes flick to Finn before I ask, "Jubilee?"

"Two sounds good."

He leans back on his stool.

"Oh, I'm sorry, I thought it was morning. So, two o'clock tomorrow afternoon?"

"Uh-uh. In de mornin'. A jubilee happens early. Dem fish come in lookin' for a breath."

What the hell?

Finn lets out a little snort, reading my confusion, and tugs my arm.

"C'mon, Mom. I'll explain it while we set up."

He lifts a hand and waves at Dickey and calls over his shoulder, "Hey, thanks a lot, sir. See ya tonight."

"Don't forget de shoes!" Dickey's yell floats through the tattered screen door.

Marin shoots a look at me once she gets in the passenger seat. "What the hell, Penelope?"

"Marin! Language!" I say, opening the back door.

"You signed us up to go do some sort of creepy fishing party with a man in the middle of the night! Language feels appropriate!" she shrieks.

"He was nice once I realized he wasn't dead," I argue, sitting on the floor behind their seats.

"I think it's going to be fun. Plus, what are you scared of, Marin? He's old. If things go south, the three of us could take him. A jubilee is really rare, it only happens here and allegedly one other place in the world. If we are lucky enough to see it, it's going to be awesome," Finn says from the driver's seat, clearly pleased with how everything turned out.

Marin mutters under her breath while we circle around the gravel road to our site. Finn easily backs us in.

We make quick work of setting up and eating dinner—grilled cheese—before settling around a fire.

"Okay, Finn, explain what we are getting ourselves into here. If there is a jubilee, how freaked out are Marin and I going to be about it?"

He pokes a stick at the logs.

"Well, it's definitely different from fishing off a boat. Basically, a very specific set of conditions creates a situation where fish and shell-fish—usually mullet, blue crabs, and shrimp—move to the shallowest water in the middle of the night, making it easy to catch them. Obviously, I've never done it, but from what I've read, most people will wade out a bit with a tub tied to their waist and gig for mullet or just use nets to scoop the crabs and shrimp. It's a big party sometimes, drawing in a crowd if enough people find out about it."

Marin opens a bag of marshmallows and looks at him.

"Gig?"

Finn nods, "yeah, it's basically a big spear you stab at the fish."

Her face twists. "Wait, so we go out *into* this water that's overflowing with all of these things and start stabbing them... in the dark?"

"Mhmm. Basically," he says. "Or netting them."

"What's the tub for?" she asks.

"For whatever you catch."

His tone is so nonchalant, I bark out a laugh.

As terrified as I am by the idea of it all, I'm excited. We've spent a lifetime living on an island, but this feels different. Like a glimpse of a secret world I didn't know existed before now.

Finn throws another log on the fire, smoke billowing into the air before he settles back into his chair and pulls out his phone.

I yawn as I stand up.

"I'm tired and need at least four hours of sleep before I *gig* in the dark," I tell them, heading towards the camper.

As I open the door, the most beautiful thing happens—they both smile at me and say goodnight.

Ten

"FINN. SHUT THAT THING off. This is stupid."

Marin covers her head with a pillow as Finn's alarm beeps loudly at 1:45 AM.

"Shut up, Marin, this is going to be epic. Life changing. Get your ass out of bed."

I groan as I slide open my curtain. "Language."

I struggle to pry myself from my mattress, so tired my eyelids physically ache, as Finn skips around like he's had a full night's sleep.

When Marin and I make it out of the Avion, we look like we need to be resuscitated with paddles and a high dose of electricity.

As soon as we find Dickey at the office shack, he looks at our feet and nods in approval at the rubber boots we've worn. A small light on the porch is the only thing shining in the darkness.

"Well, now." Dickey lets out a low whistle. "I wadn't sure y'alls gonna make it dis mornin', but here y'are surprisin' ol' Dickey."

My tired face attempts to smile, but it is entirely too early for third-person conversations. Or any person conversations.

"I spose y'all didn't crawl outta ya beds just to hear me talk, so let's get on with it. Gotta get movin' if we wanna even see if we gonna get a jubilee. Can't just stand here all day." He waves us over to a wagon. "Now in here, we got us some nets, gigs, a coupla numba two washtubs, and headlamps. Now some dem boys like to use big lights, but dis here headlamp frees up ya hands, ya see."

Marin and I stare at the wagon like zombies while Finn goes full speed ahead and investigates every item.

"Now we gonna walk down to the wada, and we'll know right away if we gonna be havins us a rush... jubilee, as dey say. Tides comin' in. If it's gonna happen, we gonna see some critters hangin' in de shallows dat we wouldn't usually be seein'. Maybe an eel, maybe some shrimp, maybe a mullet. Just no tellin' what's gonna be lettin' us know if it's happenin'. Y'all just grab some lights, and we gonna go shine it on down de shore."

We all do as he says, Finn asking a million questions about fish and tides while Marin and I stay quiet. I swear he says something about phytoplankton, but at this crazy hour with that many syllables, I cannot compute it. We wander down a short path to the edge of Mobile Bay. The darkness is so infinite it makes my skin crawl.

"Well, whatcha'll waitin' on? Less find us some breakfast!"

He turns toward the water, and we all follow his lead, pointing our lights down toward our feet. We spread out from each other slightly. For the first few minutes, we're quiet as we carefully look in the water, or *wada*, as Dickey calls it.

"I see something!" Marin yells.

"Me too! I think a needlefish? Dickey, over here!" Finn calls.

I keep my lamp pointed at the water. A piece of seaweed and shell bits are all I see as I walk along the shore. Then my light flickers over something that moves. A leg. Another leg. *A crab.*

"Crab!" is all I can make my 2AM mouth shout.

Dickey makes the rounds to the three of us, eyeing what we find in calm silence.

"What's it mean?" Finn asks with a squint.

"Well, boy," Dickey pauses with a smile. "It means we havin' ourselves de first jubilee of de season."

Finn pumps a fist through the air with a shout, and my throat clogs at the simple beauty of it.

Dickey stands calmly before giving us directions.

"We got a little time to get ready before de rest of dem come in. Lil' Miss?" Dickey nods toward Marin. "I need ya to go ring de bell to let the folks know that we havin' ourselves a jubilee. Go eat some food or get some coffee, and we'll meet back at de wagon to take it all down to de beach."

The three of us take off running like chickens with our heads cut off while Dickey and his golden retriever walk slowly and take a seat in a rocking chair on the front porch of the office. His silence only breaks occasionally when he whistles a few notes.

Once Marin rings the bell, the campground lights up. People in pajamas—some in less than—fling doors open and start yelling. The out-of-towners wonder what the hell is going on, while the experienced locals know *exactly* what the hell is going on.

I scramble around the camper to make coffee as all the excitement hums outside the window. Marin and Finn stumble into each other as they make a fast breakfast and scream about what might happen. As tired as I am, I can't imagine not being part of this.

I leave first, wandering over to the office and the old man who sits outside of it.

"Hey, Dickey. I wanted to thank you so much for doing this. For my son, Finn, this is as exciting as Christmas morning for him."

He smiles as I sit in a rocking chair next to him, watching the excitement unfold around us.

"I shood be thankin' y'all. Ain't nobody gonna be lookin' for a jubilee fer anotha' coupla' weeks. Your son's feedin' us all today." He takes a sip of his coffee. "Now tell me, whatcha'll doin' down here gettin' fish wid an old man in de middle of de night."

It is the definition of a loaded question.

"Hmm. Well, we fixed up an old camper and decided to take the summer to see the country. We're from Florida, so we're used to fishing, just not quite like this under such magical circumstances."

I take another sip of my coffee and click my tongue at the bitter flavor.

"What makes ya call it magic?" he asks.

Even in the dark, I can see a twinkle in his eye.

"Well, the way my son explains it, this is a very precise set of circumstances that has come together to make this rare event happen. I can't even really believe it. Things like this don't just happen everywhere, ya know?"

I drop my head back on my chair.

"Well, accordin' to yer words, maybe der's a lot more magic in dis world den we give credit to," he says. "Dem kids o' yours? Perfect timin'. I don't pretend to be a smart man, but what if ya had 'em a little lata or soona? Reckin' we don't know if dey'd be de same folks. Magical, as you call it. Birds migrate. Certain flowers grow only in certain areas. Sometimes we see rainbows paint de sky after a storm. Ya boy told me y'all just got to see sponges from de floor of de Gulf. Sounds special from where I'm sittin'. Jubilees happen all 'round us if we know where to look."

He pats the dog on the head and takes another sip of his coffee as his eyes look out into the darkness of the early morning.

I soak his words up like the desert sand in a rainstorm, letting their meaning seep into every part of me.

"How'd ya husband die?" he asks nonchalantly as he takes another sip of coffee.

"How do you... why would..."

I reach instinctively to spin the ring on my finger before remembering it isn't there.

"Women don't keep weddin' bands if dey's divorced."

His eyes drop to the chain hanging around my neck.

"Eitha way. Life, death, light, darkness... it's all magic. Timing and perfect circumstances spontaneously comin' togetha for a phenomenon of one type or anotha. Funny ting about it, dough, we forget it's all temporary. It has a season. No jubilee lasts forever—hell, we lucky if it lasts til de day breaks. Dat's why it's fun," he says with a small chuckle. "If we skipped everytin' we wanted to cause we knew it was gonna come to an end, dat'd be a damn shame if ya ask me."

I stay quiet. This man with a wiry beard in overalls at some insane hour of the morning has cracked me open with the wisdom he has in him that he somehow knows I need. I suspect he's lost someone in his life and sees something familiar in me. A twin flame that burns in a way that only someone with a hole in their heart does. I sit silently, staring into the same darkness as him, knowing he doesn't need me to say anything.

Marin, Finn, and a few other folks from campers start to join us on the porch, along with cars filling the small lot. My eyebrows raise, and Dickey sees my surprise.

"When der's a jubilee, friends don't let friends fish alone."

He squints as he waves to people he recognizes through the bright headlights.

Regardless of the insane hour, the excitement is palpable in the dark, muggy morning air.

We make our way back down to the bay, Dickey guiding us through everything as dozens of people cover the beach, bright lights shining into the water. This jubilee, it seems, is bringing mostly mullet and blue crabs, but there are some shrimp mixed in as well.

With metal washtubs tied around our waists with a rope that tugs them along the top of the water behind us, we slowly wade out into the bay.

Finn takes right to gigging the mullet with a forked spear. He's completely in his element with a headlamp, knee deep in the dark water as he effortlessly jabs the fish and then drops them into the bucket that floats behind him.

When Marin screams and runs maniacally from the water more than once—everyone laughs, even Dickey.

I scoop with a net and wade only in the shallowest parts, where I drop blue crabs into my own washtub tethered to my body.

Sometime around 5AM, someone brings out the ingredients for a Bloody Mary bar and invites everyone in earshot to make one. While vodka before daybreak isn't usually my norm, neither is wading in water with a bucket of crabs tied to me, so I have one for the sake of authenticity.

Then I have one more, just because.

The locals swear by their homemade mix of homegrown horseradish and a secret variety of hot peppers. We all raise a glass and laugh as they share stories of jubilees gone by. Even Dickey has one as he sits in a chair on the shore, coaching Finn and Marin as they wade around the water.

Eventually, the tide changes. The fish start heading back out to the deeper parts of the bay and our focus shifts from catching to cleaning. The sun barely peaks over the horizon but brings enough light to show the happy faces of strangers down the beach as they look in buckets and coolers.

"I woke up too damn early not to have blue crab for breakfast!" a man yells down the shore. Everyone cheers in agreement.

Portable gas burners fire up, and the smell of fresh seafood cooking wafts in every direction at the same time the sun fully pops up into the sky.

Emotions swirl in my chest as I try to process the beauty of what we've just experienced. A local tradition most people won't encounter in a lifetime, yet here we are, with washtubs and bellies full of the freshest seafood I've ever had.

After nearly a year and a half of living my days trapped in a rerun of memories, this is my first best new one.

I don't look for Travis—I don't say his name once—but I can't help but think about how much he would have loved this kind of crazy. He would have been right beside Finn, gigging mullet, making obnoxious sound effects, and mocking the fish as he tossed them in his bucket.

He would have waded beside Marin and me, plucking blue crabs out of nets, making jokes about having crabs that I would have rolled my eyes at but secretly loved.

Dickey would have somehow told him every secret from the east coast of Mobile Bay.

"Well, Nel," he would have said, "Guess if all it takes to get you out fishing at two in the morning is a Bloody Mary, we're going to have to get their recipe."

The idea of it all makes me smile, but even more, it doesn't make me cry. I figure sometimes, that's what life after him will be—celebrating the moments I somehow stay intact.

By lunch, I'm tired, stuffed, and riding a Bloody Mary buzz so fierce, I wonder if the real secret ingredient was simply extra vodka.

We give Dickey a group hug, and his kind old face fills with happiness as we smother him in a tangle of arms.

"Ol' Dickey nevah had a hug like dat before," he says with a grin.

The next morning, we are up early once again to hit the road, all wearing t-shirts that say *Jubilee with Me* above a picture of a dancing mullet.

***

Somewhere east of Houston, I drop in a camp chair and call my dad to make sure the bar is still standing. His "Ye have little faith!" is followed by, "What have you found out about the local ingredients from the man in Maine?" which makes my eyes roll. Instead of crawling into bed and sleeping for a month like I want to, when we get off the phone, I scroll my inbox—finding the latest email from Ethan sitting unread.

Penelope,

I mention lettuce because even when it isn't in season, I keep a salad on my menu year-round. What changes are the additional ingredients which I

try to keep fresh and seasonal. So, in
the summer, I might have blueberries
in a salad, while in the winter, I
might have beets or roasted sweet
potatoes. Believe it or not, lettuce
isn't locally grown around here in
January.

I change my menu regularly, but my
menu is also small. I've found it's
easier to keep things local if you
aren't trying to make everything.
Stay in my lane, so to speak.

Tell me about what you do. I looked
up your restaurant, and I see it's
in Key Largo. I also see that if
anyone should be asking anyone for
advice, it should be me to you. I may
have gotten a couple sentences in the
magazine, but your whole article puts
mine to shame. Most fun restaurant?
That's damn impressive.

Ethan

I laugh at the same time pride swells in my chest. I've been so stuck in sadness and surviving that I forget we *have* accomplished a lot. It is *damn impressive* and has taken so much work. But he's looked me up? Not that my face is plastered on the internet, but somehow the notion has me savagely chewing my fingernail. I put my phone down and pick it up too many times to count before deciding to respond.

Ethan,

I've watched enough crime documentaries to know that your research on us is a creepy red flag. Lucky for you, I give people the benefit of the doubt and am going to assume your curiosity is just normal weird and not stalker weird.

Our fun ranking is due mostly to the fact I have kids and needed to get creative with our space to figure out ways I could bring them to work without having them drink all the vodka. Also, we rigged the voting process. I'll let you decide if I'm joking.

In all seriousness, I'm just a bartender—nothing too exciting here.

Thanks for the insight into the let-
tuce/salad situation.

Is everything always fresh, or do you
sometimes take fresh local ingredients and freeze it for a different
season? I'm thinking soups, sauces,
etc…

Penelope

Eleven

TIME MOVES SO SLOWLY as we drive across Texas, I can feel my own body starting to decay.

We stay in constant motion as we check off the boxes on Travis' list while we trudge across the huge state.

San Antonio.

Austin.

Dallas.

The greenery of the east fades sharply into the dry and dusty monochromatic landscapes of the west. Texas is a place to go to forget or be forgotten.

The days it takes for us to cross the state wear on me.

On us.

Hours of sitting behind a steering wheel with the idiotic wooden beads digging into my sticky skin have me on the brink of snapping like a dry twig.

Somewhere between the ridiculous yoga postures Marin insists on showing me at the rest areas to help me relax and the moment Johnny Cash's voice flips from soothing to completely unnerving, I rip the beads off the seat and throw them out the window as we barrel down the highway.

"I don't care if they're made of wood. It's still littering and bad for the environment," Marin says, appalled.

I don't have the heart to tell her in that moment, I don't give a flying fuck about the environment.

With every too-long mile that registers on the odometer, I mentally list and re-list every single reason the trip is the worst idea of my life.

The morning we find ourselves sitting and staring at something labeled as art at the edge of a sun-bleached field in a town called Marfa, I am certain it's the end.

We squint at the series of rusty shipping containers set in rows in the middle of a barren field. The three of us sit on a bench with a different expression on each of our faces: Marin's admiration, mine skepticism, Finn's annoyance.

"The artist who made these, a lady named Zefra Lox, said that these symbolize the obsessive need to over-consume with the balance of lonely isolation," Marin says.

I frown.

What the hell does that even mean?

"She sounds like a moron," Finn bites out, rubbing the bridge of his nose with a finger.

Last night, we had all been in good moods while we went to see some mystery lights that danced across the desert in the dark, but this morning, Finn is distant. Cold.

A woman walks by us with a flustered look on her face and tears in her eyes.

"Isn't this just so incredible?"

I bite my lip. Because no, it is not incredible.

"Inside, we got to see a bunch of empty chairs in a room of red lamps, and out here we are looking at... what is this supposed to be?"

"It's art, Penelope," Marin says as she snaps a picture with her phone. "It doesn't matter what it is. It's about a *feeling*."

"It *feels* dumb."

Finn's tone is clipped, and the way he scrolls on his phone is desperate. His jaw clenches repeatedly, and the tension rolling off him in waves is palpable.

I lower my voice and rub his tight shoulders with my palm. "Hey. You okay?"

He jerks away. "I need to make a call. I'll meet you two in the parking lot when you are done with your stupid containers."

As soon as the words are out, he's off the bench and marching across the field.

Defeat tugs on my shoulders. "What's going on with him?"

"Who knows?" She rolls her eyes. "I think it's about Abby. I saw one of the texts saying she wasn't going to wait around all summer or something. She's kind of the worst anyway, so good riddance in my opinion, but whatever."

"Why don't you like her?"

I promised myself not to push Finn, but Marin is a resource I can't refuse.

"Honestly, she's a controlling bitch. She asked Finn to stop hanging out with some of his friends because she didn't like their girlfriends. She hated it when he went fishing on the weekends with Uncle Gabe, and she told me it was cute I wore used clothes, but she said it in a way that implied she did *not* think it was cute. Especially when I told her I thought it was cute she dressed like a hooker." She shrugs. "He can do better."

She snaps another picture of the containers in front of us.

"Language," I only half-mean it. She does actually sound like a bitch, and I would pay good money to watch Marin tell someone they dress like a hooker.

I sit quietly as I consider what she said, trying to understand what Finn might be dealing with.

When the back of my shirt is soaked with sweat and my thighs stick like suction cups to the bench, I can't take it anymore.

"How long do we have to sit here and look at this before we can go? It's hot as hell out here, Marin."

"Now," she says, standing. "I actually don't think this is even that impressive."

I snort out a laugh and hook my arm through hers. "You're a funny kid."

Her nose scrunches. "And you're a funny mom."

When we find Finn in the parking lot, he's slumped on a bench with a deep crease between his eyebrows.

"Everything okay?" I ask as I sit down next to him.

"Just great." He gives a sarcastic thumbs-up, "Can we just go?" He huffs, standing up and walking toward the Avion.

I stand, following him.

"Yeah, that's fine. Did something happen? You seem upset."

He rolls his eyes while shaking his head. "You're *so* intuitive."

"Do you want to talk about it?" I ask calmly, trying to ignore the way his tone is begging for me to lose my ever-loving mind.

"Abby just broke up with me because she didn't want to spend a summer waiting for her boyfriend to get back from vacation. Happy? You drag us on this little trip to fix your life while you ruin ours in the process. Seems about right. No, I do not want to talk about it, Mom."

My breath escapes me in a gust. "Finn, that's not fair."

He scoffs. "Fair? I can't wait to hear about what *you* think is fair."

I squeeze my hands into tight fists at his emphasis. I half expect my skin to break open and bleed.

Finn's face is stamped in sadness and anger and looks every bit of what it means to be heartbroken.

My anger is replaced by sympathy.

"Finn..."

Before I can figure out what to say next, Finn's arm rears back before quickly snapping forward. He hurtles his phone against the Avion with a loud shatter and an angry yell.

His yell isn't an actual word but holds the weight of a novel's worth.

My mouth opens and then closes. Twice. Three times.

Marin scoffs and crosses her arms. "Really, Finny, you broke your phone over stupid Abby?"

Note to self, muzzle Marin in tense situations with her brother.

"Shut up, Marin! I don't need to hear it from you, too."

He runs his hand through his hair.

The wisdom I've accumulated from four decades of living on earth makes me want to explain all the reasons why these things happen—how relationships come and go before the right one clicks into place—but I don't.

As much as I know about love and loss, I also know to a seventeen-year-old, none of my advice matters. My experience is irrelevant. I know his heartbreak is real and big and like the most devastating thing there is, even if it isn't.

Finn slams the door of the Avion as I crouch down to pick up the shattered pieces of his phone, a pointless task that only serves to keep me from crying the frustrated tears I'm fighting.

Crouched down in a Marfa parking lot, it becomes painfully clear that no matter how many miles away from home we drive, we can't outrun our own heartbreak.

Twelve

THE TWANG OF A guitar floats from speakers in the middle of the campground toward our campsite as we eat a tense dinner that night.

"Yeah, so we totally have to go see what's going on over there." Marin cranes her neck to get a look at the people walking toward the small amphitheater. "This is so Texas of us. The desert, the music. I bet some people rode horses to get here!"

Her eyes twinkle brightly as she watches.

I snort between bites while Finn stays silent, pushing food around his plate.

"Hey, can you give Finn and me a few minutes to talk, Mar? Then we can go to the music?"

She shoots him a look before taking her plate and going inside.

I grab two beers from the fridge and set them on the table, taking a seat across from him.

Finn's brown eyes go wide.

My eyes.

As much as he hates me at that moment, he still looks exactly like me. It's the only thing that reminds me that no matter how far apart we get, we are still very much connected.

"Your dad and I always said we wanted to drink with you first. It was our plan for when you turned 18," I say as I pop the tops off both and hand him one. "It's only a few months away, and I feel like a breakup in a town called Marfa is a good reason to move the timeline up. Plus, considering the fact I've been living with my head in the sand, I know there's a chance this will not be your first beer."

I raise an eyebrow as his eyes bounce from me to the beer, then back to me.

I take a sip of mine and welcome the hoppy, citrusy flavor with a sigh before he does the same.

I fold my arms on the picnic table and meet his gaze. "I'm sorry Abby broke up with you, and I'm sorry I gave her a reason to. I'm not sorry we're here."

"So, is this some kind of bribe or something? You give me a beer, and I forgive you for dragging us into the desert?" He shakes his head, picking at the label on his bottle without looking at me.

"No, but I thought it might help. There's an alcohol loophole in Texas for minors with parents. I figured I'd take advantage of it on a day such as this." I twirl my finger through the air..

He laughs softly and takes another sip of his beer.

"Do you want to talk about it?" I ask.

"Not much to say. I'm gone for ten weeks. She didn't like it. Now it's over." His voice is flat, face resigned.

"Well, she might change her mind when you get back. Or you might change your mind. Time changes perspective in ways we don't expect sometimes. And sometimes people are in our lives at a certain time when we need them and fade away when we don't." I pause. "Your dad would have had something more profound to say here, I bet."

He shrugs. "Dad might not have looked up alcohol laws regarding minors and then served me a beer, though."

It's almost a compliment.

He tilts his head to the side and looks at me, raising his beer up, which I gladly clink mine against.

It's a moment I can feel being stamped on the timelines of our lives. A story he'll fall back on later, maybe if he becomes a parent and feels like he's doing a piss-poor job. Maybe he'll think about this night in a weird town called Marfa and remember me showing up in my own messy way, beer in hand.

When the door of the Avion swings open, Marin fills the doorway wearing a denim skirt and rhinestone cowboy boots.

"Oh, that's fair. The hussy breaks up with him, and he gets a beer?" She crosses her arms over her pink flannel shirt with a pout.

"Don't even think about it, Mar." I raise my eyebrows. "And how do you have such a Texas-worthy outfit?"

"Oh, Penelope, you underestimate me."

She clicks the heels of her boots together and grins.

When we finish our beer, Marin forces us to the music.

***

The singer is a big, broad-shouldered guy with a short beard, cream-colored cowboy hat, and a Texas-sized smile. He owns the night in scuffed-up boots that effortlessly slide across the worn wooden stage with the beat of the music.

His voice is bluesy, but his lyrics are pure country, an unexpectedly soulful combination I feel all the way in my bones.

"This is amazing!" Marin yells over the music.

I nod and turn to Finn. He's neither smiling nor scowling, an odd sort of victory.

Hipsters and cowboys create a kaleidoscope of denim, flannel, and leather across the crowd. The dance floor in front of the stage is filled with young girls twirling with arms overhead under strings of lights. Food trucks serving BBQ and beer are surrounded by people with happy faces. Like all the problems they have were checked at the metal gates they walked through to get here.

"We have to go dance!"

Marin's gray eyes shine as brightly as her ridiculous boots as she takes my hand and drags me out to the dance floor.

I resist, but only just slightly, because the truth is, I *want* to. Maybe it's the old-fashioned sound of the music, the beer, or the way the big Texas sky glows as the sun sets, but it's as if dancing is the only possible option. Like time won't continue if we don't give in to the urge to move to the music.

I grab Finn's reluctant hand, dragging him as Marin drags me. He shakes his head adamantly, but once the three of us are standing in the middle of a sea of denim-clad dancing bodies on the dance floor, there's no fighting it. No stopping it. The music conquers every shred of embarrassment with each chord that plays.

We dance. Playfully and like we don't have a care in the world. We dance like we aren't running into the desert from sadness or looking for something we might never find. We twirl each other around the dusty corner of the world called Marfa in a way that reminds me that we might not be as fragile as we think.

Our hair is matted with sweat on our foreheads, but we wrap our sticky arms around each other anyway. We sing. In a bluesy rendition of *Don't Stop Believin'*, every lyric reaches deep into my chest. So deep I don't know if my heart will ever beat the same way again. Loud and off-key, our voices tangle with the singing laughter of strangers to become an anthem I didn't know we needed.

When the final notes play, the music fades into a love-laced ballad, and we wander off the dance floor to make room for the lovers and strangers that take our places.

Couples cling together like magnets, and I imagine many of them feel like they are the only ones in the entirety of West Texas. A slurry of longing and sadness stirs within me as I watch, thinking how that would have been Travis and I had life not written our story so poorly.

"Isn't it romantic?" Marin sighs as she looks dreamily at the dance floor. "Love in Marfa."

"Not sure that's the kind of love story the world is ready for," I tease as I pay for drinks.

We find an open picnic table by the dance floor as one slow song turns into two. I can't pull my eyes away from all the dancing couples as much as I can't ignore the reality I might never dance with another man again.

My stomach twists. The thought of having some man wrap his arms around me makes me feel nauseous, while the alternative makes me feel devastatingly lonely.

I zip my wedding band back and forth on the gold chain around my neck until Marin's fingers wrap around my forearm and stop the motion.

Her eyes drop to the ring in my hand but don't linger. "One more dance?"

She shimmies her hips as the singer starts purring out the lyrics to an upbeat song.

I smile.

"Only if Finn's joining," I say, cutting my eyes to his.

He shakes his head, as if he's annoyed, but I don't miss the way he doesn't fight us as we drag him out onto the dance floor for one more song.

When I crawl into bed that night—so happy I could burst—there's an email waiting from Ethan.

> Penelope,
>
> I recall *you* reaching out to me after
> looking me up and doing your own
> research. If we are pointing fingers
> at creepy red flags, I'd say I'm the
> one who should be more concerned.
> I'm also shocked you opted to create
> a family-friendly environment over
> just giving your kids free rein of
> the liquor stash. Mine seemed to
> sleep really well at night after they
> spent their days running loose in my
> restaurant…
>
> I'll have to argue with you on being
> *just* a bartender. I've gone to culi-
> nary school and am a decent chef, but
> the few nights I've had to get behind

the bar have been by far the worst of
my life. I never remember what gets
shaken or stirred. It's like the Wild
West back there. What's your favorite
drink to make?

And yes, on the frozen ingredients, I
use them for soup. It's all about language at that point. You'd say local
in the description, not seasonal.

What else? I kind of like helping
restaurant royalty.

Ethan

I don't have the energy to respond, but I read it—twice. He's funny,
I'll give him that.

"Mom?" Marin calls from the other side of my curtain. "Are you
laughing?"

"Sorry, yeah," I say, realizing I *am* laughing. "Just an email. Spam."

When she doesn't respond, I read it one more time before turning my
phone off and going to sleep.

Thirteen

SWEAT COVERS ME LIKE a second layer of skin, the first sign my body knows we are in a bad situation.

It doesn't occur to me until this very moment we have only ever practiced driving the Avion on a flat island in Florida while much of the country was anything but. My ignorance of this has become perfectly clear as we barrel north on the highway toward New Mexico.

Over a fucking mountain.

Marin and I sit in the front seat, Finn napping in the back, when the engine starts to struggle.

A sign saying ENTERING THE GUADALUPE MOUNTAINS flashes by us as I grip the steering wheel for dear life and sweat drips into every crevice of my body.

Marin fidgets with the cassette deck in a way that makes my teeth grind.

"Shut it down, Marin!" I snap.

The music somehow makes it harder to see the road.

She rolls her eyes. "Yikes, Mom, take a chill pill."

"Get your brother," I demand.

I am literally pressing the gas pedal to the metal of the floor. We don't gain any speed, but the arms on the dials stagger into the red zones.

Shit.

Shitshitshitshit.

Semi-trucks crawl by with lights flashing at reduced speeds while cars whiz by us. My anxiety ratchets up to a level I didn't know possible in a mountain range I also didn't know existed.

"Marin! Now!" I snap.

My hands start to shake around the steering wheel as all the blood slowly drains from my face.

Another eyeroll, then a flat call of, "Finn! Wake up. Penelope's freaking out."

We are about to drive off a cliff and die, but my teenage daughter can't be bothered. I'd be angry if I weren't terrified.

"Finn! We got a situation." I shout. "*Now!*"

My *now* must relay that we are in some deep shit because Marin's attitude drops in an instant.

She looks over at me, no doubt noticing my ramrod-straight spine and white knuckles.

"Okay, wait, what's going on?" she asks as Finn crouches down behind her seat.

"Finn, we are in the mountains, and I don't know what to do. We are barely moving, and the gauges are all... misfiring or something, I don't know. And it's hot as hell in here," I stammer as I wipe my forehead. "Did Gabe tell us what to do? Or is there a button? Or..."

A semi buzzes by us, turning every muscle in my body to stone.

"Like, did he give us tips on how to not roll backward in the mountains or something?"

I try to ignore the cliff that's inches from the passenger door.

He scoffs. "Mom, how would Uncle Gabe know how to drive in the mountains?"

Not helpful.

I take a shaky breath. "Okay, fine. Okay. Let's just figure this out."

The engine is loud, louder than I've heard it in the previous 2,000 miles. Loud enough to tell me we are not fine.

Far from it.

"This gauge says it's hot, I guess. And do you hear how loud everything is?" I yell unintentionally.

On cue, the engine roars again like an angry lion, and the dry, jagged mountains mock me through every window like fangs.

His nose scrunches. "Maybe you should slow down?"

"Slow down?!" I snap as I grip my hands around the steering wheel. "I'm the slowest person on the road right now!"

"You should pull over. The gauge shows it's hot. We could overheat. Marin, turn off the AC. We need to relieve some of the load on the engine."

"Could we catch on fire?" Marin asks in a high-pitched voice as she fumbles with the dials of the AC.

"No fires. Finn, you're right. They have pull-offs. I'll take the next one."

A sedan flies past us, and I hold my breath. In an act of divine intervention, a gravel pull-off appears.

I slow to a stop, and we pour out of the doors like wax from a lit candle.

Finn pops the hood calmly, aware I am clearly useless as I stand on the side of the road, sweating like a whore in church while my pulse pounds in my ears.

"Let's just let it cool down and eat some lunch."

He shrugs. Like this is no big deal. Like we didn't just almost *die*.

"Lunch? Finn, we don't even have cell service!" Marin holds her phone up high in the air. "What if we can't get it fixed? We could be stranded out here forever."

She's the closest I've seen her to hysterical since we left.

"Relax, Mar, look at all these cars. Someone will help us. We just have to wait now for it to cool down," he says, his words mangled from the mouthful of sandwich he's already started chewing.

Thirty minutes later, with a cooled engine under the hood, we are back on the road, this time with Finn behind the wheel.

"No AC until we get through the mountains. Mom, you look like you went swimming."

The turn signal ticks as he waits to pull out onto the highway, and he nods toward my sweat-soaked shirt.

"Turns out I don't handle mountain driving well." I laugh with relief as I roll my window down and let the warm air smack my face.

***

We spend the next four days making our way through southern New Mexico and into Arizona.

Our first night is spent outside of Carlsbad Caverns, where we watch the nightly exodus of the bats from the mouth of the cave. Hundreds of thousands of them pour out at dusk, silently flapping in unison like a black cloud into the desert around us. The park ranger who narrates the departure talks like a ventriloquist, barely moving his mouth, which is both a distraction and highlight of the evening.

"His mouth is creepier than the bats," Finn whispers as the ranger drones on about something called white-nose disease.

I laugh.

There has been the slightest of shifts over our days on the road. Nothing happens overnight, of course, but as the minutes and miles tick by, the grief that has plagued me for so long lifts in degrees. It's the kind of change someone would only notice if they knew where to look.

Closely.

By the time we make it to Arizona, I sleep without dread and laugh without guilt.

After we check Travis' box of an O.K. Corral gunfight reenactment, Marin insists on having old-timey photos done, which we promptly hang on the fridge in the Avion. Finn dressed as a sheriff, Marin holding a shotgun, and me as my best western floozy are forever frozen in sepia tones.

Outside of Tucson, we stay in a nature preserve away from the lights of any city, with the huge saguaro cacti towering around us like giants.

Stoic and silent.

When the sun goes down behind them, it looks like the most iconic Western painting there ever was.

"They look like kind of lonely, don't they?" Marin asks as we eat dinner that night.

"I guess if you lived in a desert for three hundred years, you'd see a lot of things come and go. I wouldn't expect them to be anything but lonely." I study the big weathered cactus next to the Avion. "If you live long enough, you're bound to outlive a lot of what you love the most."

I zip the ring on the chain around my neck as I look at the desert around us. It's the kind of place that conjures sadness by simply just existing. Cracked earth, fiercely spiked cacti, and balls of dry branches scream the harsh truth that it's a place of both survival and death.

A familiar reminder that the two always seem to go hand in hand.

***

"I bet Dad wouldn't have put this on his list if he knew how awful it was going to be."

We are somewhere north of Pheonix as Finn wipes a rag across a shallow cut on his shin.

My face puckers. He's right. We're panning for gold in some mostly dried-up creek bed, and it's miserable. The sun is hot, the rocks are sharp, and the hour we've been out there has given us nothing.

"Do people ever find anything?" I ask the woman who calls herself a Gold Guide before I chug from my water bottle.

The sour woman's voice is snippy, "Of course they do! You think I'm running a scam here?"

Her skinny body sits in a lawn chair under what I assume is the only tree in the state of Arizona and her beady eyes narrow.

"If gold was that easy to find, everyone would be rich!" she says, like I'm an idiot.

I just nod as she takes a drag from her cigarette and flips the page of her magazine.

It's forty-five minutes later when Marin yells from somewhere up the creek.

She finds gold.

We leave that day with the smallest fraction of an ounce of gold flakes in a tiny plastic bag.

***

In bed that night, I finally respond to Ethan's email. I don't know why it's taken so long—that's a lie, I do. It's taken so long because even though we are writing about work, there's a personal undertone to how we talk that feels foreign. Wrong. Because he's funny. Because he's a man. Because he's not Travis.

And yet, I write an email anyway.

    Ethan,

    There's a lot to unpack here, but let
    me just say, more alarming than you
    letting your kids loose on alcohol,
    is you not knowing how to make a
    cocktail. When you own a restaurant.

    I actually forwarded your email to
    American Restaurant magazine and I'm
    sure they will be writing a redaction
    for your piece based on your lack of
    qualifications.

    My favorite drinks to make are the
    classics, and then I just barely
    tweak them to make them something spe-
    cial. Have you ever had a daiquiri?

I'm sure just reading that you imagined something that's frozen, slushy,
and entirely too sweet. That's not
how the cocktail started. It orig-
inated in Cuba, actually, and the
recipe is extremely basic and simple
but so light and fresh. You should
have one of your bartenders make one
for you and tell me what you think.

What about you? What's your favorite
meal to cook? And do you have a
simple version? I'm in a tiny kitchen
situation at the moment, but I'd
like to try it. Without the Maine
ingredients, of course.

I pause, rereading, and realize I haven't included a single thing about
my dad's request. I add:

Thanks again for all your help with
ingredient sourcing. I've sent all
the information to my dad, but knowing him, he'll either have follow-up
questions or completely abandon this
idea.

Penelope

Fourteen

WITH A BLANKET WRAPPED around my shoulders and coffee in hand, I crack the door open, eyes lifting sleepily to the horizon.

I stop, stunned. My coffee stills midair before even making it to my mouth.

Last night, we arrived in Sedona so late all we could see was darkness. Now, the morning light effortlessly reveals the hidden magic.

Red rocks shoot up across the horizon, rugged and beautiful. The fire-filled sunrise bathes everything in oranges, reds, and pinks, magnifying the colors already there.

Living on the Florida coast my whole life, I've become accustomed to the easy kind of beauty that saltwater and palm trees create. It's a straightforward escape that offers a sort of peace by just existing. But this? This is different. It's not a beauty that offers an escape—it strips the soul bare before shattering it apart and stitching it back together differently. It's all encompassing. A place you go to *feel* something.

Our site is on the slope of a mountain overlooking Sedona, which sits like a city in a terracotta bowl.

Straight across from me, where the valley makes way to the sharp cliffs, the red rocks lift out of the dirt as if willed to do so by the sun itself.

Growing up going to church, I was taught that nothing is more holy than those four walls on Sundays, but standing here feels like more of a religious sacrament than anything I've ever been privy to. Like the holiest hymn is being sung, and the most reverent prayer is being recited.

At the edge of our site is a large rock that overlooks it all and I wander over to it and sit, not taking my eyes off the scene around me.

"Mom?" Marin calls as she opens the door and rubs her eyes sleepily.

"Over here," I say over my shoulder.

"Whoa," she whispers as she sits on the rock next to me. "This is what we were missing in the dark? This is so cool."

Her eyes dance around the bowl of Sedona as she wraps part of my blanket around her shoulders.

"Amazing, right?"

Finn joins us, cup of coffee in hand. "Your coffee skills haven't improved," he says blandly before blowing on the steam.

"It's not that bad," I argue, trying to hide the way my face wants to twist as I take another sip.

"Liar." He tilts his head toward the view I've already started to memorize. "This is pretty sweet though."

I nod.

We sit there in silence as the sun lifts higher in the sky and reveals new details with every ray of light. An old friend whispering new secrets.

Eventually, our bad coffee goes cold, and the cool air turns hot. We spend the day hiking through the vibrant red rocks and then wandering the busy streets of Sedona.

Travis may have been the one who circled this spot on a map, but it's Marin who's obsessed with every mystical piece of it.

"Here," she says, dropping a bright blue stone in Finn's hands after dragging us into a New Age crystal shop.

He huffs. "What's this supposed to be?"

"Lapiz. For enlightenment." She says it like he's supposed to understand that.

His eyes narrow.

"So, you can finally see what a dirty hooker Abby was."

I have to bite my cheek to keep from laughing.

"Mom, this one's for you."

She holds up a black stone with an orange line through it.

"Do I even want to know?" I ask as she drops it in my hand.

"Tiger's eye. It will help with..." She waves her hand up and down my body. "Courage."

"What is *that* supposed to mean?" I don't even attempt to hide my offense.

She folds her arms over her chest as she narrows her eyes. "Don't be so sensitive, Penelope. You have stuck energy, and fear is a big part of that."

I scoff. "I'm not scared."

She shrugs. "You are. Scared of changing, scared of living life without Dad." Her eyes drop to my black shirt. "Of color."

Somehow, I'm both shocked and in agreement with what she says, but unless her rock can raise bodies from a watery grave, an argument over it is futile.

I press my lips between my teeth as I glare at her. She's wearing a long skirt and a cropped tank top with a purple scarf tied in her hair and dangling beaded earrings. She fits into the aisles of rocks and dream catchers so perfectly it's almost scary.

I sigh and shove my wallet at her. "I'm waiting with Finn outside."

Since Marfa, Finn has stayed quiet, but his phone being in a dozen pieces has been an unexpected gift. Even if he doesn't want to talk to me, at least he can't hide behind a screen.

"You okay?" I ask, stepping beside him on the sidewalk.

"Other than the fact my sister thinks rocks are the answer to life's problems? Just dandy."

He shakes his head with a sigh as he scrubs the toe of his shoe against the ground.

I laugh under my breath. "She told me my rock will give me courage. For $9.95, maybe she just saved me a lot of money."

His laugh is weak. "Maybe."

For all the fighting Finn and I have done, I realize we aren't so different at that moment. Both of us working to come to terms with the fact we have to forge ahead in a life that looks vastly different from the one we hoped for.

A billboard sign above us catches my eye at the same time Marin pushes the door of the store open and holds up the bag proudly. "Rocks for what ails you."

I ignore her, not listening to what her and Finn start talking about.

Fear and excitement buzz through me as I make a decision without thinking. "Guys?"

They stop talking and look at me.

"Let's watch the sunset from there tonight."

I point to the sign; their eyes follow then widen.

Finn shakes his head with a disbelieving laugh. "Are you kidding? That's everything you hate, Mom. You'll have a heart attack."

I smile. There's a very good chance he's right. "Well, that will make a good story, won't it?"

I don't let them respond before I punch the number in my phone with shaky hands.

Three hours later, with the roar of a flame and a jolt from the ground, we drift into the sky above the red rocks of Sedona by way of a rainbow-colored hot air balloon.

Marin takes an obscene number of pictures, Finn stares out quietly at the wild earth below us, and I smile through tears that feel like streams of triumph.

"I didn't think you had it in you."

Finn's lips lift into a smile as he bumps his shoulder against mine.

I'm still terrified, but I lean into him.

"And you two thought those rocks were a scam," Marin says, flicking a knowing look at me before pulling us together for a picture.

In it, Marin's smile is wide, Finn's expression is amused, and I'm mid-laugh with my mouth hanging open as tears drip down my face—my eyes on them.

It's my new favorite picture.

***

The next morning, cup of coffee in hand, I open the email waiting from Ethan.

Penelope,

My bartender did not know the classic daiquiri, but he learned it, made it,

and you were right—it's good. Oddly,
I'm not surprised.

My favorite meal to make for people is
cheeseburgers. Shocked? I know it's
simple, much like your daiquiri, but
there's so much potential to elevate
it. Now, yours won't be nearly as good
as mine for the obvious reason of your
subpar non-Maine ingredients, but
here's what you do: buy a good quality
ground sirloin (imperative), and then
into the raw meat add minced garlic
(not too much), sun-dried tomatoes
(only about a tablespoon, chopped
finely) and honey mustard (just a
little), and salt (to taste—right
before you put them on the grill).
When you're cooking, ONLY FLIP ONCE!
Why do people get so flip-happy with
burgers? I never understand it.

Also, this is a test. Ruin this
burger, and I'm done.

Ethan

On the way out of town after breakfast, we stop at a grocery store and get all the ingredients to make burgers for dinner.

Fifteen

"I DON'T UNDERSTAND WHAT the big deal is. It's just a big hole in the ground."

Week three on the road and Finn is irritated by everything as we drive. Namely, the fact that the AC in the cab of the truck isn't consistently working. And he hates my coffee. And he found out his friends are registered for a big fishing tournament this weekend he clearly can't take part in.

"Finn, are you serious? The Grand Canyon is so much more than a hole in the ground!" I argue from the driver's seat.

"Whatever," he mutters, clearly annoyed. "Are we about done with this yet? It's been two weeks, and now the dumb AC isn't working." He slams his hand against the vent closest to him. "Can we just go home? I mean, what else do you want to do here, Mom? You seem happier now. Can't we just get back to our lives yet? It's not like Dad's here to care about his stupid list of places, anyway."

The last words are nearly drowned out by the sound of him kicking his foot against the floorboard.

I grip the steering wheel and swallow hard—*inhale for four, exhale for four*—before I speak.

"You're fishing for an argument I'm not having while I have sweat dripping down my damn neck, and we are minutes to one of the most amazing things on this planet. Just because you're pissed off your friends are doing something without you, you don't get to ruin this."

When I say I don't want to argue, what I really mean is I am one response away from pulling the godforsaken Avion over and leaving him to fend for himself against whatever is out there.

He stares out the window.

The truth is, Finn isn't the only one who is frustrated. The road is slowly sucking the nice out of all of us. There's so much on Travis' list and with the distances between everything, there's little time left for us to enjoy any of it. Something like seeing the Grand Canyon should be exciting, but today, it feels like just another box to check.

Apparently, one that Finn doesn't want to check at all.

The cool breeze that meets us once we get out of the Avion is a welcome reprieve. Hints of sage and pine float in the air as we follow the signs toward an overlook. Every breath feels like the world's first oxygen as it fills my lungs.

We turn a corner, blindly following the crowd of tourists along the sidewalk, as the sun dips low and wispy clouds are sketched across the sky.

Finn points to a secluded spot tucked between two big rocks with a clear view into the canyon we've yet to see. As we walk over to it, what's hidden beyond the ledge comes into view and brings me to a stop.

Marin squeezes my arm with a whispered "Whoa!"

I've seen pictures of the Grand Canyon. I knew what to expect as far as shape and terrain. I knew it was big. I knew it was so steep on the edge that people died falling into it. I've read that pictures never capture the bigness of it all and can never prepare anyone for what it feels like to physically stand there and see it.

In that moment, I know they are right. Despite it being a moment devoid of sadness, tears fill my eyes.

Finn crouches on the rocky ground while I drink in the view like a thirsty traveler at a much-needed water fountain.

The cliff edge we sit on drops down sharply before sloping out into a jagged ledge and then dropping down once more before repeating the shape. It continues that way, a concoction of cliffs and formations sloping down into the ground, a mile below us and miles out around us. The Colorado River curves below us like an unraveled spool of thread.

"It's like looking in the belly of a mountain," Marin says, eyes wide. "I can't believe how big it is."

I turn to Finn slowly. "Still think it's just a big hole in the ground?"

"Fine, an *impressive* hole in the ground."

His smile is faint and fleeting.

I sit next to him and hug my knees to my chest.

"It's insane, really. Water flowing the way the water just flows, did all of this." I stare out into the bigness of it, trying to comprehend how such a place exists.

"Oh yeah, this place has some major jubilee vibes, right?"

Marin smiles, her short sandy hair blowing softly in the breeze. She's right. Dickey would most definitely say the formation of the Grand Canyon is no different from the random abundance of mullet on the Mobile Bay shore.

From where we sit, we can see a fenced-off lookout below us. The people that fill it—doing everything from taking photos with expensive cameras to leaning on the railing with teary eyes—are as unique as the formations they gape at. Big guys who rode in on motorcycles, covered in tattoos and leather vests, look on with the same expression as the elderly woman with a walker. Gay, straight, old, young, Mexican, Asian, and everything in between. A dozen different languages are being spoken at once as the darkness starts winning the war against the light in the sky.

Wandering souls, all pulled here for one reason or another, looking for beauty, meaning, and whatever else they can find in a cracked-open section of the earth. Beauty that exists regardless of the pain and emptiness each of us feels in the holes in our hearts that make us human.

A deluge of emotion washes over me at the enormity of it all.

"Mind if I pull up a seat?"

An old man stands behind us with a collapsed canvas chair and a wide smile.

"By all means. Seems to be big enough for all of us."

I smile, gesturing toward the canyon in front of us.

He's wearing a navy-blue Mackinac Island sweatshirt that pulls tightly across his belly and a hat that says *World's Best Grandpa!* over a head of short gray hair. He drops into his chair and sighs at the view.

"Don't see stuff like this in Iowa!" he says with a chuckle.

"Florida either," I reply.

"My wife always wanted to see this place, but we never made it. Cancer took her in January," he says to the emptiness.

I don't say anything, thinking of Travis and him also never seeing it.

"My wife always said that the Grand Canyon proved God is a glass half-full kind of guy."

"How so?"

"My wife, Margie, she said that you wouldn't go to the Grand Canyon and look for what's not there. You'd look for what's left. Said the Colorado River ran through here and took a lot, but what it left behind is the real treasure. She'd say, 'Ned, canyons aren't about the absence. They are about what remains. Artifacts of survival and patience and slow weathering. If people looked over that edge and only looked for the missing ground, they wouldn't see the beauty. It's God's glass half-full.' She was ever the optimist, right until the end."

His friendly eyes look sad, but still—he smiles.

"My husband wanted to come here but also never made it. He would have probably agreed with Margie."

"Then you know," he says.

I look at him, not sure I do, and he reads my silence as his signal to go on.

"You know about the people who come into our lives with their love and change us as much as the Colorado River changed this unforgiving landscape. The ones that cut right through you and carve you into who you are supposed to be. They move slow and steady, eroding what we were away. What they leave behind are the ruggedly beautiful remains that remind us forever of their existence."

"The rivers that run through us," I say.

"The rivers that run through us."

Then we're quiet, because ultimately, words don't matter when sitting in a place like this. My days have been easier, but as I stare out into the humongous gorge that stretches out in front of us, I feel Travis' absence as much as I feel the ground beneath me. As sure as I'm sitting on this ledge, he is not.

"Mom, listen, about earlier." Finn fumbles with a small rock in his hands. "I shouldn't have said that stuff. I was just hot and..."

His face looks as tired as mine.

"It *was* hot, Finn."

I squeeze his knee, hoping it says everything I need to say.

Marin yawns as the sun dips almost completely under the horizon line.

"How about we get going and make those burgers we got ingredients for?"

I don't need to ask twice—they both nod before standing and immediately start toward the Avion.

As I start to follow them, I stop, turning to Ned.

"What happens now?" I ask.

"Now? We figure out a way to live without them. But it won't be the same for us. I'm an old man. I'll spend my days happily dancing in the cracks she left behind, but you're young. You won't ever have another Colorado River, of course, but I have a feeling there's more than one kind of river that runs through us in our lifetimes, anyway. Every river can't make the Grand Canyon, but that's not how it's supposed to be. Margie was my second wife. She came through and smoothed out the edges from my first wife, who I lost twenty years ago. They carved me differently. The way they loved, and I loved them—it's all part of it. You'll see."

He smiles sagely, like he knows something I don't, before giving me a small salute and turning back to the amazing view.

The kitschy tourist traps that line the entrance road out of the park slowly give way to the now dark, empty desert roads—like all that beauty is trying to stay a secret.

I drop my head back to the headrest and let out a breath the wind steals as it blows through the windows. I smile and turn up the music as I chase the last drops of daylight down the highway.

***

"This is the best burger I've ever eaten," Finn says between bites.

I laugh, because of course it is, even without the Maine ingredients.

"He's right, Mom," Marin says before taking another bite. "What is this?"

I clear my throat, shifting behind the dinette. "A guy I emailed for grandpa about the restaurant sent it to me." Then, "Not about the restaurant, just a recipe, you know?"

Marin's eyes narrow. "Of course it's a recipe, what kind of comment is that? Either way it's good."

I smile. *Right.*

That night in bed, without overthinking it too much, I grab my phone and send Ethan the review.

```
Ethan,
```

```
I hate it when a recipe says 'salt
to taste.' What the hell does that
even mean? Are you supposed to taste
it raw? How am I supposed to know
how much salt will make an entire
pound of beef taste good? I think
it's something people put in recipes
because they are either lazy or want
to make sure nobody else's food turns
out as good as theirs. Or maybe it's
because their recipe isn't actually
good, but they can always fall back on
'you must have used too much/little
salt' when there's a complaint.
```

But.

Somehow, I got it right because my
kids said they were the best burgers
they've ever had.

Go figure.

And if you didn't like the daiquiri,
I would have been done. It's a per-
sonality flaw at that point and one
I just can't get over.

Penelope

It's only after I push send I realize I didn't ask a single question about
the restaurant.

Sixteen

AT 107 DEGREES, DEATH Valley is every bit what I imagine hell to feel like.

Marin's hair is pulled back in a bandana, little blonde spikes sticking up with sweat in the back, and Finn's face is flushed from the heat. The t-shirts and shorts we wear are parkas against our already hot skin.

We look like melted crayons.

The bright white ground below us makes the deadly rays of the sun bouncing off it blindingly disorienting. We squint as we follow the other foolishly hot tourists into the middle of the harsh, flat wilderness of Badwater Basin. Where we were walking to, I have no clue. On the horizon, bodies blur into blobs, and it looks like the land itself has liquified from the heat.

"Why are we doing this again?" Finn asks before chugging his water.

Marin and I reply in annoyed unison with, "Dad."

I almost laugh at the absurdity of it. If Travis were here, we'd be arguing over how much I did *not* want to be here, but here we are, marching out into the fiery pits of hell, all in his name.

A family of four walks in the opposite direction as us as the two young kids are whining and red-faced. I catch the mom's eye.

"Hey, what's there to see out there? Like what are we walking toward?" I ask.

Her hair mirrors mine, sweaty and matted to her face, and she's no doubt internally preferring death to her current situation as much as I am.

Her hands shoot up in the air. "Nothing! Not a damn thing! You walk and walk and walk in this fucking heat for nothing! I can see ground this flat in Indiana!"

Her eyes have the flame of crazy burning in them as she yells, but her kids and husband don't react. They either aren't surprised by her tirade or agree with her completely.

"Thanks," I murmur, watching as she angrily stomps off into the crowd with her family jogging after her.

I look over at Finn and Marin and don't have to say a word. We spin around and walk right back to the parking lot.

***

"Guys, this is real camping!" I say as we park the Avion between a sea of big round rocks, the only RV in sight. "And look, Finn, we don't even have to argue about me not backing into anything!"

We are off-grid on public land. Our first time ever. No electricity, cell service, or water. It feels adventurous. Dangerous, even.

They don't match my enthusiasm, only exchange unimpressed looks before getting out and setting up.

I lean forward to look out the windshield. Large, round rocks cover hills at the base of the Sierra Nevada mountains in every direction. It's as if balls of clay have been splattered against the ground by a drunken potter, then left to dry.

Even exhausted, we can't resist the call to play on them.

"Mom! Over here! Try this one," Marin calls from at least ten feet above me.

I wedge between two rocks as she had, pushing a foot to one while using my hands to pull myself up on the other one just enough to bring my other leg up. I shift my weight back and forth like a teeter-totter and inch my feet higher up the middle of the rocks until I finally peek out of the top between the two and fling my body over one of them. Even with the sandpaper coarseness of the rocks that make it impossible to slip, my muscles are screaming.

From there, the rocks that pile up just require steps instead of full body maneuvers. Within a few hops, I'm standing next to Marin, looking out over the field of rocky hills and the jagged peaks of the mountains, snowcapped even in June.

"Wow," I huff, looking at the scene set on fire by the low sun.

Finn is a couple rocks away from us, standing on top of an arched formation.

"Amazing, huh?" Marin asks.

"Amazing," I say.

It really is.

***

By the time I make it back to the Avion, it's dark. I pour a glass of wine and drop into a chair while Finn and Marin wander the rocks with flashlights. Between the sounds of their laughter, effects of the wine, and the brightness of the stars—I'm the definition of relaxed.

The easy feeling is short-lived.

The thing we learn about camping off the grid that night is that no electricity actually means *no electricity*. Or AC. Or fans. So, while it's slightly cooler at night than during the day, it is also very still. Even with all the windows open, not a single breeze blows through to cool us that night. The air hangs heavy, and frustration is laced into every loud exhale as nobody sleeps.

When the sun rises, we aren't rested.

Breakfast is curt.

I'm defeated.

Camping sucks.

The big rocks on the rolling hills around us offer none of the joyful reprieve they had last night. This morning, they are just another reminder of how far away we are from home.

What we need to do is painfully obvious. Turn around. We've seen almost half of the places Travis had written. As much as I hate to give up, I'm tired. We all are.

I sigh as I ask, "Should we go home?"

I'm already sweating as I work to roll the awning in.

Marin and Finn look up from where they eat their breakfast, perched on big rocks, quiet.

Their silence says yes. It stings, even though I don't blame them. I agree.

"Never quit on your worst day," Marin says matter-of-factly. "Dad told me that once. He said your worst day wasn't the time to make big decisions because you won't look at things from every angle or how you can improve your situation." She lifts a shoulder.

Finn shakes his head. "Yeah, well, maybe this isn't our worst day, so it's a good day to quit to me. Marin, we could have the rest of our summer!"

He doesn't bother to hide the desperation in his voice. "Mom's proven whatever point she was trying to prove by taking this trip, and now we are in the middle of the desert and miserable—it's not even the end of June—it's going to get even hotter! Aren't you ready for a real bathroom that doesn't have a doll-sized shower?!"

Mom's proven whatever point she was trying to prove by taking this trip.

I wince at his words while I busy myself with packing up. The smell of hot dust clogs my throat. Or maybe that's the pang of failure. Or both.

"Nope," Marin replies, shaking her head. "We are *so* close to the Pacific Ocean, Finn. And there are other fun things to see. So it's hot. And it sucks right now. But it's stupid to turn back. Let's give it another week. We'll be at the ocean by then. People act crazy when they are hot and hungry, so let's cool down and then decide."

She takes another bite of her yogurt as if it's settled.

Finn groans but doesn't argue. Even if he doesn't agree, she at least makes a valid point.

Which is why, five hours later, instead of being that much closer to Florida, we park the Avion under tall trees with a view of shimmering Lake Tahoe. From our chairs under our awning, the air is seventy-seven beautiful degrees. It smells like a dozen burning pine-scented candles, and the dewy freshness of the mountain breeze washes over me like a well-needed shower.

The next day will bring the start of a long drive to the Oregon coast, but for this one afternoon, everything is simple.

The turquoise-blue water hidden in the rugged California mountains is the distraction we need. We swim in the cold water and lay in the sand under the warm sun. For an afternoon, it feels like a vacation.

Relaxed and refreshed when I crawl into bed, my now nearly nightly routine of reading emails from Ethan and poorly stifling laughs comes with something else—sheer terror.

```
Penelope,


Guess we aren't done yet, huh?


There's a science to salt, one that
I'm sure would bore you, but the
only advice I can give on its usage
is when you know, you know. It's a
secret until it isn't. Salt's just
like that.


You know, if you ever find yourself
in the White Mountains of Maine, I'd
love to show you around, and I'd be
happy to tell you all my secrets.


In the kitchen, of course.


Ethan
```

I read it a dozen times. *Is he flirting?!* I'm appalled at the thought yet somehow smiling. I do the only thing I can think of, I don't respond.

Seventeen

I HAVE TO BE dreaming. It's the only explanation for how I can smell coffee while lying in bed.

"Finn, can you stir that?"

Marin's voice sounds as real as the nutty aroma in my nostrils.

I pull the curtain around my bed back and blink my eyes open and shut.

Marin and Finn are moving around the kitchen, making breakfast, and Finn has an actual cup of coffee in his hand.

"Is this real life?" I croak as I roll onto my side and watch them.

"Good morning, Penelope." Marin hums as she scoops oatmeal into bowls.

I squint. "What is happening in here?"

"Mar made breakfast, and I made coffee," Finn says, like it's obvious.

"You made coffee?"

I sit up with a start, banging my head on the ceiling.

"You are going to kill someone with that toxic crap," he responds, leaning his hip against a small space of countertop.

I reach my hands out as I fumble down the ladder. "Gimme."

Gone is the bitter bite that was on the brink of making me sprout chest hair, and instead is a taste of smooth nuttiness.

"I've died and gone to a caffeinated heaven, Finn James!" I gasp dramatically. "How did you learn to make this, and why have you been making me suffer all this time?"

"Google, Mom. This isn't that impressive."

He lifts his chin and shakes his hair out of his eyes.

Marin puts a bowl of cinnamon oatmeal in front of me, and I eye it suspiciously.

"Did you poison this?" I demand. "Why are you two being so *nice*?"

Yesterday was a disaster. The AC completely broke in the Avion in the middle of our thirteen-hour drive, and by the time we finished setting up camp last night, we were all the very worst versions of ourselves. Putting poison in my breakfast doesn't seem that farfetched in the light of day.

"We can be *nice* when we aren't having our souls boiled out on the interstate," Marin says, sitting next to me, smiling, popping a spoonful of oatmeal into her mouth.

Outside is cool and glorious. There's a renewed sense of excitement when we finish breakfast and head out for a walk wearing sweatshirts with warm drinks cradled in our hands. If we didn't just spend so many days melting in the desert, maybe I wouldn't love it so much, but I do. God, I do. The earthy smell and the way the cool air wraps its fingers around my skin are everything I don't know I need.

"Haystack Rock is supposed to be lit. I think we should check it out."

Finn thumbs through a pamphlet as we walk.

"Lit, Finn?" I chuckle, taking another sip of my coffee. "I don't think such hip words apply to such old formations."

"Don't be such a grandma," he scoffs.

"Believe me, I think if I was your grandma, I'd be *saying* lit."

At this, they both laugh, because yes—Poppy would be saying *lit*.

Lost in the conversation and the feeling of the crisp air on my skin, we end up on the beach facing the Pacific Ocean.

The gravity of the moment crushes down on me like a tidal wave, heavy and all at once.

We made it. *I* made it. We had gotten in a vehicle and driven across the country to another ocean without Travis.

The gray sky and rolling waves in front of me seem to perfectly capture the mood. In the distance, Haystack Rock shoots up out of the Pacific like a symbol of survival.

Marin's eyes meet mine. "Mom?"

I don't try to hide it—I let tears fall and make lines like the roads on the maps we've been following down my face.

"I don't know if I thought we would make it. If *I* could make it. But here we are, without your dad, an entire country-length away from home. It kind of feels like... I don't know... an open wound that's starting to heal."

I zip my ring along the chain as I stare at the ocean.

Marin squeezes my arm. "He would have been so proud of you," she says, leaning on me. "Especially of the fact you didn't wreck once."

My laugh is damp but true.

"Mom! Mar! Over here!" Finn calls from the rocks at the water, holding up a starfish.

Marin doesn't hesitate. She squeals and takes off, running toward him while I slowly walk behind.

Watching their joy bubble over like fountains as they wade in a tidepool, a brand-new truth crystalizes before me: even without Travis, I'm still here. Living, breathing, and able to watch my kids do incredible things if I let myself look.

After hours at the beach with our hands in the cold saltwater and Marin taking way too many pictures, I walk back to the campsite alone. I start a pot of chili over the fire, and when there's nothing else to do, I open the American Restaurant magazine we'd been featured in. The first time since I stumbled on Travis' map all those months ago.

But it's not us I'm looking for in the glossy pages this time—it's Ethan.

We've been emailing for months, but the one I got last night is different.

Flirtatious almost.

It's a ridiculous thought. He doesn't know anything about me, but still, I can't shake it.

When I land on his page, I see it differently than I did before.

He's leaning against his restaurant with the sleeves of his flannel shirt rolled up, arms crossed over his chest, and a slight scruff sloping across his jaw. It suits him.

Fine, *really* suits him. He's an attractive man.

I read the caption.

Ethan Mills prides himself on using both seasonal and local ingredients at his flagship restaurant in Bethel, Maine, Mainely Local. "I wouldn't be where I am without the farmers here and the people that keep eating the fresh food we serve. It's an honor, and I'm happy to be feeding people in a way that makes a difference." Between the menu that changes with the seasons and the cozy atmosphere, Mainely Local feels a little bit like home to anyone who visits.

Maybe it's because he's in the same business or maybe it's because he doesn't talk to me like I'm the woman who lost her husband, but something about our short emails makes me... curious.

It's as if I know him. Ultimately, I know it's just my grief—the quiet loneliness that makes me desperate for connection.

My cheeks heat with the pitiful realization of it.

I close the magazine and pick up my phone, rereading the last line of his latest email.

You know, if you ever find yourself in the White Mountains of Maine, I'd love to show you around, and I'd be happy to tell you all my secrets.

In the kitchen, of course.

I know he's just being nice, I know that, but I can't stop reading it.

It's been so long since I've interacted with a man that this is where I'm at—stumbling because of an email.

I groan, humiliated.

I've always wanted to see Maine, and while it isn't happening this summer, someday. Maybe.

Maybe someday, I'll be ready to go somewhere I want to see and think of what it means to *want* a man to be flirting with me.

When that time comes, I can only hope it takes more than a stranger in a magazine sending a friendly email to get me worked up.

God, I'm pathetic.

***

The kids return, plus three.

"Mom, this is Donny, Garret, and Mike. They're up from San Francisco for the weekend," Finn says, introducing them as I stand up.

"I'm Nel." I smile, shaking their hands. "You boys should stay for dinner. I made enough to feed the state of Oregon."

I lift the lid of the Dutch oven, and wafts of chili billow out. I know enough about traveling in college to know that money is tight and the food mediocre.

"I won't turn down any mom's cooking," Donny says with a lazy smile.

He has a mop of blonde curly hair and looks every bit the California boy he is.

Around the table with bowls of food, the boys entertain us with stories of their freshman year of college.

"What about you, Ms. C? What kind of stories do you have from your heyday?" Garret asks between bites.

Finn eyes me with doubtful curiosity. Like I won't be able to deliver because I can't possibly have had a heyday.

I know youthful secrets are supposed to be locked away with youth—it's the responsible place to keep them. But the look on Finn's face says it all—he thinks I'm boring.

I have no choice—I have to prove him wrong.

"Thursday nights always had the best drink specials around USF, and as a poor college kid, I wasn't one to pass up a bargain," I tell them, taking a sip of my beer. "One Thursday, 10PM turned into 1AM, and somehow, my best friend and I decided we needed to go to the fountain on campus. It was this shallow pool with these big bull statues. Anyway, she bet me $50 I wouldn't get into the fountain and sit on one of the bulls for a full minute. Naked."

Finn groans. "Tell me you did *not* do this."

I nod solemnly. "Sadly, I did."

"Oh, Mom!" Finn groans again at the same time Mike says, "Get it, Ms. C!"

"So, what happened?" Marin asks.

"I was ten seconds away from the minute mark when blue lights start flashing across my naked bull-riding body."

"Oh my God, Mom, the cops?" Marin gasps, putting a hand over her mouth.

I nod.

"*The cops*. I got arrested for indecent exposure. Poppy and Grandpa had to come bail me out the next morning because your stupid Uncle Gabe wouldn't answer his phone. I had to do volunteer hours picking up trash on the side of the road in a neon vest and everything." I smile at how ridiculous it all was.

"Thanks for ruining my appetite," Finn says, pushing his bowl away with a shake of his head that makes the California boys laugh harder.

"Your ole mom used to be pretty *lit*, huh, Finn?"

He covers his now red face with his hands, and everyone howls.

The conversation sets the tone for the rest of the night. Us sitting around the table, laughing, and playing cards.

When I grab the ring hanging around my neck, I think of how much Travis would have loved this. The kids, the stories, the food made over the fire. He would have loved it all. *Well, Nel,* I imagine him saying, *looks like all the hot days you whined about were worth it.*

Tears never come, and sadness doesn't lurch in the shadows that night. For the first night in a very long time, I'm not only without grief—I'm happy. *Really* happy.

When I fall asleep, it's with a smile on my face and the muffled sounds of laughter around the campfire as my lullaby.

Eighteen

"How do you look like you were made for every place we've gone to with your outfits?" I ask Marin between bites of my scone.

Finn is spending the day kayaking with the California boys, so she and I opt for breakfast in town.

Her short blonde hair is tied back in a colorful vintage scarf, and an oversized cream-colored sweater hangs loosely from her slim shoulders while her slouchy jeans are rolled up just enough to showcase bright red rubber boots. She is somehow functional and trendy, and it's an anomaly that we're related.

"It's a gift!" She smiles and puts a hand under her chin as if posing for a photo. When her eyes drop to my outfit, her face puckers.

"You know, Mom, we don't live in traditional Italy or wherever it is where grieving wives are bound by duty to wear black for the rest of their lives after their husbands die. I watched this girl on YouTube say that black is very unflattering for women in their 40s because it showcases the unevenness of their skin."

She delivers the words without an ounce of concern for my feelings, then licks the icing off her fingers.

"Hey!" It's the only argument I make as I look down at my clothes and frown.

Gray sweatshirt, black leggings, black rubber ankle boots.

I'm the embodiment of depression.

"And when's the last time you had a haircut? It's a bit…" She picks up my faded braid between her fingers and drops it like a hot potato. "Dull."

"What I love about you, Marin, is that you really know how to crush a woman's ego in a deceivingly sweet voice." My voice is flat as I bring my coffee to my lips.

"Mom, that's what all this whole trip is about, right? You starting a life after Dad or whatever? Well, if you want to start any kind of life that has people in it who aren't perpetually crying, you need to look the part. You have sad vibes, Mommy dearest, very *very* sad vibes."

"Thanks," I deadpan.

She wipes her hands together and crumbs drop to the table.

"All I'm saying is, I can help you. I saw a fun thrift store on our walk here and a salon I'm sure in a town this size can take you as a walk in. We could give you a makeover. You're beautiful, Mother, but you're letting all this sadness hide it. Then you're *really* going to be sad when you wake up an old lady one day and realize you spent the best years of your sexual energy wearing black and moping."

"What the hell, Mar! What do you know about *sexual energy*?!" I hiss, leaning over the table toward her.

A woman with young kids shoots me a glare from the next table, and I make a face I hope translates as an apology.

Marin rolls her eyes. "I read. A lot. I know many women have the best sex in their forties, which means you are in the thick of it, but as far as I can tell, doing nothing about it."

She shrugs. As if she isn't giving her mother sex advice.

What the actual hell is happening?

"Okay, so we are *not* talking about this." I hold my hands up in protest. "But I'll let you take me shopping if it will make you happy. God forbid I continue to walk around radiating my *sad vibes.*"

"Oh please, Penelope," she says. "It will make *you* happy."

***

Marin hates every item I pick out at Lucy's Closet. After too many *you aren't eighty*, *you look like a sack of potatoes*, and my personal favorite— *gross*— I relent and let her take charge.

"Mom, you have a great body, but you pick clothes that hide it like you are covered in weird lumps and boils." She hands me a low-neck sweater.

"It's called being age appropriate," I argue, balking at the sweater.

"You kiss your mother with that mouth?" She scoffs. "I'm disappointed in you."

"I feel guilty," I confess, without looking at her, making her go still next to me. "I feel guilty for wearing happy, cheery colors when your dad isn't here. Like people will think I'm glad he's gone or something." I fidget with a dress on a hanger.

"Mom!" Her voice is uncharacteristically harsh as she grabs my shoulders firmly. "Nobody would *ever* think that. *Dad* would *never* think that. If every person who lost someone thought that way, this world would be a horrible place." She shoves a turquoise skirt at me as I nod.

She softens. "And no matter what you wear, Mom, he's gone just the same."

She's right. Whether I wear black or blue, I'm still alone. He's still gone.

I clear my throat and eye the pink dress she's holding.

"Fine. But no pink."

Once again, she grins then shoves me into the dressing room with a pile of clothes.

Marin is in her element. Like the actual clothes, good or bad, give her some kind of supernatural energy.

By the time we step out of the store with stuffed bags, she's beaming.

"You're good at this, you know?" I say as we walk down the sidewalk.

"Of course, I know."

She tilts her head as she strolls lightly. "Have you thought at all about what you want to do after high school? You have time to figure it out, of course, I jus—"

"No," she cuts me off, almost defensively, "And I don't think regular college is for me if that's what you're asking."

"Gosh, no, Marin. I don't care about that. If I could do it all again…" I pause, not even sure what I want to say next. I shake my head. "I just know paths to happiness look different, and it's okay if yours doesn't involve college."

"You would have done something different?" she asks, surprise leaking into her voice.

I shrug. "I did what I thought everyone wanted, I guess. I just want you to know you don't have to."

She smiles. "Good."

Then as if the conversation isn't happening, she pulls me through the open doors of a salon and loudly announces, "My mother is in dire need of a makeover."

If Marin was in her element shopping for clothes, what happens to her in this place is otherworldly. She never stops asking questions about techniques and trends. I've never seen her so passionate—another thing I missed in the last year—but sitting in this chair watching her come to life with joy feels like a special type of forgiveness I didn't even know to ask for.

When the stylist, a red-lipped woman named Shay, finally spins me around to face the mirror two hours later—I laugh. Gone is the neglected dull hair that hung sadly to the middle of my back. The woman in the mirror has a textured cut that hits just below her shoulders.

With the now rich chocolate color framing my face, I barely look like the same person.

Marin squeals with a clap. "Mom!" she gasps, "Do you love it?!"

She runs her fingers through my hair, and the face I see in the mirror is one I don't even recognize.

I've spent the last weeks working to be different, to figure out how to show up for my kids, but today, Marin is reminding me how to look—*live*—like I have an actual pulse still thumping under my skin.

I'm speechless. It's as if I had no idea this woman in the reflection had been lying dormant. Waiting.

As soon as we're outside, I wrap Marin in a hug. My voice cracks as I whisper into her ear, "Thank you, Marin. Really... I know I haven't been..."

She squeezes me tightly, saying everything I need to hear. "Love you, Mom."

Arm in arm, we make our way down the sidewalk toward the campground.

At the edge of town, the last business is Haystack Rock Distillery. *HOME TO THE MOST UNFAMOUS CRAFT COCKTAILS OF THE PACIFIC NORTHWEST*, the sign says. My heart skips a silly beat as I read and re-read it.

It's been nearly a year and a half since I've let my mind dance with the idea of creating any kind of cocktail for the bar, but seeing this little wood-shingled building on the Oregon Coast makes me miss it fiercely.

"What are you waiting for?" Marin stands at the door as if she can read my mind. "Inspiration awaits, Mother."

Despite the boulder lodged in my throat, a happy laugh bubbles out of me. I climb the stairs to meet the best Old Fashioned I've ever had.

Nineteen

"I SWEAR, I THOUGHT we were going to capsize, it was *so* rough." Finn shakes his head with a laugh. "And that water was freaking cold, like give you hypothermia cold. I did *not* want to end up swimming."

Around the fire, eating hotdogs and s'mores for dinner, I've never seen him so animated.

"That's nothing compared to the fright I had helping Mom with her wardrobe," Marin says as she squishes a marshmallow between two graham crackers.

"Funny." I cut my eyes to her as I poke a stick at the fire.

Tomorrow will be our last full day on the Pacific, and the word bittersweet barely touches the surface of how I feel. Even though we have six more weeks on the road, leaving feels like it's the beginning of going home. I'm not ready for it.

"I'm pooped." Marin yawns with a stretch as she stands. "I'm going to read a book and call Harper to catch up."

"Thanks again for today."

She leans down to hug me before disappearing into the Avion, and I snuggle deeper into my chair.

"You mind if I go hang out at the guys' site at their fire? They head out tomorrow," Finn asks.

"Go. Sounds fun. I'm going to make some calls."

I pull out my phone, smiling as I watch him leave.

It has to be a dream because everything feels easy.

So easy.

I sip a glass of wine as I dial my parents.

"I was worried you forgot about us, Penelope," my mom sings as she answers.

"Mom, it's been four weeks, and I've texted you almost every day. Will you relax?"

She *tsks* me then says, "You can't blame a mother for wanting to hear her only daughter's voice, sweetheart. Now, where are you? Here, I'll put you on speaker so your dad can hear."

"We are in Oregon, and it's beautiful here."

"How's that camper holding up?"

I blow out an amused breath. "The Avion hasn't died on us yet, but the AC did stop working, so it's hot as hell when we drive. That's been a fun character-building experience."

"It's a miracle you haven't killed each other," my dad chimes in with a chuckle from the background.

"Hi, Dad. How's the bar? Did you get all those notes I sent you from that guy in Maine I've been talking to?"

"Nel, I was running the bar before you came in with all your fancy ideas. I can manage one summer, thank you very much." He huffs playfully. "And I did get your notes. Sounds involved, like maybe too much work for me this late in the game. But I'm thinking about it. Maybe ask him for his advice on making small changes." He pauses long enough for my heart to flip-flop. "Or maybe schedule a call with him."

I choke on my wine at the suggestion. "A call? Dad, no. *You* call him!" My throat feels constricted. I can't *call* him!

"Richard," my mom interrupts. "She's on vacation, remember? Penelope, you can call him when you get home, sweetheart. Ignore your dad."

The tension in my shoulders loosens slightly.

"Listen, love you guys, I'm going to let you go. Thanks for helping me do this."

"Thanks, Nelly. Love you."

"Love you, sweetheart. Tell the kids hi!"

I hang up, sigh lightly, and smile.

I'm happy. It's as big and small as those two words. For the first time since Travis left, it finally feels easy. Mind, body, and soul—I'm calm like flat water.

I sit, breathing in that ease until I've burned through all the firewood and my eyelids are so heavy, I can barely keep them open. Finn is still gone, and with his phone in pieces in Marfa, I have to go get him.

It's black and quiet as I walk on the damp leaves and pine needles, the faint smell of marijuana floating in the air. The earthy, skunky scent has become such a staple in almost every campground we've been to, I've almost stopped noticing it.

As I get closer, the boys' voices float through the night—muffled conversation followed by an outburst of laughter. I smile.

Their campsite, the same as ours, is an enclave of trees that opens in the center. Three small tents surround a small fire, and a rope hangs between trees with towels and swim shorts hanging from it.

I open my mouth to let them know I'm here when the smell of marijuana, stronger this time, slams into me.

Then I see it.

A joint in Finn's pinched fingers as he brings it up to his mouth.

A long inhale.

A tight, "Thanks."

A small cough.

A pass to Donny.

Oh, for fuck's sake.

I have never cared about marijuana until this very moment, seeing it through the harsh lens of motherhood.

I stop behind a tree, waiting for what happens next.

The boys pass it around, each taking a drag.

Then, "Finn?"

"Sure, man," he says, arm outstretched.

He takes the joint and another giant hit.

Jesus Christ!

This is happening. My son is doing drugs while I watch from the woods like a creep.

I've always imagined how these big moments of parenthood would go. I'd make a dramatic entrance, deliver a wise monologue, and stomp away, leaving in my wake a child who was wiser for having had the life experience. But in this moment, my mortality and lack of confidence bubble to the surface, rendering me dumbfounded and desperately wishing I could call in some backup.

I clear my throat to let them know I'm here. Finn's spine stiffens, eyes widening as I walk into the site.

He drops the joint behind him on the ground, a failed attempt at discretion. I'd laugh if I didn't want to scream.

"Boys." I say it like I'm not about to attack my son with guns blazing once out of earshot. Then, turning to Finn and miraculously keeping my voice level, I say, "Time to head back."

"Yeah, sounds good." He turns and gives them a nod. "See you tomor-row?"

"Yeah, man, we head out late morning. We'll see ya before," Donny responds with heavy eyelids and a drawl to his voice.

I force a smile, but the walk to the Avion is a fury-filled silence. Finn may be stoned, but I have no doubt he also knows I'm livid.

He walks right to the door like he's simply going to go to bed. I could laugh at his nerve.

I grab his bicep to stop him.

"Are you kidding me right now, Finn? You're stoned!" I hiss.

He looks at me, eyes dilated nearly black. "Mom, relax. It's just a little pot."

He shrugs my arm off. A subtle yet unnerving move that makes my blood nearly boil through my skin.

"Just a little pot?" I ask in disbelief. "Finn, it's illegal!"

"Not here, Mom. It's Oregon. This isn't a big deal. We were sitting around a fire—I don't know what you're so upset about."

His tone is lazily defensive.

"One, you're a minor, so yes, it's still illegal. And two, is this who you want to be? Some... some... stoner?" I stutter the words out and barely recognize my hysterical voice as it cuts through the air.

The truth is, I don't know if I actually care about the marijuana—hell, I grew up on a chain of islands where it's tradition to smoke and walk around in bare feet—but this is different. This is yet another reminder I have no control over my son.

Over anything.

All traces of the playful little boy I know are gone, replaced by a stoned teen I don't recognize. Finn could be a stranger as he stands in front of me.

Is he smoking pot at home? Is he using any other drugs? My mind races in a million different directions, and my pulse matches it.

"First, I'll be eighteen in six months, so that's dumb. And second, you're making a big deal out of something that isn't. Everyone smokes sometimes, Mom. *You* should try it."

My mouth drops open. Stoned Finn has rendered me speechless.

Marin, now awake, stands in the doorway with confusion filling her sleepy face.

"Dad never would have reacted like this," Finn mumbles.

My heart collapses in on itself.

Guilt is a sharp weapon, and even now, Finn knows how to use it.

"Well, unfortunately, Finn, he's *dead*, and I'm the one here to deal with this, so I guess you're shit out of luck."

The words roll off my tongue and drop to the ground like a cinder block.

He looks away.

There it is.

Dead.

The ugly truth stings like acid in the middle of a marijuana-fueled argument in a campground on the Oregon coast.

I pick up the empty wineglass on the table. I want to scream or cry or break the damn glass.

So, I do.

With a guttural cry, I hurtle it against the Avion, and it shatters into a million pieces.

Marin and Finn stand like unbreathing statues as they stare at me, stunned.

"I said it. Are you happy now?" I bite out. "Finn, I know I didn't handle losing him in the best way. I know I checked out. But I'm trying my ass off here. I'm trying not to obsess over the fact that I failed you for a year. And yet, the only time you want to talk to me is to tell me how badly I suck as a mother, and every look you give me is filled with annoyed disappointment."

The words pour out of my mouth like water pushing through a broken dam.

"I know Dad was the fun one. He was a pilot, for God's sake, I can't compete with that! I can't be him, but he's not coming back. You know that, and so do I. And it's shitty. You lost your dad. I lost my best friend. Neither of us can begin to know what the other one feels like with that specific piece of their puzzle missing.

"So maybe you were right when you said I was trying to prove a point with this trip. I wanted to prove we could still be happy without him. That I could be a mom you're happy to be around and we could make memories that were our own. But even that feels impossible. You don't want to be here, and you won't give me a chance."

Then, I'm quiet, the weight of it all threatening to drag my whole body down into the damp dirt.

There's nothing else to say.

Travis isn't going to walk up to play mediator. Not now, not ever again. We are on our own. Travis' death may have made the mess, but it's ours to clean up.

I squeeze Marin's arm. "Let's not quit on our worst day," I say finally. "I'm going to bed."

I don't wait for a response before I push through the screen door and let the loud slam of the spring pulling it closed snap through the quiet night air.

Twenty

CANNON BEACH IS QUIET the next morning with only a few cars on the street and even fewer people on the sidewalk. The tree-covered mountains surround the small downtown like a hug, and the misty air hangs heavily as I carry two coffees and a chamomile tea toward the Avion.

A peace offering.

Last night's conversation replays on a loop as I walk. As awful as the whole thing was, I didn't wake up feeling angry, resentful, or even sad. I'm ready. Ready to not let Travis be the thing that keeps us stuck in this depressing place.

When I open the door, Marin is banging a bowl around while Finn fumbles with coffee grounds. The smells of vanilla and cinnamon blend in the air to make the small space smell like a café.

I make a show of holding up the coffee to them.

"Bless you, Mother," Marin says as she grabs her cup. "You will be rewarded with French toast."

She blows the steam from her tea and wraps her fingers cozily around the cup with a smile.

"I'll help," I offer as I hand Finn his coffee and grab a slice of bread.

We work for a few minutes in silence. Sipping our drinks and dunking bread in an egg wash.

"So," I start without looking at them. "That wine glass never stood a chance, did it?"

Marin snorts as she drops a piece of egg-covered bread into the pan with a sizzle, and Finn rumbles with a laugh that doesn't meet his lips.

I lean a hip against the counter and look at both of them before my eyes focus on Finn.

"I'm done doing this. Done feeling sad and guilty. Done apologizing for the year I was the world's most absent mom. I'm just done."

Finn's throat bobs as he swallows slowly.

"You have to decide, Finn, if you are moving forward with me or staying here in this God-awful hamster wheel. Because I can't. I won't."

I stare at him until my next blink then turn back to the French toast assembly line.

"Okay?" I tilt my head toward him.

"Okay."

With full plates of food, we sit at the table.

"And Finn?" I point a fork of French toast at him before taking my first bite. "No more weed. I know it's not that big of a deal—though all the propaganda from my childhood still has me believing it might be a gateway drug—but that's not the point. It's not legal. You're a minor. My answer is firm."

His mouth opens like he wants to argue, but he doesn't.

"And maybe Dad would have handled it better. But there's also a chance he would have knocked the joint out of your hand in front of your friends and caused a scene. I do know he wouldn't have just given you the green light to smoke. So, when you're eighteen, and you want to take up this..." I swirl my syrupy fork in the air, "habit, then that's on you. Deal?"

For the first time, his lips turn up into the slightest smile. "Deal."

"Gateway drug, Mom?" Marin groans, bringing a hand to her forehead. "You are such a dork."

With her words, we laugh our way through the rest of breakfast and spend our last day on the Oregon coast at the beach, holding starfish in the tidepools.

Together.

That night, I'm wine lubricated enough to summon the courage to reply to Ethan's last email. I don't let myself overanalyze—I let my thumbs type out whatever they decide.

Ethan,

Does anyone ever just *find* themselves in the White Mountains of Maine? I didn't even know that was a place until this very moment. And while I've always wanted to see Maine, I picture myself on the coast, not the mountains.

You should know, before you go around making these kinds of promises, I'm not good at keeping secrets because I'm a terrible liar. It's true. You

```
tell me one secret, and it's basical-
ly written across my face. I might as
well be one of those airplanes that
pulls messages behind it, blasting
information all over the place. It's
just who I am.



I'll prove it—you tell me a secret,
and if I ever find myself in the White
Mountains of Maine, we'll see if I
can keep a straight face about it.



Menu changes are at a standstill.
Apparently, my boss is scared of work
now that he made me go through all
this trouble.


Penelope
```

When I fall asleep that night, it's only after I've refreshed my email twenty times in hopes of getting a response that doesn't come.

Twenty-one

WE ARE LOST.

In Idaho.

Looking for dinosaur bones nobody wants to see.

Because Travis wrote it on his list.

The sweat that streams down my back is a constant reminder of how annoyed I am and how much I hate the Avion.

And dinosaurs.

"Are you sure this is right, Finn? This seems like private property."

I lean forward as we bump down a dusty road, and my eyes linger on a fence and sign that clearly says *No Trespassing*.

"It says we turn right in a half-mile." He holds up my phone. "We're only a couple miles away. I can see the dot. Shoot. I lost service."

He moves his arm around the cab, trying to find service that clearly doesn't exist.

If Travis were here, I'd punch him square in the nose.

Finn points to a patch of grass. "Turn here."

"Finn, there's no road. I can't drive on that." I bounce with a jolt as the rocks beneath us get bigger. "Okay, you know what?" I slam on the breaks. "I'm turning around. This is stupid. It's too hot to look for bones we don't even know if we're going to find."

"Thank God!" Marin blurts as she fans herself with a book in the back.

I slowly work to do a three-point turn on the narrow rocky road while Finn fumbles with the phone, ultimately dropping it in the crack between the seat and door.

"Now where?"

Finn's head is smashed against the door, and his voice is a muffled shout.

"How am I supposed to know? I can't reach the phone."

"Do you hear that?" Marin's eyebrows pinch together in my rearview mirror.

"Wha—" I hear it before I can finish the word. There's a hiss. *A snake?*

The hissing is loud, steady, and completely out of place as we wobble to a stop.

Finn's head shoots up, eyes wide.

"No!" he shouts. "No, no, no."

He flings the door open and runs around to the back of Avion. I see him in my side mirror. He looks down, shoves his palms in his eyes, then drops his head back with a groan.

I swing my door open and walk to him.

Now I groan.

There, lodged in the driver's side rear tire, is a sharp rock ripping through the tread as air angrily blows out of it.

"Ahhhhhhhhh!"

I lean my head back and yell before dropping my arms by my side. My hands clench into fists, and I scream like an actual lunatic in the middle of nowhere. We have a flat tire. We're lost. It's million damn degrees.

I take a long breath and a longer blink.

Marin's here.

She groans.

Our groans all mean the same thing—this fucking sucks.

"Okay," I finally say, knowing as the adult I have to keep us moving forward somehow. "Okay, we can handle this. Finn, you know how to change the tire, right? I mean, the basic steps? Marin and I can help you with whatever you need."

"Yeah, I can get it started. Let me just dig the jack out from the storage under my bed, and the tire on the back should be easy enough to get off."

There is no enthusiasm in his voice.

"Great. Marin—you make us some snacks while Finn gets started, okay? And I think there's a map or something in the glove box. I'll see if I can find where we are and get us the hell out of here."

My confidence is a lie.

I doubt this is even a marked road, much less one on a map. For all I know, this was where we are going to sit until we die and then ironically someone will find *our* bones.

When I click open the glove box, the crammed-in worn road atlas pops free. Before spreading it across the hood, I give into the sudden urge to slam the ripped-up book down.

I do it again.

Somehow, in this Idaho wilderness-induced breakdown, I find relief in beating the hell out of the Avion with a book so old the cover is faded beyond recognition filled with stained yellow pages no longer bound together.

I raise the atlas up and slam it back down.

"Stupid!" *Thwack.* "Dinosaur!" *Thwack.* "Bones!" *Thwack.*

"Want to throw a wine glass next?" Marin stands holding a plate of fruit and cheese, unamused as she watches my tantrum.

I level her with a glare as I snatch the plate from her and set it on the hood.

"Real mature, Penelope," she says before walking back to help Finn.

I fumble to pick up pages that have scattered across the ground when I see it—a piece of notebook paper.

The handwriting makes me stop breathing.

Travis.

The sun no longer feels hot, and my heart no longer beats as I pick it up, praying it won't slip like the desert sand through my fingers.

Well, Nel, it starts, and my heart wilts like a flower at the two familiar words.

We must be in some kind of trouble if you're reading this. I purposefully tucked this note in the atlas, somewhere I know you'd never willingly look unless we were lost. So, we must be lost, and you must be pretty pissed.

I can only hope we are at least somewhere fun, so if you make me hitchhike, I'll come home with a good story.

I pause to laugh. This dusty road in Idaho is as far from fun as it gets.

I have no doubt wherever we are supposed to be going is some-where I picked. I want you to know, wherever it is, I don't care if we go. We can turn around right now. I have you—there's nothing else I need to see.

You decide where we go from here—I can find a t-shirt anywhere.
Love you,
Travis

I stare at the paper, speechless. Emotion erupts in me like a volcano as I clench the paper so tightly my hand shakes.

I can see him—leaning on the hood and trying not to smile about how mad I am.

But he isn't here. The letter is years old, and he's gone. Lost to the sky and the sea. Life yanks the rug out from underneath me all over again.

I re-read it, every sentence a needle in my heart.

I try to breathe, but the oxygen feels like it's laced with shards of glass that slice every part of me when I inhale. My knees give out, and I hit the jagged rock-covered road as a sob rips out of my throat.

I look at the letter in my hand like it is both the thing that will kill me and the elixir of life.

Then a question crashes into me like a meteor—what were we doing here?

This trip, all our planning, has been an ode to Travis. We've gone to all the places he had wanted to go. Why? Am I looking for him? Do I expect to find him standing in a fossil bed?

Of course not.

I've been holding onto him. I've been going to the places he wanted to go, not so I can move on, but so I can *hold* on—to him, to us, to the future that was robbed from us by a fluke storm over the Gulf of Mexico.

I read the words again and wipe the final tears that fall down my face.

You decide where we go from here.

I sit on the ground, jagged rocks digging into the backs of my thighs, and force my eyes shut.

Inhale for four, exhale for four.

The Avion jolts angrily behind my back from something Finn does with the tire.

I look out at the beautifully lonely Idaho landscape, the red tips of the grass sway just barely from a breeze so soft I'd miss it if I wasn't paying attention.

I know where I want to go.

***

"Maine?" Finn yells over the wind as we barrel down the highway. "Was that even on Dad's list?"

"It was not. But you know, I've always wanted to go there and have never made it. And if we look at the list, how many of those places do *we* actually want to see?" I ask him as I point us east.

As if I even need to remind him of the dinosaur bones we tried to find just hours ago.

It took an hour and a half to get the tire changed and figure out where the hell we were, but we're finally back on the road.

Maine bound.

"I was just thinking, we spent the first half of this trip doing what your dad wanted, which was great. But I don't care if we see something called the Corn Palace or the World's Biggest Truck Stop or Carhenge, do you?"

Windy silence.

"We can get to Maine in three days and spend the rest of the summer on the coast and eating lobster. Doesn't that sound..." I search for a convincing word. "Relaxing?"

"Sure, Mom."

He leans his head on the seat and looks out the window as the wind blows his hair around.

If I'd been traveling to hold on to Travis, this was my opportunity to let him go. To find a way to move forward, even if it's just a step.

My eyes look toward the horizon.

I smile. We're going to Maine.

It's only after the decision is made and we are somewhere in Wyoming when Ethan's next email comes through.

>
> Penelope,
>
>
>
> The coast is great, but the mountains are better. If you get close enough, they pull you in and never let you go.
>
>
>
> I'm nervous about your secret-keeping skills but seeing as you're at the opposite end of the country from me and you've already made it clear you have no intention of *finding* yourself here, I'll tell you an easy one: I sleep naked.

What?! I drop the phone like it's on fire with an audible gasp before working up the nerve to finish reading it.

```
If our paths ever cross and I bring
it up, you'll have to keep a straight
face, or I'll consider it a secret
spilled. Then you'll owe me one.
```

```
Maybe it's been trouble to you, but
it hasn't to me.
```

```
Ethan
```

I only read it once—because what the hell am I even supposed to do with that?

Twenty-two

IT TAKES US THREE grueling days on the highway before we make it to Maine.

The relentless mountains of the west make way to the plains of the Midwest before rolling into the hills of the east. This country is nothing if not diverse in its landscapes.

I tell myself we are staying in the mountain town of Bethel because it will make for a short drive to the coastal town of Bar Harbor the next day.

I say it's serendipity we've ended up in the town where Ethan Mills lives and owns a restaurant.

I say all this because I am a pathological liar.

Yes, our destination is the coast, but our stop in the mountains is because I'm just a little bit intrigued to find out who the man I've been emailing for four months is.

MAINE'S MOST BEAUTIFUL MOUNTAIN VILLAGE, the sign that welcomes us into the city limits, says.

Even though it's the first day of July, the air mimics fall as it blows through the open windows.

Driving through the town is like stepping into a postcard. The colorful shops and restaurants line Main Street along with maple trees donning still new bright green leaves. The rolling hills of the White Mountains ripple in the background.

It's idyllic.

I look at Marin and Finn as I pump gas.

"You two look like we walked here from Idaho."

They are greasy, stained, and tired—a summary of our entire summer.

"Gee, Mom, sorry we couldn't pull off that whole stuck-in-an-old-camper-with-no-AC-for-three-days-of-driving-across-this-hot-ass-country look better," Finn says, rolling his eyes as he crosses his arms over his ketchup-stained shirt.

"Let's just get in there and get whatever food we need and then park this thing and not ever get in it again," Marin adds as she swipes a line of ChapStick across her lips.

I put the gas pump back in its holder.

"You know what? Let's not do this." I'm just as miserable as they are. "I'm tired, and I'd kill for a shower and a bed I can sit up in without getting a concussion. There's an inn." I point diagonally down the street. "If they have rooms, let's stay there. We can go to Bar Harbor tomorrow."

"Yes!" Finn drops his head back with a relieved groan. "That's the best idea you've ever had."

He's already walking down the street.

"Finn! We can drive!" I call toward his retreating back.

"I don't want to get back in that thing ever again," he shouts over his shoulder.

Two hours later, we're showered, dressed, and each sprawled out on our own king-sized beds. We could have shared one room, but after the month we've spent crammed together, separation is a luxury we can't pass up.

I throw on a pair of jeans, a t-shirt from the O.K. Corral with a picture of a horse wearing a cowboy hat, and an unbuttoned red flannel shirt. My hair isn't as cute as it was the day I'd gotten it cut, but the layers have a casually messy look. Or maybe it's just messy.

I don't want to look like I'm trying too hard. I'm casual. Laid back. I want to appear as though I just accidentally wandered into his restaurant after a day of... what? Casually driving across the country to eat dinner at his restaurant?

From every angle, I hate this idea. No matter how many ways I spin it, I look completely crazy. And desperate.

No.

This is research.

For my dad.

Basically, a business trip.

Ethan could be married. Or in a relationship.

No.

People who are married don't tell strange women they sleep naked.

Not that I care how he sleeps. Or if he's in a relationship.

This is an email business friendship situation.

"So, listen." I lean my hip against the doorway to Finn's room. "I've been talking with the owner of a restaurant here in town, and I want us to go there for dinner tonight. Grandpa wants to add some local ingredients to the menu, and apparently, this guy knows how to do it."

I pick at my cuticles as I talk.

"No way, I'm not leaving this place until tomorrow," Marin flops onto her bed already in her sleep shirt before her head pops up, eyebrows raised. "And that's a pretty big coincidence we end up in some random town where a guy you've been emailing lives."

She's annoyingly perceptive.

"Yeah. well, I just saw it was on the way..."

If I can't explain it to her, I'll never be able to explain it to him.

"I'm not leaving, either," Finn says, not looking away from his TV while he sits in bed propped up against the headboard.

One of my fingers starts to bleed from my aggressive picking.

"What? What about food?"

I can't do this alone!

"There's a pizza place that delivers here," Marin says, holding up a menu. "Pizza. De-liv-er-y. Doesn't that sound amazing? It's been over a month!"

As if she's been without running water and electricity.

I shake my head. "If I don't meet him today, I won't meet him. Plus, my arteries want healthy food."

"Fine, *we'll* get pizza, and *you* can go eat something *your* arteries like." Finn clicks the remote.

"Ugh! Okay. It's just down the street." Neither of them look at me. "And I'll have my phone. And don't open the door for anyone."

"What about the guy that brings the pizza, *Penelope*?" Marin mocks.

"Text me if you need me. I mean it. And don't leave the rooms."

I zip my wedding band along the chain around my neck and wait for them to change their minds.

They don't.

Without a plan, I leave my kids and walk to meet a man who doesn't know I'm here.

Twenty-three

I END UP IN the worst seat in the entire restaurant of Mainely Local.

It's slammed. Every table is full and there's a line out the door.

When I asked the hostess if Ethan was in, she pointed silently toward the bar as she held a phone to her ear, taking down a reservation.

I'm sitting between an exposed brick wall that's rubbing me like a pumice stone and a woman that smells like my dead grandma.

The bartender has been at the other end of the bar the minutes I've been there, and all my surveys of the room haven't given me anyone that looks like Ethan did in the magazine.

My current plan is to just lay it all on the line when I see him. Something like, *"Hey! I'm not crazy, but we've been emailing. Surprise! I'm here to take that kitchen tour and learn all your secrets."*

I wave my hand again to get the bartender's attention, to no avail. Still.

The man is struggling to keep up. Several people at the bar have empty glasses, and the drink printer, no doubt orders from the waitstaff, is spitting out so many orders the tickets are falling on the floor.

"Moosehead IPA!" someone calls.

The bartender nods before opening every cooler until he finds the beer.

He still hasn't looked at me.

A brunette woman with bright red lips and a low-cut top squeezes between two stools and waves slightly. Instantly, he's in front of her, leaning casually with his back to me and saying something closely as he fills her wine. She laughs. He acts as if the bar isn't imploding around him and people aren't waiting for drinks.

Like me.

That move pushes me from patient to pissed.

I'm trying to give him the benefit of the doubt for being ignored. Maybe he's new. Or blind, I had considered after seeing the state of the bar around him. The way he's giving all his attention to the woman with melons taking up precious real estate at the bar while I'm smothered between the wall and the scent of bad perfume lets me know he's able to see just fine.

I bring two fingers to my mouth and let a whistle fly.

The bartender's head snaps away from the red-lipped lady, and our eyes meet.

Mine narrow before widening.

I can barely breathe.

The woman next to me shifts her weight and somehow pushes me closer to the wall, but I don't feel it.

Ethan Mills is at the bar because he's the bad bartender.

He swallows up the distance between us with long strides until he is directly across from me.

"You got my attention. What?" he snaps.

What?

Of all the scenarios I imagined, this was not one of them.

I open my mouth then snap it shut, stunned to silence.

"You make a big show of whistling me over here. You ordering?"

His eyes shoot from me down the busy line of people on stools.

My nostrils flare.

Real-life Ethan is not the same as email Ethan, and I think I might hate him.

I fold my hands on the menu.

"If *you* weren't making such a big show of letting your bar sink, I wouldn't have had to break out my whistle. But you seem to be having a bad day, so I'm going to let it slide. I'll have the Mountain Mojito and the grilled chicken salad with feta and the house dressing."

I smile.

"No specialty drinks tonight," he says.

"I'll have a regular mojito then," I order it to be petty.

He's being a jerk. He's admitted to me he hates working behind the bar, and there's nothing I want to see more than him having to muddle mint while people shout drink orders at him.

Which is why my smile widens.

"A regular mojito?" He drops his head back with an incredulous laugh. "No. No mojitos. You can have beer, wine, or a cocktail that requires less than two ingredients."

His jaw tics.

"What the hell kind of bar has that stupid rule? You have an entire menu called specialty drinks."

I hold it up to him to prove my point.

"Fine," he snaps, yanking the menu out of my hand before marching away.

"What's the deal with him?" I ask the lady sitting next to me, breathing through my mouth.

She shrugs. "Apparently, the regular guy called out tonight."

"He's kind of the worst," I say, watching as Ethan fumbles with an herb that does not look like mint.

Is that basil?

"Honey, look at him. Who cares if he's the worst?" Perfume lady says with a cocked eyebrow.

I look back at him and study the features I'd already memorized from his magazine photo. His thick head of dark hair has more hints of salt than I could see but his jaw also has a harder edge under the day-old scruff.

"I don't see it," I say, trying to convince myself.

She snorts with a shake of her head. "You're the only one."

Still, I watch him.

The mojito he finally delivers to me is an abomination.

I take one awful sip before I push back to him. "I'm not going to drink this."

Rage ignites in his eyes. "Why not?"

His voice is deep and has the slightest tinge of a Maine accent.

I raise my eyebrows. "I watched you use basil. In a *mojito*. I'm not drinking it. It tastes like gasoline and mouthwash... with basil."

He starts to argue, but I hold up my hand.

"But." I smile. "I'm going to help you. I'm a bartender, an *impressive* one, and you need help."

His chin jerks back, but he doesn't look away.

"You're going to have a mutiny if all those drink tickets don't get made. Every server here is going to blame you for their bad tips tonight."

I point to the line of tickets hanging from the printer and the servers waiting at the end of the bar.

"Why would you do that?" His eyes search mine before looking down the bar at the chaos waiting for him.

I shrug. "I don't have anything else to do."

"Okay," he says, somewhat reluctantly.

"Okay."

I shoot Marin a text before I slide off my stool and circle around to the back of the bar.

"I'm Nel, by the way."

"Okay, Nel," he says, slight smirk ghosting his lips, "let's see how *impressive* you really are."

Twenty-four

"YOU AREN'T ALLOWED TO touch anything unless I say," I tell him, pulling my hair up into a messy bun and rolling the sleeves of my flannel shirt up. "You're a disaster."

I assess the bar. Tickets are still hanging from the printer and at least five empty glasses sit in front of customers.

"What the hell have you been doing back here?" I grab a couple of empty bottles set on a random ledge and drop them into the trash. "It looks like you let a bunch of frat boys run rampant."

I pluck the line of tickets out of the printer and skim through them.

"Look." He grinds his teeth and rubs the back of his head. "Obviously, I know this isn't going well, or I wouldn't accept your help. So, please. Just. Help!"

He emphasizes the last words with an irritated bark in his voice, which I ignore.

"Take this." I hand him a highlighter. "I want you to go through and mark off the ones you can handle, which, based on what I've seen, is only beer or wine. Maybe." I shoot him a doubtful look. "Leave the cocktail tickets here." I point to a ledge. "I'll catch the bar up while you do that.

I'm not bothering to learn the computer system; you can eat the cost of these drinks until we get caught up."

He snatches the highlighter from my hand with a curt, "Fine."

"Miss, do you know how to make a cocktail that doesn't taste like piss?" a man with an amused look asks across the bar, loudly enough for Ethan to hear.

Ethan shoots him a glare.

I grin.

"As a matter of fact, I do."

"Then we'll take a couple of Manhattans, and the ladies here would like some margaritas on the rocks."

"You got it," I say, feeling a sweet buzz of adrenaline crackle through me.

The bar is a mess, but I make myself at home, switching bottles out on the well rack and making a mental note of the garnishes. My rubber boots squeak as I move across the thick mats that cover the floor. As far as I am from home, it feels just as familiar.

I grab the shaker, making a show of spinning it in my palm then throwing it from one hand to the other before grabbing the tequila and pouring it in.

I laugh and take a playful bow as I get small applause, then make quick work of halving and juicing limes before adding the rest of the ingredients. I shake, strain, garnish, and serve the margaritas like I have hundreds of times before.

Only this time, it's different. Like I'm a musician making my comeback tour, it's my hour of reinvention. I'm not the sad, stuck bartender on Key Largo that everyone knows. I'm just... me.

"Margaritas."

I hold them up proudly and place them on the napkins in front of the two women, then move quickly to make the Manhattans.

The man who ordered sips his and hums out a moan.

"That's damn good, miss. A helluva lot better than whatever Ethan made me."

He mockingly lifts his glass toward Ethan and laughs.

"Funny, Mike," Ethan says flatly over his shoulder as he highlights tickets and puts bottles of beer on trays.

"You have a name?" the man asks me.

"Thank you very much." I beam. "And my name is Nel."

"Well, Nel." He pauses, taking another sip.

I freeze, waiting for the fallout from hearing those two familiar words stitched together, shocked when it never comes.

He smacks his lips with an *ah!* "You make a mean drink." He holds up his glass in approval before turning back to the group he's with.

I continue to work like it's the most thrilling thing in life while Ethan stays quiet aside from random mutterings I ignore. I'm having too much fun—feeling far too alive—to deal with his devolved personality.

When four men sit at the bar, I drop napkins in front of them.

"What can I get you boys tonight?" I ask.

They're around my age, maybe a little younger, each handsome enough. They eye me curiously.

"Four Coors," one of them says before looking past me to Ethan. "What are *you* doing back there, man? I thought last time was the last time."

He reaches a hand toward him over the bar with an amused smile.

I grab their beer and pop the tops off before sitting them down in front of them, curious as to how Ethan will respond.

"Don't remind me," he grumbles, grabbing the man's hand across the bar and giving it a quick shake.

I start making a martini from a new order on a ticket as Ethan leans a hip against the bar.

"Who's the woman?" one asks, nodding toward me.

"Someone saving my ass," Ethan says.

"Where'd you find her?"

He scoffs. "Sitting on a stool, pissed off at me."

I bite back the smile and look away as I shake the cocktail over my shoulder.

Eventually, we find a rhythm. He's not exactly friendly, but he's not completely unfriendly either. We get the bar caught up, and every order that comes through the printer for the guests at tables is immediately taken care of and given off to a server.

I don't dare look at him too long, or at all, out of fear of him realizing who I am.

We're so busy I don't have time to think about how I'll explain it when the time comes. Maybe I won't. Maybe this will just be how we meet, and he'll never know. I'll work his bar, then I'll go to the coast of Maine and never talk to him again. Knowing my dad, this idea will pass, and I'll never send him another email.

"Nel! Can we get another round of those margaritas, please?"

I pop up quickly from the cooler I'm organizing at the same time Ethan walks by. My head collides with the tray he's holding and sends a bottle of beer flying through the air before it lands with a foamy crash.

He runs his hand through the thick hair on the top of his head.

"Can you pay attention?" he snaps.

With this, I realize—he's not unfriendly, Ethan Mills is an asshole.

My eyes widen before narrowing sharply.

"Look, for whatever reason, I'm doing you a favor." I flick a finger against his chest, which annoys me to notice is very broad. "Maybe try to not be so... pissed off. You'd be a lot better back here if you took out that stick you've shoved up your ass!"

I cross my arms as I hear the boys sitting across the bar, poorly attempting to stifle their laughs.

"Ethan, is it?" I ask like I don't already know way more than I should about him.

"Yeah," he mumbles, looking away and scrubbing a hand over his scruff-covered jaw.

"Ok, *Ethan.* Maybe try to be less of a dick when someone is helping you."

I grab a few pieces of glass off the ground before washing my hands and grabbing the tequila. The boys at the bar break out into full-blown laughter as I flip the bottle in the air before pouring it into the shaker.

"And gentlemen?" I say, eyeing the four guys. "Your friend Ethan here didn't tell you I'm not ringing any drinks up tonight, so I'd order top-shelf if I were you."

Then I give them a wink before moving down the bar, only stopping to smile sweetly at Ethan as his lethal look pivots from me to them when they start to howl.

Thank you very much.

***

"Part of your problem is this isn't very organized," I say, scrunching my nose at the chaos.

The crowd has thinned out just enough for a teaching moment that he desperately needs.

I point to an area of randomly open bottles and mixers. "Do you have some kind of system here or...?" My voice trails off as we look around. It looks like the bar was teleported from a warzone.

"Maybe?" he says, scratching his neck. "This clearly isn't my area of expertise. Usually I'm in the kitchen."

For the first time, I notice his eyes. They're a color that can't decide if it wants to be blue or green, and they sit on his face like two small pools of the ocean. It's a color so intense I have to look away.

"Well, you can learn how to make a drink, but I'll tell you that knowing where everything is can help you a ton when you get in a situation like this. For the sake of all these poor people, I hope you never have to get back here again, but at least learning the layout can help." I pause, considering the situation. "And I typically take an order and work the easiest drinks first, then the more complicated ones. If you do that, you won't drown... as fast."

His eyes meet mine, and there's the faintest flicker of something. Admiration?

"Hi, Ethan," a woman's voice cuts in. With long dark hair, big blue eyes, and lips she's licking like a fox in a henhouse, she slides coolly onto a stool.

Turning away from me, he leans against the bar to face her.

"Hey, you." His voice comes out as smooth as velvet.

"Ethan." She giggles. "It's Megan, silly. I got a haircut since the last time we went out." She flicks her hair around.

"I know. I like it," he says with that *smirk*, wiping the bar in front of her.

"You haven't returned my calls. I thought we had a connection." She taps her fingernail on his forearm that rests on the bar, and I'm instantly annoyed.

Irrationally annoyed.

His eyes meet mine, and I snort a laugh as I drop an empty bottle into the trash.

"Haven't I? I've been busy." He scratches the back of his head. "Can I get you a drink?" he asks.

She pouts. "No, I'm with friends. I just wanted to say hi. I didn't know you were so busy. I'm free after this..." her voice trails off, but her eyes linger long enough to relay everything she's thinking, earning a smile from him before she walks away.

An obvious fact reveals itself at that moment. Ethan *has* been flirting with me in his emails, but it's because Ethan flirts with *all* women.

I can't tell if all the blood leaves or rushes toward my head as I look at him. I'm mortified.

I know I can't run away, so instead I hand him a ticket and hear myself say, "For such an ass, you certainly have a lot of women fawning over you."

I don't wait for him to respond before I greet the next people who take their seats at the bar.

Twenty-five

"I WAS A DICK," Ethan says as he clears dishes from the bar.

I laugh under my breath but don't look at him as I wash glasses in the sink.

Over the last hour and a half, it has become painfully obvious he's a good-looking man. Fine, a *very* good-looking man. His thick hair looks as if he's been running his hands through it all day, and the few strands of silver that sweep through it somehow add to his appeal. I've never liked facial hair, but the way the slightest stubble covers his jaw is borderline delicious.

I'm not even going to think about his eyes. Or forearms. Or the low timbre of his voice that combines with the faintest of Maine accents.

The realization this man is, in fact, hot, makes heat crawl up my neck.

What the hell is wrong with me?

The shift that happens is instant and destructive. Gone is Nel, the confident bartender. In her place is a teenage girl who's only recently discovered the opposite sex.

"Well, the bar is a disaster. I would be a dick too, probably. You know, it just happens like that sometimes." When I think I've finished talking, my voice lifts to a strange throaty sound and unfortunately adds, "You never know when a dick is going to fly out of the woodwork."

He laughs at what I've said at the same time I cringe.

"Yes, those dicks do just fly out of the woodwork, don't they," he jokes, and for the first time, directs one of his deadly smirks toward me.

"I'm Ethan Mills, by the way. Officially."

He reaches out a hand.

An introduction—the moment I've been dreading.

His outstretched hand has me gaping and blinking.

"This is where you usually shake my hand," he teases, moving his hand just slightly through the air.

"Ha! Right!" I say, reaching out my hand to shake his. "Well, officially, Ethan, I'm Nel. Penelope, really, but also just Nel. Or Nelly if you're my dad." My mouth decides to make some kind of deep voice that it's never made before, saying, "Which you are definitely not my dad." I wave my hand up and down, gesturing to his torso and flush instantly.

"Penelope," he says with a knowing pause.

A pause that says he's putting pieces together. I see recognition strike him like a hammer to a nail before I look away.

He clears his throat. "Well, Penelope, I'm sorry. You saved my ass tonight. I was just..." he looks around the now half-empty bar and dining room. "A disaster."

I nod through my discomfort.

"So, are you from around here? I don't think I've seen you before," Ethan asks like he doesn't already know as he pulls a beer out of the cooler and sets it on a tray.

"No." I pause as my mouth fills with cotton balls. "I'm a widow, so..."

I'm a widow?

A line forms between his eyebrows.

I close my eyes and push a palm to my forehead as I release a slow breath.

"No, I'm sorry. That was awkward. I don't know why I said that. I'm not local," I say, pretending he doesn't already know that.

Thankfully, a woman sits down at the nearly empty bar that ends the conversation and steals our attention.

I drop a napkin on the bar, smiling at her. "What can I get for ya tonight?"

She returns the smile, but her eyes latch onto Ethan. "Hi, Ethan," she purrs.

The man is like a lighthouse calling to everyone with ovaries in the state of Maine.

"Brooke." He nods. "What are you drinking tonight?" he asks coolly, leaning a hip against the edge of the bar.

"Hmmm. That sounds like a loaded question." She bats her thick eyelashes at him. "But why don't you surprise me with something special."

"As enticing as *that* sounds, I recently was informed my drink-making skills are pretty horrible. Nel here is helping me out, and she's some kind of wizard behind the bar. She can whip up something great for you, I'm sure."

Her face puckers in disappointment.

"Nel, how about you make Brooke here one of your famous daiquiris?"

The look he gives me is pure evil and smug as hell.

He knows. He knows that I know he knows.

I want to die.

My mouth hangs open.

"That doesn't ring a bell," I lie. "Do you like blueberries?" I ask her.

"Whatever, that's fine."

She doesn't pull her eyes off Ethan. He doesn't pull his eyes off me.

Every butterfly on planet earth flaps from my stomach to my throat as I grab mint leaves, blueberries, and start muddling them together then mix them with gin and tonic.

I plug the end of a straw with my finger before lifting it to my mouth and getting a drop off the other end to taste. Even just drops, the subtle freshness of the mint blends with the sweetness of the berries and the juniper bite of the gin to play like a symphony across my taste buds.

I smile, pleased, and stick a fresh straw in the drink before sliding it across the bar to Brooke.

"So, Ethan," she says as her lips curl into a smile. Without warning, she takes the straw in her mouth and provocatively twirls her tongue around it. Repeatedly.

I watch like a deer in the headlights. She's clearly on a mission to get laid and doesn't care who knows it.

The amount of time she spends licking her straw has me flabbergasted—like at any moment, the drink itself might start to moan.

I clear my throat to remind her I'm standing there. "Ethan, I think you can handle what's left. I'm famished and..." I look at the almost empty dining room, then Brooke. "I could use a drink."

"Stay," he insists. "Let me get your food."

He nods to an empty stool on the other side of the bar, and I hesitate. I do not want to stay. On the contrary, I want to run back to Idaho and undo this whole plan.

But, like the fool I am, I do as he says.

I browse the menu while Brooke giggles with Ethan. When she flirts, he leans closer.

A curdling feeling twists my stomach at the scene.

I know how it feels to have someone look at me the way they look at each other. The way he laughs, the way she smiles. They interact in a way I never will again, and I feel all my aloneness as I watch them.

After the last guests leave—including Brooke—Ethan brings me a salad and a glass of wine and stands across the bar from me washing glasses. Watching me.

"So," I say. "She was really getting weird with that straw, huh?"

He chuckles.

I point a salad-filled fork at him. "Are any of those women your girl-friend or what? You have quite the revolving door situation going on."

"That's a personal question, isn't it, Penelope?"

I snort. "It seemed pretty public with the way they came in here ready to burn their panties for you."

"*That* is an interesting visual." He dunks another glass into the soapy sink. "They're all friends. Some of them I dated a couple times. Nothing serious. And Brooke is just..." He blows out his breath. "Persistent."

"Persistent is one way to describe what she was doing with her tongue."

Another laugh rumbles in his chest as he tosses a couple empty bottles in the trash.

"So," he says as he leans over the bar, too far into my space.

"So," I say, looking at my salad like it's the most fascinating food ever made.

"What do I wear when I sleep, Penelope?"

There is an amused fire in his eyes that makes my fork drop and eyes close.

My face might actually be on fire, and he laughs.

Bastard!

"You *are* bad at keeping secrets," he says, resting his ropey forearms on the bar, smirking. *Again.* I don't have to know him long to know Ethan's smirk is like the heat of the desert or the coolness of the Pacific: it just is.

"It's not what you think," I argue, braving a look at him. "I'm here because my husband died, not because of you. Or the nakedness. Or whatever."

"Your husband died, so you came to Bethel, Maine?" He laughs incredulously and shakes his head, sliding a clean wineglass onto the rack overhead.

"In so many words, yes. My kids and I fixed up an old RV and planned to drive it around the country this summer. So, I could, I don't know, fix myself or something. After a very unfortunate day with dinosaur bones last week, I decided I'd always wanted to see Maine, so we will be here the rest of the summer. Specifically, the coast, Bethel, is just a stop for the night. So, yes. My husband died, grief turned me into the island recluse, and here we are in Maine." I raise my glass at the confession. "And maybe I noticed that Bethel could be on the way, so we stopped here for the night so I could..."

I don't even know the ending of that sentence. And yet, I lift my chin in defiance.

"Anyway. I fell in love with experimenting with flavors and the combinations that came from fresh ingredients behind the bar. Markets are my muse—or were. My husband died in a plane crash, and that part of me shut down. I was intrigued by you, I guess. About how you centered a restaurant around that same concept. And tonight was... fun."

"When did he die?" he asks.

"Umm... well, almost a year and a half ago."

I shift in my seat, suddenly uncomfortable.

"Did it work?"

My eyes pinch in confusion.

"Did you fix yourself?"

I'm stripped bare by his question. "Maybe?" A small laugh puffs out of me.

I finish my last bites of dinner as he finishes cleaning the bar, and he takes a seat next to me, topping my wine off before pouring himself a glass.

Our arms rest next to each other without touching as the music plays softly over the speakers through the empty dining room. For the first time in nearly eighteen months, I'm not a sad widow or failing mom trying to mend bridges.

I'm a woman in a bar with a man.

It feels like the first breath of air after being held underwater for too long.

"Penelope is an unusual name," he says over the rim of his wineglass before taking a sip.

"Ahh, yes. Well, to know my mother would be to understand it all. She's an artist and has gone through many phases in life. I was named during her phase of Greek appreciation, and my brother, Gabe, was named during her devout Catholic phase." I laugh. "It's all very inspired."

"Which one was Penelope? I don't know Greek mythology."

"She was married to Odysseus and stayed loyal to him while he was gone for years and years in the Trojan War. Apparently, she was beautiful, so beautiful she had over a hundred suitors in that time, but she stayed faithful for twenty years until he returned."

I zip the ring on my necklace. "Sometimes I wonder if my name sealed my fate in life," I say softly.

"Because of the beauty?" he asks with a nudge.

"Something like that." A small smile tugs at my lips.

"What kind of art does your mom make?"

"*That* is a fascinating topic. My mom is a painter. Until recently, she painted landscapes with lots of color, but now she paints nudes. Of my dad. Still with lots of color." My eyes widen to emphasize the trauma of this.

I shudder. He laughs.

I look around. The restaurant is empty, and almost every light is off. Even the staff has left.

"Ethan, I'm so sorry. I didn't realize the time. I'm sure you would rather be anywhere but at work." I start to stand, but he stops me with a hand on my arm.

His eyes meet mine and crinkle in the corners as he smiles.

"I actually can't think of anywhere I'd rather be. And I owe you dessert. And a tour of the kitchen."

He slides off his stool and disappears before returning with a thick slice of carrot cake and two forks.

"Oh my God!" I put a hand over my mouth after my first bite. "How is this so good?"

"Maine carrots," he says seriously before putting a fork full of cake in his mouth.

A loud knock cuts off anything I want to say next, and my head snaps toward the sound. Behind a large window, a woman in a pair of skintight jeans and a low-cut top smiles as she waves through the glass.

"Do you know her?" My wide eyes bounce from her to Ethan.

"Damn. Yeah. Zoey's my date tonight. I didn't notice the time, I guess."

He avoids my gaze as he gets up to let her in.

Date?

Every emotion that makes no sense ricochets through me. Disappointment. Anger. Jealousy. Embarrassment... more disappointment. Apparently, every single woman in Bethel, Maine, has perfect boobs and Ethan's number.

He doesn't get the door fully open before *Zoey* has her arms around him and attacks his mouth with hers like a snorkel. I choke on a bite of cake, shocked. Her manicured fingers claw at his chest like she's performing an animal mating ritual.

Ethan's eyes widen and meet mine across the room before he scrapes her off him.

"Zoey," he says, wiping his mouth with the back of his hand. "I lost track of time. I'm almost finished up."

He gestures to the bar and where I sit like a frump.

I stand up awkwardly and try to gather my thoughts. When my purse keeps dropping, I consider just leaving it. A casualty of my stupidity.

"What kind of date starts at 11:30?" I want to take the question back as soon as I ask.

Zoey smiles like a Cheshire cat. "The kind where nobody sleeps, I hope."

Ethan smirks, and dammit if I don't hate them both for it.

"Of course. Right." I force a smile that physically hurts my mouth. "Well, it is late, and I was just going anyway, so this is perfect timing, right? And I love your outfit. So cute. Very..." I clear my throat. "Tight." I wince. "I mean, it looks great on you." I wave my hand around. "I have to go."

Die.

I have to go die is what I mean.

"Penelope." Ethan's voice interrupts the actual crash and burn that's happening right in front of him.

"Hmm?"

I look at him as I fumble, again, with my purse.

"Thank you for your help tonight. I wouldn't have survived without you."

I hate how handsome he is at that moment, and I hate more that I notice his arm is around a pretty woman named Zoey, who doesn't want to sleep all night while I wear a stupid cowboy t-shirt and rubber boots.

"Of course. I had nothing else going on. Glad I could help. It was great meeting you both."

I bow like an awkward karate student, and Ethan bites back a smile.

Bastard!

Zoey takes a seat at the bar where I had been sitting as if signaling my dismissal.

"Well, bye. You two have a fun night. Not sleeping and all."

I smile weakly before I walk across the empty dining room, my rubber boots squeaking loudly against the floor the whole way.

The instant the door opens, the cool night air blasts my hot face like a fire extinguisher to a flame. I don't take a full breath until I get to the inn, where Finn and Marin are dead asleep.

I go to the bathroom and splash water on my face, searching my reflection for an explanation. My gold wedding ring swings through the air like a pendulum as I bend over the sink.

I grab it.

Just like the fluorescent lights don't hide all the places of my complexion I wish they would, I can't hide what had just happened from myself. I was attracted to a man, albeit an extremely off-limits man who possibly invented the red flag, who wasn't Travis.

I blot my face with a towel.

Whatever is happening, I'll figure it out tomorrow when we drive very far away from Ethan and this town.

Twenty-six

"MOM? WHAT DID THEY say?"

Marin looks at me expectantly from the other side of the booth, and I have no clue what she's just said.

"The guy at the campground in Bar Harbor—does he have space for us?"

Right.

"Yes, the campground. Not until next weekend once the Fourth of July is over, and even then, it's on a first come basis. So, we can look for somewhere else this morning to go in the meantime."

I drink my coffee in gulps, scorching my mouth, desperately needing the caffeine to kick in.

Not surprisingly, I didn't sleep well. My thoughts bounced between the same overplayed scenarios. Imagining what Ethan and Zoey were doing, absurdly hating Ethan for what he and Zoey were doing, and my personal favorite, feeling guilty for betraying Travis with the first two thoughts.

"Let's just stay here—there's so much to do in the mountains, and this weather is awesome," Finn chimes in between bites of an omelet.

"Are you sure? Seems kind of sleepy if you ask me." My chest tightens.

"I think it's perfect. Let's do something outdoorsy today." Marin sips her tea. "Oh! And how did it go last night? Did you meet the owner?"

"It was fun helping out behind the bar. I haven't had a challenge like that in a while. The owner was a letdown, though. A jerk, really." I pause. "But I liked making the drinks and joking with the customers. They had blueberries—you know I love a good fresh ingredient. I made up a drink on the spot, even."

I wiggle my fingers playfully.

"Look at you, Penelope." She smiles through her bite of French toast. "What was the deal with the owner?"

"Hmm." My throat pinches as I picture Ethan's face. "He was greasy and looked a little like an ogre. You know the type. Kind of one of those creepy old men. And weird teeth—like the kind with all that yellow film that makes it look like there's one weird massive tooth." I twist my face in disgust.

"Okay, that's gross."

"Right?" I nod too many times.

"I found a company that does guided floats down the Androscoggin River. Anyone up for that today?"

Bless you, Finn, for this subject change.

"It's supposed to be the hottest day all week, a steamy eighty-seven."

Finn holds up my phone. "Says it's a gentle float down the river on a tube, kayak, canoe, or paddle board, and the guide helps you spot wildlife." He shrugs.

"Maybe we can see a moose!"

Marin taps her fingers together in excitement.

"Sounds fun to me." I take another bite of bacon as I look out of the window. "Do you guys want to move to the campground or stay at the inn a couple more nights?"

Finn scoffs. "What do you think?"

Inn it is.

***

When we make it to the launch site on the river, I convince myself it will be a fun and relaxing day on the water. It's going to feel like vacation. Being here is a *good* thing.

"Mom, don't be such a prude." Marin scoffs as I tug at the swimsuit she insisted I wear. "You're acting like you're naked."

It's a too-bright red, too high on the thigh, and way too low in the chest scrap of fabric and the opposite of age appropriate. I look like an idiot.

"I feel naked," I hiss at her, wishing the fabric would multiply, as a young guy walks down to greet us on the riverbank.

He looks to be about Finn's age. A good-looking kid with long brown hair pulled back in a bun wearing a tie-dyed t-shirt with the sleeves cut off and swim shorts. He could be in California as much as Maine.

"'Sup guys?" He lifts his chin. "I'm Derek. I'll be your guide this morning."

Finn gives him a nod. "Finn," he says. "This is my sister, Marin, and my mom, Nel."

I smile.

"Sweet. So, you can pick whatever you want to float on." He points to the racks of tubes, kayaks, and paddle boards. "We will be gone for about three hours. You can bring a cooler if you want, but we are very much a pack-it-in, pack-it-out outfit, so there is no throwing the empties in the water. We'll catch a ride in the van at the end to get back." He drops a canvas bag into a kayak. "I take a kayak so I can keep things dry, so you can put any cellphones or wallets in there."

We make quick work of choosing our floats. I go with a paddleboard. Marin and Finn both pick tubes.

"Are we waiting for anyone else?" I ask, tugging at the too-tight fabric that both pulls into a perma-wedgie and threatens to expose my chest to the free world before dropping my dry clothes into his kayak.

"Actually," he says shyly. "This is my first solo guide. Ergo, the group is going to be small. We have two more people coming, but that's it." There's an awkward silence. "But I promise I totally know what I'm doing. I grew up swimming on this river."

He smiles eagerly.

I want to laugh, but the mom in me feels incredibly proud even though I don't even know the kid.

I open my mouth to say something encouraging but am stopped by a deep, "They let anyone go down this river, don't they?" from behind me.

I spin so fast, I stumble over my paddleboard.

Holy mother of God.

Ethan?

"Har! Har! Dad," Derek says dryly. "Very funny." He looks back to us. "My annoying dad and less annoying brother will be the other two joining us today."

Derek rolls his eyes toward Ethan, but Ethan's eyes widen and lock with mine.

I can't breathe.

"Penelope?"

I look away, feeling such an intense heat rise up my neck I expect to see smoke puff out of my pores.

"Mom?" Marin stands next to me. "Do you know each other?"

"No!" I shout at the same time Ethan casually says, "Yes."

Marin and Finn look at me, each other, then Ethan.

"I mean, yes," I rasp out.

Ethan smirks.

"I mean kind of." I backtrack. "I met him at the restaurant I went to last night. Remember?"

I shake my head slightly and pin Marin with a warning look. She squints at me, her way of silently telling me *I know you're lying*, before dropping it.

We make introductions, and I purposefully stand as far away from Ethan as possible in every situation. Austin, Derek's older brother, looks exactly like Derek, just slightly taller with buzzed short hair and no tie-dye.

Ethan, on the other hand, looks like he belongs on the cover of an outdoor magazine. A gray t-shirt that clings across his chest like it was custom-made for him reveals arms possibly made with a chisel, not in the bulky way that comes from hours in the gym, but in the way that comes from living life and chopping firewood.

I can barely see straight between his broad chest, backward hat, and blue swim trunks slung low on his hips.

Hips that Zoey probably wrapped her....

I jam my eyes shut and send the thought down the river.

Derek instructs us all to follow him into the water. The kids take the lead and dive headfirst while I hang back and wade in slowly. The water is one degree warmer than ice, and goosebumps cover my skin. The flimsy material that clings to my chest does nothing to hide how the chill affects me.

Ethan wades through the water, and his eyes flick to my chest and back up.

"Nice suit."

My face heats, and I make a mental note to ground Marin for life for making me wear this ridiculous thing.

In the least dramatic way possible, I want to drown myself in the river.

"What are you doing?" I demand as I fumble onto my board.

"Umm. Supporting my son at his new job?"

He raises his eyebrows, and the green flecks in his eyes catch the sun.

"You know what? Never mind," I snap.

"Are you mad at me?" he asks, dropping the paddle onto his board before effortlessly hopping on.

"Shouldn't you still be with *Zoey*?" Jealousy is not my best look.

"Are you kidding me, Nel?" He scoffs. "I forgot I had that planned. What did you want me to do, send her away?"

Yes.

"No. Forget it. You didn't do anything wrong, I'm just... tired."

Kneeling on my board, I start paddling away from him, knowing damn well there's nowhere to go.

"If you remember, Nel, you're the one who just showed up," he says as he effortlessly catches up to me. "After telling me people don't *find* themselves in the White Mountains of Maine, you found yourself here. What did you want me to do? Clear my calendar until that happened?"

Worse than me not having an answer to his questions is the fact there's amusement in his voice.

He thinks this is funny.

I try with desperate, angry chops of my paddle to get away from him, but he's like a barnacle that won't let himself get scraped off. He's everywhere I am with a few smooth, calm strokes.

I give up and accept that for three hours, he'll be next to me, looking like he does, while I try to pretend I don't look like I do.

Ahead on the river, Austin, Marin, and Finn tie their tubes together and cluster next to Derek, who paddles his kayak. We're far back enough I can't hear their conversation, but their regular bursts of laughter bounce off the water toward me and wrap around me like a cozy sweater. They're having fun. That fact alone makes everything a little more tolerable.

"So, you're still here," Ethan says as he paddles.

"Aren't you observant?"

"Well, you said last night you were leaving today. Unless that's just what women say that drive across the country to see men they find in magazines."

Bastard.

"That's not what happened!" I snap. "And we were *supposed* to leave, but the spot in Bar Harbor we're going to doesn't have a spot for us until next weekend. Finn wanted to stay and do stuff in the mountains, and I think they like being at the Inn instead of the camper anyway—not that I blame them there."

I tilt my paddle to follow the slight bend in the river.

"I see."

His board gently nudges into mine.

We're quiet for a few minutes as we float, long enough for some of the tension to leave my shoulders.

"The trees are so thick across the hills and mountains here. It doesn't look real. It's beautiful. You were right when you said there's a pull."

Willow branches gently bow along the riverbank in the breeze.

A fly fisherman stands up to his knees in the water and waves to us before casting. The quiet whizzing sound of the line and soft splash of the fly hitting the water play on repeat as we quietly float by. It's an ethereal kind of beauty.

"I love it; it's home," he finally says. "I know you saw places more impressive than the Androscoggin out west."

He rests his paddle on his lap and faces me.

"Hmm. The Colorado River in the Grand Canyon comes to mind. Most of us won't see anything like that again, but this is more peaceful in a way. Different."

"I would imagine the Grand Canyon is a *lot* more exciting than this," he says, chest rumbling with a laugh.

I turn to look at him.

"Different rivers dance differently with the earth, I guess. Some carve huge canyons and leave crazy rock formations. Some move sand quietly and smooth rocks. It's not about the river or the land. It's about how the two of them work together to become what they will." I pause, imagining the smooth pebbles that lay on the bottom of this river and specks of sand that no doubt started their journey somewhere else. "If the Colorado River was in Maine, it never would have made the Grand Canyon. The ground wouldn't have allowed it, I don't think. It's hard to say one is more impressive than the other. Just... different."

"Like the people we meet," he says, surprising me enough that I turn to face him.

"A man I met said the people we meet and how they shape us—love us—were the rivers that ran through us. I liked that. Understood it somehow," I say, looking off into the distance, letting myself travel back to that rocky ledge at the Grand Canyon, feeling the slightest tinge of Travis' absence.

A swell of laughter and sequence of splashes from the kids brings me back to the moment. I smile as I watch them—Marin twirling her tube around as her legs dangle over one edge, head dropped back toward the sky on the other. Finn's long arms fold under his chin as his body drops through the center of his own.

"So, how was your date?"

I thoroughly hate myself for caring enough to ask.

"Last night was one of the best nights I've had in a while," he responds, smugly.

"That's nice," I say, meaning anything but.

Derek points at something on the shore everyone looks at. I do the same—it's a house. I can't make out his words, but the home is stunning.

The exterior is wood, maybe cedar, with black trim all around it. It's two stories, built into the gentle slope of the land. The entire backside of the house that faces the river is covered in windows. The single-angle roofline and thick wire railings give it a modern feel without being cold.

There's an ATV in the yard and a couple of kayaks lying in the grass on the shore. It's not huge, but it's the kind of place you can imagine drinking coffee on the porch or skipping rocks into the river.

"What do you think?" Ethan asks, bumping my board gently with his.

"It's beautiful."

His response is an annoying whistle as he paddles.

"So, you have two sons, it seems. And dates at 11:30 with people named Zoey. Were you ever married?"

"I was. To their mom."

"What happened?"

He puffs out his breath before dropping his head back to face the sky.

"If you would have asked me that right after it happened, I would have said my wife had an affair, but now, because there's been some time, that was just one part."

I'm astonished that he says it without an ounce of animosity. Like he isn't the least bit angry.

"Early on in our marriage, I was building my name, and my life was my work. That's hard enough on a marriage, especially with the hours, but she left her career to be home with the kids. As they got older, she got lonely, and I wasn't there." He shrugs. "We got married young and grew up into different people. The normal progression of life, ya know?"

He faces me, and his eyes are a clear blue against the sky.

"I would never expect someone to be the same person at forty as they were at twenty. We all change as life chips away at us. Some couples have what it takes to make it through those changes—to put in the effort—some don't."

"Are you close with her now?" I ask.

"Very," he says with a nod. "She told me about the affair. Said she was in love, and it wasn't with me. Obviously, I didn't enjoy that, but somehow, I got over it and owned my part in it all. She's a great mom, and we co-parent well together. And she married the man." He shrugs again. As if it's just the way things are supposed to be.

"So, is that why you go on dates at 11:30 at night and flirt with every woman that struts up to your bar?" I tease.

The slightest of smiles pulls at his lips as he cuts the blade of his paddle through the water.

"Part of it. I did a lot of things wrong as a husband—I can own that. My focus now is on finding a balance between work and the boys. Casual is manageable. Dates at 11:30 don't usually interfere with family dinners."

I snort at his honesty then we fall into silence. Ethan doesn't try to fill it with chatter, and surprisingly, neither do I. We paddle and pause, paddle and pause, breaking the pattern only when our eyes hook for a blink until one of us—me—looks away.

Minutes upon minutes pass with him next to me.

"Want to race?"

There's a playful spark in his eyes that makes my own narrow.

"Race?" I scoff. "What are you, twelve? What's in it for me?"

"Bragging rights, of course." He grins like it's the best idea he's ever had.

There's no way I can beat him. He's much stronger than me, but if my night behind the bar proves anything, it's that I appreciate a challenge. I look down the river and back at him as I weigh my options.

I spin my board around so it's even with his and touch it almost completely along the entire length. My eyes meet his, and I bite my lip shyly and lean close to him. I'm thankful for the first time I'm wearing a ridiculous scrap of fabric for a suit.

"Ethan," I whisper.

His eyes widen in surprise as he takes the bait. His eyes drop to my mouth, my small excuse for cleavage, then back to my face.

Gotcha!

I grin and push his board away from mine before I start to paddle fiercely.

"Hey!" he yells through a laugh.

He's a hell of a lot stronger than me, but with his paddle on my board, he doesn't stand a chance.

"I play dirty, Ethan!" I call over my shoulder with a smile as I stand on my board and paddle as hard as I can.

I hear a splash but don't turn to look. Seconds later, my board jolts, a hand wraps around my ankle, and Ethan's head pops out of the river next to me.

"So do I, Nel."

He grins maniacally and gives a tug just enough to falter my balance. I fly off the board with a scream, and the cold water nearly knocks the breath out of me as I go under.

I laugh when my head comes to the surface. Ethan faces me, chin just above the water, eyes shining.

"You're an ass," I say as I dip my head back in the water to smooth my hair away from my face.

"Says the woman who stole my paddle."

He shakes his head and laughs. Drops of water run down his neck and bare shoulders.

"Were you just trying to get me to take my shirt off, Nel? Because all you had to do was ask." He lifts his chin, and droplets of water drip from the scruff of his jaw.

"You're insufferable. You challenged me, remember?"

I splash him with a handful of water before pulling myself up onto my board and trying to make my suit cover more skin.

"Nel?"

"Hmm?"

He pulls himself up on his own board, water dripping down his chest that I force myself not to stare at.

"You know I said I had a great time last night?" he asks.

"Yeah, we definitely don't need to talk about this. I shouldn't have asked. I was just—"

"It's just that I had such a great time. By the time Zoey showed up, I was ready to call it a night."

Oh.

"I just wanted you to know." He says it like it's important.

"Well, now I know."

I tell myself it doesn't matter, that I don't care, but the weirdest feeling of hope blooms in my belly, along with a smile I never quite shake from my lips.

Twenty-seven

I'M CERTAIN MY HEART is pounding so loudly that the people in Canada can hear it. The smirking, the muscles, and the way he says my name like warm honey—Ethan is giving my nervous system whiplash.

"Heading down to Bar Harbor next weekend, right, Mom?" Finn asks as I pull my board onto the beach next to him.

"That's the plan. Stay there for three weeks or so and then head home after that."

I grab my dry clothes from Derek's kayak, grateful to be covering myself.

"That's so funny, Dad—" Derek starts.

"Dad," Ethan interrupts, "is starving."

Derek's chin pulls back as he looks at him, then shrugs.

"If only we knew somewhere to get a burger in this town," Austin chimes in, tapping a finger against his chin.

Marin eyes him curiously as she dries off with a towel.

I brace for impact.

"Dad owns Mainely Local, and they've got the best burgers around," Austin offers.

Marin's eyebrows shoot to the sky, and she gives me a look.

"Oh, does he now?"

Saw that coming.

"Yeah, yeah," Ethan says beside me. "No need to suck up. Burgers it is. Derek, this van know how to get us there?"

With so many thoughts bouncing into each other in my skull I can barely think straight, Marin and I climb in the van first and sit in the far back seats.

"Mom!" she whispers as soon as we sit down. "That—" She points her finger toward the back of Ethan's head in the row ahead of us. "—is who you were with last night?!"

I cringe. "Shh! Yes, okay," I say as quietly as I can, bending down slightly to get farther away from him. "Nothing happened."

"Why not? He's far from a greasy guy with bad teeth. That guy is obsessed with you! He couldn't get enough of you in that bathing suit."

She makes the motion of cat claws scratching through the air.

"You're grounded for this, first of all," I hiss at her as I pull at the strap of my suit while struggling to keep my voice low. "And he is not obsessed with me. He's... I don't know what he is. Confused. Complicated. A walking red flag. Obsessed with anything with a vagina—not me."

"Mom, you should go on a date with him. C'mon. Just try it out, go out to dinner, get dressed up, have some fun. You know Finn and I don't care, right? Plus, we're like a million miles away from home. It's a good way to practice dating without having to do the walk of shame in front of people you know."

She is dead serious in her whisper voice.

"Marin!" I croak. "No. We are not having this conversation, and we are not going on a date, and what the hell do you even know about walks of shame? Jesus Christ! You and I need to have a long talk about these books you're reading when we get home." My throat burns from whispering.

"Hey," Ethan's deep voice says from above. "You don't have to whisper."

I look up to see his annoying face and groan into my hands.

"I won't make you beg, Penelope. If you want me to take you on a date, I will."

Ethan is a smug bastard.

"No!" I yell at the same time Marin blurts, "Absolutely she would!"

"Marin. No. Ethan, thank you for asking and for trying to... whatever." I gesture toward Marin. "But this is..." I wave my hands and bang my fingers loudly on the metal ceiling of the van. "Ridiculous."

"Ignore her. She'll be ready by six." Marin holds up a hand, palm facing me. "No more words, Mom. You're going."

Ethan's smile is instant, triumphant, and annoying as hell.

When Derek parks in front of the familiar restaurant, Ethan waits for me outside the van.

"Look, if you don't want to go out tonight, I won't make you go. But Marin is right." He leans in close, like he's going to kiss me, but his face slides around to my ear where he whispers, "I am kind of obsessed with you."

At this, my face feels so hot it's as if it was blasted by a blow torch.

"Fine. I'll go," I choke out. "But please stop saying things like that."

"No promises," he says as he puts his hand on the small of my back to guide me into the restaurant. A move so subtle it shouldn't make me feel like I've been lit on fire.

Yet here I am, burning alive.

***

"Mom? Hey, can you hear me?" I'm whispering, pacing, and officially freaking out.

"Hi, honey! It's great to hear your voice! I'm painting. Let me just clean my brushes off so we can talk." I hear the familiar tapping sound against her brush cup. "Why are we whispering?" she whispers.

"Sorry, I'm in the bathroom. In Maine. I'm in the bathroom in Maine." I let out a shaky breath and reset. "Sorry, I'm hiding. I need to ask you a question, and I need you to give me a brutally honest answer."

"From the bathroom? I'm intrigued." I can hear the smile in her voice.

I ignore her.

"I met a guy here last night, a restaurant owner. The one I've been emailing. We kind of talked and had a great time, even though he might be some kind of womanizer, and then we ran into him and his kids today on a river, and Marin opened her big fat mouth, and now I'm supposed to go on a date with this man."

Silence.

"So, I'm wondering what you think about that. I'm dressed in the bathroom with actual makeup and adult clothing on, but I feel. I don't know. Guilty? Like I'm betraying Travis, or something. I need you to tell me what to do."

Anxiety lives in every part of my body as I pace.

"Penelope." Her voice is soft. "You could come back married, and nobody would question your loyalty to Travis. You know that, right? You two were a dream team, but we have all watched you drag around this island with a dark cloud over your head, missing him long enough. It's what Travis would have wanted, even if it involved another guy in a bathroom in Maine."

"First of all, he's not in the bathroom. But thank you. Really. I know I get in my head, and I just—I don't know how to do this. I'm really incredibly awkward. Did you know that?" I puff out a self-deprecating laugh.

"Of course I know that, but do this. Go out with this guy. Don't worry about what you should or shouldn't do. Just have fun, Penelope. Laugh. Flirt. Get naked in a backseat."

"Mom." I massage my temple. "I was sixteen, and I wasn't *naked*. That cop exaggerated," I argue.

Her laugh fills my speaker as I cringe over my teenage antics.

"And I'm not taking any advice on getting naked from the woman who is painting dick pics of my father." I spit the words out like bitter berries.

"Have fun, sweetheart."

She means it.

I hang up and look in the mirror.

I'm wearing one of the sweaters I bought in Oregon. It's bright green with a wide neckline that slides off one shoulder, and my wedding band takes center stage around my neck. My pair of fitted black jeans stop just above my black rubber ankle boots—my only shoe option other than flip-flops.

My eyes have a smokey color around them, and my cheeks have the slightest tinge of pink.

I either look ridiculous or amazing.

"Finn, are you sure about this? I can cancel right now, and I won't be mad or anything. I just..." I stand by the door and reach for any excuse not to go.

"Marin said you'd do this." He clicks his tongue.

"I did say that!" she calls from the other room.

"Go, Mom. I know you loved Dad. But please. Go. I like him." He drops onto his bed. "Nobody will be Dad, but there's also a lot of great people in the world that aren't."

I rub my hand through his hair. "You got smart, kid."

He grins. "I know."

Then, against my better judgment, I walk out the door to meet my date.

Twenty-eight

ETHAN IS WAITING ON the sidewalk in front of the inn, looking in a way I can only describe as hot as hell. He's in blue jeans and a flannel shirt rolled up on his forearms. Forearms that are apparently my kryptonite because all I can think about is what they would feel like if I reached out and touched one.

His eyes drop from my face to my body in a way that makes me feel like he's stripped me naked and pinned me to the wall.

I disregard how my body reacts, as if it would very much like if that's what he would do and roll my eyes as heat swallows my head. "Stop looking at me like that."

"Like what?" he says innocently.

"Like you're trying to give me a stroke with those ridiculous eyes of yours." I fan myself with my hand. "I'm not one of your toys, Ethan. I'm here because you and Marin pressured me. This isn't going anywhere."

"We'll see about that," he says, holding out his elbow with a grin.

I eye it like it's a snake slithering around a forbidden fruit, hesitating.

"I won't bite. This is a date, remember?"

He takes a step closer to me, his woodsy scent making my brain misfire. "I wouldn't put it past you to bite on your dates." I reluctantly slip my arm through his and ignore how it fits like the clicking of two puzzle pieces that interlock perfectly.

"So where are we going?" I ask as we stroll down the street.

The sun hasn't quite set, but it's low in the sky, and a cool breeze blows my hair.

"It's a surprise." He pulls me closer as we pass people walking in the opposite direction, and my breath catches.

He notices. "Are you nervous?"

"Yes." I laugh at my own honesty. "I know this isn't a *date* date, but I haven't done anything like this in a long time. And I don't know if you've noticed, but I'm awkward and not very..."

My voice trails off.

"You are *very*," he says, looking at me.

I laugh a disbelieving snort. "You're relentless." I say, rolling my eyes once again and looking away.

When we stop, it's at a park at the edge of the small downtown in front of a wooden sign that sticks in the ground, BETHEL NIGHT MARKET.

Vendors sit at tables under lamps with strands of Edison bulbs wrapped around the trees. The sound of a harmonica, followed by a woman's raspy voice, floats in the air as people with canvas bags and strollers sip plastic cups of wine and beer.

"Is this where we're going?" My voice is barely above a whisper as I bring a hand up to my mouth.

He grins. "The night market only happens twice a summer. I thought we could grab food and find some ingredients to create a cocktail. The restaurant is closed on Tuesdays. We'll have the place to ourselves." He says it so casually it's as though he doesn't realize how perfect this is.

I laugh. "Ethan, this is incredible."

His response comes in the form of his hand to my back, leading me into the crowd.

We stop at every table and talk about ingredients, both with vendors and each other. I smell every herb and flower I can get my hands on while Ethan makes small talk with the farmers about recipes. We taste baked goods and cheese cubes and sip wine as we walk. We eat donuts from a local bakery and smoked fish from a local river. The folksy bluegrass music playing in the background makes it all feel like a cheesy movie—one I never want to stop watching.

Everyone looks at the man I'm with, especially the women. Not that I blame them. If my mother were here, I have no doubt she'd tell him he was a fine piece of meat and then ask to paint him nude.

"You know, if we turned this into a game where we had to drink every time a woman eye-fucked you when you walked by, we'd be drunk in less than ten minutes," I say with a smile and sip of my wine.

He scoffs. "That's ridiculous."

"That's what I'm saying," I tease. "If only these women tried one of your cocktails."

"Funny," he deadpans.

Then we're quiet as we walk, but it isn't awkward—it's comfortable. Familiar. *Easy.*

A group of kids play hide-and-seek around trees in a section of the park while couples lounge on blankets in front of the band.

"This is the first farmers market I've been to since before Travis died. I didn't know how much I missed it until now," I say while we walk. "Like this part of me has just been hiding in the shadows, waiting for someone to shine a light on it. Thank you, seriously. This is amazing."

"I'm glad you like it," he says, bumping his shoulder against mine.

When his hand brushes against mine, the feeling it gives me is all-consuming.

And stupid.

He's him, I'm me.

I'll be gone in days, and I'll never see him again.

If I just move over an inch, I'll avoid him altogether, but the need to feel his skin against mine is as strong as the pull of the opposite ends of a magnet.

On the third time our knuckles brush, he wraps his fingers around mine, squeezing my hand in his, and says, "Gotcha."

I press my lips together in a poor attempt to hide the smile that shatters my face and look down at our intertwined fingers before looking up at him.

"Careful, Ethan, people might get the wrong idea."

He cocks an eyebrow. "And what would that be?"

"That you don't only go on dates that start at 11:30 at night."

He laughs under his breath. "Maybe I don't care if they think that."

I allow myself three seconds of imagining what that means before shoving the thoughts aside.

At the last table of the market, covered in colorfully painted Maine landscapes on canvases, we stop. Every piece is filled with bright colors and bold strokes. Instead of green trees, they've been layered in shades of yellow and pink. They're stunning.

The artist, Rhonda Donalds as written on the sign, is an older woman with a kind round face. She stands from her chair, smiling, and greets us.

"I love these," I tell her as I trace the lines of one of the abnormally bright trees. "My mom's an artist. She also favors bright colors."

"I always say I paint the world as it ought to be. Maybe your mom would agree," she says, dark eyes shining in the reflection of the lights.

Then, she walks me around her booth and tells me about each painting. She's painted everything from busy Maine cities to rocky coastlines near Canada.

We stop in front of a large canvas. "This one is the Androscoggin River. Flows right through the heart of Maine. This river is as much a part of us as it is the state," she says.

"We were here?" I turn to Ethan, and he nods.

The painting shows the scene we had floated through. Tree-covered mountains are depicted in explosive color, with a river flowing through. Hues of yellows and reds dot the water. It's both exactly and nothing what it looks like.

"I'll take it," I say, surprising myself. "I want to remember my time here just exactly how you have painted it—filled with color and light and unexpected beauty."

I run a finger along the curve of the river on the canvas.

Ethan clears his throat, but I don't dare look at him.

It's absurd, but I buy it anyway.

It's way too big, and I'm leaving in two days, but part of me knows it's as much about Ethan as it is the beauty of the painting. Like something important is happening I won't be able to comprehend until much later.

In the twenty-four hours since I've been here, I'm awake. *Alive*.

Somehow, Ethan's presence has started dredging up the pieces of who I used to be, who I desperately still want to be, and shoved them to the surface.

"Ready?" I step next to him with a bulging bag of ingredients and a canvas almost half as tall as I am.

He shakes his head. "You look ridiculous."

"Shockingly, I get that a lot." My face is fixed with a permanent smile.

He takes the painting from me, interlaces his fingers with mine, and leads me across the park to his empty restaurant.

Twenty-nine

WITH SPRIGS OF LAVENDER, lemon, and a bottle of local honey, once again I make myself at home behind Ethan's bar.

"Hey!" I say, shielding the ingredients from his eyes with my hands. "No peeking!"

He pulls a loaf of bread and a block of cheese out of a bag across from me.

"I was at the same market you were. I have no idea how you found something so secretive."

"It's not like that." I cut a lemon into wedges. "For me, it's about taking one ingredient that's common yet special, figuring out a way to plug it into a drink, and making it a different experience.

"Take the blueberry gin and tonic I made last night. Blueberries aren't inherently special, right? But they are very Maine, and they do make you feel like you've had something magical when you've had them in a cocktail."

"Blueberries aren't special?" His eyebrows shoot up. "Watch what you say in Maine, Penelope." He waves a loaf of bread at me. "That's grounds for some serious punishment."

I laugh and roll my eyes. "Yeah. Yeah. My point is, don't expect some exotic item you've never heard of."

He starts cutting the bread, and I can't help but watch him. Study him. His good looks are obvious but also nuanced in the way random strands of silver hide throughout his dark hair, the soft scruff on his jaw covers the sharpness of it, and eyes that sometimes look blue, sometimes green always seem to be plotting something. I could look at him for hours and still not learn every detail that makes him *him*.

"You're staring at me," he hums.

My gaze drops back to the counter I'm working at. "You're easy to stare at," I admit, laughing at my honesty, before trying again. "It's just, everyone stares at you, and it's kind of a lot to wrap my brain around."

"What is?" He drops the bread on the plate and squares his shoulders to me across the bar.

"You know, you have girls that deep throat straws like Brooke and show up for 11:30 dates like Zoey. I don't know why it's possible you would want to spend a night at a market with me. I feel like I might ruin your image or something." I put the lid on the stainless-steel shaker, shaking it over my shoulder.

"And don't say anything. When I make embarrassing confessions, it's just easier on my ego for us to not talk about it."

I pour the drink into two rocks glasses with ice then top them with club soda and a sprig of lavender before sprinkling purple powder over top.

"Nel, it's not—" I hold up my hand.

"No. Talking. Now close your eyes."

I clap my hands together as he does as I say and slide the drink in front of him.

The glass is mostly filled with a pale-yellow mixture, but it gives way to a deep purple layer that swirls around the ice at the top. A sprig of lavender nestles lightly against the rim as little bubbles race toward the top.

"Open!" I smile as I slip onto the stool next to him with my drink. "Taste it. Tell me what you think."

I want it to be good. I want *him* to think it's good.

He opens his eyes, lips tugging to one side as he looks from the drink to me, then takes a sip and smacks his lips together.

"Mmm!" He brings a hand to his chest. "Gin, lavender... Lemonade?" He takes another sip and laughs under his breath. "Damn, Nel. That's a good drink."

My heart skips at the compliment. "Really?"

I take a sip. The tang of the lemon mixes with the sweet honey, the lavender's floral notes, and the gin's gentle pine sing like a choir on my tastebuds as the carbonated bubbles pop on my tongue.

"But how did you get this purple? Is that... not food coloring?"

"Food coloring?" I act offended. "No." I wiggle a finger at him. "One of the vendors was selling tea, and she had butterfly pea pollen. It's from a flower that grows in Asia and one of the properties is this beautiful color. I added a little at the end for dramatic effect."

He takes another sip and rests his hand on his chest. "Damn good."

I hum, pleased, as I look around the restaurant and notice all the things I hadn't before.

One wall is fully covered with ends of raw logs, adding rustic texture to an otherwise modern space. The remaining walls are white and tastefully lined with black-and-white photos of what I assume are local landscapes. A huge antler chandelier hangs perfectly in the middle of the exposed beamed ceilings.

It's stunning.

"It's kind of impressive you own a restaurant this beautiful, and you make the worst drink I've ever had," I tease.

"Here we go again," he groans. "How about this—we finish this round, and you teach me how to make the next one?"

I grin. "I'm always up for a challenge."

***

"Gently, Ethan. You're taking out some serious rage on that thing."

He's smashing the lavender petals and leaves to death, and I cringe, laying my own hand on his to soften his force.

"Better," I say, "now, instead of traditional lemonade, I used fresh lemon juice from two lemons." I juice them and add them to a glass. "And a simple syrup made with local honey."

He adds the gin, shakes the contents, pours it into two glasses, and then tops both with club soda. I sprinkle the pea pollen that makes the purple color, and we tuck a sprig of lavender in each.

I sip mine first. "Perfect!" I nudge him. "Maybe you aren't such a lost cause after all."

"Maybe I just needed the right teacher."

The low, serious tone of his voice makes something warm and gooey happen in my belly at the same time the gravity of the situation pulls down on me.

We are in a dark bar with music, drinking cocktails. Alone. My wedding band suddenly burns into my chest like a branding iron. Travis' face flashes in my mind and guilt floods over me like an unexpected tidal wave.

I'm with Ethan because Travis is gone. The thought almost takes me down to my knees.

"Hey, you okay?" he asks it softly, his face etched in concern as he sets his drink down and looks at me.

His eyes flicker between mine.

"I'm sorry." I trace my fingers down the side of my neck. "I haven't been with a man since... you know... and it still feels... like I'm doing something wrong. Not that I'm *with you*, with you, or anything." I laugh despite my warring emotions. "I'm so bad at this." I drop my head with a groan.

"You aren't *bad* at this," he says, lifting my chin with his thumb and forefinger. Then, "Choosing to be with someone and promise forever only to realize forever isn't that long is hard to swallow for anyone. It takes time to figure out how to keep living in a life that doesn't feel like yours."

I nod slightly. He's right—righter than he knows.

"Is that why you didn't tell me you were coming here? Because you feel guilty?" he asks, eyes searching mine.

"Maybe." An unexpected laugh passes through my lips. "But also because it was kind of a sporadic decision. And I wasn't sure if I'd come across as being... psychotic." I shake my head. "It felt like you were flirting with me, but now that I've seen you in person, I can see that's just how you are. I'm glad I'm here either way." I pause. "For the mountains."

He puffs out a soft laugh. "For the mountains." His gaze holds mine, and the only sound is the music playing. "You know, Nel," he finally says, playfulness returning to his voice. "It really isn't a date without dancing."

He sighs like he has absolutely no choice in the matter as my stomach plummets to the ground like a broken elevator.

Dance?

The thought of all that full-body contact with him is enough to make me self-combust.

"Are you kidding me? Here? No." I face my palms toward him. "No dancing. That's... that's..." My voice is a high-pitched stuttery sound and the music that's playing has turned to something upbeat, which makes me add, "and who dances to this kind of music?"

"We do," he takes my hand. "Marin was adamant you have fun, and this be a date," his pause is sly—methodical—and accompanied with a smug look. "Maybe even a walk of shame."

I try to argue but my mouth doesn't comply. I stay silent, and he pulls me close.

There, behind Ethan's bar, I don't resist. When the full line of his body presses up against mine, warmth shoots a path down the length of me.

What is wrong with me?

One of his hands finds the small of my back while the other takes my hand in his. I slide my other hand up his chest, around his neck and into his hair. Our hips sway and against every smart thing I should do, I lean into him.

Chest to chest, stomach to stomach, hips to hips.

The beat of the music is fast but the way we sway is slow—somehow it feels like it's the only way to dance to this song even though it makes zero rhythmic sense.

The deep voice of a man croons into the quiet space over the speaker, and I'm not sure if I'm even breathing. I need to leave, but as if he can hear my skittish thoughts, Ethan pulls me closer.

I feel *every* hard line of his body.

Especially the one against my low belly that shoots a wanting panic firing through me.

His breath skims across my ear and shivers ripple down my spine. He's so warm. The slight scruff of his jaw scrapes against me again, and all I can think about is touching his face with my fingers. It's as though my fingertips have no use because they haven't traced the lines of him.

I lift my chin with a shallow breath and search his face. His eyes drop to my lips, and on instinct, I lick them. The way my body physically reacts to this man is abnormal.

I need a doctor, a diagnosis, and more drugs than one pharmacy can legally provide.

I move a hand and place it on his chest—his heart galloping like a racehorse.

Thank God.

"Your heart is pounding."

It's a grateful whisper and laugh.

He mirrors my position. The only thing between his palm and my skin is the wedding band that suddenly weighs three hundred pounds.

"So is yours."

His voice is as deep as the bottom of the ocean. The heated tension suffocating.

We stop moving and just stand in the low light.

He leans closer.

My breath hitches.

His parted lips skim mine, and I have to grip my hand around his neck to keep from physically collapsing.

His lips hover over mine, not in a kiss, but in something that's so much more intimate I might die from the severity of it.

I could move one more millimeter and taste him. One. He waits. His pause tells me volumes about who Ethan Mills is.

It's my decision.

I start to lean in and the bubble of amnesia I'm living in pops. All I can think is: *Travis.*

Travis Travis Travis Travis.

His name scrolls through my mind like the credits of a movie.

"I should go," I whisper, hating the words as soon as they're out but push away from his chest anyway.

His eyes close, shoulders drop, grip around me loosens.

I gather my things in silence as the room closes in around me. It's too much for me to process.

He's too much for me to process.

I'm at the door, fumbling with my painting like a clown trying to get into one of those ridiculous little cars. Except I'm a full-grown woman at a full-sized door, too damn flustered to see straight.

"Spend tomorrow with me," he says.

I stop, mid-struggle at the door. "Excuse me?"

"You, your kids. I'll be with the boys. My house is on enough land for your RV, and we can see the fireworks from the back porch. I was going to take them fly fishing during the day. You could join us."

"You want me to stay the night with you?" I scoff. "Are you insane?"

He leans on the bar casually, crosses his arms over his chest, and licks his lips slowly. Deviously.

"First, you would be in your own bed in my yard. I hardly consider that staying the night... unless that's what you want." His lips curl. "Second, you're leaving the next day, and then that's it. And the kids like each other."

He shrugs casually. As if to say, *what's so insane about this?*

My brain bounces back and forth like a tennis match. It's either the best idea I've ever heard or the worst thing that could possibly happen.

He uses the time I consider to close the space between us until he's standing next to me at the door.

"Please, Nel," he coos.

"Ugh!" I sigh. "Okay, you know what?" I hold my hand up. "Maybe. I'll talk to Finn and Marin tomorrow and see what they think about sleeping in the yard of a stranger."

He grins triumphantly. "I knew you'd see it my way."

"I said maybe, Ethan. *May. Be.*"

I shove the door open.

"Maybe means yes," he says, leaning against the door like he knows he has me.

"I'm leaving now."

And before he can say one more thing or make me change my mind or rip my clothes off, I slip through the door, hurry to the inn, and go right into a cold shower.

Thirty

"WAIT, WHAT?" MY EARS deceive me, along with my firstborn.

"I said I think it's a great idea. I've always wanted to try fly fishing in a river like that."

Finn lifts his hands over his head, doing a mock cast through the air with sound effects.

I pinch the bridge of my nose.

"But we don't know them. Isn't that a little... weird?"

"Mom." Marin laughs as she sips her tea. "We spent hours with them on the river, and you spent two nights with the man. And you've been emailing him for months! Is he giving off serial killer vibes or something?"

"Okay, I did not *spend the night* with him. And no, it just doesn't feel responsible. Plus, it's the Fourth of July. Don't you want to do something festive?"

As much as I hope they agree, I don't want them to, which confuses me.

Finn scoffs. "We aren't ten-year-olds that need a fair, Mom. I think this sounds amazing." He pours syrup over his pancakes.

I groan.

"Fine. But if this goes terribly wrong and we all end up in coolers somewhere, I'm blaming both of you."

We take our last bites of breakfast as my phone pings with a text, *What time will you be here?*

Sonofabitch.

Me: *How did you get this number?*

Ethan: *I know the owner of the inn. What time will you be here?*

I rub a hand on my forehead. He's just so arrogant.

Me: *What time would you like us to get there?*

Ethan: *Now.*

Bastard.

Me: *I'll see you in a couple of hours.*

Me: *And wipe that stupid grin off your face by then.*

Ethan: *No promises.*

***

When we arrive at the address he sends a couple hours later, I mentally give him the middle finger. He lives in the cedar house on the river.

Of course.

"This is the house on the river," I say to the windshield more than anyone else.

Marin chuckles as she cranes her neck from the back.

"Duh, Mom. Derek pointed it out to us as we floated by."

"Well, Ethan left that detail out," I say dryly.

Derek meets us outside in what seems to be his tie-dyed t-shirt and swim short uniform, flicking us a wave before guiding us into a flat space to park.

"Hey, man," Finn says as he opens his door, giving him a very teenage handshake that involves too many steps. Marin gives him a hug and tugs at his t-shirt, saying something that makes them laugh.

Austin wanders off the back porch slowly, looking like the stereotypical college student who has slept until noon wearing athletic shorts, t-shirt, and a sleepy face. The kids laugh as they drag the cord from the Avion to plug us in and unroll the awning before wandering down to the river's edge.

I stand, leaning on the side of the cab, taking in the view. The river flows by like a keeper of secrets as the midday light dances off its ripples. In the distance, green rolling mountains stretch out as far as the eye can see. The way the summer breeze slithers across my neck and the smell of clean air hangs in my nostrils is both a feeling and a place.

Marin's loud laugh pulls me back to my body at the same time Ethan steps down from the porch.

He strolls toward me casually, like his only destination is his next step, and there's a smirk angled across his face that irks me.

"Fancy seeing you here," he drawls as he leans against the cab to face me.

I roll my eyes.

"Nice house," I deadpan.

He shrugs casually. "You think?"

I pin him with an unamused look. "Well, it's just as beautiful as it was yesterday," I say, looking towards the kids instead of him.

"So, this is the home on wheels." He nods at the Avion. "Do I get a tour?"

He doesn't wait for the answer, walking toward the door.

"Umm, sure. I mean, it's not much to see," I say, swallowing too many times.

I walk up the steps first, he follows. Closely.

"The tour is really long," I say with mock seriousness. "Kitchen, dining room, my bed, kids' beds, bathroom." I point in rapid succession. "The end." I smile despite the fact his presence feels like death by strangulation.

He looks around, studying the details as he makes a slow circle in place. He stops when he faces the loft, walking to the small curtain that separates my bed from everything else and pauses, looking over his shoulder with a feral grin.

"Looks big enough for two," he says, pulling back the curtain back.

"It's not." My mouth goes bone dry at the notion. "Now get out! I feel like I can't breathe." I put my hands on his back and bulldoze him out as he laughs.

"You're blushing," he says once we're outside.

"It's an allergic reaction." The lie makes my skin burn hotter. "Anyway, what's the plan here? Are we fishing, or did you just lie about that to lure us out here so you could do God knows what?"

He laughs louder this time.

"I've had you alone for two nights in a row. Luring is a stretch. But let's fish. I have the gear set up in the garage. You want to see the inside of the house, or is that too dangerous for you?"

"Yes." I say quickly. "I mean, no. I mean—" I let out a long exhale. "Fine."

The man turns the ground beneath me to quicksand and makes it impossible to find solid footing anywhere.

"Tour it is," he says with a smile.

We walk toward the back of the house to the porch that faces the river. The beautiful wood siding exterior is even more gorgeous up close. It's rough and grainy as I rub my fingers across it.

The porch is spacious, with several chairs and a large table. It's just a deck—boards and simple furniture—but it feels like a place you sit while life slowly unfurls like the leaves of a fern.

Marin waves up at me from the shore, and I wiggle my fingers back with a smile as Ethan pushes the sliding glass doors open. I turn and follow him inside. We step into a great room that absolutely lives up to the name. It's big, open, and smells like fresh-cut wood and spices.

A large river rock-covered fireplace fills one wall while the others are painted in a creamy shade of white. A few mounted animal heads and fish hang on the walls along with black and white photos like he has in his restaurant. The chairs and sofa are a masculine light brown leather with dark wooden details.

Connected to this room is a kitchen that looks like it came right off the set of a cooking show. Huge stainless-steel appliances and black stone countertops are framed by rich walnut cabinets.

I walk around, silently running my hand over every surface available, using my fingers to learn the space.

It's stunning.

I circle back around to where he leans against the large island in the kitchen.

"Do you like it?"

"It's awful." I say, unable to hide the smile that tugs at my lips.

He snorts. "Upstairs," he points to a railing above us. "Is a loft space with a TV and a ping-pong table. It's where the boys usually hang out. Their bedrooms are up there as well. Mine is down here, down the hall."

He gestures down the hall and looks at me with a kind of intensity that makes my insides leap into one another.

In my mind, walking down that hall is the equivalent of walking off a cliff and absolutely not happening.

With every second we stand in his house, my body feels more and more like a rubber band being pulled too tightly. I need water. And a therapist. And to get the hell out of here.

He must see my struggle, because the next thing he says is, "Let's get the kids and fish."

***

It turns out, Marin and I are terrible at fly fishing, and we have absolutely no shame as we stand in the river in our oversized hip waders.

"Okay, let your lines out, ladies," Ethan says, standing knee deep in the water next to us.

Surprisingly, we manage this step and the neon-colored string floats down the river with the current.

"Good, now tip the rod down. No, not in the water, Marin—" He wades over to her and gently guides her hands to the correct position. "Like this."

I mirror what he shows her before he moves onto the next step.

"Ready? Now comes the magic. Lift up, pull back, pause, snap forward." He demonstrates the motion, making his line dance through the sky with a graceful loop. "Just back and forth, not too much movement of the shoulder. It should be in the elbow and wrist. See that?"

He does it again.

We both try—repeatedly—but God, we're awful. We lose every fly Ethan ties on and can't stop laughing about it.

"Ethan, I promise we're trying." Between the snort I let out and the way Marin cackles like it's the funniest thing I've ever said, it's hard for him to believe us.

He scrubs a hand over his jaw.

"Got a trout!" Austin calls as he holds up a fish from farther down the river.

"I wanna see!" Marin shouts back, reeling in her line, and wading down to them.

I turn to Ethan and shrug hopelessly, fishing rod in hand, feeling ridiculous in the oversized waders.

"You go down there with them. I'm a lost cause," I tell him.

He shakes his head. "I'm not letting you off that easy. Try again."

He wades over behind me and guides my casting movements with his arms locked around mine. He smells like sandalwood and pine trees, which are apparently my new favorite scents because I can't stop inhaling.

I stand, caged in his arms as he controls the movements, and I can't help myself—I lean into him. His arm rubs against me every time he casts the line and warms me by degrees. It's a slow form of torture.

"Ethan, you work the rod like it's part of your body. I have no idea what I'm doing," I say as the line flies through the air.

"If working a rod that's part of my body is what you want help with, I assure you I have better ideas than fishing, Penelope."

Between his warm breath on my ear and the meaning behind his words, I stagger back into his chest as he vibrates with a chuckle.

"Okay, you know what? That is not what I meant. Don't say things like that when you're all cagey around me and smelling like you do. Let me out of here."

I duck under his arm and gasp for air as he grins, clearly enjoying how he gets to me.

"You just look like you belong here. *Fishing*. It suits you."

I plop down on the grassy shore and watch as he sends the line soaring through the air, making another beautiful arch.

Then another.

"I've spent a lot of time out in this river. I've learned a thing or two," he says over his shoulder.

Even in ridiculous fishing gear, he's a treat to watch.

I close my eyes and let the sun warm my face. The sounds of the water flowing, the birds singing, and the leaves rustling stitch together like scraps of fabric that form a mismatched quilt of the memory that's forming. A memory I desperately want to be a tangible thing I carry with me.

Ethan plops down beside me in the grass. "What are you thinking about?"

"Hmm. That's a loaded question." My head tilts toward him. "I'm thinking about how I can understand why you live here. I'm thinking I wish moments like this lasted hours instead of seconds."

If my words scare him, he doesn't show it. He just nods and looks out at the same river I do, neither of us moving closer to the other.

Our reality doesn't allow for it.

I live 1,723 miles away from this house, and a dead man's ring hangs around my neck. I'm leaving tomorrow—never seeing him again. It's a fact that dents my heart enough to make my chest ache.

He snaps a blade of grass in his fingers. "So, Bar Harbor, huh? Any big plans?"

"Of course! Hiking the national park, lobsters, whales, puffins, sailing, more lobster." I tick the items off on my fingers. "I know I sound like a stupid tourist, but I've always wanted to see the coast of Maine."

I hug my wader covered knees to my chest and look at him.

"Do you ever leave your mountain and go to the coast, or are you bound here by some kind of magic?"

"I do leave the mountain, thank you very much." He tosses the grass he's holding at me. "I get a lot of seafood from the fisherman in Bar Harbor, actually."

I hold his gaze. I want to tell him to make a trip there next week. I want to say, *let's go meet the fisherman together.* But hope is a sweet con, and I know there's no use. The words that linger on the tip of my tongue die without ever being said.

"Your porch come with wine?" I ask, bumping my shoulder against his.

He laughs. "Actually, it does." He grabs my hand and pulls me up.

I don't let go as we start to walk to his house.

Neither does he.

Thirty-one

WHEN THE KIDS GET back, it's with a cooler full of brook trout.

Derek slings his hip waders over the railing of the porch. "I found a recipe I want to try to cook them, Dad. You mind?"

Ethan's eyes widen slightly. "You? Cook?"

Derek rolls his eyes. "Yes, Dad. *Me. Cook.* You aren't the only one in the family that knows how to make food."

The frustration that flickers across Ethan's face is gone as fast as it comes.

"Right. Just let me know if you need help with anything."

"I can make a salad," Marin offers.

"Listen, I'm not arguing with anyone to cook," I announce as I top my glass of wine off. "If anyone needs me, I'll be sitting here looking at this *awful* view."

Ethan's teeth grind when he sits in the chair next to me and the kids walk inside.

"You okay?" I ask.

He nods. "You ever think having kids is a real pain in the ass?"

A laugh bursts out of me. "I do," I confess. "But it's a hard time in life, right? Being a teen at the brink of adulthood. There's so much pressure to decide who you are and what you want to do with your life, but I laugh when I think about it now. I'm forty-one and feel more confused than ever. I don't know why we think an eighteen-year-old should have a clue. They crave independence but have no idea what that means. Neither did we, yet here we are."

I pause, staring at the sun that's dipping low on the horizon.

"I'm pretty sure my kids are going to have nightmares about our time in the Avion for the rest of their lives. None of us know how to do this."

He laughs dryly, lifting his glass. "I'll drink to that."

A bird swoops by, and its song is the only sound other than the muffled laughs of the kids inside when it lands on a nearby branch. It's so peaceful.

"Would you ever leave Maine?" I ask.

"Would you ever leave Key Largo?" he shoots back.

Sitting here staring at all the green, I want to say yes. I want to say I can live in a place like this. But we will both know it'll be a lie as soon as the words come out. They'll be the wishful dreams of a perfect day with good company and wine. Everything I know is miles and miles away.

He kicks his bare feet up on the railing. "Tell me something I don't know about you."

"I'm horrible at making coffee," I say instantly. "You?"

His lips tug. "I'm great at making coffee."

"That's cheating, tell me something different."

"I've only ever danced with one woman in my restaurant." His face is toward the sky when he says it.

My heart flat lines, and I look at the same sky as him. "Well, I've only ever danced with one man in your restaurant, so it seems we have something in common."

With that, I zip the ring across my necklace.

***

Dinner is amazing.

Derek, despite the fact he looks like he just got home from Woodstock, is an incredible cook.

We sit around the table—all talking at once and eating food so good I'm sure my taste buds are ruined forever—like it's something we always do. Always will do.

It's so easy with the kids, with Ethan, it physically hurts. Like it would be just a little more enjoyable if we hated each other.

When Ethan's knee brushes against mine under the table, I don't pull away despite the hopelessness it makes me feel.

We laugh through countless stories. We don't ask questions about the future. We talk about who we are at this very moment. We get to know each other like it matters. Like we aren't just passing through town but are going to be permanent fixtures in each other's lives.

Long after the food is gone and the second bottle of wine is opened, we roll dice and yell at each other in the degradingly playful way that only the closest friends can. It's a scene as beautiful as an old snapshot—a moment made to be remembered.

When the sky is dark, the only sounds besides our voices are a choir of frogs singing like it's their last song on earth. A faraway boom roars toward us, followed by blue lights that explode across the sky. The fireworks from the town's Fourth of July celebration light up the night and dance across the river.

We watch, calling out our favorite ones, until the grand finale, where we all clap.

Austin stands and wriggles his eyebrows challengingly toward the table. "Ping-pong tournament of champions, anyone?"

The kids jump up, tossing insults at each other, and file inside in a bubble of laughter.

Once again, Ethan and I are left alone, this time in the dark.

"Alone again, Nel." He rests his forearms on the railing as he bends slightly at the waist.

I mirror his position. "It appears so."

"The boys like you."

I smile. "I like the boys."

He turns his head to face mine and our eyes hook. "If you weren't getting in that time machine sitting in my yard and driving away tomorrow, what would you do about this?" He wiggles a finger between us.

"Umm." My voice shakes. "I don't know. I try not to think like that because, you know, those are our circumstances. I am leaving tomorrow, and I do live 1,723 miles away, not that I checked the exact distance from your house to mine." I laugh softly. "I don't know what I would do, but I know what I wouldn't do. I wouldn't let your lips just brush mine without finding out how it would taste to kiss you or fight wanting to lean my head on your shoulder when you sit next to me. And I wouldn't shy away from looking at you because the fact it feels like you are looking straight into my soul wouldn't be such a big deal. And I sure as hell wouldn't be dreading waking up tomorrow because I wouldn't be driving away and living the rest of my life not knowing any more about you."

I turn away and fix my eyes on the dark river as forcefully as I feel his still fixed on me. The silence between us is so thick I could hold it in my hand.

"Well, say something already," I blurt, forcing myself to look back at him.

He moves his face close to mine, so close I can feel his breath on my skin, shaking me to my core like aftershocks of an earthquake. My eyes drop to his lips, and the realization slams into me that I want to kiss him. I want him to kiss me.

I couldn't summon the nerve to lean in last night, but dammit if I won't regret it for the rest of my life if it doesn't happen just once before I leave him.

I lick my lips.

Please move closer. Please. Please. Please.

My mind is chanting the words my mouth isn't brave enough to say.

He's close. So close, I smell the wine on his breath as it mixes with his woodsy scent I will forever associate with him, Maine, and summer.

I swallow.

He leans.

Close.

Closer.

My breath stops.

A ring slices through the air.

Once.

Twice.

My phone.

The moment is cut in half.

I close my eyes and pull it out of my back pocket. Poppy's name flashes across the screen.

I look at Ethan desperately. "I'm so sorry." Then I answer with a breathless, "Mom? Hey!"

"Penelope! I haven't heard from you. How was your date?"

Her voice blares through the speaker loud enough for Ethan to hear.

I wince at her jarring loudness.

"Mom, it was fine. Can I call you back tomorrow or something?"

She ignores me. "Did you get naked like I suggested?"

"Mom! No!" I hiss. "And can we plea—"

"You know, Penelope, as your mother, I should tell you if you don't keep using all the parts of your body, they will not be happy with you. The fewer orgasms you have, the harder it is to have them."

Ethan laughs next to me into his wine glass, and I want to die. Again.

"Mom!"

"I'm serious, your dad isn't here. This is just girl talk. When was the last time you experienced the gift of your feminine pleasure? It's a natural part of life to have those needs."

My pulse pounds in my temples. I'm going to kill her. Slowly.

Ethan chokes on his next sip.

I haven't had an orgasm since Travis died, but I'm not having that conversation with my mother. Sadness doesn't exactly set the tone for me to tap into the gift of my *feminine pleasure*.

"Mom. Stop," I demand. "I cannot have this conversation with you right now. I love you, tell Dad happy Fourth. I'll call you when I've mentally recovered from this in three years."

She's still talking when I hang up and my entire body burns in embarrassment.

"I'm going to go check on the kids and pretend that didn't just happen."

I don't wait for him to respond before sliding the door open and disappearing inside.

Thirty-two

THE LAST THING I need is more heat, but Ethan builds a fire in the yard with two chairs next to it.

"Marin's already sleeping on a couch," I say as I drop into one of the chairs. "And my guess is the boys are going to fall asleep with game controllers in their hands the way they were yelling at each other."

He laughs, standing across the fire from me poking a log with a stick.

"I'm sorry about my mom. And my awkward confession." I stare at the growing flames. "Turns out making people uncomfortable is genetic."

"I liked listening to your mom," he says, his voice overly serious. "I think she made some very valid points I would be more than happy to help you with."

I slap him on the arm as he sits next to me. "Funny."

"And I liked your confession." He smiles, dropping his elbows to his knees and looking at me with an intensity that makes me look away.

Again.

"You looked away, Penelope," he says in a teasing hum as he taps my boot with his.

"Well, you know. The whole soul-seeing thing and all." I blow out a half breath-half laugh.

I drop my head back and look up at the sky, the heat from the fire warming the already scorching skin from my chin to my chest.

He pokes at the fire with a stick. "Do you ever filter yourself?"

"Sources close to me would say no." I laugh, looking at him. "Do you?"

"Maybe." He shrugs. "I like saying what people want to hear."

My eyes narrow. "Do you think you'd filter the answer to any question I'd ask?"

I search his face as the reflection of the fire dances in his eyes. My urge to touch him—feel him—is as strong as my resistance against it. It's as though I'm tied in a straitjacket with the laces pulled too tight.

"What would you ask?" he asks, throat moving with his slow swallow, pulling all the moisture right out of my mouth at the sight of it. *Is swallowing attractive?* I've never considered it until this moment where I find myself staring at the column of his throat, watching his Adam's apple bob along the length of it.

I shift in my seat, feeling a friction in my bloodstream. "I don't know. Nothing..."

"Oh really, Penelope?" he asks, smirk tugging at his lips. "There's nothing you want to ask me?"

"Is there something you *want* me to ask you?" I try to ask it defensively, but my voice is suddenly thick and my breathing shallow. Like we're playing some kind of game and I don't know the rules.

His eyes drop to my throat and linger. On instinct, my hand grabs the ring that hangs there.

I flinch.

He notices. Another moment is split in two.

His head slowly turns back toward the fire, and his jaw clenches before he leans back in his chair and faces the sky.

"Do you know the constellations?" he asks.

"No? Not really? Just the basics, I guess. Love me a good dipper." I hide my smile with a sip of wine before angling my face back to the sky. "You?"

"Not really."

He looks at me, and I laugh at the ridiculous subject change.

Our arms drape on the armrests of the chairs, the closest they can be without touching, and I hate the distance and need more all at once.

I hook my pinky around his. I can't not.

Setting my wine down, I face him.

"Ethan." His name barely makes it out of the tightness of throat. "If you don't kiss me, I think I might die. Like not in the melodramatic way, in the actual way. My body is physically aching, and I know that sounds..."—a breath whooshes out of me— "crazy or desperate or something. Maybe I am, but I just can't leave without—"

He doesn't let me finish my ramble before he cups his hands around my face and presses his mouth to mine. I freeze for a split second before wrapping my fingers around his arms and softening. His tongue swipes across my lip, and mine does the same, testing the waters before diving so deep into the kiss I don't know if we'll ever come up for air again. The way every cell of my body reacts to his mouth on mine is a bone-melting, life-altering experience.

The taste of the wine and smell of the campfire engulf me, and I know it will be a very long time before I can ever have either of those things without thinking of this kiss being permanently imprinted on my tongue.

He drops a hand from my face and traces the line of my neck before it rests across my throat. My pulse ricochets between my body and his palm.

When we finally pull our mouths apart, we're panting. We'd run a marathon without leaving our chairs. I drop my forehead to his with a breathy laugh.

"That was—Wow. I didn't know." I shake my head slightly. "Thank you." I close my eyes.

"I don't think I've ever been thanked after a kiss before, Penelope," he says, kissing my bottom lip and smiling against it.

I want to crawl on top of him and spend the night feeling him kiss me like that, over and over again. I need it. My body *really* needs it.

Instead, I sag back into my chair, my lips still tingling from where his just were.

"So, you haven't dated anyone since your husband died?"

I snap my head in his direction at the unexpected question.

"Do people that date usually have to beg other people to kiss them?" I ask, raising my eyebrows.

"Why not?" He traces the lines of my palm with his finger.

"Guilt, grief. The fact every man I know is either happily married or a skeevy friend of my brother. It just hasn't been on my radar."

"Is it on your radar now?"

I look at him until I can't and this time, I deflect. "It's late, and I have an early day tomorrow." Like a coward, I stand up without answering him.

He follows me to the Avion and leans against it, arms crossed over his chest.

"Nel—"

I don't let him finish.

With two fistfuls of his shirt, I yank him to me, pressing my mouth to his. When we collide, I know I'm not saying goodbye—I'm ignoring it. I need to feel him one more time.

He takes a pivoting step that pins me against the wall with a force so strong it takes my breath away. His knee spreads my legs until they're far enough apart for his thigh to wedge between them. When I move against it, the most sensitive and aching part of me I've been desperately trying to ignore flips on like a switch.

Like I need the kiss, I need the relief of his body against mine. One rub is all it takes for my hips to buck instinctively against him, rushing after a feeling I haven't felt in so long. *Too* long.

"Ethan, you can't touch me like that." I pant as he runs a trail of kisses along my neck.

"Like what?" His thigh rubs me *there*—again—and I can't control the whimper that passes my lips.

"Like *that*," I say through clenched teeth. "I haven't had a... I can't... I won't be able to..."

I can't form a complete sentence.

It just feels so *good*.

The way his thigh rubs against me and how my hips move against him is without any instruction from my brain—it's all instinct and unfiltered desire, and I don't think I could stop it even if I wanted to.

"What are you doing to me?" he whispers, and I feel it on every inch of my body like coarse sandpaper.

His hands drop to my hips, fingers digging in tighter. He rocks me against his thigh as his mouth devours mine. Between the pressure of me grinding on his leg and the way his hands grip my hips, I'm on the brink of going up in flames.

I moan into his mouth as my hips rock faster.

I drop my head back as my thighs clench around his leg. I'm so close to plummeting over the edge that I can barely control my movements.

He pulls my bottom lip between his teeth, grips my hips tighter, and then tugs me down forcefully onto his muscular thigh as his rocking rhythm matches mine.

I'm embarrassingly close.

So close I can feel the release swirling from the base of my spine to the back of my throat.

"Ethan..." His name is a gasp or a plea or both. "I can't... I haven't..."

I want to stop.

My first orgasm in over a year can't be against a leg. *His* leg. I refuse.

"Penelope." My name is so deep on his lips that it hits straight between my thighs. "Let go."

Against every logical thought, I do.

Fully dressed.

Against his leg.

In his yard.

Like a horny teenager.

The orgasm screams through me, and the fireworks that explode in my eyes put the town of Bethel's display to shame.

I gasp for air, barely standing upright, while Ethan cages his arms around me, not bothering to hide how how hard he is pressed against me.

Tomorrow, I'll be embarrassed over the fact I just got off on his leg, but right now, I feel like a goddess that's just been released from captivity.

I'm a panting puddle being held together only by my skin, and it feels fucking amazing.

"I haven't been touched like that in a really long time," I say between shallow breaths. "Actually, ever. I've never *ever* done that."

My laugh is a husky sound as he ghosts a kiss on my neck and chuckles against my skin.

This time, when his lips find mine, it's long and slow, like we have all night. Like there's nothing more important than the way his tongue moves against mine. Like we are going to stand here forever with our mouths melting together.

He pulls away slightly, my body still coming down from the high, and then touches me softly, rubbing his nose against my cheek.

"No filter. If I wasn't driving away tomorrow and I didn't live 1,723 miles away, what would you do about this," I ask, even though I know the answer will be a curse on my heart no matter what.

His fingers trace the line of the chain around my neck before stopping at the ring in the center of my chest. He holds it in his hand and stares at it as my chest rises and falls with my breath.

His eyes meet mine, and there's an unexpected turbulence in them. "Nothing," he says, voice guarded as he drops the ring and takes a step back with a shrug. "If you weren't leaving tomorrow, I wouldn't do anything. It's not who I am."

His words dump over me like a bucket of ice-cold water. "Right." My stupid heart crumbles. "Of course not."

Ethan is a man who dates pretty women late at night. There would never be a future, even a hypothetical one, between someone like him and someone like me.

Even knowing that, he's still shocked me.

I fumble to get the door open and force myself to smile, though my lips feel like lead. "Goodnight, Ethan. I'll see you in the morning," I say softly.

"Night, Nel."

He shoves his hands into his pockets, taking another step back.

I close the door and press my back to it. The only sound is my heavy breathing and pounding heart in the darkness of the Avion.

The man who just gave me my first orgasm in over a year would never want anything more. I grab the ring in my hand and let every opposing feeling rip me apart as I slide down the door and land on the floor.

I don't bother wiping the tears that fall next.

Thirty-three

THE SEVEN HOURS I spend not sleeping are the perfect amount of time for me to convince myself that Ethan misspoke.

Or misunderstood the question.

Like maybe he meant he'd do nothing differently than what we were already doing, which is dry humping and making out like horny teenagers.

A chilly rain falls, but I barely feel it. Heat feeds on my entire body as I walk toward the house, remnants of the pleasure he'd given me curdling with the sting of his words.

I'm going to walk in, tell him thanks for the thighgasm, then demand an explanation.

And sure, I'm leaving and living a world away, but the idea in a hypothetical world he wouldn't do *anything* differently is ridiculous. Who thinks like that?

Marin, Finn, and Derek stand in the kitchen as I slide open the glass door.

"You're up," I say too loudly with a smile too big.

"Don't remind me," Derek groans, running a hand through his long hair. "I have a float trip this morning, and I need about fifteen hours more sleep."

Marin and Finn yawn in agreement.

"We are heading out in just a bit. Is your dad up yet? I want to say goodbye, of course, but I don't want to wake him or anything."

I look around and try not to seem too eager.

"Uhh..." Derek clears his throat. "He left."

"Left?"

My voice is a strangled kind of sound.

"Yeah..." His eyes bounce from Marin to Finn, then back to me. "He had some, uhh, stuff with the restaurant, I guess. I dunno, I think it was planned?"

"Yes, right. Of course!" I force a laugh that sounds like a robotic *ha ha ha*. "I mean, the day after a holiday is always a big cleanup in a restaurant, so I totally get that. I mean, gotta start early, right? People need to eat, right? Crowds can sometimes be bigger on the fifth of July than they are on the fourth, did you know that? I mean, it's the darndest thing. I guess everyone is just so burned out from all the celebrations they just want someone else to cook for them. And not do the dishes, of course."

I babble like a moron.

Marin's eyes are wide as Finn presses a finger to his lips while Derek just stands, confused and uncomfortable. Clearly, he's never dealt with a shocked woman who just had a much-needed sexual experience on his dad's leg in the yard before.

"Right." I smack my lips together. "Derek, thank you. You are an amazing cook, guide, and host. If you ever find yourself in Key Largo, please look us up. And thank Austin for us, and your dad, of course. Or not. You know, just whatever feels..."

I wave my hand around as if it's an understood signal that this conversation is over.

He left.

He left?

I must have missed something. Like maybe he told me this last night, but I had too much wine to remember. Or he said it, but it was during the fireworks, so I didn't hear him.

It can't be right.

I didn't expect him to throw himself in the middle of the street and beg me not to leave, but no goodbye? It feels like a knife is being twisted straight through my chest.

Was this because I used his leg? I cringe at the thought of that possibility.

I bounce between feeling incredibly sad and ferociously angry. I knew what I was getting with him. He's a man who dates a lot of women, and it's ridiculous to read anything deeper into what happened.

Hell, it was probably just another night for Ethan Mills!

To hell with him.

I only start to breathe easy after we pull out of the driveway and head east toward the coast.

Finn immediately crawls back into bed, and Marin sits next to me in the passenger seat. Our eyes are glued to the hazy road in front of us. It starts to rain harder, and a thick fog covers everything like a blanket.

The weather is an actual representation of my mood.

"Mom..." Marin taps her fingers on her lap and drops her head onto the headrest. "I'm sorry about Ethan. I know you... enjoyed spending time with him. I'm sure there's a reason he left."

I shake my head and swallow down all the tears that I want to cry but refuse to give to him. "Oh, Marin, don't be silly. Did I like spending time with him? Sure. But that's it. He has a life. I didn't expect him to base his schedule on us leaving or anything."

Lie.

I did expect that.

"Plus, we are going to see whales! And puffins! And lobster!" I feign enthusiasm, but the way she looks at me lets me know she's not buying it. I reach my hand over to hers and give it a squeeze.

"I'm fine, promise."

She returns the squeeze before closing her eyes.

I stare through the windshield and imagine each droplet of rain is a memory of Ethan the angrily squeaking wiper can purge from my mind.

Making drinks behind the bar. *Wipe.*

Paddle boarding down the river. *Wipe.*

The blue-green color of his eyes. *Wipe.*

Holding hands in the night market. *Wipe.*

The way he kisses. *Wipe.*

The wiper clears the windshield long enough between awful memories for me to see something big and brown flash in front of us.

"What the—"

My words are cut off by a slam.

Everything that happens next is a blur.

A metallic crunch.

Sudden pop.

The dig of the seatbelt across my chest.

Exploding airbags.

My grunt on impact.

Marin's yell.

We spin like a top in the middle of the road, smoke billowing out of the engine as dust fills our lungs.

Then—stillness.

And shock.

Marin garbles out a sound next to me that I can't make out as I fumble with a seatbelt that's digging into my skin.

"Marin!" I shout. "Marin, are you okay?"

My pulse pounds in my ears as she sobs something next to me and I climb to the space between our seats.

I crouch down next to her on the dishes that have flown from the cabinets.

"Marin, talk to me."

Panic surges through me as I cup her face in my hands.

She blinks her eyes open and scrunches her dust-covered face.

"I'm fine. What happened?" she croaks.

"Mom?" Finn calls from the back.

"Finn! Are you okay?" I yell to him before turning back to Marin. "Can you get out?"

She nods—slowly—and I rush to the back where Finn is sprawled on the floor between the beds, moaning and rubbing his head.

"Finn, are you okay?" My voice is desperate as I search for blood, relieved when there is none.

"Mom?" he groans. "What the hell happened?"

"I don't know. We hit something. It was fine, and then it wasn't. The cab is destroyed. Can you walk?"

He reaches an arm out to me with an *oof*, and I help him up and out the side door, where we find Marin standing in the middle of the road with an angry red mark from her seatbelt slashed across her chest.

"Marin?" I cough, walking toward her through the light rain. "Do you see anything?"

Then I see it. A lifeless mountain of hair with a huge rack of smooth antlers that takes up most of the road.

"A moose?" I whisper. "We hit a fucking moose?"

My eyes are wide as I bring a hand up to my open mouth.

"Language, Mom," Marin rasps out, rubbing a hand across the line on her chest from the seatbelt.

Finn coughs out a laugh that echoes across the quiet road as soon as it escapes his mouth. It spreads from him to me to Marin in a chain reaction, all of us looking between the moose and the ball of aluminum that was once the Avion. We laugh until tears run down our faces.

It's ridiculous how hard we laugh about getting in an accident in the middle of a quiet mountain road in Maine, but we do.

"Now what?" Finn asks once he can speak clearly.

"Now." I sigh, wiping the tears from my eyes. "We call a tow truck and get the hell out of here."

Thirty-four

THE TOW TRUCK DRIVER is a man named Tony. Tony is a large, hairy man who wears a stained t-shirt and chain-smokes cigarettes in the cab of his truck with the windows up. He has more hair coming out of the collar of his shirt than most men have on their entire bodies.

His voice is reflective of how much he likes cigarettes and sounds like someone ran a hand mixer over his larynx. His northeastern accent is thick, and he ends almost every other sentence with the phrase, *ya see.*

Tony drives me fucking crazy.

"I don't usually come up this far north, ya see. It's lucky you got a hold of me. Bar Harbor's nice if you're into that sort of thing. My old lady and I don't go there much because it's for rich people, ya see. You folks rich or something?" He pauses but not long enough for anyone to answer. "Judging by that hunk of junk I'm hauling behind me, I don't take yous as rich folks."

He blows smoke into my face, causing me to fall into yet another coughing fit.

"Sorry about the smell," he continues. "Had some old McDonalds on the floorboard, ya see." He's oblivious to the fact we might as well be riding in a hearse with the cancer he's forcing down our lungs.

We sit crammed into the front seat like sardines—me next to Tony's large belly, Finn squished next to me, and Marin wedged against the door.

"We come up to these mountains sometimes, ya see. My old lady and I like it up there, nice and quiet. Found a spot you can get all-you-can-eat ribs, ya see. Worth the trip every time."

Another puff of smoke fills the cab.

"Tony, not to be a pain, but could you roll the windows down when you smoke? I'm just a little sensitive to it." I try to swallow my cough, but it hacks out anyway.

"You one of those health freaks from the city? You're not my first high-maintenance passenger, ya see. I think it's a government conspiracy that they say smoking isn't good for you. My uncle lived to be a hundred and smoked a pack a day, ya see. A pack a day!"

He shakes his head as if my request is absurd.

Ten minutes later, he lights another cigarette and does not roll the windows down.

When we finally arrive at the mechanic shop in Bar Harbor four hours later, we topple out of the cab of the tow truck in a cloud of smoke and smelling like we've been rolled in tobacco.

I thank Tony for his time. He smiles at me proudly and reveals a large silver tooth in the front of his mouth, then drives away.

Finn pinches the chest of his shirt and lifts it to his nose to sniff.

"God, we smell like ashtrays," he says, face twisting in disgust.

"Wow," I mutter, turning to the kids. "Okay. I'm going to go in and talk to these people, see what our options are. You can stick around, or there's a welcome center across the street." I point to the building. "Maybe something like that will be a little more entertaining and less depressing than what I'm about to deal with."

They turn toward the welcome center; I drag myself into the mechanic's office.

A woman behind the counter with a beehive of yellow hair, loudly smacking a piece of gum, smiles at me when I walk in.

"My RV got towed in. The Avion." I point to the mangled mess of metal through the window. "A moose decided to run into it this morning and meet an untimely death. Anyway, I'm wondering if anyone will have a chance to look at it or tell me what can be done?"

I bite my lip as she looks at me and then out the window to the disaster of an RV sitting outside. Her face puckers like she's sucked on a lemon.

"We don't have anybody that can work on it today, but I have someone that can at least take a look—Jimmy!" she shouts the name without turning away, making me jump. "What do you think of the camper in the parking lot?" She smiles, lowering her voice. "He'll take a look, and I'll let you know."

Minutes later, in walks a guy with a shaved head and a blue mechanic's uniform with a nametag that says Jimmy.

"You got the RV?" he says, walking up to me, wiping his hands with a rag.

"Guilty." I laugh half-heartedly.

"Yeah, so that thing's totaled."

He says it matter-of-factly. Like I'm not almost two thousand miles from home and any other running vehicle I own. Like he isn't completely destroying all of my plans.

"Totaled?"

I squint, trying to process his words.

"Yeah, there's no fixing that thing. I mean, you can if you want to, but you're talking about a whole rebuild and lots of money." He rubs his fingers together and whistles. "Vintage ride like that, parts are hard to come by and pricey. My opinion, you're better off buying a new one. You'd probably save money."

Then he lifts two fingers in a salute, spins around, and gives the girl at the counter a slap on the ass before disappearing through a door into the garage.

When Marin and Finn come back from the visitor's center, they find me lying on a bench outside.

Crying.

"Oh, my God, Mom? What's wrong?" Marin looks me up and down as if she expects to find gunshot wounds.

"The Avion's totaled," I say flatly, staring at the sky as tears drip down and pool into my ears.

Finn sits by my feet on the bench.

"Mom, it's okay," he says gently. "We all kind of hated that thing, anyway."

I laugh meekly through my tears.

"What do you want to do now?" Marin asks.

"Right. *Now*," I say, forcing myself to sit up. "I seem to forget when there's a disaster, you have to do something next."

The irony of the situation is not lost on me. Me not being able to cope after losing my husband led to me sitting on a bench, not being able to cope with losing his stupid camper. God has the sick sense of humor of a sociopath sometimes.

"Let's get an Airbnb." I wipe the snot from my nose with my smoke-laden shirt. "Let me see if I can find one. I'm not leaving this place without eating some damn lobster."

"That's the spirit!" Marin says with too much enthusiasm.

I click around on my phone until I find an available house.

"I found one! It's perfect. Three bedrooms, two bathrooms... walka-
ble to downtown!"

I perk up.

"Tony wasn't wrong about how expensive it is, but it's totally fine."

Marin and Finn lean over my shoulder and look at the pictures.

"It has a washer and dryer. God bless America. I need to put my head
in there after that ride with Tony," Marin says.

A few clicks on my screen and a disgusting amount of money later, we
have a mint green house with cheery floral landscaping in the middle of
downtown Bar Harbor reserved for the next three weeks. I'm so excited I
almost forget about all our stuff, mangled up RV, lack of transportation,
and all-around terrible situation.

Eventually, we have a plan.

Using trash bags for luggage, we grab all our clothes, shoes, and a
couple of the blankets that Marin and I had fallen in love with. Marin
gets her microscopic bag of gold and the old-timey photo. I take the
enormous canvas from the farmer's market.

Finn gives me a look like, *seriously?* And I raise my eyebrows, daring
him to challenge me on it.

I negotiate with the owner of the repair shop for him to keep the
camper and scrap out the pieces if he just takes it off our hands.

While we wait for the Uber to come, a crushing feeling sweeps over me
as I look at the Avion. I had come to hate the stupid camper—the size,
heat, and all-around inconvenience of it—but it was also the vehicle that
had carried all my broken pieces around and allowed me to slowly start
putting them back together.

The air conditioner breaking while driving across the desert is one of the more awful things I have experienced in life, but it was Travis' dream. He had picked it up, brought it home, and planned a trip. Now it's going to be ripped to pieces and sent to a junkyard. It seems as if the most depressing moments of my life revolve around wreckage.

We'll figure out how to get home, but this is the end of something. Surrounded by trash bags on the side of this Maine road, it feels an awful lot like goodbye.

"Mom?"

Sadness makes me sluggish as Marin leans on me.

"It's goodbye, Mar."

She looks at the Avion and wraps her arm around me.

"It is. But you know what?" She tilts her face toward me. "He would have loved everything we did and didn't do."

Finn stands next to us and looks at the mangled mess of metal in shades of 70s whites and browns and smiles.

"Thanks for the fun, Dad."

Marin loops her arm through his, and we all stand there, knowing without saying it, something is changing.

"Uber's here."

Finn holds up my phone and points to the SUV that's parked beside us.

"Goodbye, Travis." It's barely a whisper.

Holding the too-big canvas in the backseat, I stare out the window at the camper until it's out of sight.

As guilty as I feel, there's an unexpected relief, too.

Thirty-five

THE SHOWERS WE TAKE when we get to the rental house are so long that we run out of hot water twice. I splurge on a bath in the claw-foot tub and want to spend the entire three weeks there.

Exhausted, we order pizza. The whales and puffins and lobsters will have to wait for another day.

"So, I never asked you guys what you found at the visitor's center earlier. Anything fun we need to add to our list?"

I drop a slice of mushroom on my plate.

Marin clears her throat, and Finn gives her a long look before they both turn to me.

"Actually, Mom, we did."

"Okay." I wipe my face with a napkin and narrow my eyes towards them. "And? Don't keep me waiting all day here, people. If there's something cool to see, I want to see it already."

"Well, the thing is, it's a wilderness experience."

My eyes widen, and I drop my pizza on my plate.

"Oh no!" I shake my head adamantly. "We just got out of a camper you told me you were sick of, and you want to do a wilderness experience?

What does that even mean? I want to hike in Acadia National Park and then sleep in this bed right upstairs."

I point to the ceiling.

"Well, the thing is, Mom, it's not for you." Marin says, twisting the napkin in her lap.

"What are you even talking about, Marin? Finn?"

My eyebrows pinch.

Finn hands me a pamphlet.

"There's an Acadia Wilderness Experience. It's for fourteen nights for teens ages fifteen to seventeen. A guide would take us out and teach us about foraging, building shelters, fishing, and tracking. We get to make a canoe even. And then there's an option to learn to sail if we wanted at the end."

The blood drains from my face as I open it. Teens out acting like Bear Grylls, smiling in every picture I flip over like they are living their best lives.

"But what about the whales? And puffins?"

My eyes burn with everything this implies.

"Well, we might get to see them, and you could obviously still go on the tours here. We wouldn't be gone the whole time—just two weeks. We'd have a few days together after."

"Marin, *you* want to do this? I mean, Finn, I'm not surprised—but you?" My ears are ringing as I try to process this information.

"Being up in Bethel, Mom, it made me appreciate it out here. I'll admit, sleeping in a handmade shelter if it rains doesn't sound appealing, and I would never do it alone, but I don't know, doing it with Finn sounds, I don't know, fun. Like one of those experiences people talk about years later as being a source of inspiration, you know?"

Her words make me dizzy, but I also understand them deep in my bones.

I'll never be able to say no to them, not after stealing their summer and dragging them around this country like a crazy woman who broke out of the local asylum. They want to do this, and I'm going to let them. It might wreck me, but I'll do it.

I shove down every emotion that wells up in me with several hard swallows and long blinks.

"Is there space?" I ask. "I mean, this seems really last minute."

"They had two brothers back out last minute, so those spots are ours if we want them," Finn says between bites of pizza.

"When would you leave?" I ask, thumbing through the pamphlet again, reading about the skills and invaluable lessons they will learn in their two weeks.

"The day after tomorrow."

The day after tomorrow.

I nod, waiting for the burn in my eyes to subside. All I can say is, "Let's get you signed up."

Marin and Finn explode with words of gratitude and hugs and high-fives. For the first time in my life, my heart somehow fills while flattening. A paradox.

I can survive two weeks without them just like they survived the last year, watching me move through this world like a ghost. I *can* do this.

I'll still be in Bar Harbor. The puffins and whales and lobsters won't care if I'm alone or not—though now I realize I don't care about most of what we had planned. It was for *us*, not me.

I watch Marin and Finn as they point to different pages and talk wildly. They are growing up. As much as I need time with them, they need time without me.

There's no choice. I celebrate with them.

"It says here you have to dig a hole for your toilet." I wave the pamphlet at them and smile genuinely. "I can't wait to hear those stories."

***

It's a scramble to get everything done the next day.

Large backpacks, canteens, lighters, several pairs of socks, good hiking shoes, some sort of all-in-one pan thing, and a pocketknife.

Finn will thrive, I know that, but I still can't believe Marin is going through with this.

"Are you sure about this, Marin?" I ask in the sock aisle.

She laughs. "Mom, I know, I just... it's hard to explain. We are going to come back from this jaunt across the country, and everyone will see instantly how different you are. Not just your clothes and your hair, but *you*. You're happy. You went out on a date and made cocktails. Even Finny is less of an asshole. But me? I haven't done anything. I'm still just happy Marin that loves everything. I just want... I want to push myself the way you have."

Her eyes search my face for approval—I give it to her wholeheartedly and wrap my arms around her in a hug. "I love you, Marin, always and forever," I say into her hair. "I hope you don't get eaten by a bear."

She laughs then drops four pairs of socks in the basket.

***

The visitor's center for Acadia National Park is buzzing with teens and parents at 8AM.

"Take a picture, Mom," Marin says. "Finny and I at our last ever summer camp."

She laughs, and Finn rolls his eyes as she hooks an arm around his neck.

After signing a few papers at the registration desk, I give them both hugs.

"Please don't cry, Mom. I can see it coming from a mile away."

Finn's voice is a groan as his eyes dart around to make sure nobody sees me getting emotional.

"I would never." I say, water already lining my eyes. "I love you both, I'm proud of you, and I'll see you in two weeks." I grab Finn's arm. "Take care of her, okay?"

He smiles, giving me another hug, and lightly says, "Maybe."

I laugh despite the emptiness I feel.

"Love you, Mom!" They call as they disappear into a sea of teens ready to set off on an adventure out in the woods with oversized packs on their backs.

Then, I'm alone.

No kids.

No camper.

No plan.

I remember when my kids were demon-driven toddlers—I would have given a limb to get time alone. Now the empty house that isn't mine is so loud with silence I'm scared my ears will bleed. I've never known a quiet like this.

I fill the clawfoot tub with steaming hot water, bubbles, and pour myself a glass of breakfast wine.

Staring at the ceiling as the warm water washes over me, the bubbles pop under my fingers, and I blow out a breath.

When I drop my head back and look at the ceiling, for the first time since we ruined that poor moose's life, I think of Ethan. He hasn't called, texted, or emailed me to explain why he left without saying goodbye.

Every sip of wine reminds me of the taste of him.

As much as I don't want to think about it, I wonder what he's doing. Is he on a date? Probably not at 9:30 in the morning. Unless he stayed the night with a woman.

Nope. Not letting my mind go there.

I close my eyes and slide under the water, letting the warmth wrap around me and wash all the sadness away.

When I finally pull myself out of the tub, I wipe the condensation off the mirror and stare at my reflection.

I trace the lines of my face with my finger and try to see who I was before they were there. When I was young and naïve. When the idea that life might not work out the way I planned was an impossible notion.

I see her, but not really. Life isn't designed to keep us the same versions of ourselves.

My eyes land on the gold ring that dangles around my neck—the last reminder that keeps me clinging to a life I'm never going to have again while stopping me from moving any further into a new one.

When Travis died, it was as if I was forced awake from a sweet dream I didn't know I was having—the gold band a constant reminder I can never go back to it.

I can't keep wearing it. If I do, I'll keep considering him every time I feel it on my flesh. It's not that I don't want to remember him, I do desperately, but I know I've taken it too far.

I don't just remember him—I live for him.

Marin was right when she told me I've changed. With every breath I take, I feel I'm different from the person who set out on the road at the beginning of summer. I think of Travis when I see airplanes and watch Finn do something exactly like him, but somewhere out on the road, I stopped looking for him. I delight in the times I catch glimpses of him, but I'm no longer mourning the moments I don't.

I unclasp the necklace and drop it on the counter.

I have an idea.

Thirty-six

I SOMEHOW MAKE MYSELF look like a living being by the time I step out onto the sidewalk and head toward the bustling downtown.

I wander the side streets, taking in the unique architecture designs. Huge mansions and small cottages make the entire town feel like there's something for everyone.

Well, in the words of Smokey Tony, anyone with money.

Flowers are in full bloom in every picket fence garden box as trees wave green leaves so bright they rival the sun. Remnants of the Fourth of July banners and buntings hang on houses in a kind of picturesque patriotism.

Bar Harbor is a rainbow, realized.

Even the yards where bushes explode chaotically look like they're by design.

My first stop is a jeweler where a man smiles kindly when I hand him my ring, the gold chain, and the smallest remnants of Arizona gold flakes and explain my idea.

"I need a week," he tells me, looking at me over the top of his glasses.

I wait for an unbearable wave of sadness to wash me away when I walk away from everything I've handed him, but it never comes. Instead—peace.

Three stores later, I'm staring at myself in a fitting room wearing an emerald green dress that cuts low in the front, ties in the back, and hits mid-calf with a pair of ankle boots that are not made of rubber and a set of gold bracelets dangling off my wrist.

I look damn good.

I'm not buying something to hide myself like I have been for the last year, and there is nobody I need to impress. This is all me. My ode to surviving the worst heartbreak of my life and being able to come out alive on the other side.

I doubt anyone notices the forty-one-year-old woman in the green dress attempting to strut, but I do it anyway. I do it with my chin up, my shoulders back, and the slightest smile on my face.

And when I realize I'm hungry, I decide to take myself out on a date.

I walk into the first place I come to, with music playing from inside and the smells of a hot grill. I open the large doors without even looking at the name or menu that's posted outside. I simply don't care because I don't have to.

I'm alone but alive.

A hostess smiles at me from behind a podium. Her dark hair hangs in two braids and there's a bright pink tint on her lips.

"Just one?" she asks, grabbing a menu.

"Umm, yeah. I can sit at the bar..."

I look and see there isn't a single available stool except one against the wall—not doing that again.

"Oh, God. That looks packed, and I'm so hungry I might die. So yes, a table for one is fine."

I smile at her and follow as she walks to a table at the edge of the big room.

I take in the space. The décor is nautical, reminding me of the Crow's Nest a little, in a New England way. Colorful buoys and lobster traps hang from the walls as strings of lights twist around thick nautical lines of rope across the ceiling. Black and white pictures of puffins, whales, and local lighthouses line the walls.

It screams coastal Maine without being kitschy. A man and a woman sit on stools on a small stage with guitars, singing.

The place is packed. Between the music, the breeze blowing through open shutters, and the smell of seafood, the energy is a life force.

My waiter, a young guy with dark skin and baby dreadlocks, is at my table immediately.

"I'm Dion, and I'll be taking care of you. Do you know what you'd like to drink? We have a full bar, and our specialty drinks are here." He smiles and points to a section of the menu.

"Oh gosh, I'm a sucker for a specialty drink. I'll have..."

I quickly skim the menu. Margarita, mojito, mule, all the usuals. Some with blueberries, because of course.

Then I stop. The *Market Made* is made with gin, lavender, lemons, and local Maine honey.

It's a too-familiar combination.

"This is so crazy," I say, looking up at Dion. "Who makes your specialty drinks? Like, who comes up with them? I swear to you, I just made this same one you have on here, and I have never ever seen the combination before."

"Ahh. You got me there." He overemphasizes a slow shrug. "I would say the bartender, but it might also be one of the managers. I can ask for you?"

"I hate to be a bother, but would you? I just can't not know how someone else came up with that. And I'll have one—a Market Made."

I re-read the drink description to make sure I haven't missed something.

What are the odds?

Dion returns a few minutes later and puts the drink in front of me. A foggy yellow liquid with small fizzy bubbles float up through the ice toward a swirling layer of purple and a sprig of lavender. The coincidence of it sends a chill up my spine.

"The bartender said this one came from the owner. He's here tonight. I can ask him to come over if he has time?"

His head tilts to the side.

"I don't want to be a pain, but if he has time, I'd love that. This is the weirdest thing that's ever happened. Like I'm telling you, I wouldn't be surprised if this is just a crazy dream."

Dion pushes his lips together in a line, clearly not seeing—or caring—how crazy it is.

I give him an apologetic smile. "I haven't looked at the menu, so I need more time."

"Enjoy your drink. I'll check back on you in a few minutes." He tucks his notebook into his apron before walking away.

I stare at the drink sitting on the table while moody chords of music fill the air.

Almost the whole menu is seasonal and locally sourced.

I roll my eyes. *Ethan would love this*, I think bitterly.

I look at the drink again and swirl it with my straw, the purple dripping to the bottom of the glass. The flavors roll across my tongue with familiarity.

This unique combination, and the man I tasted them with, will not easily be forgotten.

Dion appears again.

"The owner is helping in the kitchen right now. He said he'll come out as soon as he's finished."

"Great." I smile and hand him my menu. "And I'll have the lobster mac and cheese with a house salad, please."

I take another sip of my drink, lean back in my chair, cross my legs, and let my head bob to the music.

As devastatingly sad and alone as I felt this morning, this moment is somehow its polar opposite. I'm relaxed. Even though I'm at a table for one, I don't notice. I don't care. I have music and a cocktail—in Maine.

"Ma'am?" Dion's back less than a song later. "The owner's here."

He gestures toward someone standing behind me.

I smile as I set the glass down and stand up, turning to introduce myself.

"Thank y—" My gaze lifts slowly but my smile drops instantly.

I see the eyes before the smirk.

"You've got to be kidding me."

Thirty-seven

"Hello, Penelope," Ethan drawls.

In this light, Ethan's eyes look more green than blue, and it's now my least favorite color.

"Hello, Penelope?" I repeat through clenched teeth.

Ethan's eyes drop from my face down the length of my body, and satisfaction competes with rage for a split second.

"I'm serious, Ethan. What are you doing here?" I demand, slowly lowering myself into my chair.

He casually takes a seat across from me. Like I invite him. Which I don't.

"Dion mentioned you ordered the newest cocktail on the menu. What do you think?" he asks, tongue in cheek.

"You?" My voice is now louder than the woman singing.

"Actually, *you*. If you're mad that I didn't give you credit, I can if you want."

Like, *that* is why my blood is boiling.

"That's not what... that's not why."

I smack my lips loudly and blow out a frustrated breath. I lower my voice and fake calmness. "I saw it and wanted to ask how they got the idea. I wasn't pissed because I didn't get credit. Jesus, Ethan. Why are you here?"

I look around the restaurant, and the pieces fall into place. It's different but also very much the same.

Bastard.

"I figured you'd know by the name. It's not exactly creative," he says, leaning back in his seat casually.

"I didn't look at the name. I was hungry and picked the first place on my walk."

I look at the wall beside me, and big as the broad side of the barn, Mainely Local is painted onto the exposed brick wall in big letters.

I groan.

"Look, this is a mistake," I say in a huff. "I'm sorry Dion wasted your time. Just let me eat my food because I'm about to die of starvation and forget you ever saw me."

He stares at me in that way of his, and I feel like a caged lion.

"Where are Marin and Finn?" he asks, resting his forearms on the table across from me and leaning too close—deliberately ignoring me.

"Not here," I snap. "What are you doing, Ethan? I got the picture loud and clear you don't..." I hold up a hand. "No, never mind. I'm not doing this. I jus—"

"Where are Marin and Finn?" he asks again, ignoring me, leaning back in his chair like he's never leaving.

"God, you're arrogant! They found some wilderness camp thing they wanted to do in Acadia, so I dropped them off this morning."

"Where are you staying?"

I hate how good he looks.

"Not that it's any of your business, but I have an Airbnb a couple blocks away. We hit a moose when we left your house and were towed here, only to be told the beloved Avion was totaled. The kids will be gone for two weeks, and now here I am. Anything else you want to know before I call the cops and have you removed from my table for harassment?"

I suck the rest of my drink down with a long, loud slurp and raise my glass toward Dion across the room.

"You hit a moose? Christ! Nel, why didn't you call me?" His concern is hysterical. Maybe, the funniest thing I've ever heard.

"Tell me that's a joke," I scoff. "You leave without saying goodbye, and you think I'm going to just call you when I'm stranded on the side of the road? What, so you can rescue me? You must be delusional."

"It wasn't like that."

"Oh really? Well, I'm sure Derek had a lot to say about how I handled the news that you were gone. How I babbled on like a moron in the middle of your kitchen." I laugh bitterly as the music of the song fades into silence. "I get it. Women are disposable to you, Ethan. Fine. But I thought you would at least have the courtesy to say goodbye. If anything, it should have been ideal for you. You gave me a screaming orgasm in my pants, told me you have no hypothetical feelings for me, and then I was going to drive away the next day. Isn't that a near-perfect no-strings-attached scenario for you?"

The people at the next table stop their conversation and gawk at me as Ethan scrubs a hand over his face in a failed attempt to hide his laugh.

Dion puts a salad and fresh cocktail down in front of me and smiles nervously at Ethan.

"Dion?" My voice is sweet as aspartame. "Please keep the drinks coming. And Mr. Mills here will be paying for my tab and tipping you generously for your efforts."

I shoot Ethan a trying glare, daring him to argue, but he just keeps a stupid smirk on his face giving Dion a nod before waving him away.

I take a bite of my salad while Ethan watches me. I ignore him until my skin starts to burn off my bones from the intensity.

I drop my fork and lock eyes with his.

"Listen, Ethan, if you have something to say, just fucking say it. I spent the morning crying because my kids left me for two weeks, but then, I miraculously stopped and decided to enjoy my time here. I went for a walk. Went shopping. Bought myself this ridiculously expensive dress. Tomorrow, maybe I'll go find whales. Or maybe I'll lay in a bathtub all day. I'm trying here. I'm trying to have fun even though none of this is how I hoped it would be. So please, if there's one little sliver of humanity in you, put me out of my misery and tell me how I can get you to leave me the hell alone."

His eyes fall to my neck—my bare neck—where his expression falters. He notices. "Don't leave before I come to talk to you again." When he doesn't have a smug look, my eyes narrow.

"Excuse me?"

"I have to go back to the kitchen, but please don't leave until I talk to you again. So I can explain. And then I'll leave you alone. Please."

His eyes search mine and I want to tell him no. Desperately.

"Fine." I lift my fork. "But I'm not staying here all night."

Without another word, he stands up and walks to the kitchen, leaving me stunned.

Thirty-eight

ETHAN IS BACK AT my table less than an hour later, somehow looking better than before, and I curse my stomach for the acrobatics it's doing.

"How was everything?" he asks, taking a seat across from me like he owns it.

Which he technically does.

"Awful. Now tell me why I waited here. I don't want to drag this out." I look around impatiently. Like I have somewhere else to be.

"Where do you have to be?" he asks, making a face that says *liar*.

I roll my eyes, annoyed by the question—and his face—and refuse to answer.

He picks up a fork and reaches over the table to scoop a bite of tiramisu off my plate, moaning with pleasure.

I push the plate toward him with another roll of my eyes. "Please, help yourself."

He smirks as he takes another bite.

"C'mon, Ethan. Just tell me what this is about."

"Dance with me."

His voice is so velvety smooth I hate him even more.

I scoff. "Oh no, not this again."

He pouts out his bottom lip.

My teeth clench.

"Ethan, there are people still eating, and nobody else is dancing." I gesture toward the other tables of the dining room. "Why can't you just talk to me like a normal man over this bad espresso and mediocre tiramisu?"

"You know that tiramisu is good. Some people even say it's better than sex."

His lips curl sinfully.

"Don't say *sex* to me," I hiss. I throw my napkin on the table. "Fine." I jerk to a stand. "Let's get this over with."

His smirk as he stands tells me he sees this as a victory, and it makes my blood boil.

He walks us over to a corner of the room with a small opening between the tables. The couple singing croons on about love lost, and it makes the taste in my mouth sour.

Ethan grips the small of my back and pulls me close to him. His scent envelopes me—woodsy aromas mixed with the smokey smells of the kitchen—and his rough hand grabs mine.

"Talk," I snap. "You have a harem of women staring at us, and being so close to you is making me nauseous."

I nod toward the hostess stand at the entrance where several of the female staff members are staring, no doubt wondering who I am and why I'm dancing like an idiot with their boss.

"You took your ring off." His whispered voice combines with the scruff of his jaw rubbing against me to send chills down my neck like ripples on a pond. My body is a traitor.

"Irrelevant. What do you want?" I ask, clipped.

"This restaurant is open from May to October, and I spend a lot of that time here. I try to stay in Bar Harbor from the Fourth of July to Labor Day, popping in otherwise as needed. I left a day later this year to be with you. And I didn't tell you about this place because I just didn't think you were ready."

His grip tightens around my waist, but I don't look at him. His logic pisses me off.

"Fine, you have a restaurant here, and you're here. Ethan, that's not even the biggest thing. Why the hell did you just leave? You just let me spend a whole day at your house, *with my kids*, and then disappear. Why? I cannot wrap my brain around that."

His shoulders tense under my palm.

The song ends, and the blurred sounds of conversations combine with the scratching of chairs moving across the floor to fill the quiet pause before the music plays again.

"Since the night I met you, I can't stop wishing the world was smaller and a mile wasn't so far. Because you belong in Maine as much as I belong in Florida, but I keep trying to convince myself that maybe they aren't so different." His mouth is next to my ear as he continues, "and because Nel, if I had said goodbye, I would have also asked you for time I knew you couldn't give me because of a wedding band around your neck that I didn't want to compete with."

Somewhere in the letters of all those words, the façade of fury I had tried so hard to maintain shatters. He rests his forehead on mine, and the look in his eyes makes my own burn.

"You said that if I wasn't leaving—"

"I lied," he confesses.

We stop dancing, but neither of us let go, frozen like a statue of two bodies carved as one.

My breath is labored, like I just ran uphill with boulders tied to my legs, and if my heart adds one more beat into the mix, it's going to give out.

"I dropped my ring off at a jeweler, and he's melting it down into a gift for Finn and Marin."

He doesn't move—doesn't speak—just looks at me like he can see every thought I have and ever will have.

"Hey, Ethan?" a girl's voice breaks whatever spell we've been standing in. "Sorry to interrupt, Boss, but Chef has a question about the menu before he shuts it all down for the night."

He loosens his grip and glances at her. "Right, thanks, Emily. I'll be right there." He looks back at me. "Wait for me, and I'll walk you home?"

"Yes. Fine. I mean..." I shake my head and smile. "I'll wait."

***

I wait outside on the sidewalk, vibrating with anxiety.

My brain doesn't know what to do with everything Ethan just said, while my body seems very confident with what it wants to do based on the pressure that's rapidly building up in me.

It is a battle of my brain versus my vagina, and I'm *really* hoping my vagina wins. I am Team Vagina so much that I would wear a jersey and wave a pompom if I had one.

Our reality hasn't changed. I'm still leaving. He still changes women like I change underwear. The whole thing is a horrible idea, but dammit, if that man doesn't know how to make me want to bulldoze down logic and reasoning.

"Fancy seeing you here," he says, looking at me like I'm his favorite thing—the only thing.

I don't bother to hide my smile.

He grabs my hand without hesitating, intertwining our fingers in a way that feels different from before. Like there's no going back. Like it means something.

"What was your plan here? You thought I'd see the name of the restaurant and come throw myself at you? Were you ever going to call?" I ask as we start walking.

"I hoped. You said you were coming to Bar Harbor and that you'd be here for three weeks. It's not a big town. I thought you'd see the sign and know. I didn't know if you'd *want* to see me, but I figured I gave you a way to make the choice. Plus, you have been known to drive across the country to find me after I send a couple of emails. I decided it wasn't such a long shot."

I laugh.

Then he adds, "I don't know if I would have called, but I would have waited."

My eyes search his, trying to understand the enormity of what that might mean, before I blink away.

Maybe it's because we've both said everything we needed to say, or maybe we don't want to ruin whatever this is, but neither of us says another word the rest of the walk. Our two hands are a single shape right until we stop in front of the house and step onto the porch.

"So," I say.

"So," he echoes.

I look up at the night sky.

Do you want to come inside?

I can't get the words to come out of my mouth. They are trapped in my throat by bars made of fear.

His hands settle on my hips, and it feels like a surge of electricity.

"Penelope..." His mouth hovers over my jaw. "You take my breath away in that dress."

My thighs clench together on reflex, and some kind of garbled sound comes out of my mouth.

He laughs against my skin and grazes the side of my neck with his tongue.

Holy hell.

"Ethan." I press my hands against his chest. "You are about to burn down the damn neighborhood with your mouth!"

I push him away. "I'm going to invite you in, but I'm still mad at you, so there will be no funny business tonight."

Unfortunately.

"Define funny business." His fingers dance across my shoulders as I fumble to unlock the door.

"I will not be naked, and you will not be naked, for starters."

I flick the light on as we walk inside.

"According to the way your body behaves, I don't need to get you naked."

My body purrs.

No.

"And none of that. No comments that make me feel like there's lava in my underwear."

Every word I say is the opposite of what I want.

He raises his eyebrows. "Lava in your underwear, Nel?"

"You know exactly what I'm saying. Deal? Or you can leave and see if I decide to show up in your little restaurant again." I cross my arms as we stand inside the doorway.

My body may want to do very dirty things to him, but I need him to prove something to me. That he wants to stay. That he knows how to stay.

He takes a step closer. "I'll be on my best behavior. I won't even touch you."

I hope he's lying.

"Perfect. Grab a beer, and I'll go get changed."

Before either of us can change our minds, I walk out of the room and up the stairs.

Much to my dismay, my brain wins the battle against my vagina's best efforts.

Thirty-nine

I SQUINT AT THE bright morning light as I point my toes to stretch my legs with a groan. I'm on the couch.

Ethan stayed here.

I scramble to stand, and my eyes dart around the living room.

"Ethan?" I call.

His name echoes through the quiet house.

I jog to every room, pushing open doors and calling his name.

In the middle of the kitchen, I know I'm alone.

The dappling light that trickles between outside branches and through the windows is the only movement in the house.

He left.

Without saying goodbye.

Again.

The realization hollows me out. I close my eyes and try to piece it all together. We sat on the couch for hours.

"Is your dad any closer to localizing the menu at the Crow's Nest?" he asked.

I laughed. "My dad gets these ideas sometimes. Who knows?"

"Who takes care of the bar while you're gone all summer?" he asked.

"Nobody gets behind my bar unless I teach them." I shrugged. "The bartenders can handle it."

"That confident, huh?"

I nodded. "I like making drinks, but I love teaching others how to do it." I paused. "I might even be decent at it."

"You taught me to make one—you're better than decent," he said with a smile.

Then we turned on the TV, the cooking channel, and Ethan criticized every chef on there.

When he yelled, "What the hell are you doing with all that vinegar?" I couldn't contain my laugh.

I was already in my sleepshirt when he yawned.

"Stay," I said.

Then I climbed on him and kissed him as I ran my fingers through his thick, dark hair.

"I thought you said no funny business." He was smug.

"I'm not being funny," I said into his mouth.

But it didn't go any further. I laid my head on his lap, where I must have fallen asleep.

Did he leave then?

No.

I woke up in the middle of the night with his arms around me and thought how right it felt. I watched him sleep, listening to the rhythm of his breath, and felt the cadence of his heart before falling back to sleep.

And after all that, he couldn't stay.

I rub my temples. Confusion turning to sadness.

I'm still leaving, this is still temporary, and my expectations are still too high.

I stare at the warm light dancing through the window.

There's a scrape against the front door before the knob turns, and my head jerks.

Ethan steps into the house, arms full of groceries, and my heart flip-flops like a fish out of water as relief pumps it back to life.

"Morning," he says with an earth shattering full-wattage smile as he puts the bags on the table. "I didn't want to wake you. I got stuff for breakfast."

I bite my lip sheepishly, pulling at the hem of my oversized t-shirt. "I thought you left."

"I guess technically I did." He pecks a kiss on my forehead. "But I came back."

His gaze rakes down my nightshirt and bare legs, and the smile I try to hide is fully exposed.

"Sit," he orders as he covers the counter in ingredients and pulls a French press out of one of the cabinets.

My eyes widen. "Do you know how to use that thing?"

"Yes?"

His chin dips as he scoops coffee grounds out of a canister. My mouth waters instantly as the nutty smell wafts around me.

"Ethan! I'm as bad at making coffee as you are at making cocktails. Teach me, please."

I put my palms together and bob up and down.

His chest rumbles as his lips lift in amusement, and he lifts his chin in a silent *get over here*.

"What do you usually do?" he asks.

"I usually fill a coffee filter with coffee and push the button."

"*Fill* it?" His eyes widen. "With how much water?"

"I usually drink a cup or so, and now Finn drinks a cup..."

I shrug.

"Nel, no."

Hands on the counter, he bends at his waist and drops his head between his arms.

"This French press holds 32oz of water. I would use about 8-10 tablespoons—*tablespoons!*—with this."

I tap a finger on my chin. "That could be part of my issue."

He scoops grounds into the French press and then fills it with hot water before putting the lid on.

"How can you make the best cocktail I've ever had but not know how to do this?" He's genuinely baffled.

"I've had a life with enablers. My college roommates always made coffee, then Travis, then I spent a year fumbling through it until Finn couldn't take it and took matters into his own hands."

I shrug as if to say, *don't blame me.*

He slowly pushes the plunger through the dark liquid and grabs two mugs, pouring us each one before sending me to a stool.

"Tell me how you learned to cook?" I ask.

I blow the steam on my mug while Ethan somehow makes chopping bell peppers look pornographic in jeans, a t-shirt, and bare feet.

"I grew up hunting and fishing the way my boys have." His knife rocks in a steady rhythm across the cutting board. "I realized really young how much I appreciated I could provide food to myself and my family, and that led me to experiment with ways of cooking it."

He scoops up the pile of diced peppers with the blade and drops them into a bowl.

"After culinary school, I learned a lot of restaurants have no idea where their food is coming from. There's a lot of ordering from wholesalers with frozen deliveries from some faraway place—it just felt so disconnected to me." He turns to look at me. "So I decided to open a restaurant and see if I could do it differently. See if I could source things as fresh and local as possible while also building a relationship with farmers. I started out with a menu of five items and was only open for dinner four nights a week while I worked part time with a construction company in town." He smiles, as if he's remembering those days in vivid color, and shrugs. "It just kind of grew from there."

My response is in the form of a quiet nod, surprised at how passionate he is about it. How clear of his purpose.

"What are you thinking?" he asks, whisking eggs in a bowl.

"I don't know. You light up when you talk about it. Like you are doing exactly what you are supposed to be. It's... nice. Like you have this special gift and mission that propels you forward with clarity. Everyone doesn't have that when it comes to their career."

"Don't you feel the same way about what you do? You're a helluva bartender."

"Maybe?"

I rarely let myself think about my career regrets, and I never talk about them.

"I was basically born behind the bar. It's what I've always known. I got a degree in business so I could help my dad. College wasn't really what I wanted to do, but it seemed to be the natural progression of things at the time, so I just went along with it because I wasn't really passionate about any other plan. Then, moving back to Key Largo seemed like the next thing to do because that's where my family was. Once I met Travis, things just kind of fell into place for me there. My career was the easy choice, I guess."

Butter simmers in the pan as he pours the eggs in.

"I like creating drinks and seeing people enjoy them. I don't know if I ever imagined I'd be a bartender with a side hustle of managing my dad's restaurant when I grew up, but I guess that's how life is sometimes."

Giving life to those words seems a bit like stepping out onto a tightrope with no net. I've thought of them before, but never once have I said them to another living being, not even Travis.

"How do you mean?" he asks.

"I mean, there are people like you, with passion and vision, that know exactly what they are supposed to be doing. I, on the other hand, did not have any idea what that looked like for me at eighteen when it was time to make grown-up choices. I think I just kind of let the easy route guide me for a lot of those early big decisions. My dad never told me I needed to come back and help him, I just always assumed that would make him happy and it would be easier than forging some life on my own." I sip my coffee as my thoughts start to spiral. "I don't know. With Travis gone and the kids getting older, I just kind of wonder if I missed the boat somehow."

"If you could change it all right now, what would you do instead?" he asks, folding the omelet in half in the pan.

"Is a cocktail consultant a real thing?" I laugh honestly. "I like creating drinks and making specialty cocktails. I love that. Maybe I would teach bartenders or work with restaurant owners on creating drink menus. There's probably no market for that, but I think I'd like it."

He sets a plate with an oversized omelet in front of me with two forks.

"This smells amazing, Ethan. No wonder all those women hunt you down at all hours of the night," I tease, picking up one of the forks.

"I haven't made breakfast for any woman since I was married."

The confession stops me mid-bite while he easily plucks a forkful of omelet into his mouth.

"I think you should try it," he says.

"Try what?" I ask, taking a bite.

"I think you should try being a cocktail consultant. I would hire you, and I can think of several other restaurant owners who would love to have someone like that help them."

I search his face for a joke, but there isn't one. He's serious.

"Maybe." I look down at the plate. "But first, I was thinking I could teach *you* how to make drinks. I can't leave here knowing that sometime in your future you're going to get behind a bar—that you own—and have you replay that scene from last week. Turns out I have two weeks here and nothing to do."

"What about the puffins and whales and lobsters?" There's a playfulness in his eyes as he takes his last bite of breakfast.

The moment Finn and Marin decided to go to that camp, I stopped caring about puffins or whales. The lobster? I definitely still want that, but everything else were plans for them.

"I just want lobster. Lots of it. But I realized for the first part of this trip, I went to a lot of places because I thought it was what Travis wanted, and then when we were coming here, I planned a lot of things because of some idea of what it would be like with the kids. Now that I'm alone..." My voice trails off. "I guess I just see it differently."

"Good."

"Good?" I ask, eyebrows raised.

"I have to go to the restaurant for a few hours this morning, but I want to show you something...with lobster." His mouth curves into a smile that renders me powerless. "And pack a bag—just in case."

Forty

JUST BEFORE TWO O'CLOCK, Ethan pulls up in his shiny silver truck, and I'm waiting for him on the porch wearing casual jeans and a plain white shirt.

He eyes the bottle of vodka sticking out of the box I hand him as he opens the door for me.

A smile tugs at my lips.

"I didn't know what you had planned, so I brought stuff for your first lesson."

I sink back into the passenger seat, toe off my flip-flops, and prop my feet on the dash as he climbs into the driver's seat.

He smiles, then reaches across the center console to wrap his hand around my thigh. It's a nothing move, ordinary, but the simple gesture feels a bit like a free fall.

"Let's get you some lobster."

With the windows down and the briny smell of the ocean blowing across my face, I don't even ask where we're going. I don't care.

I want to stay in this truck with the warm wind whipping my hair around my face and Ethan's hand on my leg forever.

The sun warms my skin as I watch evergreen trees fade to rocky coastlines and then back to trees as we drive.

When we come to a small coastal town, the water shimmers like sequins, and fishing boats bob playfully in the waves. There's not much to it. A post office, grocery store, marina, and a few small businesses, but what's there is picturesque. The houses, mostly big block rectangles, are painted in a color palette I can only describe as New England.

"This place looks like a picture that's used to make a puzzle," I say as we drive through town.

He snorts. "I've never heard anything described like that."

"All I'm saying is, they don't put trash on puzzles. This is the cutest town I've ever seen. People probably walk around singing sea shanties."

As if scripted, a man in a striped blue and white shirt tips his old captain's hat as we drive by. I shoot Ethan a look that says, *see.*

When we park, it's under a big sign with bright red letters that say, *POUND IT! MAINE'S BEST LOBSTER POUND.*

I squeal as I get out of his truck, walking toward a cute white building with bright red trim.

It's perfect.

We're greeted at the counter by a round woman with a mouth that only knows how to smile.

"Ethan Mills, leave your fancy restaurant long enough to come to eat some real food?" she asks with a cackle.

Her frizzy red hair is pulled back in a ponytail, showcasing bright, rosy cheeks.

He brings a hand to his chest in mock pain. "Marlene, it hurts when you say things like that."

"The truth hurts, honey," she says, her smiley eyes flicking to me and then back to him.

"Marlene, Nel here wants a true Maine lobster pound experience, and I knew we had to come here. Unlike you, I'm not threatened by the competition."

He rests his hand on the counter and gives Marlene a smile that even she can't resist blushing at. His effect is universal.

"Two soft shells, please, and..." he turns to look at me, holding up two fingers. "Two beers?"

I nod.

He waits for the food while flirting relentlessly with Marlene as I walk around.

There's a large screened-in porch with a yellow canvas roof that shoots out over the bay. People sit happily snapping tails and claws off lobsters and making a mess with corn on the cob while wearing silly bibs that say *Pound It!* in red loopy letters at brightly painted picnic tables.

The smells of butter, seafood, salt water, and fryer grease remind me of Key Largo and all my hours in the restaurant. The scene is as familiar as my own face. Only it isn't. I'm on an island a world away from my own.

I ache as I think about how far away my real life is.

I walk toward the picnic table where Ethan is putting the tray down, and stop in front of a shelf of t-shirts. *Pound It!* is written in the same loopy letters as everything else and has a lobster holding a hammer. I smile. I think of Travis.

As fast as the thought comes, it's gone. Without tears. Without guilt.

When I sit across from Ethan and tie on my own ridiculous paper bib, I grin.

"I feel so Maine right now."

The spread of food is so simple yet completely novel. A whole lobster lays next to an ear of corn on the cob with a ramekin of melted butter on a big metal pan.

He holds his lobster up like a puppet and makes it dance.

"Let's teach Nel how to eat a lobster."

I never stop laughing as he walks me through the entire process.

I snap the tail off as he does, clean the meat like him, and dig through the claws and other secret spots of the body to get the rest out. The sweet and salty taste is ecstasy to my taste buds.

"Oh my God," I groan between bites. "This is the best thing I've ever had in my mouth."

I know the mistake I've made the instant I look at him. Elbows propped on the table, there's a look in his eyes that could have melted the butter.

"Oh really, Nel? That you've *ever* had in your mouth?"

"Okay." I hold my butter-covered hands up. "Don't be so literal, Ethan. Or... intense. God, you're like some kind of walking... walking... stick!" I stutter.

"A walking stick? Is that what you call it?" He drops his head back and laughs.

"No, that did not come out right. I don't even know why I said that." I huff out a flustered breath. "All I meant is, you are an attractive man, and women notice it. Hell, I'm sure you've had men notice it. And as if that's not enough, you have this smolder that makes women say stupid things because it gets too hot to think straight when you get all smoldery and sexual. So put on some sunglasses or something. And maybe a Halloween mask. I want to enjoy a meal without getting third-degree burns from you." I throw an empty claw at him.

"Ethan?" a female voice calls from over my shoulder. "Ethan Mills, it is you. Must be officially summer if you're on the coast." The voice giggles.

I turn to see a beautiful blonde in a sleeveless dress with shiny hair and clear porcelain skin that glows in the sun. Her perfect looks seem photoshopped.

"Hey Rachel, good to see you." He stands up and gives her a hug. "Rachel, this is my friend, Nel."

"Hi!" I wave my butter-covered fingers towards her perfectly manicured hand. "I would shake, but I'm probably contagious." I laugh.

She doesn't.

Ethan bites back a smile. Looking at Rachel look at Ethan, there's an obvious look of longing on her face. Like she's spent her entire life in the dark, and he's the first rays of light she's seen. She looks how I feel—something I'm not prepared for.

My eyes bounce from him to her as I ask, "So, Rachel, how do you know my *friend* Ethan here?"

She smiles as though she has a million secrets to share as Ethan shoots me a look with an unspoken *stop talking* that I fully ignore.

"Hmm, now how would you explain *that*, Ethan?" she asks him coyly. "I would call us... summer friends, right?"

When she bats her long, thick eyelashes at him, I finish my beer in a single gulp, tipping the bottle straight toward the sky for good measure.

"That's nice," I say dryly.

"How do you two know each other?"

Her gaze goes from me back to Ethan, where it lingers.

"Oh, you know, the usual. He pinned me up against my silly RV, and I dry-humped his leg until I moaned his name. So... *friends,* I suppose, would describe us too."

Both Ethan and Rachel stare at me with mouths hanging open as I snap a lobster claw with a nonchalant smile.

"You know Rachel, it was great to see you, but we have to finish this up and get going," he finally says, scratching his neck. When she walks away—speechless—he looks every bit as uncomfortable as I hope he feels.

He holds his hands up defensively. "I can explain that."

"No need," I say, ripping another piece of shell off my lobster too aggressively. "I'm leaving in a couple weeks, remember? You're allowed to have summer *friends* named Rachel." I shrug before continuing. "Plus, it also explains why you didn't tell me you would be here—you didn't want to miss out on all your seasonal... what's the word? Ah yes—friend-ships!"

I emphasize the *s* with a hiss as I snap a leg off the already angrily demolished lobster's body.

I don't wait for him to respond before I scrub my hands with the smallest wet wipe I've ever seen that does nothing against the sheen of butter that covers my fingers. I stand up slowly, rip off my bib, and march out of the restaurant without looking back.

Forty-one

"I KNOW THAT LOOKED bad."

Ethan is still wearing his bib when he finds me wandering the docks of the marina, and it would have been funny if I wasn't plotting his death.

"Oh, do ya now?" I pick up my pace only for him to match it. "Look. I have no reason to be mad at you. We are *friends,* and I know you're a walking stick." My laugh is self-deprecating and unamused. "I know we're nothing, not really. It's just that she was perfect, like a thirty-five-year-old Barbie, and I'm... I'm... like Tom Hanks in that movie where he's been stranded on an island with a soccer ball."

"Volleyball," he says, correcting me like it's funny.

"You know what I mean."

"Nel, listen to me." He grabs my arm and stops me. "Rachel and I went on a few dates last summer. That's all she was. My excuse for ending it was that the season was over, and it was, but I also just wasn't interested. If you weren't standing here with me, nobody would be, got it?"

He rounds his back and bends his knees so his eyes are level with mine.

I look away like a scolded child.

"Nel, I need you to tell me you believe me."

I want to slap him and then push him in the water so a boat motor can chop some of the perfect off his face, but dammit, I believe him. Maybe I'm a fool, but I trust him.

"Fine." I cross my arms and face him. "I believe you."

He grabs my hands and tugs them gently.

"I have something to show you while you think of all the ways I'll be punished." The smile on his face is contagious and tramples my best efforts to stay mad.

He drags me up and down a series of docks until we finally stop.

A houseboat?

The exterior is a deep hunter-green with black trim and a set of steep steps that lead to a railing-wrapped rooftop. Facing the dock is a small porch with two chairs and a small table in front of a sliding glass door.

It's modern, sleek, and nicer than any I've seen.

I look at him. "A houseboat?"

He leans against a piling, casual as ever, nodding.

My eyes narrow. "And?"

"Do you like it?" he asks.

"What kind of question is that? Sure. It looks nice. New. I've never been on one actually. The ones I've seen in marinas in the Keys give off more of that on the run from the law vibe, but I'm sure this one is great. It doesn't look like bricks of cocaine are being smuggled on it." I hold up my hands as if to say, *why do I care?*

"I was hoping you'd say that." He grabs my hand, steps off the dock and onto the boat, pulling me behind him.

"What—" I pause as understanding clicks. "Of course. It's yours." I blink, irritated, and his smile only widens.

"Why can't you just say that like a normal person? *Nel, I have a houseboat. Do you want to see it?*" I lower my voice to mock his. "And I would have said, *sure, Ethan, let's go*. Then it wouldn't be this whole annoying thing you do."

"It's more fun this way," he says.

He slides open the door, and we move from the small porch into the surprisingly spacious living area. There's a couch, TV, kitchen area with a few cabinets, and a table with four chairs. Like his house, it's creamy white with expensive leather and wood finishings and a few landscape photos on the wall.

He leads me through the space in slow yet deliberate strides.

"Back here is the bathroom."

He pushes open a door, revealing a toilet, shower stall, and vanity, all larger than what we had in the Avion.

"And my bedroom."

I walk in behind him. He leans against the wall, puts his arms over his chest, and crosses his ankles. He says every word he doesn't speak with the way his head tilts toward me and tracks my movements.

I wander around his room, touching every surface I walk by. When my hand moves from the smoothness of his nightstand to the softness of his white cotton comforter, my cheeks burn. When I get to the window, I can see the other boats in the marina as the thick, textured dark blue material of the curtains scrapes through my fingers before I turn to look back at him.

The churning sound of an engine from a passing boat hums by before the room gently rocks from its wake.

It's hard to swallow through the tightness of my throat.

Between the effect he has on me and my lack of experience in these situations, every thought in my head is probably written all over me as clearly as the words scrolling across a news ticker.

He pushes off the wall and takes a step my way, triggering something between sheer terror and primordial need to bounce through me.

I can't handle it.

"I feel hot," I say, clearing my throat. "Are you hot? You know, it's probably from earlier. I just want to go see the outside again—for air."

I rub my palm against my forehead as I try to squeeze past him without touching him.

He grabs my wrist and anchors me to a halt as his mouth moves close to my ear, and his voice lowers. "Stay with me tonight."

I can't breathe and I definitely can't look at him. My nod is so subtle, so slight, he might have missed it if he wasn't paying such close attention.

I yank away from him and rush toward the open door, where the coastal breeze is a welcome relief. My first breath of air is a gasp.

Ethan, relaxed and unaffected, appears with two beers and lifts his chin.

"Up?" he asks.

"Up," I say, feeling my nerves settle just slightly.

The view from the roof is stunning—the bay to one side and the picturesque town to the other. The sun, low in the sky, coats everything with gold.

"Well, this is amazing," I say.

He hums in agreement.

"So, what's the story here? How did you end up with a houseboat?" I take a sip of the beer he hands me.

"It's not that interesting. I had a place here for a while, but as the kids got older, they didn't want to spend their summers away from friends, so they stopped coming. It seemed silly to keep a big house for just me, so I sold it. I'm only here a few months a year. This seemed like a great solution. It's big enough for me, and if the boys come, I'll put them in a room at the hotel." He points his beer toward the largest building in town.

A sailboat cuts across the horizon.

"This view is incredible. Better than most people will have in a whole lifetime." My eyes move to the boats around us—nearly identical to his. "Do people live in all of these?"

He nods.

"A cop." He points to the one closest to us before moving on to the other. "A plumber, a retired doctor, and I'm pretty sure that guy does something illegal."

I laugh softly with a shake of my head as I lean against the railing.

"How do you think Finn and Marin are doing in Acadia?" he asks, mirroring my position.

My cheeks puff up with air before deflating.

"Gosh, I don't know. Finn is probably loving every second, but Marin shocked me with this. I kept reading about the bathroom situation, but she insisted." My lips lift in the slightest of smiles. "But I guess this is part of it, right? Holding onto them tightly just to ultimately let go."

Another boat goes by, and again, we bob gently in the wake.

"The first summer the boys didn't want to spend on the coast with me, I was shocked. It took some getting used to, not having their trail of clothes or dirty dishes to clean up and the days off to spend fishing with them. Eventually, I figured it out and accepted they were growing up. They usually come for at least one weekend now, and I go home for at least one. It's a wild thing, seeing it happen. The change of watching kids grow is slow until you notice it, then it happens all at once, like a lightning strike."

I nod, knowing exactly what he's talking about.

"What's that for?" I point at a half-eaten loaf of bread in a bag tucked in a corner.

His eyes slide in my direction with a playful glint as he picks up the bag. He pulls out a slice of bread, balls up a small piece, and says, "A game," with a small smile.

Leaning over the railing, he whistles before he tosses the bread ball over the water. Within seconds a seagull swoops down to grab it out of the air in its beak.

His small smile morphs into something bright and full blown as he hands me a piece of bread that I refuse.

"Too grown up to play with the birds, Nel?" he asks, tossing another bread ball into the air, another bird swooping to catch it.

"No, this is just stupid," I say, only half meaning it.

"Really? Too stupid for someone who wears squeaky rubber boots around?" he mocks.

I cross my arms, nostrils flaring. "My luggage is a trash bag. Give the wardrobe a break."

His smile doesn't leave his face and his voice is an annoying sing-song sound when he responds with, "Don't knock it 'til you try it."

He tosses another piece of bread, a bird swoops in to catch it, and dammit if it doesn't feel like a little bit of a privilege to watch this man play like an overgrown child.

I hesitate only a second longer before relenting and taking a piece, tossing it the same way he does. A bird dives across the sky and catches it. I bite my cheek to hide my smile.

"Told ya," he hums, tossing another one.

It's stupid really, laughing this hard throwing bread to birds, yet somehow, it feels like I've been missing out. Like it should be part of every day. Like a day where I don't do this just can't possibly be as good.

When the loaf is gone, dark clouds roll in and mushroom across the sky. I smell the rain just before the first drop lands on my arm. The once clear horizon looks almost black as thunder rumbles in the distance.

"Storm's coming," he says.

"Looks like it."

The only place to go is in.

Forty-two

IN THE MIDDLE OF the houseboat in damp clothes, I'm terrified. It's smaller than before, like the rain is making it shrink, and soon, there won't be enough oxygen for both of us.

As the drops pelt on the metal walls, its rhythm races that of my pulse. I don't need to ask what's about to happen. I already know.

Despite all the ways my body is begging for this man to make it feel good, I'm frozen. I haven't had sex in eighteen months, and suddenly, I am both highly aware of this and extremely self-conscious.

Ethan is a perfect specimen, and I'm just... not. For two decades, the only man who's seen me naked is Travis. By the time he died, we were far from the nervous kids we were when we met. He knew my body better than I did. He watched me stretch and soften with pregnancy and age, yet always seemed to know what I needed without me ever using words to say it. We fit like a favorite pair of faded blue jeans.

The wild anticipation that drove us when we were younger had been replaced by a comfortable longing after years of practice. And while I expected that to be boring when I had imagined growing old with someone, it wasn't. It was a familiar kind of pleasure.

Here, in this room, I'm an inexperienced kid all over again. Only this time, I'm forty-one and hyperaware of the lines that have been drawn on me with a paintbrush wielded by the hands of time.

I watch his chest rise and fall with his breath as he closes the space between us with a small step. We aren't touching, but it's the only thing I can think about. His hands on me. My mouth on him.

"I... I haven't done this in a while and..." My voice is a trembling mess. "I might be, you know, bad, or something." I pull at the hem of my shirt.

He lifts my chin with his knuckles, his gorgeous eyes meeting mine. "You could never be bad, Nel," he says, barely above a whisper.

Then his eyes drop to my mouth and my lips part like an unspoken invitation.

That's all it takes. He knows. He presses his mouth against mine in a kiss that steals away what little breath I have left. Every swipe of his tongue feels like water in my lungs, drowning me slowly into the entirety of him.

Heart be damned, I want this more than I need to walk away from him unscathed.

The softness of our kiss turns to a frantic fury of tangled tongues and nipping teeth. His hand fists my hair, and the way he tugs it, just enough to let me know he has me, makes the blood in my veins turn hot.

We knock into the table and a chair falls as we stumble past. When I laugh into his mouth, it's only for him to steal it with another deep, hungry kiss.

Arms overhead, my shirt is off. Hands at my waist, my jeans drop.

A trail of what we're doing covers the short distance to the bedroom.

"Nel," he says against my skin, making my whole-body clench at the rough way he says my name. "I've wanted to do this from the first night we met."

I say something, but I'm not sure what. The ache that's forming in me is the only thing I can focus on.

My bra drops next. Before I can even think about feeling uncomfortable, his hands replace it while his lips, tongue, and teeth never stop scraping across my skin.

The fact that I'm nearly naked, and he is fully clothed is both extremely unfair and undeniably hot.

When he gently pulls and pinches my nipple, I whimper. Once again, he's undoing me with just a touch. Once again, I don't care. He gives me everything I don't know to ask for in every way as his fingers glide across my skin.

His hungry mouth replaces his hand, and I run my fingers through the thick hair on top of his head.

"Ethan..." His name is a breathy beg on my lips as my head drops back. I want more. I *need* more.

His hands are everywhere, his mouth is everywhere, and I can feel how hard he is for me. For *us*.

He pulls his shirt over his head, and I trace the dusting of hair that covers his broad chest and subtle ripple of abs. When I get to the bulge in his pants that is making my entire body throb, I drag my fingers along the outline of it.

The guttural moan he gives me from that touch alone feels like a reward across every inch of my skin.

His hands grip my ass, lifting me up, and dropping me onto the bed—there's an urgency in the way he moves. A neediness.

My back to the bed, he kneels in between my legs, leans over, and cages me in with his arms. His normally bright eyes are dark as he hovers over me, and the way he kisses me isn't polished or practiced—it's wild.

Frantic.

Desperate.

His kiss is my mood.

He skims one hand down the line of my breast, the dip of my waist, and in between my thighs, where he rubs lazy circles around the spot that needs him the most.

"You like this."

It's not a question. It's a statement. A fact proven by how my body writhes beneath him, how the thin piece of fabric of my underwear gets wetter as he rubs, and how the only sounds coming out of my mouth are gasps and whimpers.

My back arches off the bed as his hand works me to the edge with the help of his mouth, sucking his way across my breasts and up my neck.

"Ethan, I'm not going to last very long." The words are as strangled as the sensation I feel, and it's so severe it's borderline painful.

"You don't have to," he says, breathy and hot against my skin, driving me to rock against his hand frantically and on reflex—primal reflex.

He pulls my underwear to the side and slides in one finger, then two. That's all it takes. I shatter with a scream that fills the room while he watches me fall apart like it's the most interesting thing he's ever seen. My fingers dig into his back as the orgasm sweeps through me, fierce and fast.

His lips find the tender spot on my neck where he works his tongue in a way that sends chills across my already satisfied body, and the beginnings of a second orgasm start to swirl from that alone.

The way Ethan Mills uses his hands and mouth on my body is a religious experience. He kisses the spot between my breasts, resting his lips softly just above my heartbeat.

"You're so pretty, Penelope."

The simple sentence makes warmth curl in my chest and spread in every direction.

I reach down with shaking hands to unbuckle his belt and fumble with his zipper. I'm struggling to get air in my lungs, but he's hard and ready, and I can't wait one minute longer to know how he's going to feel inside of me.

Clothed, the man is hard to look away from, but naked, Ethan makes me physically quiver.

He kneels above me, hooking his fingers in the sides of my underwear before slowly sliding them down my legs, studying every inch of me like he's trying to commit my body to memory. When he swipes a finger in between my thighs, a fresh shot of desire burns through me.

He leans off the bed, opens the drawer of his nightstand, and grabs a square foil wrapper.

A condom.

A condom?

Despite every hot thing he's done, and I have no doubt what he is still planning to do, a laugh bubbles out of me.

"Is that a condom?" I ask, hiding my smile with my fist as I lay back on the bed.

"What else would it be?" His eyes narrow as he bites the edge to rip it open.

I laugh as I say, "I didn't know anyone over the age of twenty-two used these."

"What are you saying, Penelope?" His face is so tense with desire it's almost dark.

The laugh dies on my lips, and I swallow hard at the view of his very hot, very naked, very turned-on body that's above mine.

"Nothing, I don't know. I just never thought about it. I mean, I've only been with one person for a really long time and then no person for a really long time. But you're you, so I guess that makes sense, you know? And I've already made sure I'm not having a baby this late in the game but—"

My words come out a nervous babble. During sex. I would have thrown myself overboard if I didn't want him so badly.

"I'm clean," he cuts me off. "Just tell me what you want me to do right now because I don't think I will last another second with you being perfect and naked and me not being inside you."

I don't think—I can't. I grab the condom, drop it on the floor, and wrap a hand around his neck to pull his mouth against mine. It's reckless, but fuck it. I'm already being burned alive, and if we're doing this, there isn't one part of him I'm not going to feel.

He's at my entrance, concern etched on his face as he hovers above me. "I'll be gentle."

No. I shake my head. "Don't."

So, he doesn't. With a firm push of his hips, he's in me, stretching me slowly, and I arch off the bed with a cry.

It hurts but in the best kind of way.

He pauses and searches my face. He's waiting for me to tell him I'm okay. Damn him for being considerate when I want him to be anything but.

"Don't you dare stop." The words are a needy demand as I tilt my hips and pull him in deeper.

With a low growl in his chest, he's in me—moving in ways that make me sob out his name. When he withdraws, it's only to fill me up again. And again. Any shred of self-consciousness melts away with every rock of his hips and hungry kiss he brands on my skin.

My body molds into his as he thrusts into me. Over and over and over. It's too much and not nearly enough.

Our mouths are gaspy mingles interrupted only by desperate pleas.

He grips my hips, flips us over, and digs his fingers into my skin as he moves me on top of him. My rocking starts slow, adjusting to the new position and how he fills me up so fully I might die. I lift off him until just the tip of him remains inside me before sliding down on him so hard it's difficult to differentiate between pleasure and pain.

Then I do it again.

And again.

"Fuck, Nel."

His fingers dig deeper into my hips, and his head drops back.

Every move pushes me closer to my undoing.

In another flash of movement, I'm on my back, and he crashes into me with a thrust so hard it feels like I'm being ripped in two. But if the hard length of him doesn't break me, the orgasm that shatters through me afterward certainly does. The scream that comes out of my mouth is as foreign to me as the blurred edges of my vision.

He slams into me one more time before he shudders, emptying completely into me with one last rock of his hips. He rounds forward, his skin slick with sweat and his breath shallow, dropping his forehead to mine as we roll to our sides.

His eyes search mine as we face each other, and my palm settles on his chest. Breaths steadying.

"Your heart is pounding." I smile.

He mirrors my movement. "So is yours."

His eyes crinkle as he nudges my nose with his.

"That was amazing."

"Eh." I say, with a bored tone, biting my cheek to hide a satisfied smile.

"Oh really, Penelope?"

His fingers trace the line of my hip gently before grabbing my ass with a squeeze that makes me yelp.

"Guess we'll just have to keep trying until I get it right."

Then his hands, mouth, and body are on mine, and we do it all over again.

Forty-three

WHEN WE FINALLY LEAVE the bedroom, it's after dark and the rain has stopped. I'm wearing one of Ethan's long-sleeved shirts that hits the middle of my thighs, and he's only wearing sweatpants and a t-shirt. The scene we create is familiar—easy—and it doesn't seem possible that we've never been here before.

I guzzle down a glass of water as he minces garlic on a cutting board. "Are we supposed to talk about what just happened?"

The question comes out in an awkward blurt, but I'm so far removed from this kind of scenario I have no idea what protocol is.

He shoots me an amused look over his shoulder and raises his eyebrows.

"I would *love* to talk about what just happened."

"Ha. Ha," I say dryly. "I'm serious, Ethan. Are we supposed to have some kind of discussion or make any weird speeches about what it means or doesn't mean?" I spin the empty glass on the counter. "What do you usually do in these casual situations of yours?"

I'm being serious—I genuinely don't know what I'm supposed to do and desperately don't want to get it wrong.

He drops the knife on the cutting board and covers the small space between us in two quick steps.

"Stop right there." He lifts my chin with his index finger until my eyes meet his. "You were amazing. *We* were amazing. I'm *very* happy to talk about all the things I thought were amazing if you want." He dusts a light kiss on my lips, absorbing some of the tension pulling at my shoulders. "But my casual situations are nothing like this, Penelope. Women don't meet the boys, and I definitely don't mince garlic for them in my sweatpants."

I smile deliriously from how his words make something warm pump through my veins.

"Do *you* want to talk about what just happened?" he asks, rubbing his palm against my bicep.

"I liked it, if that's what you mean." My cheeks flush with the confession, and I have to look away as all the things I *liked* so much start dancing in my head.

"Good."

He kisses me, deeper this time, before pulling away and getting back to work at the stove.

***

With a satisfied belly full of shrimp scampi, I wave the bottle of vodka at Ethan.

"The Moscow mule might have peaked a few years ago, but it's still popular enough I think you should know it."

I pull a recognizable copper mug out of my box and hand it to him.

"I remember," he says looking at it. "We have sets of these at both restaurants."

"The reasoning behind the copper material is it keeps the drinks cold-
er, but its novelty makes a lot of people order the cocktail. The mug alone
makes it feel like a different experience. I would say if you are going to
serve the Moscow Mule in your bar, the mug is non-negotiable. If you
have the space, some people like to keep them in a freezer, so they are
chilled when they serve the drink in them, but we don't have that space
at our bar, so they are always used at room temperature."

I spread the rest of the ingredients across the counter before filling
both mugs with ice.

He nods but doesn't say anything.

"I always recommend a better-quality liquor whenever possible, but
every bar is different, and you have to learn your customers and the
price they are willing to pay. I like Tito's. It has a more subtle flavor
that doesn't overpower the other ingredients, but you can also explore
flavored vodkas or something from a local distillery. I know how you
don't like to deviate from Maine." I tease, pouring a shot of vodka into
my mug before passing it to him.

He chuckles, then does the same.

I hold up two limes. "Now the lime."

We each cut and squeeze the juice over the ice and the familiar smell
of the bright citrus smells like a million hours in the Florida sun.

"The easy way to make the drink is a bottled lime juice, but it is
absolutely worth it to use fresh ingredients wherever you can, including
limes, a sentiment I'm sure you can relate to in the kitchen. I guarantee
it's worth the time and effort to use fresh juice. I have no proof, of course,
but I would bet money that people are more likely to order a second
drink when a fresh lime is used over a bottled mix. It's *that* powerful."

He silently nods, but there's an amused look on his face.

"Ginger beer comes next," I say, popping the top of the small bottle. "There are a few popular brands, but I always try to find one that isn't overly sweet or syrupy. Corn syrup is never my friend, but sometimes it's hard to be that picky. If you are going through the effort of juicing a fresh lime, it's for nothing if the main mixer tastes artificial and overly sweet."

I top off my mug with it and pass it to Ethan to finish his before stirring the drinks with spoons.

"Last but not least, we come to the garnishes. This is where I see a lot of bartenders get carried away. My rule of thumb is if it doesn't add to the flavor or experience of the drink, don't use it. Some people put mint on a mule, but a single leaf isn't going to add flavor to the drink, and most people aren't going to eat it straight, so I consider it worthless. I use a lime wedge."

I hug a green sliver onto the rim of the mug.

"And a piece of candied ginger."

I open the bag and inhale the spicy scent that follows before grabbing a piece and nestling it next to the lime. Ethan mimics my movement, still in silence.

I hold up my finished drink proudly before taking a sip and smacking my lips in approval. "And there you have it." I smile proudly, watching him quietly study his mug before shifting his gaze to my face, an emotion I can't read in his eyes.

My eyebrows pinch together. "Why are you being so quiet and weird? Drink it."

"You lit up." He neither picks up his mug nor looks away.

"What's that supposed to mean? I did not." I pull my chin back.

"When you talked about every ingredient and how the cocktail was built, you lit up. Like you were doing something you loved. I've never seen someone talk about lime juice with such passion," he teases.

"Okay," I say, drawling out the word and rolling my eyes.

The pit in my stomach tells me this is leading to something I'm not ready to address.

"So, I like limes? Are you serving canned green beans in your kitchen, Mr. Mills?"

"You know that's not what I'm saying. You don't just like talking about limes, you like talking about what the limes can do. You told me yesterday you don't know if you are doing what you should be. I'm saying from where I'm standing, *this* looks like what you should be doing." He finally takes a sip of his drink and grins. "And you just taught me to make a drink that doesn't taste like piss." The implications of what he's saying are radical.

Leave my dad's bar?

The thought alone feels like a punch in the gut, no matter how much I love the idea of seeing where something different might lead.

His tone softens. "I'm just saying that if you are looking for confirmation this is something you could do, I know it is."

The soft ping of raindrops against the boat picks up again as we stand in a quiet that feels charged.

"It's raining again," I say the obvious because I don't know what else to say.

"Mhm."

I face him, leaning back on the counter and press my palms against it. "Now what?" I ask, my gaze hooking with his.

"I can think of a few things," he says as he maneuvers around until he's leaning against me.

The scruff on his jaw rubs against my neck as he kisses a slow, savory line until his mouth finds mine. He tastes like ginger and lime, and his tongue is cold from the ice.

His fingers slide down my waist and grip the back of my thighs—picking me up effortlessly. Our mouths stay fused as my legs wrap around him. He walks us across the room.

It's three quick steps before my back hits a wall, feet dropping to the floor.

With a hook of his fingers and a flick of his wrists, my underwear slides down my legs, and I squeak with a laugh.

"Pants. Off." I gasp between hungry kisses.

"Are you going to use my leg to get what you need again, Penelope?"

His voice is a low gravely sound that makes my brain break.

Jesus, Mary, and Joseph.

His mouth is so close to my ear that between his hot breath and deep voice, I almost pass out. I'll be embarrassed by the reference later, but in this hot moment, the reminder of how his leg had given me exactly what I needed winds me tighter than a spring.

His sweatpants are off, and he's so ready that my thighs squeeze in a vain attempt to ease the ache that throbs.

"Open."

It is one, deep, demanding word I absolutely obey.

My legs spread, and within seconds, he's stretching me open with his first delicious inches and digging his fingers into the back of my thighs. One leg around his waist and the other pushing against the ground on my tiptoes, my body trembles.

The carnal look in his eyes lets me know this isn't going to be a sensual journey of learning each other's bodies, this is going to be a hot, quick fuck, and it has me burning.

I'm already sore. Earlier, I wondered if I'd ever be able to sit again after our time in his bed, but back to the wall, I will gladly beg this man to destroy me. I let him stretch me open and slam into me with enough force we might take down the wall.

We strike a rhythm—his life-altering thrusts pinning me to the wall with the grinding of my hips—and he hits a spot inside of me that's so deep, I can't see straight. It's an aching kind of bliss that vibrates through me with every filling slam.

When he speaks, it's only to have the sentences broken by the movement of his hips.

"The way... you're moving... is the hottest thing... I've ever felt." His teeth are clenched in restraint like he's holding himself back, and it's the last thing I want.

My back arches off the wall, and when our eyes meet, I nod—he knows.

His next thrust is so unhinged I feel it in my throat.

Between the rain and the breathing and the slamming against the wall, it's an erotic symphony that sounds like angels singing. Dirty, filthy, smutty angels.

He trembles—he's close. I use the wall as leverage and drive my hips against him as hard as I can. With one final soul-shattering thrust, we climax together, exploding like two asteroids crashing in the night sky. The only thing I can do is let out an unpracticed, unfiltered, unrestrained cry.

His movement slows but doesn't stop, rocking slowly until we both ride out the last waves of bliss. My body goes limp at the same time his forehead drops against the wall.

If he wasn't holding me upright, I would have dripped into a puddle on the floor.

"Apparently, I like sex against the wall more than against your leg," I say in a husky voice with a laugh.

His mouth hovers over my skin as his whole body vibrates.

"I've never met anyone like you, Nel," he says, making me grin like the idiot he turns me into. Then, "You'll be hard to say goodbye to."

He says it like he means it, and my grin is replaced by the urge to cry.

"You'll be hard to say goodbye to, too," I say softly.

Then we're quiet.

Because ultimately, that's all there is to say.

Forty-four

ETHAN DOES, IN FACT, sleep naked.

It's one of the many things I learn in the next twelve days in Bar Harbor that are blissfully similar to our first one.

He works a few hours every morning at his restaurant, and we spend every night together. Every night, I think it might be the time that finally satisfies my appetite for him, but every night, he proves me wrong. He becomes the drug, and I need just one more hit.

I teach him to make cocktails, but the things he teaches me can't be boxed in by words. He pushes me, in that playful way of his, to be just a little bit uncomfortable, all the while waiting with a hand reached out until I get there.

"It's beautiful here," I say as we hike one of the last afternoons we have alone together.

The trail we're on feels like a secret—we haven't seen another person. Most of it had been tall trees and jagged rocks, but now we stand in the open at a lake that reflects the sky like a mirror. Trees cover the hills around us in a serene beauty that spreads as far as the eye can see.

"I love it here. I'm always alone—best spot to clear my head," he says as he unties a boot by the edge of the water and pulls it off.

My eyes narrow as I watch him.

"What are you doing?"

"What does it look like I'm doing?"

He slips off his other boot and works to unbuckle his belt before pushing his jeans down his legs.

My mouth drops.

"You're *swimming*?"

I look around, like maybe I missed something. Like a pool. And bathing suits.

He peels off his socks.

Then shirt.

Then briefs.

When he stands in front of me wearing only a cocky smile, my heart stutters.

"*We're* swimming. Strip," he says, making a quick swiping motion with his index finger through the air.

I shake my head. "You've lost your mind. I'm not swimming! This is a public trail, Ethan. Anyone could walk up! And God, we're adults—adults don't swim *naked* in lakes. I have kids!" I sound as panicked as I feel.

"I'm an adult, and I'm swimming naked in a lake. And in case you haven't noticed, your kids aren't here."

As nonchalantly as he says the words, he walks toward the water, the muscles of his bare back flexing with every step.

I can't do this.

Can I do this?

When he's up to his shoulders in the water, he turns to look at me—still fully clothed on the shore.

"What are you waiting for, Penelope?" His echoed voice is a taunt across the flat water.

What *am* I waiting for?

Maybe it's the way he looks naked in that lake, or maybe it's because it feels daring and scandalous, but I do it. I do it without thinking or trying to talk myself out of it. I kick my boots off, shed my clothes, and laugh wildly as I run into the water with a splash.

Naked.

I'm forty-one and skinny dipping, and I've never felt so ridiculous or alive.

I swim out to him. He lifts me up, and my legs wrap around him and his nakedness. Then, in a lake in the middle of nowhere in Maine, he kisses me.

If I weren't leaving in days and a mile wasn't so far, I might think I've just fallen in love with him. I might think for the first time since Travis died, this is the happiest I've been. As fast as the thoughts invade me, I push them away. Because I know love takes longer than weeks to happen, and a mile really is far, especially when there are nearly two thousand of them linked together.

Even when the hikers he promised me would never come walk by and obscenely catcall us, we stay in that lake. We swim until our fingers wrinkle and our stomachs growl.

It's one of the best days of my life.

***

On the second to last morning, before Marin and Finn are back, I watch Ethan sleep and study how the warm light reflects off hidden strands of silver in his hair. I watch him for so long my eyes start to burn.

When his eyes flutter open, it's with a sleepy, "Hi."

He half yawns and reaches his arms overhead in a stretch before turning to face me. Lines of shadow and light stripe across his beautiful body, half-covered with a sheet.

I hug the pillow underneath me and face him. I try to smile, but the sadness carved on my skin moves like concrete.

"Hi."

"What's in here this morning?"

He gently taps my forehead as his bottomless eyes search mine.

I roll onto my back and stare at the ceiling.

"On the east coast of Mobile Bay, there's this thing that happens that they call a jubilee. I won't even bother trying to tell you the exact details of what has to occur for the whole thing to happen because I'd butcher them, but it involves tides, temperature, oxygen levels, and winds doing all the exact right thing. Anyway, when all these things cooperate, the shallow shoreline is flooded with gobs of fish and crabs, and the people all come together and celebrate the harvest in the middle of the night." I don't know why I think of that night in Alabama lying in Ethan's bed that morning, but I do. "As you can imagine, it's an extremely rare phenomenon, but we got to see it by some weird stroke of luck." I almost laugh thinking of us wading through that dark water in the middle of the night with those ridiculous washtubs.

"The man that took us out that night told me jubilees weren't any more special than anything else in life. That everything is a magical phenomenon of one kind or another. He told me that what makes jubilees fun is they are rare and eventually stop, and we shouldn't pass anything up just to avoid the pain of the ending.

"For some reason, this morning, I was thinking after looking back on everything I've seen this summer, jubilees really are everywhere. The way Sedona has red rocks, and the lonely saguaros grow for hundreds of years in the desert. The way mystery lights dance in Marfa and the Colorado River made the Grand Canyon. The way we make a perfect series of unrelated choices that hand deliver us to something that feels like the rarest magic in all the world."

I don't need to clarify the last part. We both know what I'm talking about.

Us.

His fingers interlace with mine as I blink back the tears that want to fall.

"Let's have coffee on the roof this morning," he says.

I nod. "And feed the birds," I say.

Because I'll miss that, too.

***

Ethan doesn't go into the restaurant that day.

We go through the motions of doing everything we had done in the days before, except there's a somber undercurrent that won't be ignored. We speak less and stare off into the distance more. I'm so lost in my own head I can't exist in the present, no matter how little of it we have left together.

Marin and Finn will be back tomorrow, and before they left, we planned it out to spend four days in Bar Harbor before flying home. All I can think about is the end.

I cling pathetically to his side as we walk around downtown that afternoon. As if the more I touch him, the longer I'll be able to feel him when I leave.

There's a game people play where they ask what you would do if you only had one week to live. I've always answered it by stating grandiose plans of seeing something exotic or doing something crazy with the people I love. I now know I would just mope, exactly the way I've been doing since I woke up this morning.

I'm not seizing the day. I'm losing it.

I stop in the middle of the sidewalk.

"Cancel the dinner reservation, Ethan. This day has been awful. You know it just as much as I do. As much as I hoped not talking about it would make it better, it feels worse—like we are in some kind of depressing funeral march on a treadmill that won't stop." I blink through the burn that's piercing my eyes. "I can't share you with anyone tonight. Not the strangers we walk by on the street or the waitress who will take our order or anyone else. The bubble we've lived in for the last two weeks is going to pop the minute I pick my kids up tomorrow, and I hate myself for how sick it's making me feel and how needy I'm acting."

He smiles, but it doesn't meet his eyes. He knows.

In the middle of the busy Bar Harbor sidewalk, he cups his hands around my face and pulls me into a kiss that's so devastatingly heartbreaking I almost collapse.

"If you weren't leaving next week Nel—"

I shake my head. "Don't," I say firmly. "Let's just go to the house."

Hand in hand, that's exactly where we go.

That night, after he cooks us salmon, and I study every move he makes in the kitchen, there's a heaviness in the air.

When we strip off our clothes and crawl into bed, we're silent—sadness digs its claws into every ounce of pleasure. Ethan touches and kisses me with a gentle intensity he hasn't before. It isn't playful sex with laughter or a quick slam against the wall. He makes love to me in a way that wrecks every cell that glues me together.

More than once, I have to look away from the way his eyes burn into mine and pull every secret out of me without a single word. When his gentle rocking pushes my body to a shattering climax, the sob that escapes my throat is mixed with hot tears that stain my face.

I'm destroyed.

He stays quiet.

He knows.

Whether he feels what I do or not doesn't matter. He knows the losing battle I'm fighting.

He kisses every tear that streams down my face until they stop.

With my head on his chest, nearly asleep, he swirls circles across my bare back with his finger.

"Penelope?" His voice is barely above a whisper.

I keep my eyes closed and pretend to sleep. I don't have the strength to say what needs to be said.

"If you weren't leaving, I would have loved you."

Then, my newly mended heart shatters into a million pieces all over again.

Forty-five

THE SADNESS OF LAST night is eclipsed this morning by the excitement of seeing Finn and Marin.

In the kitchen of the house, I tap my toes on a stool while rubbing my sweaty palms against my jeans.

"Is it weird I'm nervous?"

"Nervous?" Ethan laughs as he makes coffee. "What the hell for?"

"I don't know. Because I spent the whole time they were gone naked with you." I twist my hair with my fingers.

"First of all, they don't know that."

He puts a cup of coffee in front of me, his ropey forearms on full display under the pushed-up sleeves of his shirt. "Second of all, I don't think they would care, anyway. They seemed to like me, and they like the boys. And I know for a fact Marin wanted you to have a walk of shame." He raises an eyebrow as he presses a light kiss on my temple.

"You're right. I'm being ridiculous. I can play this cool. It'll be fine. Wonderful, even."

He gives me a skeptical look before he cracks an egg into the pan.

An hour later, Ethan is at work, and I'm in a large room in Acadia National Park with twenty other sets of parents. I bounce anxiously as a line of matching t-shirts and oversized backpacks finally bobs into view.

Then here they are, grubby and smiling. Happy tears drip down my face as I grab Marin and Finn in a hug that can never last long enough.

They laugh, smell horrible, and look like different people but the same kids all at once. Touching them reminds me of how much I missed them.

"Mom," Finn croaks. "It's been weeks, not years."

Marin's arms wrap tightly around my waist as I laugh and swipe the tears away. "I can't help it. I missed you!" I look at Marin. "And you survived a hole for a toilet!"

She grins. "With flying colors, Penelope."

"I want to hear every single detail," I say as we start to walk toward the parking lot.

"You won't believe it all, Mom, but I need a real shower and dry clothes before I can think straight. And maybe ice cream. And pizza."

Marin shifts her bag on her shoulders.

"Are we getting an Uber?" Finn asks, tugging at the straps of his backpack and looking around the parking lot.

"Actually," I clear my throat. "I ran into Ethan, and he let me borrow his truck s—"

"I told you she'd find him!" Marin squeals, slapping Finn on the arm and cutting the rest of my words off.

"What?" I stop, mid stride across the lot. "You knew?" My mouth drops open.

"Mom, of course," she grins. "It was part of the reason I didn't feel guilty leaving you here alone while we went to camp. I knew you'd find him, or he'd find you or something. How did you figure it out? Oh my gosh, Finn! Isn't this so romantic?"

Finn rolls his eyes, and I shake my head with a laugh as we walk up to
Ethan's truck.

"Get in," I say. "We're meeting him for dinner tonight, and he can tell
you all about it."

***

They talk all at once—a tangle of yelled, "Tell her about the time…" and
cackling laughs. I don't follow most of the stories they tell, but I'm so
deliriously happy to have them back, the smile never leaves my face.

After extremely long showers and too much time reading reviews on
where to find the best ice cream, we're sitting at a picnic table with cups
filled with chocolatey frozen goodness.

I pull the box out of my purse I picked up from the jeweler and take a
steadying breath.

"I have something for you guys." I slide it across the table to them.

Marin looks at me before pulling the lid off, her mouth opening
slightly as she tilts it toward Finn. He takes one of the medallion-sized key
chains out and dangles it in the air. Travis' signature of 'Dad' scribbled
on one side catches the light from the sun.

"It's my ring—well, was my ring—and the pitiful bag of gold we found
in Arizona." I smile. "And the chain my dad gave me. I had them melted
down, so you each had a piece of him and the love that made you."

I pause, trying to find words that don't seem to exist.

"I couldn't keep wearing it—the ring. My dad told me it kept me sad,
and I think he was right. Every time I felt it on my body, I was teleported
to my grief and… I don't know, I thought this would…" My voice trails
off, hoping they understand what I'm trying to say. "They're not solid

gold. We didn't have enough. It's plated, not that it matters, I guess... And this wasn't about Ethan. I did it before I knew he was here."

"Mom, it's perfect," Finn says as he lays the keychain in his palm.

"It is, Mom. I love it."

Marin traces the signature on her own, over and over.

Relief tumbles over me like a waterfall.

The ring had been my life preserver, but to have it off my body and in their hands feels right.

"So, did you and Ethan go do any of the things on your list? Puffins? Whales?" Marin asks when she finally tucks the keychain back in the box.

I squint at them, a weird kind of guilt simmering in my gut. "We ate lobster. And Ethan showed me around the island." *Among other things.*

"But puffins and whales didn't seem as exciting without you two, so I kind of abandoned that plan. Next time, maybe."

"Next time," she says, eying me skeptically.

Whatever she's thinking disappears with the next spoonful of ice cream she sticks in her mouth.

Forty-six

WE MEET ETHAN AT Mainely Local, and as usual, I'm taken aback by how damn handsome he is in scuffed-up boots, jeans, and a t-shirt. I see him before he sees us—watching him guide the staff and talk to customers in his casually wide, authoritative stance.

A woman strolls over to him, beautiful, of course, and he says something that makes her laugh while his hands stay glued across his chest. When his eyes meet mine across the room, I raise my eyebrows at him, and he does the same, the slightest of smirks lifting his lips.

Marin nudges me. "Mom, you're staring at him."

"Am not," I lie.

When he makes his way over to our table, he gives Marin a big hug with goofy noises and Finn a fist bump.

"Penelope." He nods his head toward me and reaches out to give me a hug as I stick my hand out to shake his, slamming it right into his chest. I grimace, and he bites back a smile.

"Really, Mom? You spend two weeks together, and you shake hands at dinner? If that's real, Poppy's going to be so disappointed in you."

Embarrassment swallows me whole as I fumble to get into my seat.

"So, how was camp? You both survived, I see."

Ethan doesn't miss a beat at settling into a chair and changing the subject.

"Awesome. Only one night of rain, which was very soggy, but at least it was only once," Finn says, thumbing through his menu.

I choke on my water, a fresh wave of heat crawling up my neck as I recall the day it rained and *exactly* what I was doing when it fell.

"Mom? What's going on with you? You're acting so weird."

Marin's eyes narrow over her menu, and Ethan doesn't even try to hide his smile. I hate them both.

"No, I'm just thinking how hard it would be in the rain."

I squeeze my eyes shut with a cringe at the accidental innuendo, and Ethan snorts.

"I'm starving. Would you believe I've been here all day and have only had a salad?" he says, flipping his menu and then tapping my foot under the table.

His hand finds my knee and gives it a squeeze.

I look at him.

Relax, he mouths silently.

Like it's just that easy.

Finn grabs a roll from a basket on the table and starts slathering butter on it. "I'm so glad to have real food. We had these dehydrated meals that were god-awful and then foraged for berries. I thought I was going to die."

I can't get comfortable in my seat, and no matter how much I rub my hands against my jeans, their moisture is endless. Two leaky faucets connected to my arms.

When the waitress takes our drink order, I ask for the largest glass of the best tequila they have, straight, earning a look from everyone at the table.

Even Ethan.

Especially Marin.

"So, how did you two run into each other once we left?" I think Marin says it, but I can't be sure.

"Your mom came in here and yelled at me in front of the dining room," Ethan says it so matter-of-factly both kids laugh.

"She has a tendency to do that," Finn says.

In the next few minutes, I mentally check out as they talk about camp, and Ethan tells stories from when his boys went to the same one a couple of years ago. I can't retell a single thing they say if my life depended on it.

When my drink finally arrives, I throw it back in a single gulp, and a loud gag from the hostile burn as it scorches down my throat.

Marin's eyebrows pinch together. "Mom, why are you so crazy right now?"

"Ethan and I had sex." I blurt the words, then slap my hand over my mouth.

"I knew it!" Marin yells at the same time Finn drops his napkin and yells, "Gross!"

Ethan covers his mouth with his hand but says nothing.

"I'm sorry, I just felt guilty and like you should know. And he didn't force me or anything. It was my idea completely, like I *really* wanted it. If anything, I forced him. And then it just kept happening. Every day, sometimes several times. Sitting here with both of you makes me feel like I was hiding this thing like I should be ashamed of it. But let me tell you, it was really very good. Great." I pause, cutting my eyes to Ethan. "Or at least I thought so."

The kids are still groaning when I stop. Ethan's eyebrows are sky high, hand still over his mouth.

Then I add, "I don't want to keep this weird secret or anything so... now you know, and I can probably relax a little and lay off the tequila." I smile and take a sip of my water.

The tension immediately melts from my shoulders as soon as my confession is out.

Finn's face is so pale I almost laugh. "Mom, we aren't kids," he says, running a palm across his forehead. "We know what happens when adults date. You never ever have to share that with us ever again. Ever. Again."

Ethan clears his throat. "So, your mom is a hard act to follow, but the special tonight is local mussels in a white wine sauce if that sounds good to anyone." Ethan barely keeps a straight face as I squeeze his knee under the table.

"You two are so obvious." Marin rolls her eyes and drops her menu. "And I ate clams I had to dig up for two weeks. I want a steak."

***

After my most inappropriate confession, dinner is perfect. To anyone watching who doesn't know us, they'd mistake us for a family by the way we laugh and talk all at once.

On the walk home, Ethan grabs my hand, and the fact I don't pull away confuses me from every angle. We're leaving. This is ending. But I hold his hand in front of my kids like neither of those things are real. Like we aren't in a losing race with the ticks of the clock. Like I have feelings that are going to last much longer than the time we have left together.

"So, you guys have a few days here—what are you going to do with them?" Ethan asks, tilting his head toward the kids. His question slinks around my heart and tightens.

"Sleep," Finn says.

"And take baths," Marin adds.

"Thank goodness I didn't hold out hope on you two seeing whales and puffins with me," I tease.

We stop in front of the mint green house, and Marin leans into Ethan with a hug.

"Thanks for dinner, Ethan. It was very entertaining," she says, pegging me with an amused look.

"Anything for a girl who survived two weeks in the wilderness."

His smile is as genuine as hers. They like each other, which makes what's coming next that much worse.

"Yeah, thanks."

Finn bumps his fist against Ethan's before him, and Marin walk up the steps to the house.

"I'll be right in," I say.

Finn nods, then they both disappear into the house.

Alone on the sidewalk, dread is a heavy ball in my stomach as I turn to face Ethan.

"Nel, I have to say I've never witnessed anything quite like that confession." The streetlight flickers in his eyes as his lips lift.

"I like to stay on brand," I say, shaking my head with a small laugh.

Then we're quiet, and the urgency I feel to memorize him becomes visceral.

I trace my fingers across his scruffy jaw, taking note of how every coarse piece of hair feels against my skin. My hand skims down the line of his throat, then the edge of his collarbone, before feeling the slope of every muscle down his arm.

His jaw tics at the movement, but he stays silent and still as I do the same thing up his other arm, collarbone, and jawline before settling my fingers at the longest of his hair at the top of his head. His eyes close, and he leans his cheek against my palm.

"What are you doing?" he says, voice deeper than usual.

"Memorizing you," I say. "So, I can see you when I can't. So, when you're gone, I can pretend you aren't."

It's hard to breathe. Hard to stand. Hard to stay glued together. Everything I feel standing next to Ethan on this sidewalk is driven by desperation—want, sadness, dread, hope, guilt, joy—it's all desperate. Devastatingly desperate.

No emotion exists alone.

"Nel—"

I cut my name off with my mouth, hoping the way I kiss him says everything I can't.

He grips his hands firmly in my hair, as if trying to hold me in place.

When I finally pull away, I'm wrecked.

His face fills with concern as he brushes a thumb across my face.

"You're crying," he says, dropping his forehead to mine.

I swipe my hand across my cheek and feel it covered in moisture.

Then he hugs me, tightly, and I sob into his chest. I don't try to hide it or minimize it. My cries come with shakes and gasps for air. My whole body is a sinking ship of sorrow.

"It's okay," he hums into my ear as he rubs circles on my back. "It's going to be okay. We have a few more days, and we can figure it out then."

He makes it sound so easy, like a mathematical equation we can solve with a calculator. Like he has no fucking clue how *not* okay this all is.

I don't try to convince him otherwise. I wipe my eyes and force a pained smile.

"I should go. The kids are probably worried I'm out here forcing you into sex again." I laugh despite my distress.

He chuckles and kisses me on the forehead. "I'll see you in the morning to make everyone breakfast. Nine?"

I nod, take a step away from him, and give him one last look.

"Goodnight, Ethan. Thank you... for everything."

Then, before I fall apart again, I hurry inside and close the door without looking back at him.

Back pressed to the inside of the door, Marin sees me over the top of her phone from the couch.

"Mom? What's wrong? Are you crying?" She stands and walks toward me.

I shake my head, wiping my eyes, waiting for my breathing to steady or my heart to give out.

"I'm fine, it's fine," I say, forcing yet another smile I don't feel. "I have a surprise for you guys. I knew when you got back, you wouldn't be up for much more of all of this, so we are actually flying home tomorrow. It's early. We have to be at the airport at 6:30, but we'll be in our own beds by tomorrow night. Grandpa and Poppy are picking us up in Miami."

"Hallelujah!" Finn drops his head back on the couch in relief. "No offense, Mom, this has been great, but I can't wait to be home."

His honesty makes me laugh.

Marin lowers her voice. "Is that why you're upset? You said goodbye to Ethan?"

"Something like that." I say, smiling for real this time, running my fingers through her hair. "Now, you two go pack your backpacks with as much as you can. I didn't buy luggage so let's just pray that the airline will accept our trash bags." I sniff through the last of my tears. "Uber will be here early."

When they scramble up the stairs, I grab a piece of paper and a pen.

Ethan,

This note is me taking the coward's way out. By the time you read this, we will be on a plane bound for Miami, and I will have probably cried myself to dehydration. I couldn't face a goodbye with you, not after the last two weeks. Not after the way you changed the way the sun rises and sets on my horizon by simply just existing on the same planet as me.

I need to finish what I've started with my kids—showing up in their lives actively and on purpose every day, not just when we are trapped in a camper—and I need to learn how to stand on my own two feet without needing someone to constantly prop me up.

I wanted to ask you to wait for me to find my way a hundred times, but I knew it wouldn't be fair to you. You have an amazing life and a line of women who do very dirty things to straws that I'd never want you to pass up on my account. Please know I will hate all those women fiercely until the day I die.

Of every beautiful mile we drove this summer, my favorite are the ones that led to you. You brought me back to life and made me remember who I am. A river that ran through me, changing me forever.

If I didn't have to leave, I would have loved you with every broken piece of me.

Nel

The next morning, our car pulls up, and we lug our bags and my oversized painting into the trunk. Then I tape the paper to the front door, Ethan's name scribbled across it.

Forty-seven

MY MOM KNOWS THE second she sees me something is off. I smile, I laugh, and I hug with gusto at the conveyor belt of baggage claim, but she sees every secret I can't keep.

"You love him." It's not a question. It's a statement of her delusion.

I scoff, shifting my luggage trash bag on my shoulder as we walk through the airport. "Love, Mom? That's a bit extreme."

"I knew I loved your dad the minute I met him. What's so ridiculous about you spending a few weeks with a man and feeling the same thing?" She looks entirely bewildered at the thought.

I shake my head. "It doesn't matter what it was or wasn't, not really. I'm here, and he's there, and each mile that separates us seems longer than the next. I want to focus on the kids now—enjoy our time together before Finn moves away and never wants to come back." I try for a joke, but nothing feels funny.

She hums knowingly. "Just remember, Penelope, no two loves are the same."

Piled into the car with my dad behind the wheel in a shirt covered in parrots, we spend the next hour driving toward the island we left behind almost two months ago. I crack the window as we cross the bridge from the mainland and let the familiar smells of saltwater that blow across water the color of Ethan's eyes, welcome us home.

It's after we're settled and starting loads of laundry that I work up the nerve to turn my phone on, holding my breath as the messages come through from Ethan in rapid fire.

A note? Really?

Nel, it doesn't have to be like this. We can figure it out.

Dammit, answer your phone.

Will you at least let me know you made it home?

My eyes burn like hot coals are jammed into them as I read and re-read his messages.

Finally, I find the courage to respond. *Hi* is all I can write.

A minute passes, then two, then finally three dots appear and disappear several times before a text.

Ethan: *Hi.*

My bones go soft just reading the word.

Ethan: *Did you mean what you wrote in your note?*

Me: *I did.*

Ethan: *Okay.*

Me: *Okay.*

When Marin finds me folding laundry late that night, I'm lost in the tangled web of my mind. She stands next to me and starts sorting.

"Do you think the trip worked, Mom?" She pinches two blue socks together and folds them in on each other.

"I think I'm done feeding you boxed food if that's what you mean," I say with a slight laugh.

She smiles. "Well, that's progress."

"Did camp work? You said you were looking for something to change and inspire you. Do you think it did?" I shake wrinkles out of a shirt with a loud snap of the fabric in the air.

She laughs softly under her breath.

"I don't know. It was one of those things I'm proud I did because it was hard, but I'm not on track to be a park ranger or anything."

"Well, that's too bad. You'd rock a ranger uniform," I tease.

She abandons folding the clothes and faces me. "What are you going to do about Ethan?"

I shrug. "There's nothing to do."

"I loved Maine," she says.

"Me too, kid."

***

The next morning, the kids are gone so early it's like they didn't just get home from a summer spent trekking around the country. Finn goes to baseball practice, and Marin goes to her friend's house.

Alone, with a coffee in hand that surprisingly doesn't taste nearly as bad as it used to, I replace the paintings in our living room with the one of the Androscoggin River. The corners and edges are tattered from being tossed around the Avion in the accident and then shoved with luggage on the plane ride to get home, but the bright colors that dapple the water and the vibrant lines that slope the mountains are still perfect.

I stare at it until I feel like I'm there. Until I can hear the whir of a fly rod and smell the smoke from a fire. I stare at it for so long that when the loud ring of my phone slices through the air, it makes me jump so high I spill coffee across my lap.

Dad flashes across the screen. I yelp from the heat of the coffee on my crotch as I answer, "Hey, Dad."

I pinch the phone between my ear and shoulder as I fumble to pull too many paper towels off the roll.

"Nelly! If you're up and moving, why don't you come by the bar? We can talk about menu changes and some ideas I have. Catch up."

What he means is, *time for work*, but I can hear his smile through the phone.

"Sure thing, Dad," I say as I blot madly at the brown liquid on my shorts. "Let me finish up here, and I'll be right over."

I end the call and give one last longing look at the painting.

After I change my shorts, I go meet my dad.

Not even twenty-four hours home, and summer already feels like a dream that never really happened.

***

We are back in my dad's office—the table he randomly selects next to the Gulf of Mexico under the palm frond thatched roof of the Crow's Nest. Only this time, in his shirt covered with coconuts wearing sunglasses, it's him who is speechless.

I didn't plan it, but sometimes ideas are like that. They are just seeds until they take root and start to grow so rapidly they overpower everything with their bigness.

There's a deep crease between my dad's eyes as his mustache twitches.

"Explain this to me one more time, Nelly. I'm struggling here. I didn't really fire you. I just wanted you to take the summer off—the summer!" he says, stunned.

"Dad, you know I love the bar, and you've always been good to me, so this isn't anything personal. It's just that when I was in Maine, I had the opportunity to teach someone how to run a bar better—just a glimpse of it—and I liked it. Loved it even. I thought maybe other bars would want to hire me to learn how to make what we have here. How to make drinks that are special to their target audiences. And nothing will ever be as fun as our place, but maybe I can show people how to make their own fun." I take a long sip of water as he looks out at the horizon and shakes his head.

"So, you're going to leave the Crow's Nest and do this full-time?" He drags his hand down the side of his face.

"Yes. No. I don't know!" I shake my head. "Maybe? Dad, I just want to try this. I love you and the people here, but sometimes it feels like someone else's dream I was dropped in. I've never done anything like this on my own, and it just seems like this big thing I'll always regret not trying."

His eyes fill with panic. "But what about when I retire? Who runs it then? I only have one year left in me before—"

I bark out a laugh without letting him finish, and a fresh shot of conviction lights up my chest.

"Dad, you've been threatening to retire for five years! And I'm not waiting—I don't want to—not because I don't love you, but because it's not what I want to wait for. I don't want to run this restaurant for the rest of my life."

My dad stares at me like he's seeing me for the first time, and I swear there's something like pride in his eyes. He sags back in his seat with a resigned sigh.

I soften. "I just need to try this. I won't leave you high and dry." I reach over and squeeze his arm as excitement and fear dance together in the pit of my stomach.

"The summer was good to you, Nelly," he says, studying me again as if he's trying to confirm it's really me sitting here.

"It was, Dad, it really was." I swallow the lump that's trying to form in my throat.

"Well, you can forget about adding any of those fancy fresh ingredients on the menu," he says before taking a sip of his beer.

And then, like I didn't just do one of the most difficult things of my life, I laugh.

Forty-eight

IN OUR FIRST WEEKS home, the kids and I find a new rhythm together. One where we sit around a table every night, with food I cook, and laugh about the day. Finn talks *(talks!)* about his life, including the fact that Abby has a new boyfriend, no surprise to Marin, without any of the resentment he had for me just months before.

Our trip forms a line of demarcation in our relationship that marks the us before and after.

The *me* before and after.

"So, I wanted to talk to you guys about something I've been thinking about. You know I love making drinks and Grandpa's bar, but lately, I've been wondering if I want to do something different," I say one night over dinner. I take a long sip of water and note Marin's saucer-sized eyes.

"When we were in Maine, and I went in and helped Ethan clean up his mess that first night, it was fun—a challenge. Different from what I do every day here. The idea of helping bar owners turn their business into something uniquely well-oiled might be a fun change for me. And with you guys getting older and getting ready to figure things out without me, I wondered if maybe I should give it a try."

I puff my cheeks up with air and wait.

"Mom, that's amazing! You would be so great at that. Maybe you could have one of those reality TV shows where you go in and yell at everyone until they get it together." Marin rubs her palms together maniacally. "Ohh! Or meet Gordon Ramsey!"

"God, your dad loved his show," I say, the words rolling off my tongue effortlessly and with a laugh. No wince, no dreaded prick behind my eyes, just a fond memory.

Marin snorts. "And always did a bad British accent when he watched."

"Remember that time he tried to make one of his recipes, and the oven caught on fire?" Finn shakes his head. "Lamb, right?"

I nod, nobody else saying anything as we look off in silence for a beat, reliving that ridiculous night of cooking.

"Anyway, what do you think, Finn? About consulting?"

Finn laughs. "Grandpa's going to flip."

I shake my head and watch the familiar wide leaves rustle in the breeze.

"I actually told him already, and there was no flipping. Plus, it's just a silly idea now. I've emailed a couple of my connections and lined up some trial consults. Then I guess we'll see what comes of it. I'll still be working at Grandpa's, at least part-time."

Marin's phone is out before I can finish my sentence. She swipes across the screen, typing at warp speed.

"Not silly, Penelope. Let's get you on social media."

***

In the middle of August, I drive up to the market in Homestead, a place I'd avoided since Travis died.

I stand at the entrance and freeze. The last steps—the ones that will take me into the bustling scene—feel almost impossible.

Somehow, I take them. I take them and don't bother to hide the way I, a forty-one-year-old woman, have tears running down her cheeks while smiling proudly because she's standing in the middle of a crowded market.

The sounds, smells, and tastes are all the same, like nineteen months haven't passed. Like it's just been standing here waiting for me to come back all along.

As much as I'm standing here in the middle of the crowd with bags of produce, I miss Ethan. I think of our date at the night market and the way he slipped his fingers through mine. With my eyes closed in the scorching heat in the middle of the crowd outside of Miami, I can almost taste the wine in the plastic cup and hear the bluesy music playing in the cool Maine air.

Without giving myself time to change my mind, I pull my phone out.

Me: *Hi.*

I bite my lip in the seconds that feel like an eternity it takes for him to respond.

Ethan: *Hi.*

I smile and snap a picture of one of the tables covered in peaches, then send it to him.

Me: *Peaches are in season.*

Ethan: *What are you going to do with them?*

Me: *Something with rum.*

Ethan: *You went to a market.*

Me: *I went to a market.*

My thumbs buzz to type more, but I don't.

I slide my phone back into my pocket right before I buy a bag of peaches.

That night, after several experiments, the peach mojito becomes the specialty drink for the rest of August. Pride swells as I write it in big loopy letters on the board with colorful chalk.

Proof that I had more living left to do.

Forty-nine

FINN SPENDS THE FIRST weekend of September fishing and surprises Marin and me with a full spread of fish tacos and homemade Pico de Gallo for dinner.

"Finn. This is amazing. What's this recipe?"

Every spicy and sweet flavor he used compliments the other perfectly.

"Derek sent it to me."

"Derek?" I choke mid-swallow. "I didn't know you kept in touch," I pause. "How are they? Him? He?"

Marin laughs. "Mom, you're so obvious. Why don't you just call Ethan? People have long-distance relationships all the time. It's not impossible. And July in Maine is a lot better than July in this hot inferno."

I scoff. "That's dramatic." I turn to Finn. "Either way, it's great. Tell Derek it's a winner."

How's Ethan? The question sits in my mouth until it dissolves.

I change the subject. "My first consulting gig is tomorrow. I'm helping a bar down near Key West revamp their drink menu."

"That's awesome. How does it work? Are you trucking the entire farmers market with you?" Marin teases before she takes her last bite of taco.

"Funny," I say, shooting her a look. "No. He sent me his menu already. I made notes and have some ideas on what would work." I shrug. "And I'm going to take it down there and pretend I know what I'm doing."

I laugh nervously.

"You know what you're doing," Finn says. It's a compliment. One that warms me from the inside out.

***

The next night, lying in bed, I'm riding a high I can't come down from. My first consult went so perfectly I had to pinch myself multiple times to make sure it was real.

The owner loved my ideas.

"I've never thought of cocktail flavors like that before. It's brilliant really!" he said after I suggested we complement the flavors of his food menu rather than focus on the cliché island staples like frozen daiquiris.

I showed the bartenders a couple of ways to make staple drinks using a couple of mangos, pineapples, and limes.

"If consulting doesn't work out, you're hired," he told me with a smile when we finished for the day.

I laughed in response. "My dad would never let that happen."

I can't stop smiling as I stare at the dark ceiling.

I did it. I'm *doing* it.

And then—Ethan. He's attached to every exciting part of this like a shadow. Without him, I wouldn't have known I could take this big scary leap.

I roll over and grab my phone off my nightstand.

Me: *Hi.*

Ethan: *Hi.*

I swallow hard before responding.

Me: *Apples are in season.*

Ethan: *They are.*

I miss you.

Delete.

What are you doing?

Delete.

Can I call you?

Delete.

Me: *Are you heading back to Bethel?*

Ethan: *Tomorrow.*

Me: *Don't forget to feed the birds.*

Ethan: *And to think you didn't want to play my game.*

Of all the things I want to say next, the only one that makes sense is nothing.

Fifty

"PENELOPE, BELLA JENKINS HERE. American Restaurant Magazine."

It's the end of September, and I've done five consulting jobs when she calls.

"Hey, Bella." I shift the phone on my shoulders, surprised to hear her voice. "How's it going?"

"Look, I know it's late notice, but we had something fall through for our next issue, and a little birdie told me you're dabbling in consulting. Would you be game for a last-minute piece to fill the spot? Just a picture and a short article on your business if you're interested."

I almost drop the phone. I've barely gotten my feet wet. My website isn't done, and the ink is barely dry on the business cards for Twist of Lime Consulting. In no way am I prepared for something as big as this.

"Bella, I'm flattered, but it's so new. Not that I wouldn't love it, it's just that I feel like a little bit of a fraud—I haven't even proven I can do this yet, let alone deserve an article in your magazine." I pick at the skin around my thumb.

"Are you kidding me?" I hear keys clicking on a keyboard. "You've won most fun restaurant—twice! You've proven yourself. And we can spin it as one of those *taking the leap into uncharted territories* type stories if you're so worried about it. Plus, the issue is filled with men. We need a woman. Can I send a photographer down next week?"

My veins feel like they've been pumped full of champagne as a fizzy feeling flows through me.

When I hear myself say, "Let's do it!" I can't help but smile.

"Perfect. I'll email you the details."

"Hey, Bella?"

"Yeah?"

"How did you find out about this?"

"You tagged the magazine in one of your social media posts—it got our attention."

Marin.

"Great, thanks again."

Shock is the only word I can use to describe how I feel as I end the call. Telling my family I am trying this is one thing, but telling the entire industry is completely different. Bile rises in my throat at the thought of it, but there is no time for puking.

Work now, puke later.

The phone call lights a fire of urgency under me I haven't had before. I'm not about to have my name blasted out only to not be able to deliver. Even if I fail, I'm hellbent on failing looking like I know what I'm doing.

By the middle of October, I'm only working at the Crow's Nest once a week.

I've fine-tuned the packages listed on my website. They range from single-day training with the bar staff to three-day options where I observe the operations for a night before fixing what's broken and changing the menu. The largest package lasts for three months where I visit the bar several times over that period and fine-tune every aspect of the operations with the owner.

A man in Miami who gets my name from a friend of a friend of my dad books me for the entire month of November for his bars across southern Florida.

It's surreal.

When I lay in bed most nights, I feel like I've spent the days skydiving, sleeping with a dose of adrenaline that I never seem to shake.

I imagine Travis would have been proud of me for taking the risk if he'd known that this idea was lurking inside of me, but when I'm honest with myself in those moments, it isn't Travis I long to talk to every night. It's Ethan.

Since I texted him at the beginning of September, I haven't heard from him. I don't admit to myself the number of times that the buzz of a new message makes my heart skip a beat at the possibility it might be from him. I don't acknowledge that every time the phone rings, I hope it's his name that flashes across the screen.

I don't dare let my mind wander to what he's doing or who he's doing it with.

On a Saturday morning in late October, when the weather almost resembles fall, I give in and pull out my phone.

Me: *Hi.*

His response is an instant, *Hi.* and I can't help but wonder if he's checking his phone the same way I check mine.

Me: *Beets are in season.*

Ethan: *I'm not drinking that cocktail.*

I laugh.

I miss you.

Delete.

Me: *What are you doing right now?*

He sends a picture of his coffee mug sitting on the ledge around his porch, the trees in the background blazing with every fiery color of fall around the same river I stare at every morning in my living room.

My heart sputters. I can feel it, cool and crisp, probably smelling like a campfire and evergreens. I snap a picture of my mug with the clear blue sky and bright green palm trees in the background and send it in response.

We're parallel lines, living the same life, doing the same things, so many miles away we'll never intersect.

Me: *I bought a French press. Remember when you taught me to use one?*

Ethan: *Barely.*

I roll my eyes.

Me: *You're kind of a dick.*

Ethan: *I've heard those dicks just fly out of the woodwork sometimes.*

I grin like an idiot at the reference.

He doesn't send another message. Much to my dismay, neither do I.

Fifty-one

NOVEMBER COMES IN LIKE a whirlwind.

Between Marin taking a part-time job washing hair at a local salon, Finn's busy practice schedule, and my lousy attempt at balancing working at my dad's bar and consulting jobs, the dinners we sit down together that had been so regular after summer now feel like a rare treasure.

"We should make you your own hashtag so then when bartenders take photos during the training, they can use the tag."

I have no idea what this means, but I nod absently as I scoop salad into bowls.

"Maybe." I hum, suddenly extremely thankful she's the one who manages my social media account.

"There's a girl I'm thinking of asking out," Finn says as he twirls spaghetti onto a fork.

My eyes burn instantly. Not because he's growing up, those tears had been shed long ago, but because the simple statement shows how far we've come together.

"Really? Anyone I know?" I try to say it casually like this is no big deal, but I can't hide my ridiculous smile or the too-excited tone of my voice.

"Catie Johnson, I think you might know her dad." He eyes me. "And don't be weird. Your smile is creepy."

I laugh. "I went to school with her dad, Mike. He's friends with Gabe, actually. Good guy."

"Catie Johnson?!" Marin's eyes widen. "Finny, way to go. She's on the volleyball team and volunteers for beach clean-ups. She's basically the opposite of She-Who-Must-Not-Be-Named."

I snort at the Abby reference. "She sounds great, Finn. You should invite her over for dinner or something. Or now that the Avion is gone, we can do something with the shed so you can have friends over to hang out."

"Okay," he says.

"Okay."

I don't cry or hug him or do a dancing scream as my heart swells until it's too big for my body when he simply smiles at me. I just nod, twirl my spaghetti, and act like that conversation didn't just make every single hard one worth it.

***

The day the magazine comes out in the last week of November, I'm drunk on disbelief.

My dad closes The Crow's Nest to the public, and we have a big dinner with family and close friends to celebrate. When he holds up the page as he stands at the head of the table, everyone cheers.

"Penelope Crawford takes her unique cocktail-creating skills and award-winning flair for creating a fun atmosphere of her family's business to the next level, offering her skills to bar owners everywhere who want to run their business with more efficiency, fun, and creativity with her consulting services at Twist of Lime Consulting."

Despite how hard the transition has been for my dad, his voice drips with pride as he reads the words out loud.

I look at the picture in his hands and can barely believe it's me. There I am, standing in the green dress I bought in Maine, leaning against the bar with a huge grin on my face and a cocktail shaker in my hand.

"Speech!" Gabe calls through cupped hands.

The cry echoes around as fists pound against the table, making plates and silverware rattle loudly.

I stand up with a glass of wine in my hand. "Okay, okay." I face a palm toward them. "I'd like to take this moment to thank my parents for irresponsibly raising me behind a bar and helping me learn every inappropriate thing I didn't know I needed to know."

They laugh, hug each other with a kiss, and smile like I've just given them the biggest compliment of their lives.

"And to Gabe, for letting me make bad cocktails for him when he was way too young to be drinking them."

He cheeses a grin and holds up his beer like it's a trophy, earning a laugh from everyone and a playful slap to his chest from Jenny.

"To all those spring breakers who sat on barstools and ordered ridiculous shots I had to fumble my way through every single year."

My dad nods at that one, raising his glass, no doubt recalling how much of a headache that time of year can be.

"To Marin and Finn." My voice cracks in two the second I say their names. "For believing in me and loving me no matter how much I mess up. For waiting for me to get my head out of the sand. For helping me find my way. I would never have done this if I didn't know they weren't beside me."

Tears carve rivers down my face I don't bother wiping. Across the length of the table, my mom dabs her eyes. Finn gives me a small smile as Marin interlaces her fingers with mine.

"And to..."

Ethan.

His name fills my mouth with every unsaid confession.

"...to everyone that drank a cocktail I created. Thank you for believing in me enough to get me here."

I raise my glass and smile.

Then, all the glasses were in the air, clanking together in my honor, and my heart bursts at the beautiful sound of it.

***

"Penelope. I'm proud of you."

My mom leans next to the commercial sink in the restaurant's empty kitchen as I rinse the plates from dinner.

"Thanks, Mom. Really. For everything."

"I think you should go get that man in Maine."

I drop the glass I'm holding into the soapy sink with a loud crash at the unexpected statement.

"Mom..."

She shakes her head, holding her hand up to silence me.

"You listen to me, Penelope. You left this island with one kind of heartache, and you came back with another. *Unnecessarily.* Maybe it will go nowhere, maybe it will be difficult, but this will be a regret you will never recover from if you don't try."

A chain of fear tightens around me. "What if it's too late? Mom, the man is..." I flip through every word that fails to accurately describe the breadth of Ethan. "Incredible. And thoughtful. Women notice him. And I'm—"

"*Incredible,*" she interrupts. "You are too hard on yourself and see something different from everyone else. And you won't know if it's too late if you don't try." She arches an eyebrow.

I shake my head as I scrub the next plate.

"What about the kids? And the distance? And what if I'm not ready?"

"Excuses," she scoffs, drying a plate. "You don't have to be a martyr to be a mother, Penelope. They are growing up—are you going to make them choose between a relationship with you and someone else?"

I don't answer.

"And the distance?" She shrugs. "You'll figure it out. You *are* ready. You weren't a year ago, but you are today."

I chew my lip.

"So, tell me." She pauses, looking at me like she's the devil. "How was the sex?"

I snort and shake my head. "You're worse than Marin."

She eyes me, her silent *and?*

I relent, saying, "and it was amazing."

She smiles smugly. "I thought so."

***

When I get home, there's a text from Ethan.

Just a picture of the article in the magazine without anything else.

Me: Hi.

Ethan: Hi.

I think about what my mom said as I decide what to write next.

Me: *Brussels sprouts are in season this month—I'm wondering what your thoughts are on that.*

Ethan: *The magazine is going to retract the article if you keep talking like that, Penelope.*

Goosebumps cover my skin as I imagine his voice saying my name like warm honey.

I hate how much I miss him. Hate how he has stained my insides so deeply I can't scrub him away, even with all the miles between us.

I thought that leaving him behind would make it easier for me to focus on the other wobbly pieces of my life. All it does is create a weird constant ache every time I notice he isn't here.

Which is always.

Travis died, and it was against my will. I couldn't stop it any more than I could stop the endless sadness that followed. But Ethan? I walked away from him all on my own. The ache in my chest is by my own design.

Me: *I did it.*

Ethan: *You did.*

The words, *Because you told me I could,* go unsent along with every other thing I want to tell him.

Fifty-two

ROCKS GLASSES LINE THE bar as a group of jersey-clad bartenders eye them with skeptical boredom.

"Aside from making excellent cocktails and being someone people actually like talking to behind the bar, the best way to enhance the bar experience for your guests is to add a little flair to how you do it."

My voice is overly enthusiastic as I ignore the phone that's vibrating in my pocket.

"This is a sports bar, with actual sports being played while watching sports being played."

I smile, meeting each of their eyes.

"Consider what we have going on in here. We have people golfing." I point to two putting greens. "Basketball." I nod toward the arcade-style basketball hoops. "Ping-pong tables, shuffle boards... whatever that punching bag thing is called."

My finger bounces through the air and points to more sporting activities than I knew existed. While the covered seating area leads out to a courtyard of games without walls or a roof, the enclosed space around the bar is covered in team pendants and sporting equipment.

It takes the concept of sports bar to a new level. The dull staff? Not so much.

"So... who are your people? Who wants to come here?" I ask with a too-big smile, compensating for their lack of cheer with an abundance of my own.

When the Tampa sports bar owner booked this consultation, he told me there was a disconnect between the vision he had and the way the atmosphere felt. The eight blank faces that stare at me confirm his thoughts. "Anyone?"

"Sports fans," a girl answers in a monotone voice.

"Good. Sports fans. Who else?"

"Men," another one says flatly.

"Men. Good, but let's go deeper than that. Forget about gender or if they watch the Bucs every Sunday. *Who* are these people?" I raise my eyebrows.

"Competitive."

The slightest bit of enthusiasm peeks through the answer.

"Fun."

"Laid back."

"Playful."

"Bingo!" I clap my hands. "The people that come here want to *play*. You might get people who randomly complain about the volume on the TV, but for the most part, your guests come here to have some fun, and play. The bar needs to follow suit. *You* need to follow suit."

I drop a bucket of ice on the bar, and their eyes lock onto it.

"Do we get to dump it on the heads of bad tippers?" a guy with a shaved head jokes, making the others laugh.

"I won't say no, but your boss might not love it." I smile. My phone vibrates in my pocket.

Again.

This time, I pull it out to make sure it isn't a family emergency before seeing a number I don't recognize and shoving it back into my pocket.

"Sorry about that," I mumble, refocusing my attention. "If you're having fun, your guests are more likely to be having fun. According to the sales, your guests are drinking beer and basic cocktails. Specialty drinks make up a very small portion of orders. Fancy cocktail techniques will serve no real purpose. People aren't expecting fancy martinis when they walk in these doors, right?"

They nod in agreement.

"So, what we are going to do is add some play in how we make basic cocktails—rum and coke, gin and tonic, vodka and cranberry—starting with how we get ice in the cups. We'll start easy and work up to something harder."

I pick up a piece of ice with tongs and toss it from behind my back, sending it flying over my shoulder to the front of my chest, where I catch it in a glass.

"Hey-ooooh!" one of them calls with a fist up to his mouth.

I grin and hold the glass up. "Let's start by just tossing it up in front of you and catching it, then we'll go from there. Any questions?"

They shake their heads, but instead of boredom, they're now eager.

"Okay, get to work!"

In an instant, they are tossing ice, laughing at themselves and each other. The owner, leaning in the doorway on the other side of the bar, lifts his chin and smiles before walking away.

The pride that starts to burn is doused out by the overwhelm that comes with the vibration of my phone in my pocket.

Again.

I rip it out and stare at the unknown number before sending it to voicemail.

It makes seven.

Seven voicemails in three hours requesting more information about scheduling consults.

Two weeks after the magazine article came out, my life is being catapulted into an alternate universe. I knew there would be an impact, but I'm drowning as I try to navigate it. Phone calls, emails, and Marin's social media inquiries blur together on a never-ending to-do list. This is what I wanted, what I got, and now I can't handle it. It's a frustrating kind of defeat.

"Got it, Nel!" a voice calls from behind me as ice clatters against a glass, and a cheer follows.

I press my finger against the power button and turn my phone off. I'll have to deal with it, just not now.

"Excellent! Let's try it with a partner."

Then, I toss another piece of ice into the air.

***

"Hey, Mom, how did it go?" Marin's face fills my screen as I sprawl across the hotel bed.

"Hey—good. It was fun. They were a little dead in the beginning, but I think by the end, they got a lot out of it."

"You look tired." My parents flash behind her on the screen with a wave.

"I am."

My eyes drop to the notebook with names, cities, and dates scribbled across it.

"I have a list of people who have reached out to me and no clue when I'm going to call them or how I'm going to schedule all this."

She shrugs, saying, "Hire someone."

It doesn't make much financial sense yet, but with my sanity on the line, it's the best idea I've got. If someone else can deal with scheduling and emails, I can just focus on the work I want to do.

"I might have to." I look back to the endless list next to me again. "Where's Finn?"

"Practice."

I nod.

"How was school?"

"Fine."

She flips through a book I can't see on the screen.

"I'll be home tomorrow."

"Sounds good."

"Love you."

"Love you, too."

I hang up with a tired sigh. I'm exhausted and doing a shitty job of managing everything. The work is fun, but the logistics are complicated and foreign. After a lifetime of shifts of work where I just showed up at the same place at the same time, this is a problem I hadn't thought of.

Marin is right. I need help.

Despite being exhausted, I open my computer. While it powers up, I tap the screen of my phone.

Me: *Hi.*

Ethan: *Hi.*

Me: *I'm wondering if I'm supposed to feel like I'm drowning 24/7?*

Ethan: *Every entrepreneur would say yes.*

Ethan: *Anything I can help with?*

I swallow hard as I read and re-read the question.

Yes. Fly here. Call me.

As usual, I write anything but.

Me: *A warning would have been nice.*

Ethan: *It's more fun this way.*

Fifty-three

NADINE IS A PART-TIME college student who wears thick glasses, has frizzy black hair, and is possibly the most organized person on the planet. The day I hired her, she showed up with color-coded schedules and spreadsheets that changed my life. She is an organizational superhero.

"I got your travel booked for the next few months."

Nadine's perky voice comes through the phone on our now daily call.

"What are we looking at?"

"Next week, you are in Atlanta for a single day of training, then off for two weeks for the holidays if you want to squeeze in one of the local requests we have. January, I have you booked for three days in Charleston, South Carolina, then the initial meeting for an ongoing gig with an owner in Bangor, Maine."

My pulse skyrockets. "Maine? What's that one?"

I click the pen I'm holding furiously.

"Umm..." I hear Nadine click through screens on her computer. "Sounds fun. It's someone who is considering a restaurant in the city but isn't sure how it could stand out against what's already there. Very early stages. They paid the full fee already. Basically, she has a building and some ideas but nothing else. They want to get an idea of what you think would work in the environment, yada yada. Name is something Donalds."

I google Bangor, Maine, shifting my phone to my other ear. "Yeah, that does sound fun. All right, well, email all those over to me, and I'll text you anything else. Thanks, Nadine."

I hang up, looking at the map on my screen. It's just over a hundred miles from Bangor to Bethel. I could add a couple days onto the trip and go see Ethan and... What? Say hi? Dry hump his leg? Give an awkward speech declaring my love?

I rub my forehead.

Me: *Hey, can you extend my trip to Bangor for the whole week?*
Nadine: *Sure thing, Boss. Anything else?*
Me: *That's it. Thanks!*

And just like that, once again, I'm going to Maine.

***

I'll never understand why Miami sells winter clothes, but they do. This is why, the week before my trip to Maine in mid-January, I drag my mom and Marin with me to the city to go shopping.

"Penelope, show some skin. You look like a nun."

Eyes narrowed, my mom pinches at the sweater I'm wearing like it's a piece of rotten produce.

"It's twenty-three degrees in Maine, Mom. Showing skin will kill me," I argue.

She scoffs and turns up her nose. "Well, you won't win him over looking like that, that's all I'm going to say. I mean, a turtleneck?" she huffs. "It's blasphemous to a woman's body!"

With this declaration, her arms are in the air.

"Mom," Marin interjects. "How about we get a nice coat, and then whatever you wear under it can be less... nun-ish."

Ever the mediator, my Marin.

My mom eyes me over the lingerie she's holding. I don't even want to know if she's looking at that for her or me.

"So, what's the plan? Are you just going to go in there, guns blazing, with some cleavage and jump on the bar licking your lips or what?" she asks.

I roll my eyes. "What kind of plan is that, Mom? No, I'm just going to walk in and say hi. And then I'll see what happens. There's a very good chance he's dating someone. Hell, I might walk in and find him making out with another woman at the bar." My stomach twists at the visual.

"Why don't you just call him and find out?" she asks.

Like I haven't thought about that every single day since I flew from there.

"And say what? Hey Ethan, I can't stop thinking about you even though I ran away from you, and you still live in Maine?" I shake my head. "No, I'll chicken out. I just need to go see for myself and then figure it out. Maybe I'll see him, and he won't be as attractive as he was six months ago. Like maybe I was in such a different headspace that it will all be... uglier. Like desperation made me do it."

Lie.

My mom and Marin exchange a look as they send me back into the dressing room, arms full of everything that isn't a turtleneck.

***

I'm on my second day of freaking out, but there's no backing out. I'm going to do this scary thing even if I piss my pants in the process. I cycle through a million different ways how walking into Ethan's restaurant unannounced might backfire on me. Him being married is the absolute worst-case scenario, I decide, but him kissing a woman at a dark, quiet table rivals it.

What if he's not even there? Do I drive to his house? God knows what I might find there.

No.

I'll show up, he's going to be casually working as he always is, and I'm simply going to say hello, and I shouldn't have left the way I did.

I can do that.

Can I do that?

The distance between us hasn't changed, so why I think I can handle this whole situation better than I did six months before, is beyond me.

Maybe it's because I have family dinners with my kids that aren't filled with contempt.

Or because I told my dad I wanted something different in my career.

I know that's not why.

It's because, at the end of every day, I want to hear his voice and tell him everything.

Pacing the kitchen, I pull out my phone.

Me: *Hi.*

Ethan: *Hi.*

I have no clue what to say.

Me: *Isn't it kind of weird that anything is in season in January? Where does it all grow?*

I cringe.

Ethan: *It is. My guess is Florida.*

I drop my head against the kitchen cabinet with a groan. He's probably sitting casually, like this is no big deal, while I'm on the brink of dying a slow death.

Me: *Have you met anyone?*

I chew my pinky nail aggressively, drink an entire glass of water, and chew my pinky nail again while three dots appear and disappear.

Ethan: *I have.*

My heart drops straight to the floor and breaks.

Me: *Is it serious?*

His response is an instant, *It is.*

He met someone, just like I expected. Expecting and accepting, I realize, will not coexist in my body when it comes to this.

Him.

Me: *Me too.*

Ethan: *You're still a terrible liar, Penelope.*

My cheeks sting with heat.

Bastard.

The smart thing to do would be to drop it. He'll never know I'm in Maine. I can go to the meeting, stay in Bangor, and never go to Bethel.

This is one of the many lies I tell myself while I lay in bed that night and pretend to sleep.

Fifty-four

MAINE IN JANUARY IS the coldest place I have ever been. Even in the middle of the afternoon, the sun does nothing to warm this part of the earth. It's frigid.

I check my reflection in the rearview mirror. The last time I was in Bangor, I was wearing rubber boots, a flannel shirt, and had bloodshot eyes as I boarded a plane with a trash bag. Now, I stand in a creamy silk blouse, fitted dress pants, leather ankle boots, and red lipstick.

Ethan probably won't even recognize me.

Nope.

Ethan is tomorrow's problem.

I've negotiated with myself if I can keep my cool through the afternoon meeting, I'll allow myself to have a proper meltdown the moment I get back to my hotel.

I'll stay in Bangor for the night and drive to Bethel tomorrow. What I'm going to say to him, I have no idea. But I have plenty of time to over-analyze that plan tonight.

The empty brick warehouse stands at the edge of the city and looks like a human hasn't entered it in decades. Piles of plowed muddy snow sit around the parking lot while patches of ice fill in the cracks of the pavement. Summer in Maine had been beautiful, but the way the freezing wind cuts across my skin in winter is completely miserable.

I twist on the old knob, and some of the peeling paint that covers the wooden door flakes off as it creaks open. A surprising rush of warmth blows out to greet me, along with the loud hum of a furnace.

"Hello?" My voice echoes around the big, empty room.

No response.

I'm stunned by how different the inside is from the out. Outside, it looks abandoned, but inside, it has the potential to be spectacular. Exposed brick covers every wall as partially broken bulbed ropes of lights drape haphazardly across a high exposed beam ceiling. The floor is concrete, which I imagine will pop if refinished.

My boots click against the floor as I walk. There's a small bar that would maybe seat six, covered with dust and chairs. Whatever this building originally was, someone converted it into some sort of entertainment space afterward.

I click across the room and push through a set of doors that surprisingly lead to a small and very outdated kitchen. I bite my lip. A kitchen reno would be expensive, making me wonder if it would be smarter to focus on an upscale bar experience with a limited menu of small plates versus a traditional full-blown restaurant.

The door creaks open from the front of the building, and a wave of anxiety washes over me. I'm confident in what I can bring to the table, but this is a big project, my biggest one yet.

As I make my way toward the door of the kitchen, a large stack of familiar-looking canvases leans against a corner and makes me stop.

I crouch down next to them—recognition striking like a bolt of lightning.

I thumb through them. Bright colors cover mountainous landscapes, one identical to the oversized piece that now hangs in my living room, and cityscapes that I assume are of Bangor. R. Donalds is scribbled on the bottom corner of each.

Wait—*what?*

The artist is opening a bar? It doesn't seem right. She was close to seventy when I met her. Not that she couldn't tackle the project. It just seems so... big. Maybe a relative? A daughter even?

I glance at the papers for the meeting, Rhonda Donalds' name on the paper clear as day. I missed the connection.

Footsteps grow louder as they cross the big room toward the kitchen, where I'm still kneeling, attention back on the paintings. I can't move. I'm hypnotized and confused as I let my hands trace the familiar colorful strokes of each one.

Rhonda, from little Bethel, Maine, has a stack of paintings in a warehouse in Bangor owned by someone with the same name.

How?

"She sends her regards," a familiar voice says from behind me.

Time stops right along with my heart as I slowly stand and turn around.

I see the eyes before the smirk. "Ethan," I whisper shakily, taking him in.

Ethan is standing in a suit looking like every woman's fantasy, and I have zero words. I'm dumbfounded. And, against my delusional thinking, the thick hair on the top of his head, sharpness of his jaw, and hard lines and angles that make him *him* are still just as attractive.

"Penelope," he drawls.

After not hearing his voice in so long, the depth of it makes me lightheaded.

He leans against the brick wall casually, like this isn't one of the most jarring experiences of my life, as the file of papers I've been holding falls to the ground and scatters like confetti.

"How?"

I don't move. My feet are glued to the concrete floor in shock and disbelief.

"I didn't know if you'd come if I used my name, and Rhonda gave me permission to use hers. I've become one of her best customers," he says, tugging at one of his sleeves.

The room spins like a Tilt-o-Whirl.

I look around the dated kitchen. "This building?"

"Mine."

His gaze meets mine and makes my blood flow backwards in my veins.

I nod, swallow, and nod again.

"Why am I here?" I finally ask.

He studies me intensely before pushing off the wall and taking a few steps toward me.

"Because I value your opinion. I bought this building for an incredible price on a whim, but I'm not sure what to do with it. I hoped you would."

His tone is all business, and I can't help but feel the slightest bit disappointed in that.

"Right. Of course."

I shake my head to recalibrate and crouch down to pick up all the papers I'd dropped, summoning whatever sort of grace I can grasp at to make it through the rest of this meeting like the professional I claim to be.

I feign composure as I look at the ceiling and anywhere but him, heart hammering in my chest, ears, and every space in between.

"I walked around before you got here. It's a gorgeous building." My voice is shaky, but at least I'm able to speak. "I did a little research on Bangor before getting here. The population demographics make me think you could swing a couple different options in here, but the cost of renovating might be something to consider."

I thumb through the once-organized file of papers to find my notes. My fingers tremble across every piece.

"It's big enough you could do whatever you want, but my first impression is to give it a speakeasy vibe. If you extend the bar and create a menu of top-shelf cocktails, I'm imagining lots of smoky options or maybe fancy martinis. If you made the focus the bar, you wouldn't have to do a huge kitchen expansion. You could do small plates and appetizers."

I walk out of the kitchen first and look around the space again, imagining velvet couches and eclectic seating spaced all around, with Rhonda's colorful paintings on the wall.

The nervous energy surging through me makes it hard to stand still. "Do you not like it?"

"You're as good at this as I thought you'd be."

I feel my neck grow warm with the compliment, and I look in the opposite direction of him. "Thank you for saying that."

I pull on the belt of my coat as he takes a step closer to me, every cell of my body going on high alert.

"Do you like what you're doing?"

An easy smile lifts my lips. "I love it." That's the easy, honest, truth. The change of pace and time on the road had been an adjustment, but I love what I'm doing.

He nods before eyeing the bar. "Tell me what you'd do with this."

I walk around to it, and he follows closely. So close the heat that fires up my neck and burns at my cheeks forces me to shed my jacket. All the while, Ethan is casual, smug, and annoyingly handsome. Seeing him so immune to the situation unnerves me even more. He walks with ease while I'm completely coming undone. My mouth doesn't know if it wants to water like a faucet or go as dry as a bone.

"It's too small right now to be anything, really. If you want this to be the focus, you need to extend it..." I think for a second. "Actually, you know what might be interesting? Opting for high tops close by and cozy booths around the floor space. Maybe somehow having the bar not be where you have people sit but maybe more of a stage where the entertainment is seeing the bartender make the drinks."

"Hmm."

"Too weird?" I ask, laughing for the first time since he walked in.

"Maybe not." He shrugs. "Why booths?"

"Booths are shown to increase average ticket prices. People get cozy, they want to stay longer, they order more drinks." I lift my shoulder. "If this is higher end, it's a win, but if you're trying to turn tables, it might not be your best bet."

He scrubs a hand over his scruff-covered jaw and looks around the space.

Then, as if I have no control of my mouth, I hear myself ask, "So, you've met someone serious? Not that they are serious, but you know, like that you are serious with, in that kind of exclusive sort of way. Not that it's my business or that I'd expect anything like, you know, you *not* to be." I try to look disinterested as I shuffle through papers before I let my eyes flick to his face.

His lips twitch. "I have."

Two words I don't want to believe in.

"Good." I clear my throat. "I mean, that's great. For you. And her. And you as a duo." I rub my forehead and scrunch my nose. "You know what I mean."

I don't let him respond before I pivot back to business. "So typically, with these consultations, the owner is a little further along in the process. From here, we can talk about menu ideas, but I guess you need to decide what you want this to be and how much you want to spend. Obviously, you can already successfully run a restaurant, so there would just be a few things to consider if you decide you want this one to be more of a bar."

I try to squeeze by the space he takes up behind the bar to get to some distance, but even barely touching him sends awareness shooting through me.

"Is this going to be another Mainely Local business, or are you thinking about something different?" I ask.

"You look good, Nel."

The simple compliment makes my heart skip like a pebble thrown across flat water. "Thanks. Same. You look the same. Good." I laugh through an exhale, adding, "Good enough to still make me babble like an idiot."

I shake my head and relieve some of the tension that's been swelling since he walked in and wrecked my ability to think, speak, and see straight.

His eyes meet mine, familiar smirk tugging at his lips.

"There's a restaurant down the street. Let's go grab dinner. I'll tell you what I'm thinking for a menu, and we can go from there."

No.

This man admitted to being in a serious relationship. I will not be that woman. My body might be a pandemonium of hormones, lighting up with every word he says like there's a chance in hell this is going any further, but my mind is not. Dinner is the absolute worst idea. From this point forward, I can handle everything over email with my fancy letterhead.

I'll come see him when he's up and running, and there's a staff to train. End of story.

When I open my mouth, I'm adamant I'm going to walk away, but, "Sounds good," is the only thing that comes out.

My mouth betrays me right along with my body.

Fifty-five

ETHAN FOLLOWS ME TO the hotel I'm staying at and waits in the lobby while I go up to my room. I just need a few minutes to freak the hell out in peace and quiet before doing whatever stupid thing I'm doing.

Self-destructive behavior, I believe an expert would call it.

He hired me to do a job, albeit sneakily, but no matter what I feel and he doesn't, I have to figure out how to manage my feelings or refund his money.

No.

In the scheme of everything else I have done in the last two years, this project will be a small blip we can handle over a few phone calls and emails and maybe only two or three more in-person meetings once he hires a staff, which would be months and months away.

Easy.

I've seen him, he's in a relationship, and I will get over my feelings.

This is not a big deal.

Twenty minutes later, I'm in the lobby wearing a fitted green turtle-neck sweater—the only one my mom and Marin would let me buy—and black skinny jeans.

I do not let the fact his tie is loosened around his neck nor how his eyes are burning affect me.

I also ignore how he almost paralyzes me when he puts his hand on the small of my back when he leads me into the restaurant. I barely notice how my body responds to the simple act of him rolling up his sleeves as we sit at our table.

When I openly stare at him as he orders a bottle of wine, it's not because he looks good. It's because he doesn't. This is what I tell myself over and over.

He leans back in his chair, props an elbow on the table, and crosses a foot to his knee. He is the epitome of relaxation, and it makes every inch of my body itch.

"What are you thinking about?" he asks as he twirls the stem of his wine glass.

I do what I have to, I lie.

"I was thinking if you wanted to do something different, you could train the bar staff in smoked cocktails. I know a few methods, but it might be something you'd want to consider letting me bring an expert in for. I don't think any bar in Bangor does it, but I'd have to double-check."

I slide a paper I'd written out a few of my favorites on across the table to him.

"The smoked Manha—"

"You didn't tell me you were coming here." He cuts me off as he pushes my notes to the side without even as much as a glance toward them.

"Well, to be fair, neither did you." I raise an eyebrow, lifting my wine glass to my lips. "And I was planning to come see you in Bethel after this meeting I was bamboozled into."

He snorts. "Bamboozled is a stretch. There really is a business, and I really need help. I just used a different name." He shrugs as if to say, *what's the big deal?*

I sigh. "I didn't want you to tell me not to come. I wanted to show up and see you with my own two eyes, for better or worse. Though the fact you've met someone you're serious about, it's probably for the best I didn't have a chance to let some kind of weird confession fly out of my mouth."

"You?" He snorts. "Never."

I look at him until it's too uncomfortable.

Voice low, he says, "You looked away, Penelope."

The reference catches in my throat. "Well, old habits and all that," I say quietly, staring at my wine glass so long I see two of them.

"How are the kids?"

"Excellent!" I smile proudly. "Marin helped me brand my business, and Finn has a new girlfriend, is gearing up for baseball season, and apparently trades recipes with Derek."

He nods, telling me everything I need to know. Ethan knew they were staying in touch, which means *they* must also know he's seeing someone. They let me walk right into this situation with false hope.

Everyone is getting grounded when I get home.

"The boys?" I ask, pushing the feeling I've been backstabbed by my own children aside.

"Good. Austin is back at school, and Derek just told me he plans to go to culinary school after he graduates. He works with me in the kitchen a couple of nights a week and doesn't even yell at me."

He smiles the entire time he talks about them.

I'm not surprised by the news at all.

"I wanted to call you. A lot," I confess, startling myself. "When Finn told me about his girlfriend, when I started the business, and when I had my first consulting booking. The days I was at the market. I wanted to call you after all of them, but I just didn't know what to say and if it would make everything worse. I know you're with someone you care about. God help us if it's Deep Throating Brooke, but I just wanted you to know. Just so you know, I meant it all."

I rearrange the silverware in front of me.

"I would have waited, Penelope. For however long it would have taken, I would have. I meant it all, too."

His throat moves slowly as he swallows, and we sit in a loud silence, staring at each other.

"Filet mignon with a sweet potato?"

I sigh with audible relief when the waiter interrupts the tension.

As we eat, our conversation easily shifts to lighter topics. He asks about my dad, who never localized his menu. I ask about his bartending skills, which he's been working on. Talking to him is like it's always been—good, familiar, and so easy it makes my soul ache.

In that moment, I know I've missed out on one of the best things I could have had in life.

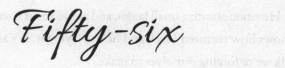

Fifty-six

WHEN OUR DINNER IS gone, and a female blues singer takes a small stage with a gritty, soulful voice, the dim lights and soft, sexy music make me feel things I don't want to. It reminds me of the nights at Ethan's restaurants, and my heart splinters in all the ways it paints a picture of a scene I'll never be part of again.

He leans back casually.

"Tell me something I've missed from the last six months."

I regret leaving Maine the way I did.

I've missed you every day for six months.

My mom thinks I love you.

I might love you.

I do love you.

I love Ethan.

I know it now.

I know it too late.

Sitting across from him, I experience a completely new kind of miserable heartbreak. It isn't the devastatingly shattering kind that hurts until

I'm numb like Travis caused. It's the kind where my heart stays intact just enough for it to dully ache every time it beats in my chest.

Worse is pretending I don't feel it.

"Hmm. Well, I'm not so horrible at making coffee anymore," I say.

He vibrates with a small laugh, and amusement covers his face. Like he knows how tortured I feel, and he's enjoying it. It's as cruel as the small talk we're forcing ourselves to make.

I lift my wine to my lips.

"What about you? Tell me something I've missed."

"I got a dog."

I snort. "I didn't expect that, but I can see it. In front of that fireplace or laying by the river."

"He does love the river." He nods and smiles, the corners of his eyes crinkling.

Without warning, I hear myself ask, "So how did you meet your... her?"

If I'm going to walk around with a knife in my soul, it might as well plunge all the way through.

"My dog? It's a he." His smugness is as permanent as the nose on his face. I don't love him, I hate him.

I narrow my eyes. "You know who I'm talking about."

He pauses, long and methodically, in a way that feels like a bomb is about to drop. "She came into my restaurant."

He props his elbows on the table and lifts his chin. Like he knows how loyal his good looks are to him in that white shirt rolled up on his forearms.

"Of course." I roll my eyes on reflex before stopping myself. I refuse to be petty. "I'm sorry. I'm happy for you."

He ignores me.

"Wait, that's not actually when I *met* her. This is kind of embarrassing Nel, but she kind of stalked me first." He holds up his hands as if to say *let me explain.* "She contacted me under the guise of needing help, but I know better."

When he smirks, I take a gulp of my wine then press my lips into a tight line, trying to hide how much I *do not* want to hear anymore.

"*Then* she came into the restaurant. On my worst night, actually. I had to work behind the bar, which, before that night, as you know, was my least favorite area to be. I swore to myself I was going to list the damn place for sale the next day because I was so miserable."

My chin pulls back—*behind the bar?*

"But in walks this woman, wearing a ridiculous t-shirt and rubber boots that squeaked like ducks, offering to help me."

At this, he grins, and I instantly feel my heartbeat at every surface point of my body.

"Being at my worst night, I was not in my best mood, but I was mesmerized as she marched around and made everyone around the bar fall in love with her as she made drinks and put me in my place."

Wait—*what?*

I'm so still I don't know if I'm even breathing. Because what he's saying...

"Then, for some reason, she took pity on me and agreed to go out with me on a date." He leans back in his chair, blue eyes dancing. "I went out on a limb and took her to a farmers market, somewhere I'd been hundreds of times, but I had never seen it quite like that. When I watched her talk to farmers and get excited about herbs, I was a goner. Stupid right? Forty-three years on this planet, and I just needed to find the one woman who giggled about mint. I fell so hard that night I knew I was never going to be the same again. I bought every painting by an artist she liked just so I would have glimpses of life the way she saw it when she wasn't with me."

Oh. My. God. My eyes burn like the winter wind is blowing straight through them.

"I knew when I kissed her, I never wanted to kiss another woman for the rest of my life. Even ones who do very naughty things to straws couldn't compare." Smug smile in place, he reaches his hand across the table to grab mine, which is trembling.

"Ethan..." I can't find my tongue.

"Please, Nel, this is getting to the good part. It's rude to interrupt."

He shakes his head solemnly as the first tear drips down my cheek.

"Then, I left. Honestly, I was scared. Really scared. That's not who I was. I went on late-night dates and kept things casual, and this woman screamed serious. But she found me again. This time, wearing this green dress—very similar to the one you wore in the magazine, actually." He licks his bottom lip slowly before a small smile makes his mouth curve upward. "Between the way she looked in that damn dress and how she once again put me in my place in a room full of people, I was ruined."

I barely hear the words he's saying from the sound of my pulse pounding in my ears. Another tear falls and another.

But he doesn't stop.

"Nel, she has this ability to always tell me exactly what's on my mind, without reservation or concern over consequences. The things she's said to me make me feel like I've only ever had relationships that never went below the surface. They were all tattoos on the skin until she came in like a blood transfusion and infiltrated every single part of me."

The graceful single tears are gone, and I am now full-blown ugly crying.

Ethan is here.

The person he's serious about is *me*.

He waited for messy, broken, babbling *me*.

In one quick move, he's out of his chair, on both knees, on the floor in front of me. When he bumps the table and his glass of wine spills, he doesn't turn to look.

His hands rest on my thighs, but his eyes are glued to mine.

"I looked up plane tickets to Miami a hundred times since you left, starting the day you flew away. Once, I made it all the way there before deciding you still weren't ready and flying back home. I wanted to give you a year to figure things out on your own, but when I saw you in that magazine, I knew I couldn't wait any longer. I would have loved you if you hadn't left, Nel, but it turns out I loved you even when you did."

I smile through the tears that keep falling.

"Yes." My voice is in a thousand pieces. "Yes. To you and this and all the messy work that comes with it." I run my fingers through his thick hair, smiling deliriously. "I love you, Ethan."

Then, with him kneeling between my legs in that damn suit, I bring my face to his and kiss him. I kiss him like my life depends on it, and he kisses me like he's trying to make up for all the ones we've missed. His taste and smell and the feel of his skin touching mine is like coming home after being gone for far too long.

When we finally pull apart, we're smiling.

"Did you really get a dog?" I ask as he stands up and pulls my hands for me to do the same.

He grins. "I did. A Golden Retriever named Odey."

"Odey?"

"It's short for Odysseus."

Penelope's husband in Greek mythology who spent ten years trying to get back to her after ten years at war.

"Dammit, Ethan."

I drop my face to his chest as I try to hide every fresh emotion that stains my skin before looking back up at him.

He curls his lips into a smug smirk I've missed so much over the last six months.

His mouth drops to my ear, and his voice lowers. "Dance with me, Nel."

I don't argue with him. After everything he's just told me, there isn't much I have the power to say no to.

Me against him with the woman's raspy voice filling the air, my body liquifies as we sway slowly in a dark corner of the restaurant.

And when the music stops, and the wine is gone, we barely make it to his truck before our clothes are off. In an icy night in Bangor, Maine, in the backseat of a truck in a parking lot, Ethan reminds me how good we are together with his hands and body and the words he never stops saying in my ear.

The next morning in the hotel lobby, our ridiculously giddy smiles are permanent—a reflection of how satisfying our night together was.

When we finally drag ourselves out of bed, we get dressed and eat breakfast while staring at each other like lovesick puppies. I'd be embarrassed if I wasn't so happy.

As he starts up his truck, I pull out my phone.

Me: Did you know?
Marin: Of course, we did, Penelope.
Finn: It was for your own good.
Me: You're both grounded.
Marin: Have fun, Mom. We love you.
Finn: And please don't tell us what you two do together.

I laugh, warmed completely despite the freezing temperatures that have iced over the windshield.

We made it to the other side of this big ugly thing together. It's different than I expected, but also so much better.

Some people are lucky enough to have one person to love for their entire life. One person they grow with, change with, and experience every big moment with. One person who knows them better than they know themselves.

Despite my best efforts, that is not how my story is written.

My story gave me two. Two great men who changed me to my bones. Without one, there could never have been the other.

It's a bittersweet truth that will probably cause the slightest ache in my chest for the rest of my life.

Ethan reaches his arm across the seat and grabs my thigh while my sock-covered feet prop up on the dash. Piles of snow line the sides of the road as we head out of the city and into the mountains. The White Mountains, which really was where I found myself.

"I was thinking." I turn to him and rest my head on the headrest. "We should spend Januarys in Key Largo."

He squeezes my leg.

"Deal."

Epilogue

Two years later...

I MARRY THE HELL out of Ethan; it's as simple as that.

When he got down on both knees and proposed to me in the middle of the first Bethel farmers market of the season, I dropped down on my knees right along with him and kissed him through tears until he knew I was saying yes.

We got married on his property in July, one year after we met, with the Androscoggin River as the backdrop. Just us and our families.

Both Finn and Marin walked me down the grassy aisle as I carried a bouquet of Maine wildflowers—from the market—and wore a simple white dress.

My dad didn't mind, he understood. This time around was different.

Hand in hand with my mom, he smiled proudly in an obnoxious shirt covered in moose and pine trees as my mom cried.

When the kids walked me to Ethan, they hugged me tightly, whispered *I love you,* then gently pushed me toward him. He was, as usual, handsome in his suit and smirk.

I barely made it through the simple vows before I jumped in his arms, wrapped my legs around his waist, and crushed my mouth to his.

Our reception happened right on his back porch. We ate burgers that Derek grilled and drank daiquiris I made... with Ethan.

Everyone smiled that day, but the one I noticed most was Finn's.

It was broad and breathtaking. He was happy. We both were.

When he graduated high school, he went to work with Gabe on the boat and started earning his captain's license. He'll never leave the island. He might look like me, but he is still his father's son. The Keys are just part of who he is. The saltwater there runs in his veins as thick as blood.

"One day," he says, "I'll have my own business and fleet of boats."

I believe him.

Marin somehow graduated a year early, which was just so Marin of her. She traveled with me back and forth to Bangor while we got Ethan's new restaurant running. One day, she told me she was never going back to Florida.

My spunky girl had met a boy in a band and was head over heels. So, she stayed. She's now in cosmetology school and spends her days being unapologetically her while stealing glances at a boy with a guitar. She reminds me of me when I was a young bartender with hearts in my eyes for a baby-faced pilot.

I still see Travis from time to time. When a plane flies low overhead or when someone wears a ridiculous t-shirt, his face flashes in my mind quickly, like a happy dream, before it's gone. There's no painful longing, just admiration for the man I was lucky enough to love and be loved by. For the man who carved me into who I was meant to be without me ever noticing.

And me and Ethan?

We figured out how to make the miles less far.

The first year of my business had some growing pains. I took on too many clients and burned out fast. Eventually, I scaled back. Now, I take only a couple of consultations a month and never stray too far from home.

Or, more accurately, *homes*.

We now split our time between Key Largo and Maine. I can't imagine I'll ever spend another summer not breathing that northeastern air as much as Ethan would say he never wants to see another skin-slicing winter there.

Sometimes, I work behind the bar at his restaurant, and I think of who I was the first time I walked in. How I had no clue my life was about to be flipped upside down by that simple decision to sit at a bar next to a woman wearing entirely too much perfume.

Women still notice Ethan—I suspect they always will—but I'm not jealous anymore. How can I be when he always looks right past them to me with a fire in his eyes and a smile on his lips?

I make our coffee every morning, and he crawls into bed with me every night.

That summer we spent out on the road, I left Key Largo one person and came back another. Every stunning place and not nearly long enough moment with my kids, pieced me together just differently enough for a new map to unfold within me—one that led to a kind of happy life I didn't know could exist without Travis.

Every beautiful mile led me to Ethan—the unexpected destination I didn't know to look for but can't imagine life without.

Acknowledgments

Right before I went to college, my parents converted a van into a camper, and we spent two weeks driving across the country. I'm sure my mom and dad would say today, I acted a lot like Finn—an annoyed teenage hostage. On our drive home, somewhere in Utah, we hit a mule deer.

The van stayed in Utah. We flew home.

Eighteen years later, my husband and I loaded up our two young kids and started out on an adventure I never saw coming. We lived in our camper for just over eighteen months and explored the United States. It was one of the most beautifully difficult things I've ever done.

Seeing the Pacific Ocean on that trip? I cried like a baby. I remember thinking, I can't believe we drove all these miles and made it to the other side.

On that same trip, I met a woman when we were staying at a campground down in the Keys. Our conversation was brief, maybe ten minutes, and she told me she was traveling alone with her five or six kids from Utah.

I was stunned. 18-months in a camper and I never drove once. She went on to tell me that they had been travelling to see the national parks for months at a time until her husband died a few months prior. She was now finishing what they set out to do, without him.

I thought of that woman for days. I don't know her name, wouldn't recognize her if she knocked on my door, but the fact she could do that is still one of the most impressive things I have ever heard.

At none of these moments did I think, "I'm going to write a book about this!"

When the time came to write, they were the stories that bubbled to the surface as I started typing. They just appeared like that's what it was all for.

Kevin gets the dedication, but my kids get the shout-out. Oak and Vale, I couldn't have done this without you. You supported me and cheered for me when nobody else in the world knew I was writing. Sorry for all the times I yelled, "Just let me finish this sentence!" I love you guys. You inspire me every single day.

To my parents, who took me and my brother on that first big road trip as I rolled my teenage eyes endlessly. Who knew it was going to be worth it twenty years later?

To my friends and first readers who pushed me hard enough that I didn't give up—thank you isn't a big enough word. Nicole, Christy, Summer, Whitney, Shelly, Tayler and Sonia—you helped write the words of these pages. And especially Morgann, who answered my texts at all insane hours in the early days of my manuscript and literally gave me thighgasm (her word—she deserves a trophy.)

TO MY ARC READERS! thankyouthankyouthankyouthankyou! You are the team of people I didn't know I needed.

To my editor—Victoria—who told me this was good and then helped make it better. If a mile wasn't so far, I'd like to think we'd have one of Nel's cocktails and a Tim Tam together.

If you're reading this,—you. Thank you for giving me and the words I put into the universe some of your precious time. I hope it was worth it.

As tears roll down my cheeks, thank you, to all of you. I love you for what you've given me simply by knowing you.

Market Made

Nel's Market Made is the ultimate locally-inspired cocktail. She made her own simple syrup with Maine honey and lavender. But we can't all be Nel. This recipe is a simplified version of her fancy one.

- 2oz gin

- Lemon juice (whole lemon)

- 1 oz lavender simple syrup (can be found at liquor stores)

- Club soda

- Optional: butterfly pea pollen (gives a purple color but doesn't change the flavor; can be found online)

Add simple syrup, lemon juice, and gin to a shaker with ice. Shake. Pour contents into glass with ice and top with club soda. Optional last step: sprinkle with pea pollen for the purple color.

For the rest of the cocktails from the book, Travis' Forced Fun Road Trip itinerary, and a bonus chapter from Ethan, visit www.ashleymanleywrites.com

About the author

Ashley Manley has no prestigious accolades and detests talking about herself in the third person. Alas, here we are.

When she isn't writing, you can find her chasing her kids, reheating her coffee, or dreaming of her next adventure under tall trees. While her and her family have lived a little bit of everywhere, North Carolina will always feel like home. For more information, visit ashleymanleywrites. com or find her on Instagram @ashleymanleywrites.

Printed in the USA
CPSIA information can be obtained
at www.ICGtesting.com
LVHW030259190524
780577LV00012B/927